THE TAIPAN AGENDA

THE TAIPAN AGENDA

Hugh T W Robertson

Writers Club Press
San Jose New York Lincoln Shanghai

the Taipan Agenda

Writers Club Press
an imprint of iUniverse, Inc.

For information address:
iUniverse, Inc.
5220 S. 16th St., Suite 200
Lincoln, NE 68512
www.iuniverse.com

ISBN: 0-595-21436-3

Printed in the United States of America

For John
and all the other good men who left us too soon.

CHAPTER 1

BANG!

The sound of leather striking mahogany resonated around the office, as David Fairbrother slammed his briefcase on to the antique desk. Throughout its life as a piece of functional furniture, the rich, deep varnished wood had suffered at the hands of tempestuous owners. Even so, if the wood had a voice, it might have cried out in surprise at this outburst. It's present custodian was not usually prone to such violent displays of emotion. He was by nature a man who believed in emotional discipline. On this bright July morning, he had obviously been driven to the point where his emotions found their own way to the surface.

'Bloody Americans! Breakfast meetings! What kind of people want to discuss business over breakfast? Breakfast! They have the audacity to call that breakfast! Fruit and some ghastly concoction of yoghurt and grains. Horse fodder!'

This uncharacteristic outburst was being directed at no one in particular. The ears which received the verbal onslaught were those of Catherine Wilson, Fairbrother's long time and, some would say, long suffering secretary. She was not one of those who would have complained about her boss. She had seen the best and the worst of this man and when the scales were released, they fell heavily on the positive side. Having given the man an opportunity to vent his obviously aggravated spleen, she allowed a small smile to form on her face and let her calm voice lighten the heavy atmosphere of the room.

'Well, now that you have that out of your system, why don't I bring you a cup of tea. While I'm off performing that vital task, you can busy yourself with the mail.'

Fairbrother looked at her under brows which gathered like storm clouds. Then, suddenly, the weather lifted. He took a very deep breath and slowly nodded his head. 'Thank you Catherine. Sorry about the profanity.' He was a man of temperate words. It took a great deal to bring even the most mildly profane utterance to his lips.

'It must have gone badly.' The concern in her voice was genuine.

David Fairbrother sighed. 'Badly is an understatement. I don't know if I am going to be able to make this joint-venture work. The cultures of the two sides are so far apart. Oh, listen to me! Cultures! I am beginning to sound like one of those Harvard clones that they churn out by the gross. Perhaps some Earl Grey will inject good English sense into me.'

'You will find a way to make it work. You always do.' With that, Catherine turned and left the office.

She was right of course. When he was calm and the deep irritation he felt had passed, he would find a way. He always did. His anger was probably more for himself than his potential business partners. He had allowed his passions to cloud his judgement. It was just not done. His control and negotiating skill had brought him to the head of this company. He was respected by his peers and probably feared and envied in equal measure. Fairbrother looked out of the ceiling to floor window of his 33rd floor office. He never tired of the view. He always held meetings in the conference room, at the rear of the building. Visitors to his office were too easily distracted by the panorama of Hong Kong harbour. In matters of business, he liked the attention to be on his speech, not on the vista.

'Aiah!'

The word came out as a sigh. Wong Yeung-man felt every one of his fifty-eight years as he struggled with the padlock. Humidity, pollution and the proximity of the harbour had taken their toll on the mechanism. At last the key turned, the click of the lock releasing the chain, which was the only protection of his livelihood. Wong straightened his aching back, as he pulled the chain free from his hawker's cart. He closed his eyes and let the early morning sun bathe his face in warmth. With his world-worn face raised to the heavens, he opened his eyes. A smile appeared among the sea of wrinkles when he saw the clear blue, cloudless sky. It would be a hot day. A good day for business. Soon the truck would arrive to fill his cart with ice and the soft drinks that he would sell to the sweating river of people passing his pitch on this busy thoroughfare. An expensive location. The triads knew a good thing and extracted their protection money accordingly. What could he do? Ask the police for help? He had heard what happened to people who went to the *Chai Lo*. He had a family who relied on him. He was no good to them dead, or so badly chopped that he could not work. He would lose his pitch if he could not work for even a single day. Even illness was impossible. He couldn't afford it.

Wong pulled the small folding stool from its nest on the side of the cart. Opening the legs like the blades of a huge pair of scissors, he placed the stool on the pavement in its usual place and sat on the hard, round seat. He patted his round belly, full of the congee and fried bread that had made up his breakfast. The taste was still on his lips. His friends, with whom he had shared the first meal of the day, had joked with him about his daughter. Why was she not yet married? A beautiful girl. She should be looking for a husband. Why had he allowed her to stay at school so long? He should have insisted that she work to help support the rest of the family. After all, her brothers all had their own families to look after. How could he explain to these men what he had in mind for his only daughter? She would be the first member of his family to go to university. She had been accepted to the Chinese University of Hong Kong. Her hard work had been rewarded with a scholarship. That would take care of the tuition fees, but he had to keep working to help pay for the other things she would need. The apple of his eye would have the opportunity to take advantage of the intelligence which the gods had decided to gift her with. Her brothers were all good boys, but they would never be as smart as Ah Ying. Wong's chest swelled every time he thought of her.

Since graduating from Oxford, over thirty years before, David Fairbrother had travelled all over the world with the company. Walker-Johnstone was one of the original *Hongs* , the British trading houses which had found and exploited the deep water harbour of the "Barren Rock", as Hong Kong was then often known. The unfortunate nature of their first commercial enterprise, the opium trade, was something everyone in the company would rather forget. Somehow, it never appeared in the company biography, published in the annual report. The company felt that it had contributed so much to the prosperity of the territory, that it could be forgiven its shameful start. Now the company had interests all over the world, but the head office remained here, in the dynamic metropolis on the flank of the largest potential market on the face of the Earth.

He had lived in Hong Kong on three previous occasions, each time the return to Head Office resulting in movement a few more rungs up the corporate ladder. Now, he had nowhere to climb. He was the *Taipan*. An archaic term for the Chief Executive of the company. In Hong Kong, though, it carried a greater meaning. He was one of the elite of the community, not just the business community.

In the world of *laissez faire* he was one of the handful of men who would be consulted on any major decision that government had to make. The ruling elite in Hong Kong were the sultans of commerce. It was a position that sometimes did not sit well with David Fairbrother. He saw himself as an egalitarian. His roots were modest. He had worked his way up and respected those with similar industry and integrity. At times he felt that corporate interest played too large a part of government policy. Then again, he had the interests of his shareholders to protect. Having such a loud voice meant that those interests were never neglected.

Fairbrother settled into the soft leather of his chair. His desk was neat, no sign of clutter. On the blotter was a pile of letters, large and small. There really was no need for him to open any of the correspondence, but it was one of his quirks. He enjoyed the ritual of opening mail addressed directly to him. Most personal correspondence would have been addressed to his home, but occasionally he received personal mail at work. For the most part, the envelopes would contain a mixture of CV's from aggressive, would be *Taipans* seeking a position with the company, invitations to social functions and the occasional surprise. Fairbrother would not deal with most of the correspondence, he just enjoyed the experience of discovery. Obvious junk mail would be filtered by his staff. The occasional piece of merchandising trash that escaped the net would irritate only as long as it took to travel from hand to waste-bin.

Catherine reappeared with the tea. She laid the bone china cup and saucer on a silver coaster to the right of the blotter. Fairbrother thanked her and lifted the cup to his lips. The secretary waited until she saw the satisfied look which always followed her employer's first sip of tea. It was an unspoken statement of gratitude. A small gesture that meant a great deal to the woman. Catherine Wilson had a husband and family of her own, but the man sitting at the desk was the head of her second family. She had been with him for 8 years, following him to Hong Kong from her first overseas posting with the company, in New Delhi. Their relationship had never been anything other than professional, but she felt that she knew this man better than her husband. They had been together longer. He was godfather to her eldest daughter and had given her away at her wedding, standing in for her late father. Without saying a word, Catherine left Fairbrother to start the working day in his usual fashion and put the nauseating memory of the breakfast meeting out of his head.

Wong slid the cover shut on the top of his cart. The belly of the metal box was full of ice and drinks. The commercial day could now start. The pavement was already busy, but the real business would be closer to noon, when the oppressive heat and humidity had done their work and sent the passing minds wandering towards thoughts of the refreshing relief which Wong had to offer. All he had to do was wait. No hard sell required. This suited Wong, as by nature he was a quiet man. He was not soft. It had not been that long since he had seen off would be invaders of his pitch. Of course, the money he paid the triads was the final insurance of his continued prosperity. The money they took meant that he had to work all the harder, but at least he could work. Even if it was under the umbrella of their malicious protection. No point on dwelling on the inevitable.

The drink seller took a wet cloth from his cart and wiped the sweat from his brow. The young driver of the delivery van had made no attempt to help the older man. Young people today had no respect for their elders, thought Wong. Except his kids, of course. They had been brought up well. He was proud of the fact that he and his wife had kept the boys out of the clutches of the local gangs, thugs who adopted the names of the Triad Societies. Some of them might actually be linked to the criminal organisations, doing their donkey work in the housing estates. Selling drugs and acting as cannon fodder for the action of the police. The real gangsters never seemed to be touched. Just stupid kids. But not his.

The letter on the top of the pile made Fairbrother smile. He recognised the writing immediately. As he picked it up, he looked towards the door of his office. The woman on the other side of the door had obviously recognised it too and placed it on top. He felt so lucky to have Catherine. She knew how much this letter would mean. The *Taipan* reached for the letter opener and eased the blade into the interior of the envelope. With one swift movement, it was open. Fairbrother eagerly pulled out the letter. Another smile graced his tanned face as he read the familiar greeting; "Dear Pops". A letter from Caroline always brightened up the gloomiest of days.

David Fairbrother worried about his only child. She was a woman now, studying at university in England. To her father she would always be the blond child around whom his whole world revolved. He had spoiled her rotten since she was a baby. Even he was amazed at how level headed she had ended up. It was certainly no thanks to him. He knew that she could take care of herself and that she was surrounded by a loving surrogate family. He had been pleased when she had chosen to study in York. He had many friends there, whom he immediately contacted and from whom he extracted blood oaths that they would look after his pride and joy. His rational side knew that there really was nothing to worry about. Rationality had little to do with how much he loved his daughter. He worried, and that was that.

The letter contained little more than chit-chat. A reminder that he was not entirely forgotten, in the midst of the busy life she led. The end of the letter contained the best news. Her exams were finished, she had spent time with her friends and was now ready to come home to her family for the rest of the summer vacation. The flight was booked, he would see her in less than a week. His heart skipped as he read the words. His eyes grew bright as they left the page to look at the silver framed photograph of Caroline, which shared the expanse of dark wood with another of his wife. All the morning's aggravations were forgotten. Yet again his daughter had spun her magic with the simplest of gestures. Fairbrother carefully replaced the letter in the envelope and put both in the left breast pocket of his jacket. It would rest close to his heart until he could share the good news with his wife.

Reluctantly he returned his attention to the pile of mail in front of him. His reluctance was magnified by the contents of the next letter. An engraved card, embossed in gold. Yet another invitation to yet another ball. It was part of his duty, as a leader of the community, to be seen to support such events. Some he gladly attended, those with a good cause, where his presence might encourage others to also attend and contribute some of their ill-gotten gains. A picture in his company, appearing in the Hong Kong Tatler, was seen by some as a passport to the dizzy heights of the social elite. Fairbrother had little time for such people, but if it made them develop a conscience, even for as long as it took to write a cheque, then he supposed that it was worth a few hours of his time. This invitation was not to a benefit for a good cause. It was to the opening of new building. One of the latest developments of Harbour Holdings, the oldest of the chinese *Hongs* and the strongest. It was much younger than Walker-Johnstone, but was growing at an extraordinary rate. Rumours abounded that the company had been close to collapse a dozen or more years before. It's current success belied that rumour, or indicated that another rumour, that outside forces had bailed the chairman out, might have some foundation in fact. A look of distaste came over Fairbrother's countenance as he thought of the man who was at the helm of Harbour Holdings. Shaking his head, Fairbrother tossed the invitation in the direction of all the other detritus to cross his desk. Taking a deep breath, he blew away the foul stench that had momentarily spoiled his mood.

Wong had made the first sale of the day. It was always a relief. He felt on edge until that first few dollars were deposited in the pouch which he carried around his waist. As he sat on the stool, his mind wandered to the evening ahead. His brother-in-law was hosting a dinner for the family. He had spent the weekend in Macau and had returned a winner. Of course he always said that he was a winner after his frequent trips to the Portuguese enclave. Most of the time it was far from the truth, but tonight's celebration could only mean that he had won back a small part of the contributions he had made over the years to the prosperity of Stanley Ho and his gambling empire.

The dinner would take place in the Sun Kwong Restaurant in Kowloon City. Three floors of cavernous restaurants and intimate private rooms. One of these rooms would play host to the party. Three tables for family and close friends; the win had not been that big! Wong sighed. Perhaps one day he would host such a party. When his daughter graduated, he would, with luck and a fair turn in business. He hoped that today would be very hot. He needed some extra income. Face demanded that he contribute something to the party, probably a bottle of brandy to share with his host. The quality of the drink would depend on the temperature and the thirst of the passing throng. Wong looked at the cloudless sky and said a silent prayer to the gods who ruled such matters.

The package was bulky, but light. Fairbrother hardly glanced at the writing, his mind was still enjoying the anticipation of his daughter's return to the family. Probably another CV, he thought briefly. They seemed to be getting more elaborate with each passing year. A couple of sheets of paper were no longer enough. He had even received videos from American graduates. When in a generous frame of mind, he had actually watched about two minutes of one self-absorbed production. Frankly, his advice to the applicant would have been to avoid showing his face until an employer had actually offered him a job. As the monotone of business school rhetoric had spewed from the mouth of the face on the screen, Fairbrother had felt an increasing desire to fling something large and hard at the television. He shook his head as he thought of another unforgivable impulse to lose his cool.

The *Taipan* eased the blade of the letter-opener under the flap of the large brown envelope. The thick paper prevented him from opening it with his customary flourish. Some effort was required to execute the four cuts necessary to expose the contents. Fairbrother rested the closed end of the package on the desk and stared at what looked like a second envelope, inside the first. This piqued his curiosity. Whatever was inside was being well protected. Knowing the abuse to which mail was subjected by the Post Office, Fairbrother considered this a prudent measure. The sender was obviously a careful individual. A favourable first impression. He reached in with three fingers and pulled the second envelope out. After half an inch he encountered some resistance.

Wong watched the receding figure of the gwailo, who was greedily consuming the soft drink he had just purchased. They really did sweat a great deal, thought Wong. Yet, they insisted on wearing suits, even in the height of summer. He felt warm enough in his T-shirt and shorts. Still, living in a large flat and making enormous amounts of money must have some cost. Wong felt that it was a price worth paying.

The noise was sudden and violent. Wong looked around as the sound reverberated off the buildings around him, making it difficult to locate the source. It was the gaze of other people that brought his eyes up to the building straight in front of him. Still, he could make little out. His friend the sun was reflecting off the glass front of the tower, straight into his eyes. It was instinct, rather than conscious thought that made him move closer to the building, at exactly the same moment that he saw something falling from the tower of glass above him. If he had stayed put, it might have missed him. As it was , he walked straight into the path of the three foot long shard of glass.

Its edge caught him at the base of the neck, its momentum drove it into his flesh, slicing its way obliquely through the muscles of the neck and severing the arteries and veins crossing its path, only coming to rest on the first rib, having shattered the clavicle.

Half the glass shattered as the body hit the hot pavement. Blood began to form a gruesome halo around the old man's head. His last, brief thought was for his daughter. What would become of her?

CHAPTER 2

'It's made of what?'

Richard Stirling smiled as the young Chinese Inspector struggled with his reply. 'Well, eh, it, well sir, it *looks* like concrete.'

'Concrete bomb, eh? Well, that's a first.'

The younger man looked nervously over his shoulder at a stern figure talking loudly to every policeman within hearing.

'What's wrong?' asked Stirling.

'I don't think that my boss is too happy about the fact that I am giving this briefing instead of him.'

'Has he been up to the device?'

'No.'

'Have you?'

'Yes sir.'

'Right. So that's why I am talking to you and not some senior officer who only gets his arse up from behind a desk so his name will appear in the morning report. I want a first hand account from someone who has travelled to and from the scene and actually seen the thing with his own eyes, i.e. you!

'So, stop worrying about him and concentrate on helping me not get killed. OK?'

'Yes sir,' said the young man with a smile.

Richard turned his attention to the large sheet of paper laid out on the bonnet of the Land Rover. His eyes scanned the floor plan of the housing estate. Kwai Chung Estate was a "resettlement estate", meant as a temporary measure, bringing members of rural communities into the urban fold. It had become a permanent, if decaying fixture. A gloomy environment. Home to honest, hardworking folk and fertile ground for predatory drug dealers, offering a short-lived release from the squalor of the surroundings. The highest buildings were only ten stories, residentiary midgets in the high-rise world of Hong Kong.

The scene hardly mattered. It could just as easily have been one of the gleaming towers of the Central business district. The job was the same. The main difference was that if he destroyed someone's home, in the process of dealing with a bomb, he would get considerably less flack than if he scratched a marble floor in some merchant banker's reception. That was Hong Kong. The economy was an engine and the people who lived in estates like this one were the silent fuel that ran it. The men with their hands on the controls were the only ones with a real voice. Richard had more sympathy for the coal than the engineer.

'OK, again, show me the route you took to the object.'

The young Inspector redrew his path, with his finger, on the diagram.

'How big was the thing?' asked Richard.

'About the size of a…'

'Show me with your hands,' said Richard.

Looking at his hands, the young man concertinaed until he came up with a size he was happy with. 'Like that, round, about the size of a football.'

Richard did a quick mental calculation, estimating the volume of the object and therefore the potential explosive yield.

'Smell anything?'

Richard looked up at the chinese policeman as there was no reply. The man looked perplexed. At last he found his voice. 'Well, sir. It is a toilet. In these old estates, the plumbing isn't very good...so there is a pretty strong stench. I mean...'

Richard held up his hand and smiled at his companion's embarrassment. 'It's alright, no need to go into any further details. I only wanted to know if there was a distinctive smell that would indicate the presence of explosive. Obviously the other scents in there would mask something so subtle. Don't worry about it.

'Now, what else did you see in the room?'

'Well, the thing has a chain coming out of the top and is padlocked to the chain that secures the door to one of the stalls. It seems pretty secure.'

Richard frowned at this news. 'What made you think that it was a bomb?'

The young man looked surprised. 'The sign, sir.'

'What sign?'

'Sorry, I thought you knew, it was in my report to control. There is a sign above the device, attached to the door. It says "Comrades, keep clear. This bomb is intended for the yellow running dog traitors who dishonour us all.".

'You can't be serious! What kind of bollocks is that?'

Words failed the Inspector. As he fumbled with his speech, trying to drag the words out, Richard put him out of his misery. 'I think someone is having us on. My guess is that some neighbours are having a dispute and this is someone's way of getting back at the owner of the toilet. Each of the toilet stalls is assigned to an individual flat, isn't that right?' The Inspector nodded. 'Right, when I have finished with you, go find the owner of the targeted toilet and we shall ask the poor bugger some questions. Chances are that we shall find the bomber, or practical joker, if this thing turns out to be a hoax.'

'Sorry sir, I should have thought of that. I hope I haven't wasted your time.'

Richard looked straight into the young man's eyes. 'Inspector Lam. Never feel bad about doing the right thing. The only thing that would piss me off is if some poor bastard was blown up by a bomb, because some silly arse didn't want to take the risk of wasting my time. This is my job and you have done the right thing by calling me out. Never be afraid of being wrong. I would rather attend a hundred hoaxes, than take the risk of missing a single bomb. Remember that.'

A smile appeared on Lam's face. 'I will sir. Thanks.'

The serious look on Richard's face melted into a softer countenance. 'Right, take this piece of paper and draw me a diagram of the toilet. I want to see the exact position of the device and the route you took into, around and out of the room. Did you notice any wires, or strings coming out of the object? Anything else that was odd, or caught your attention?' Lam shook his head. 'OK, if you think of anything, let me know. I'm just going to have a word with your boss over there. Tell him what a great help you've been. Bet that doesn't make it into his report.' The young man smiled, then turned his attention to constructing as good a diagram as possible for the man he now liked a great deal.

Richard put on his most serious "don't fuck with me" face as he approached the highly animated Superintendent, who was trying his best to let everyone know that he was in charge of the situation. Richard was just about to ruin his day by dispelling that particular myth.

'Superintendent Pang.'

Pang looked at Richard with an expression of superiority. The thought behind the mask was "So, you want to speak to me at last". Beyond the bravado, Pang was nervous. Specialists like Richard always made people like Pang uneasy. They were outside the normal chain of command and therefore unlikely to put up with rank based posturing. They were unpredictable, especially ones who dealt with bombs for a living. When you ran the risk of having your various parts fly off in all directions at high speed, upsetting senior officers was hardly likely to phase you. In the case of Richard Stirling, he had turned being bolshy into an art form. If Pang tried to exert his authority, he was in for a rough ride.

Richard broke the awkward silence that had appeared between them. 'Your young *Bong Baan* has been most helpful. From his description of the object, I think that you were wise to follow procedure and evacuate the floor above and below the toilet.'

Pang suddenly took on the look of a rabbit caught in the headlights of a car. Richard had caught him out. 'Eh...well, I didn't think that it warranted that much. I mean, chances are that it is only a hoax.'

Richard just stared at the man. His silence allowed the Superintendent to stew in his incompetence. As the gravity of his omission sank in, Richard at last spoke. 'I would advise you to correct your error. I have some preparation to do before I deal with the device. I understand that the bomb was found over an hour ago, so I am in no hurry, but there is still a chance that it has a timer, so I would suggest that you get people out as quickly as possible.' The use of the words "device" and "bomb" were very deliberate, leaving Pang in absolutely no doubt about the gravity of his error.

Richard didn't bother wasting his "nothing is a waste of my time" speech on this man. He would never learn. Richard knew the type all too well. The thing that made his blood boil was that Pang and those like him seldom suffered as a result of their incompetence and indifference. It was the poor bastards like Inspector Lam who were at the razor's edge. Richard was lucky. He could tell this prick to fuck-off, if he felt he was being put in danger. Lam was too young and too inexperienced to even consider it. He and his like relied on people like Richard to act as a buffer against men like Pang.

Pang started blustering about, shouting at junior officers, as if the failure to set up a safe area around the suspect object were their fault. Men like Pang would do almost anything to avoid accepting the blame for even the smallest mistake. To Richard, the inability to accept that you have made a mistake was one of the biggest weaknesses a person could have. Only by first admitting our mistakes can we possibly learn from them. Pang would continue to make the same mistakes for as long as he breathed air. Shaking his head at the ridiculous spectacle of one of his senior officers in action, Richard turned away and headed for his vehicle.

Taking a strip of black insulation tape from the thigh of his jeans, Richard wrapped it around the bare wire in his hands. The black strips that adorned his leg looked odd, but they saved time and the need for an extra pair of hands. Richard made a last check of the connections between the firing cable and the detonator. Ah Pau, his driver and number two, looked on. He would often prepare 'dems' for his boss, but if there was no pressure of time, Richard liked to do it himself. His trust in his number two was absolute, he just found that the preparation helped him relax. Activity distracted him from the reality of his next move; approaching an object that might just be a bomb. Bombs killed. Bombs destroyed. Bombs could really ruin your day.

'Ah Pau, please make a final check on the cordon with the incident commander and let him know that I am going in.'

The Sergeant gave Richard a questioning look, with a hint of disapproval.

'What?' asked the Scotsman.

Taking a deep breath, Ah Pau replied. 'So, you're not wearing the bomb suit?' It was half a question, half a plea.

'We've been through this before. Sometimes I just don't feel that it is appropriate. It hinders my movement and makes the situation unnecessarily dangerous. If I think it will help, I'll wear it. If not…'

Ah Pau shrugged and walked down the stairs, towards the command post. Richard had chosen the stairwell to set up his equipment. There was plenty of concrete between him and the suspect object and few corners to go round, so fewer opportunities to get snags in the command wire of his demolition charge. He had considered sending a robot in to inspect the device, but the diagram drawn by Inspector Lam had changed his mind. The length of det cord that he held was a precaution. It would be stupid to approach the object without a means of neutralizing it. The golden rule was; approach the damn thing as few times as was necessary. Well, one of the golden rules. Richard remembered the "six P's"; Proper Planning Prevents Piss Poor Performance. Having considered the nature of the object, an explosive charge seemed the only suitable weapon at his disposal. If the object was made of concrete, his best bet was to crack the casing with the detonating cord, hopefully separating the detonating mechanism from the explosive in the process. If the thing was a hoax, the damage caused by his charge would be minimal. If it was a bomb; well, some new plumbing would be needed, but no one would get hurt. That was the deciding factor in his determination of a course of action; was anyone's life at risk? Life was everything, property was irrelevant. Buildings could be rebuilt, objects replaced. Human life was another matter. Richard's job was to save life, even his own.

Ah Pau reappeared and gave Richard a nod that meant all was ready. The cordon was secure, the area clear. The size of the area cleared was probably overkill, but it was best to err on the side of caution and it had provided an opportunity to get the upper hand with an arrogant senior officer. Result! thought Richard.

While Ah Pau controlled the large reel drum of the command wire, Richard drew out three coils of wire and held them and the dem in his left hand, the one closest to the wall. With a determined, but unhurried stride, he set off on the Long and Lonely Walk.

Yes, it was made of concrete. Richard's heart was pumping hard, but his head was clear and his mind focussed. He had checked the toilet, looking for secondary devices. He always had to remember that he might just be the bomber's target. Having found nothing else out of the ordinary, his attention was now with the suspect object itself. The young Inspector's description had been right on the money. The red chinese characters on the banner across the stall door screamed out a warning, even to someone who couldn't read them. Richard's mind was aware of the fact that he should spend as little time as possible in his present situation. His eye caught what he had been looking for. A thin, almost invisible, length of fishing line dangled from the rear of the concrete ball. That could be the arming device. If so, then he would have to be careful not to disturb the thing, it could have an anti-handling device built in. Aware of the seconds ticking by, Richard thought it would be a good idea to actually do something. The EOD Officer's built in alarm clock served him well. Right now it was telling him that he should get on with it and get the hell out of there. It would be bad luck if a timer should set the thing off while he was standing over it, but why give ill fortune more of a chance?

Richard dropped the coils of wire and carefully placed his package on the surface of the ball. The det cord was laid on the underside of a length of broad duct tape. The sturdy tape was pressure sensitive, adhering with greater vigour as it was pressed harder against a surface. It was sticky enough to adhere even under modest pressure, so reducing the danger of moving an object. Richard placed the charge around the "equator" of the ball, covering about half its circumference. The idea was to crack the thing open. Taking more tape, he taped some of the trailing wire to the door frame, taking the weight of the wire off the charge, reducing the chance that charge and bomb would part company before the big pay-off. Having completed his task, Richard left the room with little ceremony. He walked back toward his command post, all the time the hairs on the back of his neck standing to attention. As he walked, he was aware of the smell of joss sticks which permeated the building. His senses were charged during these seemingly endless parades. At this moment, his focus was on getting back to the command post. Once there, he would relive every sight, sound and smell of his trip to and from the device.

Ah Pau gave him his usual smile when he rejoined him. Richard went to his kit and pulled out the Shrike. Essentially nothing more than a sophisticated battery pack, the piece of equipment had gained its name from the British Army, for whom it had been originally designed. Richard pulled the velcro fastening open and exposed the controls. Ah Pau handed him the two leads from the firing cable. Richard placed these in their terminals and pressed a button on the face of the shrike. A green light came on. Confirmation of a firing circuit.

'OK, Ah Pau, tell the IC Post that there will be a controlled explosion in two minutes from now.'

The Chinese officer hurried off, leaving his boss on his own. "Controlled explosion", thought Richard. "Cross your fingers and hope for the best" would be more like it. How many times had he heard news readers use that catch-all phrase to describe the variety of techniques employed to disrupt a bomb? In the end, it all boiled down to the same thing. It took a finite amount of time for the heating element in a detonator to reach the temperature required to set the primary explosive off. The idea was to separate it from it's power supply before it had received the 0.6 amps required to do the job. Unlike in the movies, where the intrepid bomb disposal officer cuts wires and generally farts about in the vicinity of a considerable amount of very dangerous material, the reality is that the separation is achieved with the informed application of violent force. In this case, using a length of detonating cord. Explosive against bomb. Force against force. Manual disarming was rarely an option. Only in the very last resort would it be considered. Not so in the past. There had been a time where the value of a human life was held to be lower than bricks and mortar. That was a matter of policy. Policy killed bomb disposal officers. Policy and stupidity and pure blind bad luck.

Ah Pau returned. Richard turned his attention to the Shrike. Yelling out the word 'FIRING!', he pressed the button.

The explosion rocked the walls. It was sudden and violent and then it was over. Richard looked at Ah Pau and waited. He would wait for another ten minutes, the "soak time", before approaching the room again.

Nothing happened during the silent wait. Richard nodded at his number two. The explosion had sounded like the det cord going off and only the det cord. It sounded good, but they would have to wait until Richard went to evaluate the situation, to find out what had happened. In the mean time, Richard and Ah Pau prepared another weapon, just in case further action was needed on the second Long and Lonely Walk.

CHAPTER 3

The glow from the VDUs cast ghostly shadows against the dark walls. All around the oval "pit" faces stared intently at the display in front of them. Subdued lighting created tiny oases within the darkness of the POD.

POD was not an acronym. It was a description of a space which was designed to bring forth the seeds of creativity and ingenuity. A place where ideas could be nurtured and developed. A place where the fortunes of Harbour Holdings would germinate or die, according to the quality of the thoughts of the men sitting before their computer consoles.

The POD had been designed as an environment which would aid the decision making process, particularly within a culture where the concept of "face" meant so much. In large corporations, creativity could be stifled by the fear of losing face, or worse; causing a superior to lose face. The POD was built to help release the creative thought of a naturally repressed group. As the men looked at their screens, they saw phrases appear in a hierarchical formation. Phrases attached themselves to other phrases, forming the seeds of a train of thought. A collective consciousness, following one line, then perhaps moving along a different path. The session was one of electronic brainstorming. The seemingly random inputs would later be analysed with the help of a sophisticated computer program and models constructed to aid in the decision making process. The technique was called "Cognitive Mapping". The benefit of using computers to input ideas was that the inputs were anonymous. The men were therefore more likely to "say" what they actually thought, rather than something that might curry favour with their bosses. That was the theory.

The reality was that this was only part of the function of this windowless room. At the head of the sunken console area sat one man who knew the truth of the POD. Li Keung was head of Harbour Holdings. He was one of only two men in the room who knew its greatest secret. The other sat behind him, in the shadows, a location which suited him well. Jack Garland was not a pleasant man. As head of security for Harbour Holdings, he had many unpleasant duties. He enjoyed almost all of them. Now he was sitting back, watching the room with a predator's gaze, looking for weakness in the flock.

The secret which these two men shared was that one console in the room was different to the others. It allowed its operator to see who input what phrase. It pointed the finger at the unsuspecting author. Loyalty was measured by the touch of a button. A career could be destroyed by honesty. This was the perversion of an ingenious tool. Perversion oozed from Li and his watchdog. His tactics had made him unpopular and very wealthy. Within his cocoon of power, he carried on his twisted existence without fear.

Li's eye was caught by a phrase which appeared on his screen. His expression did not change. Even in the darkness of the POD, he refused to give any outward sign of his thoughts. In his mind, a man's fate was sealed. Li logged the thought and continued his scrutiny of the mental processes of his employees. His contempt for these men was only subservient to his thirst for power. It maddened him that he had to rely on inferior creatures to do his bidding. The irony was that when one of his people showed any sign of matching the high standards that he assigned to himself, that individual was immediately dealt with as a threat. Such was the fate of the man who had just caught his merciless eye.

Li Keung pressed a button on the console in front of him and the lights in the POD slowly came up. He had seen enough. As the room grew brighter, heads looked up from VDUs. The sighs of relief were audible. Backs were straightened and necks stretched. One by one, heads turned to look at Li.

'Thank you gentlemen. A most instructive session. I think that we will adjourn for now. When our analysts have had a chance to process the material we have gathered today and I have had a chance to digest the results, we will meet again. This takeover is crucial to the long-term growth of the company. I know that you will devote all your energies to ensuring its success. That will be all.' With that, he rose and walked toward the door. Garland was on his heel. Eyes looked down as the Englishman passed. No one wanted to take the chance of catching the man's gaze. The Gorgon lived in this man.

'Well?' As he asked the question, Garland looked at Li, sitting in his high-backed chair. A chair with armour plate in the back, behind which was a window of armoured glass. Such was the paranoia which decorated the offices of Harbour Holdings.

The seat perched on a raised platform which allowed the diminutive Li to cast his gaze downwards into the room, belying his sub-five-foot stature. It had been ergonomically designed to accommodate Li's twisted spine and offer as much comfort as possible.

'It's Wu. There's no doubt now. His arrogance betrayed him. So eager to please. So transparent in his ambition. He would have betrayed himself, even without the help of the computer.' Li leveled his gaze with that of his lieutenant.

'I take it you want a discreet settlement, as usual?'

Li's eyes hardened as he spoke. 'Wu is popular with his colleagues. In this case, I think that we should send a message that will be clearly understood by all. Make it violent and painful. I want the little shit to know just who it is who has ended his ambitions, before he dies.'

'Leave it to me.'

CHAPTER 4

'Come on boy, time to go.'

Richard looked up from the typewriter. He smiled as he looked at the one man he would tolerate calling him "boy". John Gray had earned the right to call just about anyone anything he wanted. Three tours in Northern Ireland as an ATO with the Royal Army Ordnance Corps, tackling the bombs of the IRA, had earned him the respect of his peers. Anyone else didn't matter. If they objected to his careless attitude, it was just too bad. He had earned the right not to give a fuck.

'Just writing up my report on that bloody concrete bomb. I was lucky that the thing didn't go off. Very clever.' Richard continued to talk as he fell into step with his boss. The head of the Bomb Disposal Unit was obviously in a hurry. 'Turns out that the guy who was in dispute with the owner of the toilet stall was a lab technician at Hong Kong Polytechnic. Also a bit of a weekend warrior. CID found all sorts of military-style paraphernalia in his flat. Also some interesting literature, including the "Anarchist's Cookbook". Everything he needed to make the IED was in his flat. Intelligent, but not too bright.'

John Gray kept silent until the two were seated in the rear of a police staff car. As the driver left the compound at North Point Police Station, he turned to Richard.

'This morning there was an explosion in a high rise in Central. Looks like a letter bomb. The forensic people have already started their investigation, but they wanted us to have a look at the scene. Ah Pau tells me that you didn't wear your bomb suit again today.'

This was typical of John Gray. Throw a difficult topic straight into the middle of another conversation. No matter how many times you had heard it done, it always caught you off guard. Exactly the result that John wanted from his little surprise attacks. No time for you to come up with some rationalisation. Richard tried anyway.

'It was an awkward space, the suit would have slowed me down and I wanted to get in and out quickly. The approach was well guarded by walls, I was only really vulnerable over the device and as you are keen to remind everyone, in that close, all the suit is good for is keeping all the bits together.'

The older man turned to look at Richard. 'OK, I wasn't there and what you say may well be true, but there have been a dozen incidents over the last six months where you should have worn the suit. I can't force you to. If I did, the force would make it policy to wear it at all times, even when it was really inappropriate and dangerous for us. Therefore I leave it up to individual discretion, but Richard you never seem to wear the damned thing. Even the force shrink has started to take notice. You know that you are being watched, after your little incident.'

Richard's face turned very grim.

'Sorry,' said John. 'That was thoughtless, but look me old son, I am only saying this for your own good. You're the best damn BDO I've had work for me since I left the Army and you're my friend. I want to keep you around for as long as I can. After all, who else am I going to go drinking with?'

A cheerful expression forced its way on to Richard's face. 'Point taken Boss. I'll try to use the bomb suit more often. Even in this heat.'

'Like fuck you will, but at least think about it. Now, here's what I know about this letter bomb.'

'Hi Cass.'

Cassius To turned in the direction of the greeting. 'Richard. Superintendent Gray. Glad to see you. Quite a mess, eh?'

'John, you remember Cassius, don't you. We were at Training School together. Last year I had to pour him into a taxi after our Christmas party.'

John Gray extended his hand to the young Chinese Chief Inspector. 'Of course I remember Cassius and as I recall it wasn't you who were doing the pouring Richard. Cass was the one who managed to get you home in one piece.

'So, what do we have here?'

The three men surveyed the office. Most of the room was undisturbed. David Fairbrother's desk and the window behind it were a different matter.

'The body has been removed already,' said Cassius. 'There is a lot of blood. What you would expect from a decapitation I suppose. There seems to be so little damage.'

'The device was probably designed that way. Shaped charge, perhaps. The victim was probably a solo target, but I noticed a commotion on the pavement outside, what happened?' asked Richard.

Cassius looked grim. 'A hawker. Poor old guy was just in the wrong place at the wrong time. Was caught by a falling sheet of glass. Pretty gruesome sight. Don't know who I feel more sorry for.'

A young woman approached the three men. She was wearing the overalls of a forensics officer, a civilian working for the Government Chemist Department.

'Hello Alice. Looking as radiant as ever.' Richard gave the woman a beaming smile.

'Now Richard, you start flirting with me at a crime scene and I might have to make a report to a higher authority, like your girl-friend.

'Hello sir,' turning her attention to John Gray, she got down to business. 'Looks like a very professional job. The violence of the explosion suggests high explosive. It was compact, so I don't think this was made in someone's bathtub. Commercial or military sheet explosive seems a good guess, we'll know more after we have analy-sed the residues.'

Richard looked thoughtful. 'Bit odd for a man in Fairbrother's position to be opening mail.'

'Apparently it was one of his little "quirks". So, the bomber obvi-ously knew his target.'

'That fact any use in narrowing down the list of suspects?' asked Richard.

'Might be, if the fact hadn't been included in an interview in the Hong Kong Tatler a while ago. The way gossip goes around this town, even without the benefit of the article, who knows how many people are aware of his habits.'

John Gray was looking intently at the damage to the window. At length, he turned to the forensics officer. 'Where is the shrapnel?'

Alice smiled at him. 'Over here. We kept some out for you to see. I didn't think it would take you long to ask that.'

She led the men over to a table, where fragments had been laid out on a white sheet. All eyes stared at the pieces of debris which the forensics team had recovered.

John Gray picked up a twisted piece of metal.Despite the damage sustained in the intense heat of the blast, it's unusual shape was apparent. It was in the form of an octagon, with a circular hole in the centre.

'A coin?' asked John.

'Mainland Chinese coin. Old. I'll have to get an expert to verify the age and origin, but there are plenty of them in Hong Kong. People keep them as lucky charms, sometimes wear them as jewelry,' replied the scientist. 'If you look at the other side, the heat damage would suggest that the coins were imbedded in the explosive.'

'Nasty little anti-personnel device,' said Richard. 'And maybe a message?'

Cassius looked at him. 'Poetic justice? A man who has accumulated great wealth, killed by the coin of the people he has exploited? Something like that?'

'Maybe,' replied Richard. 'Or maybe it was just an easily obtainable material, difficult to trace. But the fact that it is an old Chinese coins makes me think that it is some sort of "signature". Like a painter's brush strokes. He's stopping short of actually telling us who he is, but he's singling himself out. He's saying "Look at me. Aren't I clever, certainly smarter than any of you." He didn't just want to kill Fairbrother, he wanted to send us a message and that is bad news.'

Cassius looked worried. "You're saying that this is not an isolated event, aren't you?'

'Well, I haven't seen anything similar, so I would say that this is the first, but I will be very surprised if it's the last.'

Cassius looked at John Gray, hoping to see disagreement with his colleague. He saw none, just a nod of the head. 'Aw, shit!' He turned and looked at the destroyed plate glass. 'Shit!'

CHAPTER 5

The orange dawn slowly pushed back the grey of twilight. The transition from night to day was a special time. A time shared by many in the metropolis of Hong Kong. A time for the old and the young. The old who used the dawn as a backdrop for their daily *tai chi*, the slow motion ballet of shadow combat which helps invigorate them and draw out their inner youth. The young, for whom the working day began early, or finished late.

Richard sat at the edge of the parade square and peeled the skin from a large, juicy orange. The smell of the zest hit him like a splash of cold water. The acid of the first bite of flesh drew his cheeks in. As he breathed in the cool morning air, he felt at peace with the world. Richard enjoyed the solitude of moments like this. It was a chance to think, without the disruptions of other voices. He could focus on his inner voice, the one that helped him make sense of the crazy world in which he lived. It was all too easy to get caught up in the hubbub of life and be carried along in the swell. Moments of reflection were rare and had to be used to the full.

Ford Transit vans, battered form their peculiar life, lined the edge of the parade square. Each was a different colour. None were in the familiar dark blue livery of the police force. Every vehicle had a platform on the roof. A familiar addition to work vehicles in Hong Kong. Used as a base for workmen to access the lower levels of the high rise world. Some of the roofs had black bamboo ladders strapped to them. Light and strong, the material was used as scaffolding on the tallest of structures in the territory. The hot humid climate was unkind to steel scaffolding. A visitor might be appalled at the sight of men climbing up 30 or 40 storeys of a flimsy looking bamboo lattice, but the workmen felt safe in the hands of nature's gift. The ladders that adorned the Transits were for the same purpose as any workman's; gaining access to the inaccessible. The workmen who used these ladders were anything but ordinary. The tools of their trade were the submachine gun and the pistol. Where a tradesman's passage up a ladder usually brought the repair of damage, these artisans brought violent destruction. Their aim was to save life. The paradox of the task was that more often than not, the life at risk would be saved by the scientific application of extreme violence against those who would endanger it. Might against might. Violence against violence.

The parade square was part of the New Territories Depot, NTD. Formerly the headquarters of the police force in the New Territories of Hong Kong. Now the base for the Special Duties Unit, SDU, the counter-terrorist force of the Royal Hong Kong Police. On lazy Sundays,cricket had been played on coconut matting in the middle of this square. White clad men had been encouraged by applauding wives, girlfriends and less energetic colleagues. Now, the physical exertions that took place on the square were of a more extreme type. Men were pushed to the limits of their physical abilities and then expected to go beyond them, all in an effort to show that they belonged here, among an elite group of warriors. Such descriptions embarrassed the men who made up the unit. They down-played the Trojan existence that they led. They were just doing their job. A job they chose, or perhaps which chose them. A peculiar profession populated by unusual men. A priesthood of violence.

A familiar sound intruded on the quiet of Richard's reverie. Faint, on the edge of hearing at first, steadily growing louder, closer. Richard wiped the last drops of juice from his lips as he looked toward the horizon and the approaching rhythm. The trees around the compound obscured the helicopter until the sound was a roar in Richard's ears. Finally, the Wessex, with its green camouflage and blue and red roundel, raised its nose and settled into a hover over the large white "H", painted in the middle of the parade square. The improbable looking flying machine hung in the air, supported by the alchemy of engineering and aerodynamics. Softly, it lowered to the tarmac, settling like a huge insect on hydraulic legs. Richard stood and walked to the open door on the flank of the metal Homoptera.

Richard was greeted by the smiling face of Pete Bailly, the RAF loadmaster. 'Morning Richard. Bit odd seeing you up for this duty.' Pete had to yell to make himself heard over the roar of the engines. This was flying at its most visceral.

Richard strapped himself in and accepted the headphones that the loadmaster offered him. He moved the microphone in front of his mouth and replied. 'Thought I would give my guys a break and do the dawn patrol myself. Besides, I enjoy watching you guys hang from this thing like a piece of bait.'

Pete Bailly told the pilot that their passenger was strapped in. The roar increased and the chopper began to lift its considerable weight off the landing struts and rubber separated from tarmac. Wind rushed in through the open door, bringing with it the roar of engine and wind and the smell of burning aviation fuel. Flying in an Air Force helicopter was an experience that you could touch. It involved every sense.

The journey took less than quarter of an hour. The hot air from the engine exhaust blurred the view through the door. As their objective came into view, Billy Parker, the other crewman in the belly of the chopper, prepared himself for the task in hand. With Pete's help, he climbed into a harness. Once Billy was secured, Pete took the end of the winch cable, which perched outside the top left corner of the door, and hooked it onto the D-ring on Billy's harness. As the helicopter slowed and settled into a hover, the pilot came on to the intercom and informed the three men in the passenger compartment that they had reached their first destination. Outside the door, all the men could see was hillside. Uncomfortably close hillside. Billy took the red cloth which Richard handed to him and stepped out of the door. When the cable had taken his weight, Pete handled the winch controls and lowered his younger colleague slowly towards his target. He watched over the lip of the door and with time won skill, stopped the winch at just the right moment. Billy found himself level with the top of the pole. He grabbed the rope attached to the white pole and started to tie the red flag to it. The whole process took a couple of minutes. Satisfied with his knots, Billy signalled to the loadmaster and the winch began to reverse its operation

This process would be repeated a dozen times before the morning's task was done. Labourious, but necessary. Safety was all important at a firing range. Castle Peak Field Firing Range. A natural bowl formed by a range of hills on the west side of the New Territories. A military range facility, also used by some of the units within the police force's paramilitary wing. Particularly the SDU. The size of the range complex and the topography made it necessary to use a helicopter to put the warning flags in place. They signalled that the range was in use and that no one should approach the area. It might seem a redundant warning, but it protected the government from claims of compensation from the stupid.

It took an hour to put the crimson ring in place. The final flag would be raised outside the guard room at the entrance to the range complex. The Wessex banked off on the trip back to its base at RAF Sek Kong as Richard walked into the small white gatehouse. The Gurkha on duty snapped to attention at the sight of the three "pips" on the newcomers shoulder. Richard's uniform was similar to the Disruptive Pattern Material, DPM used by the British Army. The young Nepalese soldier knew the difference, but showed the policeman the same respect that he would have shown one of his Sahibs. Richard didn't return the salute, as he was not wearing any headgear. He, like most of his unit tended to favour informality in his dress, only donning the distinctive blue beret when absolutely necessary. Nevertheless, he gratefully acknowledged the soldier's courtesy and was rewarded with a warm smile. As the officer in charge of the range practice that morning, Richard filled out the required forms and accepted the responsibility for all that would take place while his men were there. Thanking the guard, Richard walked out into the morning sun and started to jog up the twisting road that led to the range he and his men would be using. He could have waited for his men to arrive in their transport and the chopper crew had offered to drop him off at the top of the hill, near the firing point, but Richard wanted the exercise. He had been spending too much time in the office of late and not enough out with his team. It had been over a year since his promotion to Chief Inspector and his move from Assault Group Leader to Team Commander. In the beginning, he had managed to maintain his fitness, but with the increase in his administrative load, he had allowed himself to slip back a bit. A recent run with his men had convinced him that it was time for action.

Running in boots can be tough. It takes its toll on the joints and the feet. Richard had recently changed from the combat boots worn by the Army to a good old pair of "Doc Martens". One of his colleagues had suggested them. Skeptical at first, he had soon come around to the concept, as the aching in his knees and ankles became, not quite a thing of the past, but less troublesome. Wear and tear were taking their toll, he had reached the point where he had to take better care of his body. Sad prospect for a thirty-year old.

Richard pushed himself up the steep road. Sweat came quickly in the humid air. It was a daily routine. Sweat, dry out, sweat, dry out.

He took at least three showers every day. Such is outdoor life in the tropics. Using the rhythm of his breathing to set the cadence of his stride, Richard allowed his mind to wander, focussing on anything but the burning of his muscles.

It was in fact inaccurate to say that Richard's men would be turning up that morning. Richard was Bravo Team Commander. The men who would be arriving for practice were members of Charlie Team, the training team. They were men who had passed the rigorous selection course, but were not yet full members of the unit. Over the first six months of their attachment, they would be assessed and assigned duties appropriate to their individual skills. That would mean becoming part of either a sniper group, or assault group within the two land teams, Alpha and Bravo. Some might display a particular aptitude and be assigned to Delta Team, the marine counter-terrorist force. This highly specialised group tended to want seasoned officers, so often recruited men from the land teams. Sometimes though, individuals stuck out as being ideal candidates for training in water-borne counter-terrorism. An unfortunate few would prove to be unsuitable altogether and suffer the soul-destroying prospect of being returned to normal duties. After all they had been through, failing to win a place in the teams could be very hard on the men. The unit tried to make them understand that it was an achievement to have gotten as far as they had, but it was not unknown for men to quit the Force altogether as a result of being denied a place in the unit. A remarkable few endeavoured to overcome their shortcomings and reapplied for SDU selection. Sometimes they failed again. Those who succeeded were particularly valued in the unit.

The men who would be training at Castle Peak were potential snipers. Richard needed a man for his Sniper Group and had volunteered to conduct the range this morning so that he could get a look at the candidates for the place.

It was a hard twenty minute trudge to reach the top of the road. Richard was breathing heavily by the time he made it to the sniper gallery. The gallery was an open structure with three tiers, creating a series of elevated positions, looking out across the thousand yards of valley that separated the firing point from the target butts. The butts took the form of a concrete platform, with a sand bullet trap at its back. To the right of the target area was a concrete control room where the target mechanisms were operated. The targets could face and edge and traverse the butts. Snipers didn't always have the luxury of stationary targets. Richard looked at the Rolex Submariner on his wrist. He had half an hour before the team would arrive. Taking a deep breath, he set off down the shallow valley, toward the butts. He would have the targets up and the range set by the time the men arrived.

The bullet sliced through the chest of the charging soldier. The determined look on his face did not change. No flinch, no grimace. His eyes stared off into the distance, taunting his attacker. Another bullet hit home, an inch away from the first. Still the figure remained frozen, his Eastern European battledress showing not a wrinkle. A third round hit him, a fraction away from where the first had struck. The icy stare of the red menace remained unmoved.

Richard looked at the three round group in the Figure 11 target. He nodded with approval and then looked up at the face of the charging man. The target design showed the face of the enemy, at least as perceived by an army facing the massed ranks of the Warsaw Pact. The face that returned his stare was the face of communist aggression, as seen through the eyes of western paranoia. Richard had often wondered if it was a coincidence that the target paper on which this figure was printed was shaped like a coffin. Wishful thinking? He returned his attention to the damage inflicted by the 7.62 mm bullets. Good group, particularly at a thousand yards. Now to turn up the heat a bit.

The targets were almost invisible to the naked eye, as they were edged away from the firers. Richard's eyes were not on the targets, but on the young man beside him. Richard watched his breathing, the way he cradled the rifle and for any signs of tension in his body. The fact that the targets had turned to face the shooters was announced by the volley of gunfire. Richard's keen eye remained on the young man. He watched for any signs of snatching, or flinching. He watched how the shooter's body behaved after the shot had been released, any sign that tense muscles were being relaxed. Richard was pleased with what he didn't see. Another volley. The shooter's breathing remained steady, there was no sign of tension. Steady nerves, cool head, just what Richard was looking for. The Constable was aware that he was being observed, scrutinised by a man who could hold the young man's future in his hands. If Richard was impressed, there was the chance of a place in the team that everyone said was the best in the unit. A bold claim, not made lightly. If he failed to show his best, he would have blown it. Thoughts such as these are liable to cause tension in the coolest of heads. This one had ice water flowing through it.

'Not bad,' said Richard.

The man standing next to him nodded in reply. The top of his head barely reached over Richard's shoulder, but his hard face and bulging forearms were an indication that this was an extremely hard man. Station Sergeant Kwan was second in command of the unit's training team. Men first encountered Mr Kwan during selection. They grew to hate him even more if they were lucky enough to be selected for training. At the end of six months they might not call him their bosom buddy, but they would respect him and know that they had a better than even chance of surviving their dangerous duty as a result of their association with him. Some called him a sadist. None doubted his abilities.

'You were right about his shooting Mr Kwan. What about his brain? Is he smart enough to do the job?'

'He is smart. Good eyes and ears. He'll make a good sniper. His room combat skills are excellent also. He will be good as a back-up assault man. He is very fit.' Fitness was very important to Mr Kwan. He judged every individual by his fitness. To him fitness was a matter of pride. Someone who let themselves become unfit was lacking in the elements that made a man a man.

'Then it looks as though I have found my man. I'll want to see him perform in an exercise before I make up my mind. When have you scheduled the next one?'

'In about a week, an overnight exercise, the snipers will have to stalk in to a hide and report throughout the night. Good chance for you to see them all work.'

Shooting was a small, if vital, part of a sniper's job. The most important area of expertise for these men was observation. They provided intelligence that would determine the plan of attack for the assault group. Their input to the overall intelligence gathering effort was crucial. They understood what their colleagues would be up against and what they should be looking for to help lower the odds against their comrades. Terrorists were rarely stupid. These men could not afford to be any less smart.

As the two men walked back to the firing point, Kwan turned to Richard. 'Getting fat, sir?'

Richard first looked at the other man and then down at his flat stomach. He knew exactly what the older man meant. Just the thing which had been going through his own mind. Too much time behind a desk and not enough out training with his men. Richard took a back seat to his Assault Group Leader operationally. His subordinate now had the unenviable role of "the first man through the door". Richard, though was the head of the team. When he had been the Assault Group Leader, he had always led by example. His conscience was telling him that he had let that discipline slip. There were some things that, in his new role, it was inappropriate for him to do, but keeping fit wasn't one of him. Kwan had exposed a raw nerve, just as he knew he would, by confronting his senior officer. He would never do it in front of other men. One to one, he could be an absolute terrier, if he thought that one of the unit was in need of a little reminder of their duty. Rank was irrelevant. This was his job. Kwan had seen every man in the unit, from the OC down, at their worst and their best. They had no secrets left, at least none that were of any importance.

'Point taken. I promise that I will get out with my men more often and I'll do a lot more PT to get back in shape.'

'Why not join Charlie team when we get back to base?'

For a brief moment, Richard considered launching into the thousand reasons why he couldn't join the training team for a PT session. Lurking memories of sessions with Kwan fought to get a grip of his tongue. In the end, pride took hold. 'I'd love to. Just what I need to get me back on track.' Even as the words came out of his mouth, his body was groaning.

CHAPTER 6

ISS.

Keep It Simple Stupid. The acronym that I live by. Take this for example. Two pieces of wood, joined by a simple spring. A clothes peg. An innocuous object. A couple of drawing pins. More banality. Yet I put them together, just so and I have the beginnings of a versatile switch. A trigger.

Let me just wind the wires around the pins, then push the pins fully into the wooden jaws of the peg. There. Some people would leave it like that, but not me. No, I like my work to be neat. Neat and tidy. A little tape, to hold the wires along the legs of the peg. Nice. Trim a bit here, a little there. Perfect.

Simple devices targeted ingeniously, that's the trick. Bombing campaigns follow a pattern of development. In the beginning, bombs are simple and often ineffective. The problem is usually that the bomber targets his devices poorly and his skills are undeveloped. As he gains construction skills, he learns how to place the device for maximum effect. The best time. The most damage. The greatest number of kills.

Unfortunately, ego leads to more complex bombs. Stupidly complex devices, putting the bomber at greater risk than the target. A promising career can be cut short by an overly complex device. The placing of the device becomes an unnecessarily hazardous affair. Arming the device can lead to a premature explosion. Some organisations tend to have someone other than the builder place the bomb for this very reason. They miss the point. They are wasting their time. Bomb disposal techniques make a mockery of the complex device, especially when it is targeted stupidly. A waste of time, effort and resources. A high velocity blast of water and all that electronic cunning is blown apart.

I am not so stupid. My creations are reliable. I don't put myself at risk. I don't have a blindly fanatical following to do my dirty work for me. I wouldn't want one. I enjoy the process. I like to take up the challenge of a job. Put the raw materials together. Create the death. I want to see the thing through from beginning to the end. Sometimes I can't see the result of my work. That's a pity. When I can, the pleasure is indescribable. A swell of pride. Joy, pure joy.

The victims? What victims? They are part of the process, nothing more. Why should I feel anything for them. They are simply there to allow me to complete my mission. Their death is not the mission, merely an act in the play. The bomb. That is the whole of it. Having the bomb become what it is intended to be. Becoming light and heat. Blooming death. Creation in its purest form. The human players merely give the birth greater meaning.

Snip. Snip. Snip. There. Let me just make a small hole here. Good. Now, I take this fishing line and thread it through the hole. Just like that. A little knot and there we go. I place this piece of plastic between the drawing pins in the jaws of the peg and voila! A switch. Ready to be placed in any device I might think fit. Good for a tripwire. But I have something else in mind. Something special. Yes, they are going to like this one. A lesson in just what I am capable of. This one I will be able to watch. The thrill of anticipation is almost unbearable. Almost. Some people think that the anticipation of an event is better than the event itself. They have obviously never created an explosion. Seen their creation blossom and reach out for its target. Instantaneous, inescapable. Death in the blink of an eye. I must make sure that I don't blink at the crucial moment. I want every millisecond to be imprinted on my retina, so that I can play it back in my mind's eye, again and again. Of course, it will never be the same as the event itself, but it will sustain me until the next time. Give me the hunger for the next explosion. An even greater hunger than I feel now. It won't be long now. The next one will bloom soon enough.

CHAPTER 7

Ernest Blyth walked over to the low cedar cabinet sitting in the corner of his office. Producing a small key from his pocket, he unlocked the cabinet and slowly opened the two ornate doors. He breathed in the aroma which was released as the air-tight seal was broken. The mixture of fragrant wood and tobacco filled his nostrils, the pleasure of the experience flooding through his body. He took his time deciding which of the twenty drawers he would open. Each slim drawer in the humidor held a different brand of cigar to delight Ernest's palate. The front of each drawer bore the carved emblem of the brand that lay within. All had one thing in common, they were Cuban. Even the ornate humidor had been produced in the workshop of one of the island's finest craftsmen, Gerencia Ritos of Havana. Ernest had seen some of the company's work while on business in the isolated island and knew that he had to have one. This example he had commissioned on the spot. It's lines were clean and classic. His family crest discretely adorned the front. When it had been shipped form Havana, it had been accompanied by a full complement of cigars, all personally chosen by the new owner. Names like Bolivar, Hoyo de Monterrey, Montecristo, Por Larranaga and even Cohiba, Castro's brand, only available in diplomatic circles until relatively recently. The choice was never easy, but Ernest enjoyed this daily, titillating ritual.

As head of the Gillespie Group, he could afford to pamper himself in this manner. He controlled his financial empire with a tight grip, but was quite happy to spend his personal wealth on the good things in life. Unmarried, he had ensured that his fifty-two years had been filled with every experience that was necessary to satisfy his considerable appetites. His girth was evidence of his love of food. His red veined face declared that fine wine and the best malt whiskies were his companions on the road of life.

It was going to be a long afternoon in the office. Ernest had enjoyed a relatively light lunch, as he wanted to be alert for the work ahead of him. He decided to choose a Romeo y Julieta Churchill. The seven inches of aromatic tobacco would help make the reports he had to read more palatable and might make his mood more mellow by the time his first meeting started.

Ernest opened the drawer that held a selection of cigars of the same brand. Their lengths and gauges varied, but most carried the same red and gold band with white lettering. An exception was the cigar which the Taipan removed from the drawer. It had a plain gold band, with the brand and the name "Churchill". From a small drawer, he took a flat gold cigar cutter and having removed the band, cleanly sliced off the end of the cigar, careful not to remove the end-piece which firmly held the rolls of leaf together. Ernest then closed the humidor, but did not lock it. It was his custom that the last thing he did at the end of the day was to lock away his cigars. Besides, he might feel the need for another one should the rest of the day take a turn for the worse.

Back at his desk, Ernest removed a long wooden match from a box and struck it. Rolling the wooden splint in his fingers, he waited until the sulphurous flash had settled into a large orange flame and put it to the end of his cigar. He allowed the flame to caress the tobacco and then put the other end to his lips and drew the first bitter drafts of smoke through the tightly packed leaf. This he continued until he was satisfied that the cigar had taken the life from the flame and then extinguished the match with a single breath. He placed the cigar on the edge of an Edinburgh Crystal ashtray to his right and directed his attention to the papers which his secretary had left on his desk. Ernest liked to let the cigar slowly warm, only occasionally drawing on it, to keep the burning tip alive. Only when the cigar had warmed through did he pay it the attention that it deserved. Then, the tobacco would yield the best of its flavour and Ernest would ease back in his chair, relaxed and at peace with the world. Until that glorious moment, he would have to concentrate on the disappointing reports he had to wade through.

Performance in some key areas had been well below target of late. His hope was that the reports would give him an indication of the reasons behind this. The documents in his hands would brief him for his first meeting of that afternoon. He had been through the report once already and had identified three areas in which the division could do better. He wanted to ensure that he had not missed anything before he had the division head in front of him. The man was an experienced manager and his division's poor performance had surprised Ernest Blyth. The CEO hoped that the matter could be resolved, as he liked the man and would hate to lose him. Somehow the division had to be turned around, or changes would have to be made. Sometimes that meant starting from the top down.

The document was starting to give Ernest a headache. Some obvious problems. Some less obvious, but just as worrying. The thing which the report didn't tell him was why these problems had arisen. Not surprising really. If that had been identified, the division head would have dealt with the cause and would not have been summoned to see the CEO. At the back of Ernest's mind was the nagging thought that often the most difficult fault to identify was our own. Not surprising then if the author of this report could not see the problem. The Taipan genuinely hoped that his suspicions were wrong.

To ease his troubled mind, Ernest reached for the Churchill and drew on the now warm cigar. The wait had been worth it. As he drew the smoke through his mouth and into his nose, the flavours of the smoke revealed themselves to his senses. He blew a cloud of smoke into the room and watched it rise to the ceiling. The after taste in his mouth was a joy, making him relish the next draw.

A buzz from his intercom intruded on Ernest's pleasure.

'Yes, Miss Li?'

'Sorry to disturb you, sir. A package has been delivered for you, from your cigar importer. I thought you might want to be informed.'

Ernest brightened at the news. He had been expecting a shipment of "vintage" Montecristos. They were pre-Castro and had been sitting in a collectors humidor in the United States. It was rare for Americans to give up their precious cigars, especially since the ban on Cuban cigars meant that most aficionados had to travel outside the US to enjoy their obsession, or risk the wrath of the Customs Service by smuggling them in. The price that he had to pay for this box of cigars would have made the accountants on the 12th floor wince, but Ernest thought the money worth paying. He was not just buying tobacco, he was buying history. In the same way that he enjoyed drinking a good Bordeaux from a classic year, so he would relish each of these cigars. Every time he lit one, it would invoke thoughts of linen suited adventurers, gamblers and gangsters. He would think of Hemingway, enjoying a cigar and a glass of rum, after a successful fishing trip. He would imagine dusky skinned maidens, flirting with him and inviting him to join them in a wild dance, to hypnotic latin rhythms.

'Sir?'

The voice of his secretary snapped Ernest back to the present. 'Please bring the package in Miss Li.'

A few moments later the young woman entered the office, carrying a Fed-Ex box. She placed the package on her boss's desk and smiled at the look of anticipation on his face. 'I hope you enjoy them, sir. I know you have been waiting for them for some time.'

'Thank you, Miss Li. A welcome diversion from this,' said the CEO, pointing to the papers on his desk.

Mabel Li left Ernest to enjoy opening his package. How like children men could be, she thought. Even a man like Ernest Blyth. So powerful, yet a small thing gave him such pleasure. If he had bought the cigars as an investment, Mabel could understand, but he would burn them! All that money turning into smoke. Oh well, she thought. If you were that wealthy, it didn't really matter.

Ernest looked at the box. It was unusual for the importer to FedEx his cigars over. Usually the man would send one of his employees to deliver the Taipan's cigars. Perhaps no one could be spared and knowing Ernest was anxious to see his precious purchase, he used the courier instead. Certainly, his cigars would be well protected and unlikely to go missing. His enthusiasm soon wiped this thought from his mind, as he attacked the outer box, pulling the tabs at the side, causing the box to open like a clam. There was a lot of packing material inside and the contents were wrapped in thick brown paper. Ernest smiled at the care that had been taken to protect the cigars.

Each layer of paper was removed with care, to expose the box. Ernest gasped when he saw it. The colour had faded with age, the pale yellow lid bore the triangular crossed swords and fleur-de-lis that marked the contents as coming from the house of Montecristo. This was more than he had hoped for. This must be the original box. He would have to keep this as a memento of his acquisition. The box had obviously been opened, but there was no damage, other than the obvious wear that comes with age. Even the seal of the lid was tight. Ernest looked around for the letter opener which normally sat on his desk. It was not immediately obvious and he felt himself become irritated at this delay in getting to the precious contents of the box. Eventually he found the thin blade, under some of the papers he had carelessly strewn across his desk. He inserted the blade carefully under the lid and eased the box open, taking care not to damage it.

'Jesus, look at this!' said Richard.

'What is it?' asked Cassius, his voice anxious.

'The biggest bloody humidor I have ever seen in my life. Look at this! H. Upmann, Partagas, Punch, Cohiba. There must be damn nearly every major brand of Cuban cigar here. Some of them I have never seen before. This guy certainly had taste Cass and a shit load of money. There must be thousands of dollars worth of cigars here. US dollars that is and that's not even taking into account the value of this cabinet. My guess would be that it's a one-off.'

'Oh, yes?' asked Cassius with undisguised apathy. He had never understood his friend's fascination with cigars. He knew that Richard smoked some very expensive brands and couldn't understand how he could stand seeing all that cash go up in smoke. 'Well, his obsession cost him dear this time. The secretary says that the package was supposed to contain some very expensive cigars that he had imported. We're checking with the importer and Fed-Ex now. At least the secretary got a good look at the delivery man. Might just be our first lead.'

'You really think so?'

Cassius sighed. 'No, I doubt if our man would be so stupid as to deliver the package himself, or if he did he was probably disguised in some way, but I have to at least try and be positive.' The detective looked at his colleague and decided to bring up a matter which had been causing him some concern. 'Look Richard. You and John seem awfully sure that we are dealing with one man here. Why?'

Richard folded his arms and gave Cassius a thoughtful look. 'This is not a widespread bombing campaign. The targets seem to be very specific. We're not looking for some terrorist bomb factory turning out devices by the dozen. There's artistry involved here. In this part of the world, the skills that we are seeing displayed are not that common. Yes, it is often the case that different people will manufacture and plant devices. It may be the case here. But John's experience tells him that there is a "signature", if you like, about these two bombings. I think we can be pretty sure that a single pair of hands made these devices. They're far more professionally executed than the sort of IEDs we usually come across.'

Cassius shrugged. John Gray was the expert, though he would have cringed at hearing the overused term associated with him.

'Well, he wasn't relying on shrapnel this time. From the mess in here, he just wanted to blow the shit out of his target. Literally blow him up in smoke...Christ, you don't think this guy is sending out messages here?' Richard feigned a surprised look, as though he had just had a revelation.

'You mean, the coins. Money being the root of all evil, so he uses it to kill someone who loved it. This guy is passionate about cigars, so he sends him a bomb in a cigar box. Is that what you're thinking? No, it can't be that, can it?'

Richard looked at his friend. 'My opinion? No, the guy is dicking us around. Anyone smart enough to pull this off is going to do it for a much better reason than lessons in morality. The cliches are for our benefit. A game within the big game, whatever that is.'

'Well, Fed-Ex have no record of a delivery and the cigar importer is claiming ignorance of the shipment.' Cassius sat down in his chair like a man defeated. More dead ends. Each lead they came across seemed to end up at the same destination, nowhere.

Richard ran his hand across his face. He was sharing his friend's fatigue. 'He does his homework, does our man. That's at least one thing that we know about him. The letter, which Fairbrother would almost certainly open himself, for example. The bomber had to be aware of the man's habits. A package which Blyth had been waiting for and would be eager to get his hands on. That sort of information takes a long time to obtain and is almost certainly inside information.'

'Yes, we're trying to find the leaks. Could be that the guy worked for a period in both companies, so I've asked for the details of any staff who have been taken on for a short period, going back for a year. Trouble is, in Hong Kong temporary staff are common and their references are rarely checked. Unfortunately, both companies pay their temps by cheque, so we don't have bank details to chase. Only thing we can really hope for is that false details might give us a lead. It's a small chance. They didn't even require photographs. Maybe we'll get an artist's sketch, if we can find someone with a good memory. If the guy talked to people to get the office gossip, they might remember him, assuming he didn't do his reconnaissance too long ago.'

'Well, the cigars are the best hope we have. Blyth didn't become aware of them until about four months ago, so that at least gives us a time frame. Also, the number of people who would have been aware of his interest should be limited. Unless of course this guy can get into the social circle of people like Blyth and Fairbrother. Then, we are really in the shit. You just know that Hong Kong's brightest and best would love to have their lives examined by Asia's Finest!'

'Yes,' laughed Cassius. 'It's funny how some of the most vocal advocates of law and order seem to think that a totally different set of rules apply to them. Have a strong police force, but don't let them dare investigate the activities of the elite. That would never do!

'Never mind. What about the bomb?'

'Well, you saw the damage in the office. Nothing subtle about it. Just enough explosive to blow the hell out of anyone standing close. No shrapnel. From the little I could see at the scene and the nature of the package, I would guess a microswitch activated device. Open the lid and boom! I'll know more when I get the forensic results. 'Relatively simple mechanism. The clever part is the way the device was targeted. He's smart our man. Keep the device simple as possible, so reducing the chance of technical failure and concentrate the ingenuity into placing the bomb and the target in the same physical space at the time of detonation. Yes, too bloody smart by far is this guy.'

'I suppose we just have to get lucky,' said the detective.

CHAPTER 8

❦

'Right. Yes. Uhuh. And the area is secure? OK. The senior officer on scene? Ah! I see. Right. Well, I think I will handle this one myself. I'll be there as soon as I can.'

Richard entered the office just as John Gray was uttering these words.

'What's up?'

John turned and looked at Richard for a few seconds before replying. 'A call. I think you had better let me handle this one.'

'How come?' Richard frowned as he looked inquiringly at the older man. 'I'm on call. Is it something you think I can't handle?' There was no accusation in his voice. He was aware that he had a lot to learn from his boss and that John was not going to put him in a situation for which he was unprepared. 'I'd better come along as your number two. Who knows, I might even learn something.'

John Gray started to look sheepish.

'What?' asked Richard.

'It's not that I don't think you are up to the device, it's just the situation is a bit tricky. It's in the middle of Central.'

It only took a moment for the flicker of understanding to appear on Richard's face. He looked at his feet and shook his head. 'Is that what you are worried about?' He looked up, staring straight into his boss's eyes, as if trying to prove his sincerity with the strength of his gaze. 'Don't worry. I have put that all behind me. It's not a problem. Trust me.'

John Gray looked uncertain. 'Richard, there was a lot of bad blood between you and Cummings. I just thought that your mind might not be focussed when he was around. He's the commander on the scene and well, your history might make things unnecessarily complicated. Maybe it would be best if I went alone.'

'John, it's my duty. I appreciate your concern, but Senior Superintendent Cummings is going to have to get used to the idea that I am still around and that I have a job to do, just like him. If he has a problem with that, it is HIS problem. I'm fine. I'll behave, I promise. Trust me.'

John Gray shook his head. 'I know I am going to regret this, but OK. Go ahead.'

Richard smiled and raised his eyebrows. 'Have I ever let you down?'

John didn't even answer. He just closed his eyes and waited for the shitstorm.

Richard stepped out of the Ford Transit and walked up to the uniformed figure. His face showed no emotion and none appeared on the face of the other European. Richard stopped three feet in front of the other man and at last spoke. 'Hello you old bastard.'

Still no sign of feeling appeared on the other man's face. He simply replied, 'Don't you ever wear a fucking uniform?'

'Only when I go to pick up my "gongs".' A broad smile lit up Richards face and he stuck his right hand out, which was collected in a vice-like grip by Superintendent David Blair. He looked a little odd in his peaked cap, riding britches and black leather boots. Traffic cops never looked complete without their helmets. In the heat of summer, no one could blame them for discarding their head protection whenever possible. Some refused to do so, those for whom maintaining a cool persona was more important than allowing their head to get some air. David was entirely too bright to belong to the biking bimbo brigade.

David looked quickly over his right shoulder, then returned his attention to his friend. 'I'm a bit surprised to see you…given the circumstances.'

Richard thought about querying the statement, but thought better of it. David knew his history too well. He looked over the traffic policeman's shoulder at the figure which had been the subject of David's furtive over the shoulder glance. There he was. Senior Superintendent Victor Cummings. A gloom appeared over Richard's face. It only lasted a moment, as he realised that his friend had started to give him a worried look. Richard forced a smile. 'Don't worry. I had to assure John Gray that this isn't a problem for me.'

'It's not you I am worried about,' said David. 'It's what that man can do to you that worries me. Separately, your fine, but put you together and all hell breaks loose.'

'David, I'm here to do a job. As long as that son of a bitch stays out of my way, there will be no problem.'

David Blair dropped his chin on his chest. 'Oh no…that is exactly what I was afraid of.' Looking up at his friend he said, 'Richard, don't start fighting with the man. You know what he's like. Just play it cool. Listen to what he has to say and then ignore it and get on with your job. Keep your head. That thing might just be a bomb. I don't fancy having to scrape your remains off the pavement.'

Richard produced his widest, most disarming smile and put his hand on the other man's shoulder. 'Trust me.' Then he started to walk toward the command post, leaving David Blair shaking his head and feeling the tension in the air.

Cummings was talking to a middle aged Chinese man, as Richard approached the command post. The European stood head and shoulders above the other man. He was slim, to the point of being skinny. His flesh clung tightly to his face, revealing the bone structure beneath. He had the slight stoop that is common in tall men, particularly when they are addressing someone shorter.

Richard knew that Cummings was aware of his presence, even though he tried to hide it, concentrating, just a bit too hard, on the words of the man in front of him. About five feet from the conversing pair, Richard stopped and stood, not uttering a word. Richard had put on a pair of Ray Ban Wayfarers between leaving David Blair and arriving at this spot. It wasn't because of the sun reflecting off the concrete canyon he was in. It was to give away as little as possible to the man he was about to confront.

At last, Cummings and his interlocutor ran out of things to say to one another. With evident resentment, the taller man turned his attention to Richard. Cummings was breathing more heavily than his static position might have warranted. The man looked as though he had just run ten miles. His red face was breaking out in sweat. He was not enjoying this encounter. Words came with difficulty. 'So. It's you.'

Richard knew that Cummings expected him to say something, so he said nothing, just giving the man his black eyed stare. The silence between the two started to make the Chinese man uneasy. He looked between the two, waiting for some break in this bewildering impasse. It was he who broke first. 'So, Superintendent, what are you going to do about this thing in front of my shop?'

Cummings was about to speak, but Richard got his words in first. 'He's not going to do anything about it, Mr…?'

'Pang. I own the jewelry shop over there. The one with the suspicious package in front of it.' The way he said "suspicious package" made it clear that he thought that this was all an unwarranted interruption of his daily commerce. A fuss about nothing. He wanted this all taken care of as quickly as possible. Richard instantly disliked the man.

Richard turned to Cummings. 'So, I had some of the details enroute. Having seen David Blair at the outer cordon, I know that everything has been done to make the area safe. Now, if you don't have anything to add, I would like to get on with my job. I'll set up my command post here, so...'

'Just a minute,' said Cummings, with obvious relish. 'This is what I want you to do. Mr Pang is a valued part of this community. I want you to do all you can to protect his property. I shall hold you personally responsible for any damage to his shop. This is my command. I won't have you coming in and damaging property. This is Central, not some filthy housing estate in Kowloon.

'It's very unlikely that this is a real bomb. More likely to be some Triad attempt to extort money out of honest citizens like Mr Pang.' The businessman nodded his head as this explanation of the real world was laid out before Richard. 'I know that you would like to make a drama out of this situation. Get your photograph in the paper. "The valiant bomb disposal officer". But, you and I both know that this is likely to be a hoax. I therefore suggest that you move the bag to an out of the way location, preferably out of my district and do whatever it is that you do, away from the glare of publicity.'

Richard said nothing. He didn't betray what he was feeling. His face remained blank and cool. He simply uttered, 'Hmph!' and walked away from the other men, back towards the EOD vehicle. He walked past an anxious looking David Blair. He ignored his friend's pleading, 'Richard!' He opened the rear door of the Transit and climbed into the compartment. Richard opened a drawer, part of a storage space built into the side of the rear compartment. He withdrew a green and yellow box and laid it on the counter above the drawer. He then reached over to a metal box, fixed to the floor behind the front seats. Producing a key from his pocket, he opened a padlock securing the box. He lifted the lid and withdrew a Remington pump action shotgun. Turning back to the counter, he took out five shells from the box marked "Remington", Rifled Slug, 12 Gauge" and expertly fed them into the magazine of the weapon.

As he walked past Ah Pau, he ignored the 'Dai Lo!' which his number two almost screamed at him. Passing David Blair, he ignored his friend's even more dramatic entreaty. Richard's face was impassive as he approached Cummings and Pang. The Chinese man looked puzzled. Cummings looked panicked.

Before either man could utter a word, Richard raised the shotgun and noisily racked a round into the breach. He shouldered the weapon and let loose a rifled slug at the blue, red and white striped nylon bag, sitting in front of the plate glass window of the jewelry shop. The slug crossed over a hundred yards in the blink of an eye. The blast shook the air.

Richard turned to face the former shop front. A gaping hole replaced the glittering frontage. There was little debris on the street. The position of the bomb meant that the glass from the shop front had been blown back into the shop itself. Just as Richard had known it would be. He cradled the Remington in the crook of his right arm and turned to the cowering figures beside him. In a relaxed voice he said, 'Looks like it was a bomb after all!'

'Trust me! It's not a problem! Don't worry! My God! Have you any idea what you have done?' John Gray looked as though he was about to burst a blood vessel. Richard sat on the edge of a work bench. He looked at his boss, but said nothing as the agitated figure continued to pace up and down the EOD workshop. 'Jesus Christ, what a mess. I heard that Cummings was so mad that he couldn't speak. Just as well, he would probably have had you arrested. Didn't take him too long to find his voice, though. The Director of Operations was on the 'phone before you got back. The District Commander Central is demanding your head. Something about an apoplectic shop owner. The damages are in the millions.' John Gray wiped his face with his hands. 'Ohhh. What am I going to do with you? Have you nothing to say for yourself?'

'Thought I would let you get it out of your system first. Now, want to hear my side of the story?'

John Gray wearily nodded his head and settled himself into a chair. He gestured for Richard to expound his version of events.

'And what's more, not only do I support Chief Inspector Stirling's actions, if some other arrogant bastard ever insists that one of my men place themselves in danger to protect some rich wanker's property, I will personally nail their fucking balls to a wall and blow them off with a fucking shotgun, sir! Now, if anyone in Police Headquarters has a problem with that, you are welcome to find some idiot to get themselves blown up for nothing, but it won't be me, or any of the people working for me.'

Richard watched the crimson slowly drain from his boss's face, as he listened to the reply from the Director of Operations, the man who was the head of their branch of the Police Force. The reply took some time. By the end of it, John looked to have regained his composure. At length he spoke in a calmer voice. 'Thank you sir. I knew I could count on your support. Yes sir, I will pass that on. I am sure that will be a comfort to my men. Goodbye sir.'

Richard looked inquiringly at his boss as he placed the receiver on its cradle. 'Well?'

John took a deep breath before speaking. 'Well, I have to tell you that you are a stupid bastard and that you had better not pull a stunt like that again. But, he will support your actions. He trusts your judgement. He accepts that you would have had to disrupt the device and that there was a chance that it would have gone off anyway. He will be relaying his displeasure at Cummings' disregard of protocols and emphasising that the ultimate decision on how to deal with a device rests with the EOD operator. He also says to watch your back. You have a lot of friends, including him, but one day Cummings might be in a position to become a problem to you.'

'What do you think?'

John leaned back against his desk. 'I think you were lucky this time. I think Cummings is an arsehole and I wish I had been there when you decked him. I also think that you had better avoid him like the plague. Most of the Force agree with your assessment of him, but he does have friends. I wouldn't like to lose you as a result of his petty vendetta. I think that you need to let this thing between you go, before it eats the heart out of you. I think that if I had been there today, you would have been trying to get me out of the shit. I would probably have shot Cummings, not the bomb. And, I think I need a drink, come on.'

CHAPTER 9

The high pitched whine was like the sound of a steroidal mosquito, whizzing about the sky. First this way, then that. Never allowing the listener the opportunity to pin down its location. It dopplered to and fro, up and down. A common sound at the weekend, still not totally out of place early on a weekday morning. Nothing to cause concern. Part of the audible tapestry of life in Hong Kong.

Stanley, on the southern edge of Hong Kong Island, was a favourite place for families on a break from the busy urban bustle, even this early. The open spaces outside the town were ideal for flying toy helicopters. Toy was a relative term. These models were sophisticated pieces of miniature engineering. From the detailed machining of the engines, to the ingenious electronics of the control systems. Despite their ingenuity, these mechanical gnats were prone to sudden and catastrophic loss of control. There were so many radio signals flying around the territory, that stray electromagnetic fingers could reach out and pluck a couple of hundred hours of work out of the sky, before the eyes of the stricken remote pilot. This was also the reason that making a radio controlled bomb was more hazardous to the maker than the target, at least in theory.

Radio model enthusiasts tend to meet and fly in groups. Not in this case. The tiny helicopter had the skies to itself. Plenty of room to practice the most intricate moves. The small machine flicked around the sky, mocking the absurd elegance of the full sized aircraft. The man at the controls made the most of the space, but never strayed too far from the dark walls of the prison. Stanley had a captive community, one which would not be packing up barbecues at the end of an idyllic summer day. One for whom the annoying whine of the little engine was a reminder of all that was lost to them. A life outside the bleak confines of prison. Their light brown uniforms reflected the drabness of their lives. A life they dreamed of escaping.

Little did they know that the toy helicopter might bring a form of escape. One man knew. He now stood on the edge of a recreation area, within the walls of the jail. It wasn't much of a recreation area. Grass and a couple of goal posts. Just enough room for a football to be kicked around for half an hour by a lucky few of the inmates. It was also big enough for Lau's needs.

An observer might have found the scene strange, but not be able to put their finger on the reason why. Here was a prisoner enjoying a moment of relative freedom, walking in the open space, within the prison. There was a warder, watching over him. But, look again. The prison officer has his back to the prisoner. Surely not a wise thing to do. Perhaps the prisoner is trusted to that extent. Or…

The sound of the helicopter grew louder. Lau walked out into the middle of the grass area and raised his eyes to the blue heavens. There it was! Slowly, the model aircraft droped within the walls of the prison. Closer and closer it came. Finally it settled on the ground with a miniature thud. It rocked back and forth slightly, the rotors helping settle it on it's small skids. The engine note dropped and the light rotor blades quickly lost their momentum, turning slower and slower until their energy was used up.

Lau walked over to the now static machine. He bent down and lifted the model and turned it over to expose the belly of the craft. There he could see a package, taped to the plastic shell. Carefully, he removed the package and placed the helicopter back on the ground.

After a few steps, Lau heard the motor whine into action. He didn't bother turning around as the aircraft flew out of the compound and headed back to it's controller perched on a hilltop overlooking the prison. Lau slipped the drugs into the pocket of his uniform trousers. This was not for the benefit of the guard, whose back had remained turned to Lau throughout the drop. Money had secured his blindness.

Lau smiled as he thought of the chemical escape he carried in his pocket. Not for him. He wasn't that stupid or weak. The heroin would not make him a rich man, not in here. But, it made him a big man, an important man and that was more valuable than money in this place. Lau's material rewards awaited him outside. In here face and position were his rewards for the small comfort of the dragon that he offered his fellow inmates. His position secured his safety. Protection from members of rival Triad Societies. Protection from men who would gain great kudos for the killing of a senior office bearer in the 14K. Protection from those who resented the fact that he had once been a cop.

CHAPTER 10

❁

Li Keung stood before the tall doorway. A look of bitter resignation covered his face. At his side was Jack Garland, his faithful Pit Bull. Li turned and gestured with his head. Words were unnecessary, this was a regular routine. Garland nodded and walked over to take his seat with the other aides. Of all the group, Garland looked least pleased to be away from his master's side. Li drew himself up to the extent of his claimed 4'11" and walked through the portal.

The room was dominated by a huge oval table. It's bright, polished surface reflected the light, airy quality of the conference room. Double length windows on two walls provided spectacular views of the harbour and flooded the large space with natural light. The external illumination was further enhanced by unobtrusive, but effective wall lighting.

Li hated this room. He detested the brightness. Here, there were no shadows to hide in. No protection from the stares of his peers. He was exposed and on guard. In this environment the upper hand rested elsewhere. Li looked around the table. Here were Hong Kong's brightest and best, at least in their own minds. Every face was Chinese, no *Gwailo* would be allowed into this inner sanctum. This was the ruling elite of the Chinese community. Businessmen of one kind or another. Rulers in their own kingdoms. In this room they were all equal. Li smiled at the thought. No. In each man's heart he knew that he was better than everyone else at this table. A collection of equals who all thought the rest inferior, but would never voice their conviction.

At tall man stood up from his seat. His position was at the middle of the long side of the oval nearest the windows. His distinguished features were crowned by a mane of white hair, drawn back over his head. Born in Shanghai, Vincent Lo had the bearing of the northerner, broad, straight-backed and powerfully built. He was the current Chairman of The Circle.

Li despised this man. He resented that Lo had taken a western Christian name and insisted on being addressed as "Vincent", rather than with his Chinese name. To Li the man was the antithesis of everything that this group stood for. The Circle was designed to empower the Chinese business community. To prepare the future rulers of this corner of the Peoples Republic of China.

It was a remarkable gathering. Here sat the 14k. There, the Sun Yee On. In this corner, the Wo Shing Wo. Not all the members of the group were Triads, but the fact that those present could remain in the same room without trying to kill one another was remarkable in itself. Reluctantly, Li had to admit that this minor miracle had largely been brought about by the sheer force of personality of the man who now called the gathering to order. He didn't need to use words, or a gavel. The simple act of standing brought a hush over the room.

'Unsettling events have occurred,' began Lo. 'Two of the so called British Taipans has met rather sudden and violent ends.'

One of the group to Lo's left started to laugh. His mirth was brought to a sudden and heart stopping end by the cold stare of the chairman. More than a few of the gathering felt their own hearts skip a beat in sympathy with the recipient of the penetrating look.

Lo returned his attention to the group as a whole and continued. 'There is little to applaud in this matter, gentlemen. The acts were foolhardy and pointless. The fate of Hong Kong has already been sealed. British rule has a limited amount of time left to it. To provoke a response from the authorities in this way is to invite unwanted attention upon our affairs. This group exists to assure the future prosperity of its members under the new regime. Our friends in Beijing want a period of stability leading up to the return of Hong Kong to the Motherland. This kind of senseless act, if it were to be attributed to the Chinese community, would reflect badly on the ability of the Mainland authorities to control their own people.

'Personally, I have to say that Douglas Fairbrother was essentially a good man. He had a deep love for this territory and its people. Outside of business, he was not an enemy to the people of Hong Kong. His policy was one of inward investment, unlike some of his fellow Taipans, who are trying to get their money out of here before reunification.'

Li Keung sat impassively, betraying none of the contempt he felt. How could the leader of this group defend one of the *Gwailo* ? He was a Westerner and therefore the enemy of all at this table.

'It would be unfortunate,' continued Lo, 'if it were to emerge that a member of this company had any influence on this act of stupidity. It would be an act contrary to the common good of The Circle. Retribution for such an act would be swift and decisive.'

A few members of the gathering shifted in their seats on hearing this gentle warning. Li did not budge. He knew that if his involvement was known, he would not be sitting in his seat. Lo had just pronounced a death sentence on anyone inciting such an act. Perhaps not actual physical death, though it might even come to that, but certainly expulsion from the Circle, which amounted to economic death, as no other member would do business with him. His list of enemies would grow dramatically.

Vincent Lo wasted no more time. He had stated the position of the majority and woe betide anyone who stepped out of line. The Triad heads were included in this group for a reason. Some were prominent businessmen, or members of Government and as such earned their place. But they also gave the group access to resources and skills that are not part of the Harvard MBA curriculum. They lent weight to Lo's words. The meeting moved on to other business.

'So, they don't suspect?' asked Garland.

Li sat behind his desk. In response to the question he merely shook his head. The meeting had passed without incident, but Li was glad to be back in his own sphere of influence.

'Do we carry on?' asked his security chief.

Li looked at him for a few moments, before replying. 'Vincent Lo does not frighten me.' The name was spit out like a curse. 'We will carry on as planned. Is our friend ready for his next display?'

'Yes. This one he promises will be very special. The whole of Hong Kong will be talking about it. I don't know all the details, but I have not seen him so enthusiastic. God knows what the sick bastard has dreamed up.'

Li allowed a thin smile to crack through his lips. 'Good.'

CHAPTER 11

'*Yam Booi Sin!*'

The traditional toast of 'First a drink!' rang loud from the small dining room, but was lost in the overwhelming noise of the main restaurant. The door to the private room was guarded by a sign which simply stated, in chinese characters, "Kowloon City Police. Private party." Simple enough to stop any undesired intrusions and misleading enough to hide the true nature of the group occupying the room. True, the officer who had booked the room had once worked in Kowloon City, where the restaurant was situated and therefore received plenty of face, including a very reasonable price for the meal. The identity of the group was not for general broadcast. When working, they hid their identities behind Nomex Balaclavas or black rubber respirators. Within the police force it was an open secret, most people knew who they were, but there was no need to attract undue attention, particularly from a press hungry for a glimpse of members of the "*Fei Foo Dui*", the "Flying Tiger Squad", otherwise known as the Special Duties Unit of the Royal Hong Kong Police.

The party was to celebrate the promotion of Ah Fung, one of the constables within the Sniper Group of Bravo Team. He was leaving the team, a fact which had necessitated Richard Stirling's recent trip to Castle Peak. The Team Commander was delighted for the young man. They had joined the unit at the same time. Richard had moved up in rank from Inspector, now it was Ah Fung's turn. He had been selected as a potential officer by Richard and was at last joining an intake of Probationary Inspectors at Police Training School. It was a fact that the junior officers of the SDU were a cut above the norm. There were smart young men in all parts of the Force, but the SDU men had a bearing and mystique that set them apart.

Daai Sik Wooi , a "Big Chow". A time when the members of the team could forget about fitness and stuff themselves with good food. Glasses were raised in a toast at the beginning of each course. Some held beer, some tea. The brave ones drank brandy. Richard and Keith Symons, the Assault Group Leader, had each brought a bottle of Hennessy XO to honour the promotee, a measure of the high regard that they shared for Ah Fung. Keith accepted a small glass of the smooth, potent liquid. Richard joined his protégé in attacking the dark nectar with gusto.

As the night progressed, the red faces of the drinkers in the group heralded more and more enthusiastic toasting. Every conceivable reason for downing more booze was brought to the aid of the party. Before too long, Richard had contributed another two bottles of XO. The meal had been preceded by noisy games of mahjong. With the clearing of the last plates, other games began. Loss resulted in a forfeit. What else but a *Yam Shing* , bottoms up. The drinking games of the SDU tended to be a bit more boisterous than most. Everything from arm-wrestling to push-ups. These contests of strength could take some time to be resolved, as the participants were extraordinarily fit. One side effect of fitness was the sudden onset of drunkenness with the minimum intake of alcohol. By no means teetotal, the SDU officers tended to drink moderately for the sake of physical condition. But, when they let themselves go, watch out! A promotion was as good a reason as you got for diving headlong into a bucket of booze. Opportunities such as this were rare and were never wasted. This night was no exception.

Rank and file within the unit were usually addressed by nicknames. This informality masked strong discipline, which derived its strength from within individual officers. Imposed discipline was kept to a minimum. All members of the unit were volunteers. The possibility of expulsion was more than enough to ensure that each man was his own disciplinarian. Outsiders often derided the unit for slackness because of their long hair and their attitude toward some senior officers outside their tight circle. The truth was that these men respected those who had earned their respect. Men like Keith Symons and Richard Stirling.

Daai Bei Jai, "Big Nose Boy", one of Keith's Assault Group, came, a little unsteadily, up to the two European officers. Chinese nicknames could seem cruel to Westerners. Names like *Sei Ngaan Jai,* "Four-eyed Boy", or *Fei Jai,* "Fat Boy" were not intended to offend, just state the obvious. Daai Bei challenged Richard to a game of *Chai Mooi* , a game of wits. The version that SDU favoured involved the participants adopting a one-arm push-up position, while brandishing a chopstick in their free hand. As the pair matched each other in push-ups, they took turn to guess the position in which their opponent would brandish their chopstick after uttering a long chant of "unnoooooo…hut". The utensil could be placed up, down, left, right, or centre of the torso. If a player guessed correctly, they took control of the game. If they lost twice in a row, a "Yam Sing" was the forfeit. As can be expected, losing tended to become a habit, as the relative inebriation of the two players became a wider and wider gulf. Luckily for Richard, he was either fairly good at the game, or considerably less drunk than Daai Bei at the onset of hostilities. Either way, the game came to a sudden end when Daai Bei failed to raise himself from the floor after a rather sudden downward rush which ended in a sickening thud. The next day, he would really live up to his nickname. After assuring that his comrade in arms hadn't done any permanent damage, Richard returned to the table to be applauded by the other members of the team. Daai Bei snored his appreciation of his boss's prowess.

The evening progressed in this vein, until sufficient numbers of the group had reached their limit of consumption. The remainder made plans for the rest of the night and early morning. Richard and Keith were invited to join their men at a nightclub, for more brandy and convivial female company. On other occasions they would have accepted, but as the guest of honour had joined the "early bath" brigade, they felt inclined to seek entertainment elsewhere. Richard turned to Keith and declared in a surprisingly clear voice, 'Canton Road I think young man. I feel in the mood for a bit of Hot Gossip!'

'And people wonder why your men would follow you to the gates of hell,' replied Keith. 'What a decision maker! Cold beer and rampant totty, what more could a young man ask for? TAXI!!!'

'So, anyway, we get downstairs at Hot Gossip, in the disco, and the place is absolutely heaving. There are single women all over the place. Unfortunately, my lord and role model here homes in on a girl who is quite obviously being chatted up by this tall Gwailo. At first I thought he was aiming at the other girl in the party who was on her own, but Oh No! It's the one being given the heavy treatment by the would-be suitor.'

A groan emanated from the wreck that had once been Richard Stirling, as he listened to Keith Symons relate the events of the previous evening to the others at their breakast table in the Officers' mess. The fact that they had both made breakfast was testament to their stamina, but Keith had fared better as a result of his abstinence on the brandy front. Ignoring the plaintive pleading from his boss, Keith continued his description of Richard's nocturnal antics.

'Before I had a chance to grab him, he set off over the floor to these three and barged right in front of the bloke and stood facing this girl. I think I saw his lips move, but I was too busy watching the other guy. He was so gobsmacked that he didn't know what to do at first. I thought I was going to have to come to the rescue at one point as the guy obviously decided that he would have to take some action, if he was to maintain his manhood. Then I think he got a really good look at the gorilla in front of him. Thankfully the bloke must have been sober, because he got a huge case of the sensibles and backed off. Mind you, Richard here didn't stay too long, he just whipped out a name card and handed it to the poor girl, before leaving the group and heading back to me.'

'Oh nooo,' groaned Richard.

'Wait, wait, the best is yet to come!'

Richard painfully lifted his head from the table at this burst of enthusiasm. 'Just wait 'til I'm feeling better,' he said with great difficulty, but soon realised that blessed occasion was a long way off.

'Well, here is Richard strolling across the floor, trying to look cool and sophisticated. Unfortunately, he fails to spot the edge of the dance floor, trips over his own feet and goes face down into the deck. The poor sod he had burst in on didn't look so crestfallen after that. Smug is the word I would use. He looked pretty pleased with events as he continued to chat up the girl, making the odd dismissive gesture in our man here's direction. Good, aggressive entry, clumsy exit. So, expect to hear from her today?'

Richard stared at the younger man through boiling eyes. 'Just you wait you cocky sod! Extra PT for you, if I can ever summon up the strength to leave this table.' Richard blew a very weary breath through his parched lips. 'I can't even remember what I said to the poor girl. I'm lucky I didn't get my lights punched out by that bloke. Please, if we ever bump into them again, don't tell me.'

'You're not thinking of calling that guy?' Sarah Chan gave her friend a long, hard look which made no attempt to hide her displeasure at the thought of this rash action. 'He's a drunk and a cop. Bad news on both counts. And the way he barged in front of poor Toby! Thank goodness Toby is a gentleman, or who knows what would have happened.'

Natalie Lam gave her confidante a cool look and then smiled broadly. 'I think that had more to do with those bulging biceps than "poor" Toby's manners. Besides, Toby is like all the men I have met since I arrived in Hong Kong. Nice on the surface, but incredibly dull. He tries to make his latest portfolio sound like a cure for cancer. You can only look interested in conversation like that for so long.' Natalie saw little reaction to this in her friend's face. 'Well I can't get awfully worked up by it.'

Natalie let her gaze fall from Sarah's face and land somewhere in the middle distance. A curiously naughty smile came over her face. 'The one thing I don't think that Mr Richard Stirling would be is boring. At least if he were ever sober.'

The morning had passed very slowly for Richard. At last the pain in his head was starting to subside, but he still felt the edge of his hangover in every part of his body. He had managed to will himself through a seven mile run with the team, but was glad that the distance had not been greater. A smart piece of time-tabling on the part of his Station Sergeant, who had obviously guessed that many of the men would be feeling a bit fragile. Tomorrow would be a hard physical day, so he didn't feel too bad about his idleness.

Keith had been dispatched to do a recce on a building which they hoped to use for training. It was in a remote area which was due for development, so would suit their, often destructive, needs and keep them out of the public eye. Opportunities of this type were becoming difficult to find, as the pace of urbanisation increased in the New Territories. Richard had paperwork to catch up on and had reluctantly stayed behind in the office which he shared with his younger colleague and the Station Sergeant who helped with administration.

Eyes always seemed to take a long time to settle down after a drinking session. Richard's were stubbornly refusing to let him forget the excesses of the previous night.

As he struggled to make them focus on the page in front of him, a pain would shoot straight from the back of his eyes, into the centre of his throbbing head. He was seriously thinking of giving up on his task, when the telephone rang.

'216.'

This was the accepted method of answering the 'phone in the unit and in other parts of the force who did not want to announce themselves to unknown callers, a simple statement of the extension number.

A woman's voice answered in a cautious tone. 'I would like to speak to Richard Stirling please.'

'This is Stirling.' Richard had also adopted a cautious tone.

Suddenly, the voice at the other end of the line changed, becoming brighter and much more confident. 'Hi there, do you know who I am?'

All memory of his hangover suddenly vanished from Richard's mind, as he struggled to recognise the voice. His brain was letting him down. Normally he had a good memory for faces and voices on the telephone, but at this moment he was at a complete loss.

'I suppose it is a little unfair of me to ask that question. After all, you didn't give me the chance to say anything before you went back to your friend. Nice dive, by the way.'

Richard closed his eyes and gave out a low groan, which was clearly audible over the 'phone.

'Ah, I see you remember me,' said Natalie, with a hint of minxish satisfaction in her voice.

Straightening himself in his chair, Richard at last found his voice. 'I am really surprised to hear from you. An apology is an awful way to say hello, but I think I owe you one and that poor chap you were with. I'm surprised he didn't deck me for my behaviour.'

'Oh, don't worry about Toby,' laughed Natalie. 'I doubt if he would stoop to striking someone. Anyway, you did a pretty good job of "decking" yourself as I recall.'

'Yes, my "friend" took great pleasure in recounting my exploits this morning, much to the amusement of some of my colleagues. I can say that I just felt wretched.'

'Don't be too hard on yourself. There was no harm done, except perhaps to your pride. I was actually rather flattered. To have made an impression through the level of drunkenness that you displayed was good for my ego. Besides, if you hadn't interrupted Toby, I think that I would have fallen asleep where I stood. He was regaling me with the amount of bonus that he expects after his latest financial victory. Very exciting no doubt. So, what do you do?'

It may have been the after-effects of the alcohol, but this took Richard by surprise. 'Eh, well, you know, the usual sort of police things. Pretty boring really.' As soon as he said it, he cringed. This was the last thing that this girl wanted to hear. Even in his fragile condition, he realised that she had presented him with an opening. She was looking for someone who had something interesting to say for themselves.

Before he had a chance to undo his statement, Natalie gave him a break. 'I am sure that you are just being modest, or is your brain still a bit dull from the drinking?'

'You could say that,' replied Richard with a sigh of relief. 'This is proving to be a very long day. Frankly I am surprised that I have made it this far. Look, I'd like to make last night up to you. Would you like to get together, or is this Toby your boyfriend?'

Natalie laughed in a way that delighted Richard. 'No, Toby is a friend. I think he would like to be more, but as I said, his conversation leaves a lot to be desired. He may be an animal in bed, but with that chat-up line, I fear he is unlikely to have many opportunities to show off.'

'Well, I haven't exactly had a great start myself. How about Friday? Dinner?'

'How about drinks? Then we can think about dinner. By the way, are you sure you will recognise me?'

'Tell you what, I will bring my friend Keith along to point you out to me. Then he can go off and amuse himself. He owes me that much after the abuse I received this morning.'

It was Natalie's turn to pause, as she tried to work out whether or not this guy was serious. Richard put her out of her misery.

'Don't worry, I remember what you look like. How could I forget. As you said, it would have taken a lot to cut through the alcoholic haze before my eyes. You certainly did that.' Richard took a deep breath before carrying on. 'I am really glad you called. Surprised as hell, but really glad. I'll try to be much less of a bore when we meet properly. How about Someplace Else at about seven thirty, or would you rather meet on the Island?'

'No, Someplace Else is fine, but let's make it eight.'

'Alright. I'll wait for you at the upstairs bar, it's normally a bit quieter.'

'OK, see you then. Bye.'

'Wait!' Richard just managed to get the word out in time. 'You still haven't told me your name.'

There was a soft laugh coming from the receiver. 'It's Natalie Lam. See you on Friday.' Then the line went dead.

Richard placed the receiver on its cradle and leaned back in his chair. He was smiling, then the thought entered his head. 'God, I hope I do recognise her!'

CHAPTER 12

Men are most vulnerable through their passions. Find something which arouses the deepest feelings within a man and you find a doorway to his life. Engage him in conversation on the subject and he will give away more than he could know. He will reveal the way to bring about his own downfall, his own death.

It is strange, some of the things that men become passionate about. Cigars. I can understand a man enjoying cigars, but to feel genuine passion about them, that begs belief. To spend an indecent amount of money on something which has to be consumed by fire to fulfil its purpose is obscene. Yet, I can understand some of this obsession. The act of consumption is one of total indulgence. An experience which is very private and selfish in the extreme. It is perhaps fitting that one form of consumption will result in another. My indulgence will consume something more than some tobacco. It will consume a life.

The box was perfect. Of the same vintage as the one our friend was expecting. Details are important. For a man like that, anything unexpected would arouse unease, even suspicion. He must be at ease with his discovery when he unwraps it. He has to be eager to open the package, to reveal that which he desires. Desire. So many men's downfall. We must control our passions if they are not to consume us. A lesson which my target had not learned.

My passion is control. Control of the events which I bring about. All others are merely players, materials to be manipulated until I have achieved the desired result. I shall never be consumed by my passion, it consumes all others.

The box was the lure. It drew my prey to the cold hand of death. The mechanism was simple. A release switch. A microswitch under the lid of the box, held closed by the pressure of the lid. Open the box and the spring is released, closing the contacts of the switch and completing the circuit. Once the box was closed, I armed the mechanism by pulling a length of fishing line through a tiny hole in the bottom of the box. This I cut off and easily concealed the hole, which is difficult to see, even if you know it is there. The lid has to be a tight fit to hold the switch down. I used some glue to help hold it in place. Not too much. The target has to be able to open the box. He would have had to use a degree of force, so that the opening would be sudden and the surprise absolute. Not that I think he would have known much about it.

I have always wondered about that. With a bomb, does the victim have an instant of awareness, before they are consumed by the violence of the explosion? Is there understanding of what is happening to them, or merely confusion? Perhaps it depends on the individual. For those with no knowledge, the unexpected may be a total surprise. For those who know what they are dealing with, people who have chosen the job of disposing of bombs, there must surely be at least a microsecond of understanding that they have lost the game. That is my favourite sport. Those who would undo my work. Those who are arrogant enough to believe that their skills are superior to mine. The truth is that it is far more difficult to create than to destroy. They know the truth of it and yet they bask in the false glory which their actions give them. If only the public knew the truth, they might have less respect for these men and more for the artistry that they wantonly destroy.

There is an icy delight to be had from the knowledge that the target is aware of what is happening to them. The retina must register the flash of light, as the detonation takes place. Perhaps the body is blown apart before the neurones have time to deliver their impulses to the brain. Can the nerves register the searing heat from the blast wave, or again will the velocity of the destructive force outpace the pain transmission. Any pain must be short lived, I have always thought. Certainly where the body is consumed by the blast. Where the target is more remote from the bomb and I have had to resort to projectiles to inflict damage, then the agony can be considerable. I prefer not to rely on such methods. The resilience of the human body can be surprising and what might seem like more damage than any person could bear can sometimes fail to extinguish the fire of life within. Then my efforts are for nought and the failure I feel is intolerable. Seldom have I endured such humiliation and on those occasions I have managed to complete my task at a later time, but the failure remains and haunts me still. So, I take the time to ensure that objects of my skill are left in a hopeless situation. As long as my skill does not desert me, I am confident that disappointment will not tarnish the brilliance of my performance.

Preparations for my next masterpiece are complete. The details have been confirmed. This time I was able to gather all the information that I required on my own. I prefer it this way. To rely on other people is never desirable. To rely on the observations and perceptions of others is to invite disaster and failure. Unfortunately, circumstances sometimes force the hand that you are dealt. So it was with my first two performances. It was fortunate that the information which Garland provided was sound and that it allowed me to target the men efficiently. This is not to say that he told me what to do. The man is a mindless oaf. The garbage that I had to sift through to find the gems of inspiration which I required! I despaired at times when he would put forward some detail of the target's life which he considered noteworthy, but which was obviously trivial and useless. Obvious anyway to anyone with half a brain.

The way the man struts and swaggers when he visits me! Full of his own importance, he treats me in a manner which he is liable to regret. He cannot see that I am using him to my own ends. Fine. It is as well that the buffoon is blind to my manipulation. He provides me with what I need; the materials to create my work and the objects to make them come to life. Perhaps someday I shall have to turn my attention to Mr Garland, or even his mysterious master. Garland tries to pretend that he is the author of these acts, but I know better. Soon I shall have to take the time to discover the owner of the hands that are pulling the strings. He too, no doubt, is under the delusion that he is master of the proceedings. Again, perhaps I shall have to educate him as to the reality. I am my own master, but will play the puppet so long as it suits my aims.

Soon, all eyes will be on my creation. The next event will ensure that. Already the press are pushing my story onto the front page, but every man, woman and child will talk of nothing else after my next work has come into being. The emotions it will generate will be intense. Those idiots who would try to catch me will be energised by the agonising beauty of my creation. They will redouble their efforts, but it will be to no avail. I have nothing to fear from them. Should they try to reach me through Garland, I can disappear in an instant and wipe away any evidence in the blink of an eye. Including that objectionable man.

The greatest danger to me is when I am delivering the device. Garland wanted me to use a third party, but I refused. Just another thing that can go wrong. Introduce another human into the equation and the chances of failure are multiplied. People are the least trustworthy component in the process. Even the target cannot be absolutely relied upon to act as expected. The actions required have to be so simple as to be almost a reaction to a given situation. I arrange the event and they act their part. Actors of course can forget their lines or fail to hit their mark, even the simplest of tasks can be bungled. For this reason, I like to minimise the human element. Yes, it is a risk for me to show up at an office with a package and I will not do so again, for the authorities will no doubt be on their guard for a repeat performance, poor fools. But, my disguise was more than adequate. I cannot believe that anyone in that building, even the secretary, would recognise me were they standing right in front of me.

This time I have to be there to plant the device. It may be my last chance to be so close to events and there is a risk, but I must see this one come into being. It is bold and beautiful in concept. It must be perfect in execution. Perfect. Nothing less is acceptable.

CHAPTER 13

Richard looked past his driver at the wall of white off to his right. On the other side of that damp curtain, the hillside dropped off at an alarming angle. To his left, the hillside had been scooped away to provide a base for another high-rise building. As the Land-Rover dragged itself up the twisting road, Richard wondered at the need to build tower blocks on the Mid-Levels of Victoria Peak. Perhaps the upwardly-mobile types who lived here were attempting to reach the dizzy heights of those wealthy enough to live on the Peak itself. There the buildings were decidedly low-rise, setting them apart from most of Hong Kong. The buildings that lined the narrow passage to the peak of Hong Kong's social mountain were mere Towers of Babel. Presumptuous efforts to touch the gods of commerce and privilege.

Days like this always made Richard wonder what the attraction of this place was. Yes, it was a little cooler than the low-lying areas. A definite advantage in the days before air-conditioning, but when the humidity was at its peak and the cloud closed in, condensation ran down the walls of even the highest and mightiest. Richard imagined a battalion of de-humidifiers waging an un-winnable war. Vanity had its price.

The Land-Rover pulled into the driveway of the single-storey house. The grounds were already swarming with uniforms, but they all avoided an oasis of inactivity immediately in front of the entrance to the building. Richard could see his friend Cassius standing, staring at the scene, but his own attention was also focussed on the same thing. Slowly he stepped out of the vehicle, not taking his eyes off the same spot which had grabbed his attention. There was little more than a murmur from the police officers attempting to go about their business, where normally there would be loud exchanges. Richard walked to Cassius' side. They hardly acknowledged one another, but continued to stare, un-speaking at the devastation.

The car was still recognisable as such, though the front end was bulged upwards. The centre of attention, though was the passenger compartment. The driver sat, with his head tilted back over the headrest of his seat. His daughter sat next to him, her head gently resting against his shoulder. The pair looked to be asleep. Only the deathly pallor of the two faces gave a real indication that they would never awake from this slumber. The girl had the face of an angel. Richard thought that his heart was about to break, but the anger that was building inside him overshadowed the pity he felt for this unfortunate pair.

'Have the scene of crime people done their thing?' asked Richard.

It took Cassius a moment to answer, almost as though reluctant to enter the reality of the moment. 'No, we wanted you to have a look at it before we started gathering evidence.' He paused, then continued. 'Richard, who could have done this? Look at her. Was this an accident, the fact that she was there? It's pretty obvious that her father was the target. Surely no one would have done this to the kid deliberately.'

Richard did not answer. Instead he carefully walked to the rear of the vehicle and bent over, scanning the ground at his feet. Cassius followed him, with a look of curiosity on his face. After less than a minute, Richard bent down and gently lifted something off the ground. Cassius couldn't see what it was, but didn't interrupt his friend to ask. Richard walked slowly towards some bushes at the edge of the driveway. As he reached a squat light in the middle of a flowerbed, he stopped and retraced his steps towards the rear if the vehicle.

'Cass, do you have an evidence bag?'

Cassius reached into his pocket and produced a clear plastic bag, displaying the Police crest and handed it over. Carefully, Richard pulled at what Cassius could now see was a length of fishing line. Difficult to see, even up close, unless you were looking for it. As the end of the line appeared from under the car, he saw that a rectangle of what looked like plastic was attached to it. Richard pocketed the evidence bag and placed the line back on the ground. As he stood up, he turned to Cassius. Richard pointed to the mangled car.

'You'll find the remains of a clothes peg somewhere in there. A simple switch. The end of the line was tied off to the light over there. The plastic acts as an insulator between the contacts on the jaws of the clothes peg, probably used drawing pins. When the vehicle pulls away, the line goes taught, the insulator is pulled out of the jaws and contact is made, completing the circuit and boom! A simple and effective switch, especially if it comes totally out of the blue, like this.The bomb didn't have to be a big one. It was placed under the foot-well of the passenger compartment. The idea is to blow the legs off the occupants. Explosive amputation. The blood loss is sudden and in this case fatal. There may be secondary injuries to the bodies from shrapnel, but that wasn't the main intent. See the localised nature of the damage? I would guess some form of shaped charge, the blast was directed upwards. This guy knows what he's doing. He knows too damn much.'

Cassius stared at his friend, as Richard stood up and stared off into the gloom.

'We have to get this fucker, Cass. The bastard's playing with us. In answer to your questions, no, I haven't developed into a great intuitive detective and yes, the girl was meant to die.' Richard looked at his colleague and continued. 'The thing is, I've seen this gruesome tableau before.'

The meeting had been arranged in haste. Senior members of the investigating team had been annoyed by the sudden summons, especially when Cassius could offer no explanation, other than Richard's insistence that he had important information and wanted to deliver it in person. He had returned to the EOD unit to pick something up and had asked Cassius to assemble the group in the conference room of the Organised and Serious Crime Unit. The level of agitation was growing as Richard and John Gray finally appeared through the door. Cassius let out a quiet sigh of relief, he knew of his friend's tendency to agitate senior officers as a matter of principle.

Richard uncharacteristically apologised for the delay and made straight for the television and VCR that he had asked Cassius to arrange. He pushed a tape into the machine, but did not switch it on. Instead he turned to his, now more curious than annoyed, audience.

'Gentlemen, please forgive me for asking you to come here at such short notice, but I think that you will understand when I have had my say. Please bear with me.'

Richard looked at his boss, who had taken a seat at the back of the group. John gave him a slight nod of encouragement.

'In the mid seventies, the Royal Ulster Constabulary was suffering horrendous losses to terrorist bombs. One of the reasons was identified as complacency on the part of the officers themselves. After years of conflict, weariness had induced a slack attitude to safety routines. They weren't doing the checks which would have saved their lives and paid the price.

'In an effort to snap their men out of this apathy, the RUC produced a training film which was shown to every member of the force. The idea was to shock the men into adhering to the security protocols that had been developed at the cost of many lives. They did this by using real incidents. They used actual photographs and film footage to show what happened when you got lazy about safety. It worked. The casualty rate plummeted after this film was shown.

'I first saw this tape when I did my basic bomb disposal training. One incident in particular stuck in my memory.'

With that, Richard turned and pressed the play button on the VCR. As the image flickered into clarity on the TV screen, an audible gasp came from the assembled policemen. Cassius sat, open-mouthed, staring at the screen. There, was an almost identical image to that which had imprinted itself on his brain that morning. The same damage to the car. The same peaceful expression on the face of the girl, as she rested in death on her father's shoulder.

Richard pressed the pause button and turned to the group. 'This sick son of a bitch is toying with us. And, I would lay you money that he was there today when this thing went up. He may even have touched the girl to recreate this scene. It will be worth looking for fingerprints on her head and neck.'

It took a while for the stunned audience to react. Eventually the Chief Superintendent in charge of the investigation spoke. 'So, what are you saying? That this guy is a bomb disposal man?'

Richard looked straight at him. 'All I am saying is that the person who set that bomb this morning has seen this film. It has been used by security forces around the world to get over the message about the importance of procedures. What I am also saying is that the bastard is playing a game with us. He thinks he's smarter than us. He's taunting us. And worst of all, he's enjoying the game. I don't know if he is working alone, or if someone is pulling his strings. Frankly, I don't care. That's your problem. Mine is that this fucker has his own agenda. He's enjoying himself far too much to stop now. The only thing that I am certain of is that we're going to see more of this.'

David Lo, the senior officer in the room, stood up. He looked stunned. 'The shit from this is rolling all the way down from Government House. Unfortunately, it stops right here. I don't want the Police Force to be made the scapegoats in this. We at least have to be seen to be pulling out the stops. It's obvious that the targets of this campaign are the heads of British *Hongs* , but this latest one has taken the whole thing to a new level. When hews breaks about the little girl…well, none of us are going to get much sleep, until we catch whoever is behind this.

'Look, I will support all of you to the limit of my authority and I shall try to keep as much of the flack away from you as I can, but unless we start to show some sort of tangible progress in the investigation, I don't know how long I will be able to keep the wolves at bay. Besides, after seeing that horror this morning, I don't think there is a man in this room who will rest until this animal is brought to justice.'

Cassius and Richard hardly exchanged a word as they took the lift to the floor of the building which housed the Government Chemist Department. Forensic analysis on the evidence from the last bombing had yielded some results. Both men were still lost in their thoughts when they walked into the office of Alice Keung. She looked from one to the other. 'No need to ask what is going through your minds. I haven't been able to get the image out of my mind all day. Maybe this will get you thinking about other things. We've identified the explosive.'

Both men snapped into the present at this statement. At last they might get a lead.

'Cyclotrimethylene trinitramine,' stated Alice in an emotionless voice.

Cassius stared at her and then, receiving no help, turned to Richard. He was staring straight ahead, displaying no emotion.

'RDX,' said Richard. 'Does the detailed composition tell you anything?'

Alice nodded, but before she could speak, Cassius had finally had enough. 'Alright, mind giving me the layman's version? Or have you forgotten who is actually investigating this case?'

Richard gave his friend a thin smile. 'RDX, it's an explosive compound used in plastic explosive. It's mixed with oil or grease to stabilise it and give it plastic properties.' Then he spoke to Alice. 'Was it in combination with any other explosive?'

Alice Keung simply shook her head. They both knew what that meant, but Richard explained to Cassius. 'Usually, RDX on it's own means that the explosive is military in origin. Commercial explosives tend to use it as part of a "cocktail". Alice, any indication of which military?'

The importance of this suddenly hit Cassius. If it was Chinese, the implications were unthinkable.

'It looks like British, we're trying to confirm it with the office of the Commander British Forces, but as you can guess, they are taking their own sweet time looking over the evidence. I think though that the mass spectrometry results are conclusive. Question is, where did it come from. You know what the Army can be like when it comes to their stores.'

Richard looked solemn. 'Yes I do. As crazy as it sounds, it would be easy for the explosive to go missing. A little bit left over from disposing of "blinds" on a range, for example. Wouldn't take too long for a useful amount of PE 4 to be built up.'

'Excuse me?' said Cassius.

'Sorry Cass. "Blinds", unexploded ordinance. Say a grenade which failed to explode during a range course. Standard procedure would be to blow it up in situ with some plastic explosive. Or it could be an Army Bomb Disposal Officer with the left-overs of a demolition job. Could be Marines , could be just about anyone. It's tough to keep track of every bit of explosive that the Army would use. But, I suppose it's a start, assuming we can persuade the military to cooperate. You know what they're like. The one thing in our favour is that the men being killed are Brits and powerful ones. If it was Chan Fat, from some housing estate in Kwun Tong, I wouldn't hold my breath.'

The two Chinese looked at one another and then at Richard. As sad as the comment was, both knew that their colleague was right on the mark. Even in murder, prejudice existed in this town and the British Army were famous for it.

A deep frown came over Richard's face. 'Of course, there is another possibility.'

Alice and Cassius focussed their attention on him when they heard the gravity in his voice.

'We use the same plastic explosive.'

CHAPTER 14

Someplace Else. The bar, in the basement of the Sheraton Hotel, had become a favourite watering hole for members of the expatriate and local communities. Between the hours of four in the afternoon and eight in the evening the place was packed. The reason, "Happy Hour". For four hours the drinks were "two for the price of one". Every drink. From bottles of beer, to jugs of margaritas, the drinks came two by two. The scenes of alcoholic carnage could be awesome. There were Happy Hours in most bars in the territory, but for some reason this one attracted a particularly dedicated following.

The establishment was split into two levels. Each had a bar and tables where diners enjoyed a standard Tex-Mex type of fare, with Asian influences. It was a fairly typical hotel bar-diner. The decor was eclectic. A mix of "Cheers" and someone's attic. Bric-a-brac covered the walls. There was polished wood and brass in abundance. The atmosphere was welcoming and relaxed. Ideal for conversation and determined drinking.

The upper level, where Richard sat, was smaller than the downstairs imbibing arena and generally quieter. It also meant that he could avoid the company of the policemen that were almost certainly demonstrating their quaffing skills at the main bar. It wasn't that he would not enjoy their company. It was the fact that extricating himself from it would be such a chore. He was out to make a good impression with this lady. After his first encounter with Natalie, he would have a difficult enough job, without the added burden of some loutish and insistent colleagues to deal with. As happy hour was coming to an end, the crowds had started to disperse. A dedicated core of drinkers would remain, but Richard was pleased that Natalie had decided to meet later in the evening. The bar would be less frantic and the conversation easier. The crowds would return at eleven for the second Happy Hour. One surge of enthusiastic drinking in a day didn't seem to be enough for the people who ran this establishment.

Richard had been nursing his beer for a quarter of an hour. He hated being late for anything and would usually turn up for appointments well ahead of time. Being alone with his thoughts was preferable to being at an immediate disadvantage. The impatient look as you walk through the door behind schedule. The agony of trying to make up for the first impression. Richard could do without that particular angst in his life. He had plenty of other things to stress him out without adding to the burden himself. Not that he minded being kept waiting. Well not for too long. He almost expected women to be late. It seemed to be some unwritten rule. Yet they could be the most impatient creatures if kept waiting themselves.

The hands on the wall clock were close to indicating the end of happy hour. Richard thought that he might have to order another drink to replace the now tepid brew in front of him. It was an instinct that drew his attention away from the bottle towards the door. A tingle ran from the base of his spine to the crown of his head as he watched her walk through the door. Glided would be a better term, as her movements were full of poise and grace. Richard's memory did not fail him. Even in his drunken state at the disco, the image of this beautiful woman would have burned through any chemical block and ingrained itself on his mind.

Natalie was tall, perhaps five foot ten, even without the high heels, thought Richard. She was slim, but curved in all the right places. She wore a short black dress which displayed her legs to good advantage. Long and slender, with good tone, they suggested an active lifestyle. Her hair was swept back and draped over her shoulders, falling to the level of her bosom. Her face betrayed no emotion as she approached Richard, who had stood up to welcome the arrival of this apparition. She may be cool as ice, but he was getting decidedly hot under the collar.

Richard offered his hand to Natalie who, to his surprise and joy, took it and came close to give him a kiss on the cheek. A good beginning to what could have been a very awkward first few moments. Natalie's generous gesture put Richard at ease and endeared her to him immediately.

Richard led Natalie over to a vacant table and pulled out her chair. She eased herself into the seat and gave him a smile which followed him as he took up his position across from her.

'So, you do remember me,' said Natalie, with only slightly feigned surprise. 'Perhaps you weren't that drunk after all.'

'Oh, no,' sighed Richard. 'I was at least as drunk as I seemed at the time. But even half conscious, I doubt that I would have forgotten you.'

Natalie laughed. 'Flatterer and gymnast!'

Richard groaned. 'Not exactly an elegant exit, I have to admit. Not that I have a great memory of the event, thank God. Unfortunately, my friends have an exceptionally vivid picture of events. Even those who weren't there.'

'You made quite an impression on my friends as well. Sarah, you do remember Sarah?' Richard's face indicated that the answer was no, so an amused Natalie continued. 'Well, she was appalled at the thought of me calling you. She thinks I am mad. When I told her that I was going to meet you, it was all I could do to stop her coming with me. She nearly tried to physically restrain me this evening.'

'I can't say that I really blame her,' replied Richard in a serious tone. 'She sounds like a real friend. You live together?'

'No, she rushed 'round when she heard that I was getting ready to come out to meet you. I thought I would leave it to the last minute to tell her, but it made no difference, she was 'round my flat in an instant. And she lives miles away. It was a bit like Alcoholics Anonymous for suspect dates.'

'Weren't you the slightest bit nervous about meeting me? I know that I was more than a bit anxious after my disgraceful display. To be honest, I was amazed that you called me. Pleased, very pleased, but amazed none the less.'

Natalie's smile lit up her face. 'Yes, I was a bit nervous. I didn't really know what to expect. If I had walked through that door and found you in your cups again, I would have turned around and walked straight back out. I'm pleased to meet you at last. The real you.'

Richard thanked his foresight in not getting involved in a drinking session with his colleagues prior to the meeting. 'Drinking is a universal pastime in this town, you know that. On which note, what would you like?'

'Actually, I don't know much about this town. I was brought up in London. Just a typical "BBC".' The acronym stood for British Born Chinese. ABC was the American version, and so on. 'I'm over here for work. And, I'll have a vodka and tonic on the rocks, with a slice of lemon.'

Richard raised his eyebrows. Nothing like a woman who knows exactly what she wants. Punctual and decisive. He would have to be careful, or he would fall in love with this woman.

As Richard stood at the bar, Natalie took the opportunity to have a closer look at him. He was a shade over six feet tall, she thought. Just about matching her in her heels. Broad shouldered and deeply tanned. He had the look of someone who spent a lot of time working out in the sun. No real vanity, though. He had a casual appearance, very comfortable with himself. This guy had nothing to prove. His face was hard, but his eyes had a softness and were of the deepest blue that Natalie had ever seen. They matched the sheen given off by his raven hair. She continued to stare as he walked back to the table.

Richard placed the drinks on the table and sat down. He had found it hard to keep his eyes off Natalie even while he was getting the drinks from the bar. Thank heaven for mirrors!

'So, what work brought you to Hong Kong?' asked Richard.

'Art. I run a gallery in Hollywood Road. I worked for the parent company in London and when they decided to open a gallery over here, I guess my face fit the part. The fact that I had never lived here didn't seem to matter. At least I speak Cantonese and Mandarin, but my boss didn't even ask when he offered me the job. Assumption can be a dangerous thing. Thankfully things are going well, even though I have only been here about six months. People have been very helpful.'

'People like your tall friend?' asked Richard.

'Yes, Toby has been very helpful and attentive,' laughed Natalie.

Bet he wouldn't have been so helpful if you weren't this attractive, thought Richard. Despite hardly remembering the chap, he felt that he had the measure of the other man. He had met enough of his sort. Grudgingly, he had to admit that he was probably a little of the same sort. At least he made no pretence to the contrary. He was a not unattractive bloke and he liked beautiful women. Was there really anything terribly wrong with that? OK, it was a very shallow attitude. Being attractive didn't guarantee a good character, often the opposite, but as poor a fact as it was, we tend to be drawn to beauty in the first instance. No one had ever said, "Wow, look at that really plain girl over there!". At least no one that Richard knew.

'Hello!'

Richard realised that he had been staring at Natalie without uttering a word. 'Sorry, I was just having unkind thoughts about your friend Toby and men in general in fact.'

'You mean about them only being interested in the surface beauty?'

This took Richard by surprise, but then he realised that it shouldn't. This was a smart, perceptive woman. He would have to be on his toes with this one. She wouldn't let him away with a thing.

'You think that men are all that shallow?'

'Pretty much, actually,' replied Natalie. 'I can't say that women are much better. None of my friends ever told me that they met this really great ugly guy. Mind you, nor have I, so I suppose we are all guilty of that particular prejudice.'

This really knocked Richard off balance. Was this girl a mind reader? Or was it something else? Could it be that the two of them were on the same wavelength? Richard had never believed in "soul-mates", but at this moment, he was open to persuasion.

'So, Richard Stirling. You were very evasive on the 'phone when I asked you about your job. That and the way you answer the telephone with a non-committal statement and I would guess that you are not supposed to talk about your work. Am I right?' Natalie held up her hand as Richard started to speak. 'No, wait. Of course, if you can't talk about it you are going to come up with some nonsense about "just the usual sort of thing. Boring old police-work. Paper-pushing." Am I right?'

'If you would let me get a word in, yes, I have to be careful what I say. My job is fairly sensitive. If we get to know one another better, you'll know what I do, but I won't be able to tell you specifics. Is that going to be a problem?'

'"If we get to know one another better"! Don't you think we have a future? I'm already planning to have your babies!'

Richard laughed. It was a defensive laugh, as he felt his face burn. Then to deflect attention from his embarrassment, he turned serious. 'Joking apart. My work can put a strain on relationships. You may think me mad for talking about this on a first date, but experience has taught me that it's best to get things like this out in the open early on.'

'Bitter experience?'

'Sometimes. But not always. It takes a lot of trust, on both sides. Relationships are difficult enough, but when there are things that you have to keep hidden in your life, it can put a strain on the strongest of them. I've seen too many of my friends break up with their wives and girlfriends to have any illusions on that score. Cops can be a bad bet sometimes, even the ones who can tell their partners about their jobs.

'Bringing your work home with you is a danger of the job. When you can't talk about what is bothering you, well you have to be aware that the person sharing your life cares about you and isn't the one you're mad at. It takes understanding and consideration from both people.'

Natalie tilted her head to one side and considered him for a long time.

'What?' asked Richard.

'You really have thought this through, haven't you?'

Smiling, he replied. 'I've had to. It's all too easy to blame the other person when a relationship doesn't work. Truth is, it's seldom that simple. People are complex creatures. I'm as willing to accept that I can drive my girlfriend mad, as I am to accept that there are going to be things about her which drive me to distraction. I suppose all that matters is that the good vastly outweighs the bad.'

'So, you don't believe in the perfect match, that two people are made for each other?'

'I'll tell you what I believe,' said Richard, as he leaned across the table and took Natalie's hand in his. 'I believe that any relationship, even the best, needs a constant commitment on the part of the two people involved to make the thing work. It helps if they feel that they could not go on without the other, that they are incomplete when their partner is not around. That they yearn for them like a thirsty man for water and that they are never far from one another's thoughts. I believe all that and a lot more. I also believe that if I keep on talking like this, you are going to make a bolt for the door.'

Natalie tightened her grip on his hand. 'You have no idea how wrong you are. Now, how about that dinner that you offered?'

Richard's suggestion of Japanese food was well received. The Odji, in the basement of the New World Centre was close by and well known to Richard. He had come here often, both with friends and visitors from overseas. The prices were reasonable for food that was good. Even poor Japanese food could burn a hole in your wallet. They had a choice of the sushi bar or tepanyaki. They opted for the latter. The dramatic displays of the chef, as he cooked their food on the hotplate before them was perhaps a bit over the top, but Richard enjoyed the drama of the event. Besides, he enjoyed the food.

Natalie was happy with his suggestion that they drink sake with the meal. She may have been relieved at his sobriety at the start of the evening, but she was no teetotaller. As the evening progressed, she demonstrated that she could hold her own when it came to drinking. Richard was careful though not to overindulge. He was enjoying himself too much to have the night clouded by booze.

The scallops burst with flavour in the mouth. The warm sake smoothly chased the food to the stomach and left a warm glow in it's path. The Kobe beef was like butter in the mouth, chewing seeming almost a redundant act. The conversation that was possible between the mouthfuls of food was punctuated by exclamations of pure pleasure with almost every bite. Richard enjoyed this place, but it would be somewhere very special after this night.

He didn't consider himself a romantic in matters of the heart. He had always tried to be the rational man. His relationships had been warm, at times passionate, but what he was starting to feel towards Natalie was unlike anything which had struck him before. She responded to him in a way that showed that the attraction was mutual. Not merely lust, for they were two attractive people. It was more. They enjoyed one another. They talked and were genuinely interested in what the other had to say. Their conversation was not mere small talk. There seemed to be an urgency about the way they talked, as if they wanted to get to know one another as quickly as possible.

The meal ended all too quickly, but neither Natalie nor Richard wanted the night to end. The location seemed unimportant, they just wanted to be together. Richard had to rack his brain to think of a place where they were unlikely to run into a bunch of cops. The only company he desired was right by his side. In the end he decided that a trip across the harbour would not only be pleasant, but might reduce his chances of bumping into someone who would refuse to take the hint that he wanted to be alone with Natalie.

The Star Ferry crossing was still a romantic journey. No matter how many times one took it, the trip was guaranteed to heighten the emotion of the moment. This seemed hardly possible between these two travellers, as their emotions were reaching new heights. As they held hands and stared into the glittering night, they seemed to feel one another's hearts beat as one. Everything seemed right. The more they talked, the more they wanted to know. There was no end to their curiosity about one another. Somewhere in mid channel, they kissed. Neither seemed to make the first move. It just happened. It was the right thing to do. The kiss was tender, soft and held the promise of so much more. The rest of the journey passed unnoticed as they explored one another's lips. They sat at the rear of the ferry, but were oblivious to the occasional smiling glance that their fellow passengers gave them. Before the couple knew it, the propellers were churning the water in an attempt to slow the progress of the tub-like craft. The judder, as the vessel hit the sleepers lining the ferry terminal brought the pair out of their mutual involvement and back to the deck of the boat. As the ramp lowered, they smiled at one another and finding words unnecessary for the first time that night, they followed the rest of the cross-harbour mariners back onto dry land.

It was four in the morning when they parted company. As they stood outside Natalie's building, the taxi driver had to display a degree of patience not normally associated with his profession. They were reluctant to leave one another, but both knew that this would be a temporary separation. Indeed, they had already arranged to have lunch the following day. Still, their kisses lengthened as they clung on to this moment of joy. Finally, Richard summoned his will and said goodnight. He had politely refused the offer of a nightcap, deciding that he wanted things to go slowly with Natalie. He didn't want her to get the wrong idea. For her part, she was slightly put-out at first at his refusal of her offer. For a brief moment it crossed her mind that he might not desire her. It was only for a moment. Their next embrace communicated Richards feelings more eloquently than any words. So, the game of emotional chess came to an impasse, with the promise of a re-match the next day. It was unlikely that result would be as indecisive on that occasion.

CHAPTER 15

'Looks like it's going to rain.'

Ah Pau half turned to Richard and nodded his agreement. The two men were standing on a ridge overlooking an old quarry. They had been there for an hour, watching an open-air drama unfold below them.

Members of the training team were making their final preparations, ensuring that all the trainees were in place and that the plan had been followed exactly. Richard was there to watch a couple of officers in particular, men they hoped would fill gaps in his team. Ah Pau was an Acting Station Sergeant, head of Bravo Team's Sniper Group. He had been Richard's number two when he had been Assault Group Leader. After Richard's promotion, Ah Pau had moved over to lead the snipers. The two men knew one another better than brothers. They relied on each other and Richard still valued his comrade's advice on most matters, particularly personnel selection. Ah Pau had a good eye for character and had been proven right in the past, when all indicators had said that his opinion was wrong.

The exercise that was being set up was an Ambush Option. The scenario read as follows. Terrorists had been allowed to leave their stronghold with their hostages in a bus. Their destination was the airport and an awaiting 'plane. The job of the SDU trainees was to ensure that they never reached their destination and that the hostages should be released unharmed. That was the theory. This option was not a popular one, as the expectation of casualties was high. It was preferable though to allowing the enemy to escape justice. In the real world, the security forces could not guarantee that they would be able to execute military action in ideal circumstances, so they trained for the worst possible situation. No matter how difficult they made the training, they were all aware that a real incident was likely to throw things at them that they had not considered. All they could do was prepare themselves as best they could, with the resources at their disposal and all the ingenuity they could muster.

The quarry had a narrow road running down a slope, with sheer walls on both sides. This was to be the location of the ambush. Snipers were positioned around the target area. They would not only guide the operation, by feeding information on the target to the controllers, but would cover the Assault Group on their approach. They might even be able to take out some of the terrorists before they could kill the hostages. There was always hope. In this case, the target vehicle, an old bus, would have it's windows covered, making target acquisition impossible. Should one of the terrorists be foolish enough to expose himself, he would be a target for any sniper with a clear shot. Sounds simple, but the difficult part was identifying a valid target in a matter of seconds. The last thing you wanted to do was kill a hostage by mistake. Here the skill of the sniper was tested. Paper targets were one thing. Spotting a face among many, making a decision and then hitting the target, all in the space of a few seconds, that was when the truly skilled shone and the rest had to accept that their talents might lie elsewhere.

Richard looked to his right. At the base of the slope, hidden from view, sat the great blue behemoth. He loved these machines. The Saracen armoured car might be a relic of the past, but it had served the Force well for many years. They broke down and required constant maintenance, but they still held a place in the hearts of all who had anything to do with them in the course of their duties. This one had thick metal pipes welded to the nose, forming a formidable battering ram. It's job, to bring the target vehicle to a sudden and hopefully, unexpected stop. As this happened, the Assault Group would go into action, swarming over the bus, gaining entry at two points and hoping that the violence and speed of their assault would allow them to kill all the terrorists and minimise the number of hostage casualties. Simple plan, very difficult to execute successfully. It would take all the skill and determination that even experienced men could muster. Richard was looking forward to seeing how the trainees fared. Even he would hate to have to do this in a real situation. The only certainty was that it would be bloody.

Station Sergeant Kwan looked to be satisfied with the preparations. As he spoke into his radio, Richard watched the trainee snipers for any signs of tension. The odd shift of position was an indication that the heart was starting to beat a little faster, that the breathing became slightly deeper. One figure did not budge an inch. Kwan may be right about this guy, thought Richard. He would soon see.

Kwan was still talking on the radio. At the other end of the communication would be members of Richard's Team, playing enemy for this exercise. It was not only a break from routine training for these men, each took his role very seriously. "Know thine enemy" was a good rule of thumb. All the men of Bravo Team had been through this training and knew that their performance would affect the value of the exercise for the trainees. If they messed around, the new men would gain little from it. They also knew that Richard's eye would be on them. Any horseplay would be rewarded with more than angry words. Their Team Commander knew the value of training and hated to see it go to waste through stupidity. For most, though, this was not a consideration, they had a job to do and they would do it to the best of their ability.

Kwan and the other members of the training team took up their positions. They would monitor the exercise and determine the success or failure of the various elements. The most difficult aspect would be deciding if the snipers had gained a kill. This was the most artificial part of the exercise. For obvious reasons, all weapons would be loaded with blank ammunition. Determining a kill would be a decision that the exercise umpires would make. The trainees would act as if the situation was real. All training requires a degree of imagination from the participants. The SDU did train with live ammunition wherever possible, but under these circumstances the risks were too great. Dangerous training is only acceptable when it serves a useful purpose and can be strictly controlled. The aim of this exercise was to demonstrate a tactic to the trainees and monitor their performance in difficult, if somewhat artificial conditions.

Richard watched the Assault Group assemble at two locations. They would attack the bus from two angles, carefully determined to minimise the risk of cross-fire, but splitting the attention of the terrorists. An explosive charge had been set up at the side of the road, thirty meters short of and opposite the side road where the Saracen laid in wait. This would be detonated at the same time as the armoured vehicle set off, distracting and hopefully confusing the driver of the bus.

Even Richard could feel the tension in the air. Despite his experience and the fact that he was not directly involved, he could feel a slight dampness on his palms. He smiled to himself. Always the same. Anyone who said that they were not nervous before an operation was either a liar or had ice-water running through their veins. Richard enjoyed the rush of adrenalin, indeed he needed it. He felt it gave him an edge. Richard was an assault man at heart. He enjoyed the naked aggression of the attack, the man-on-man engagement. He knew he didn't have the temperament to be a sniper. He was an excellent shot, but lacked the patience to lie inactive for hour on end, maintaining a high level of awareness, observing the enemy, waiting until the opportunity came to release a deadly hail down on the unsuspecting terrorist. He admired those who could and knew that as he made his way into the stronghold, he would be relying on the quality of the intelligence gathered by the snipers and other specialists. A well aimed and timed shot might also save his life.

Richard's attention was grabbed by the sound of an approaching engine. The bus appeared suddenly around a bend in the road. The side windows were covered in sheets of newsprint, but he could clearly see one of his men at the wheel. Ah Ngau, why did they let him loose with a bus? thought Richard, he was a maniac behind the wheel of any vehicle. Richard grimaced as he watched the man struggle with the bus on the loose surface of the quarry road. He breathed a sigh of relief when the tail finally came back in line and the vehicle started down the narrow road.

On cue, there was an explosion to the left of the bus. The vehicle swerved slightly away from it. Either Ah Ngau was playing his part well, or he hadn't expected it. Within a couple of seconds, the driver was confronted by the sight of a squat blue monster blocking his path. The wheels of the bus locked as the brakes were applied with force and in haste. The bus had not been travelling very fast, but it still took a long time for the momentum of the large vehicle to dissipate. Richard held his breath as it looked as though the strength of the Saracen's ram was about to be tested. Luckily the bus came to a halt a few feet short of the aging armour.

As if from nowhere, two groups of black-clad men swarmed up to the bus. One group attacked the front, while the other headed for the rear emergency exit. Time was the problem now. The men had to affect entry as quickly as possible, to minimise the hostage casualties. The disorientation of the occupants of the vehicle would only last for a few seconds. The rear door presented few problems and the sound of gunfire rang out as the SDU men entered the bus. The group at the front were having more trouble. They would have to get the door open, but would now know that the other group were inside and that the vehicle would be swept from the rear.

It all looked very messy. That was to be expected. It always did. To Richard's trained eye, the trainees were not doing too badly, but that front door was taking far too long. There would be a lot to discuss about entry techniques at the debriefing. Suddenly, the front door burst open, taking the trainees by surprise. As it opened, a figure launched itself out of the doorway, scattering the policemen like bowling pins. In an instant the terrorist was on his feet and loosing off with a machine pistol. Richard started to smile, then he heard a shot ring out from below his position. As soon as he heard it, he knew something was wrong. So did Ah Pau, who was already moving forward, down the slope to the exercise area. Richard was on the move too, as he watched the terrorist drop to the ground like a sack of coal.

'Oh shit!' cried Richard. A nightmare was unfolding before his eyes. His mind was racing as he sprinted across the ground to the downed man. The trainees were starting to get to their feet, as they began to realise that all was not well. Kwan and his training team were already at the prostrate figure as Richard and Ah Pau reached the bus. Beng Jai, the training team medic was giving the injured man CPR. Richard saw a large patch of blood spread out down the right side of his team-mate's shirt. The Balaclava he had been wearing had been removed. It was Daai Bei. This exercise was supposed to be a bit of fun for him before he went off to start his promotion course. Richard felt a lump appear in his throat. His instinct was to go to the aid of his friend, but he knew that the best thing to do was let Beng Jai get on with the job he had been trained for. Daai Bei was in good hands.

A member of the training team arrived with the medical kit. He took over CPR as Beng Jai set up an Intra-venous drip. It was vital to get fluid into the downed man, to keep the pressure up in his circulatory system. That would greatly increase his chances of resuscitation at the hospital. Richard turned to Kwan and saw that the older man was already on another radio, calling for a medi-vac. Richard grabbed Ah Pau.

'Get the Transit,' ordered Richard. 'It'll be quicker if we take him to Fanling Hospital. Mr Kwan, tell the chopper to go to Fanling. We may still have to take Daai Bei to BMH, if the doctors at Fanling Hospital are not up to the job.'

British Military Hospital would be the first choice for all the SDU men. The Army doctors were experienced in dealing with gunshot wounds. The doctors at the government hospitals could be very good, but they could also be terrible. Richard would rather not play that mortal lottery. That aside, experience was better than good intentions.

As his orders were being carried out, Richard's eye was caught by the sight of a lone figure, standing on the ridge above. He grabbed one of the training sergeants by the arm and said 'Come on, let's go get the poor sod.'

The two men ran up the slope, trying to be calm in their approach to the isolated figure. As Richard came closer, he saw that it was the young man that he had been paying attention to earlier. He mentally cursed the bad luck and the irony. This was the lad who was supposed to replace Daai Bei in the Sniper Group. Richard slowed to a walk as he came close to the young man. The constable's face was ashen, his eyes staring into nothingness. Richard called out his name. 'Philip.' There was no response. 'Philip!' There was an edge to Richard's voice this time which came right from the parade square. It snapped the trainee to attention.

'Philip, give me the rifle. Don't worry lad, everything will be alright. Now just give me the rifle.'

Still looking stunned, but obviously back in the land of the living, the young man handed the weapon over to Richard. 'Yes sir. Oh God, what have I done?'

'Let's not worry about that right now, come on let's get you seen to. You're in shock.' Richard gripped the man's arm and gently led him back to the road.

When they arrived, Daai Bei was being loaded onto the Transit van. Beng jai was still giving CPR. The sweat was pouring off the little man, but he refused to let anyone give him a break. This was a personal matter. He was not about to let his colleague die. Richard sat up front and seeing that those in the back were secure, told Ah Pau to get moving, fast.

As the Transit sped along, Richard realised that he still had the rifle in his hand. He carefully cycled the weapon, opening the breach. An empty case was ejected and he could see the next round sitting on the top of the magazine. When he saw it, he went red with anger. 'Son of a bitch!'

Ah Pau pushed the vehicle to the limits of its performance. On the floor of the rear compartment, Beng Jai continued his battle against death. The look of determination on his face should have been enough to deter the grim reaper from his prize. Another constable tried to stem the flow of blood from the wound in Daai Bei's side with large wound dressings. Discarded dressings were starting to accumulate on the floor. Another IV was prepared in an attempt to keep up with the loss of body fluid.

Mr Kwan, who had been manning the radio, called out that an RAF helicopter was being diverted to a landing site between their current position and the hospital in Fanling. Richard had to make a decision. Take the casualty straight to the hospital, or add ten or fifteen minutes to the journey and get Daai Bei to BMH. His choice was made in seconds. 'Ah Pau, take us to the RV with the chopper.'

The Wessex was waiting for them on the parade square at Cassino Lines, an Army base on the Shataukok Road. The Gurkha gate guard had evidently been briefed, as he opened the barrier as soon as he saw the police vehicle approach. Ah Pau did not slow down, he threw the Transit towards the waiting aircraft and came to a halt far enough away to avoid the rotors. The SDU men piled out of the van with their precious burden. Richard climbed aboard and was pleased to see a friendly face in the form of Pete Bailly. The loadmaster helped bring Daai Bei on board and wasted no time in telling the pilot to get the helicopter airborne once Beng Jai had stabilised the patient.

The flight to BMH was as fast as the pilot could make it, but for Richard it was interminable. He felt useless sitting there watching Beng Jai and his assistant do their job. He had tried to take over the CPR, but the medic would have none of it. The man was drenched in his own sweat and the blood of his charge. Kwan had stayed behind to start collecting evidence on what had gone wrong and to look after the young sniper. Richard had a pretty good idea now of what had happened. He knew that it was not Philip's fault. He would make damn sure that the one who was responsible would pay for his mistake.

Doctors were waiting at the heli-pad and took over from two exhausted SDU men. Beng Jai looked on the point of collapse. One of the British doctors gave the Chinese sergeant an emphatic thumbs-up. Richard gave him a pat on the back and ushered the group to follow their comrade into the hospital.

The wait in the cold green corridors of the hospital was worse than the helicopter ride. At least then the SDU men had been busy. Keith Symons turned up with the rest of the team. All were desperate for news, but had to share the same wait as the rest of their colleagues. At last, a doctor approached the anxious group. Richard stood and tried to read some indication of the situation from the doctor's face.

'Chief Inspector Stirling?'

'Yes, doctor. What's happening?'

'Well, your man is very lucky. He's not out of the woods yet, but his chances are pretty good. The bullet stopped against the wall of his heart. Another few millimeters and it might have been a very different story. Who was the medic who worked on him before he got here?'

Richard ushered Beng Jai forward. The man still looked worn out, as much by worry as the effort he had expended on Daai Bei.

'Young man, you have done a good days work today. You saved your colleague's life. Without your efforts, he would never made it to us alive.' The doctor held out his hand. Beng Jai took the praise with a great deal of humility. He was close to tears, not because of the accolade, but because of the relief that his friend was alive.

Richard smiled at the medic. He would make sure that everyone knew what they owed this man.

'Look,' said the doctor, 'there's no point in you all hanging about here. No one will be able to see him today. We have the number of your unit. We'll call you as soon as there is any change in his condition. Now you all look as though you could do with some rest.'

Richard nodded in agreement and told his men to go home. He and Keith had some unfinished business back at base.

No words passed between the three men as they sat in the traffic-jam leading to the Lion Rock Tunnel. The continual movement of men and goods between Kowloon and the New Territories was at it's afternoon peak. Ah Pau concentrated on the nose to tail progress of the traffic. Richard and Keith were lost in their own thoughts and prayers for their fallen comrade. After much consideration, Richard decided that he needed to share his thoughts with his friend. He reached into his pocket and took out the object of his anger.

'Recognise this?' Richard handed over the object to Keith.

'Looks like a blank 7.62 round, but there's something not quite right about it,' replied the younger man. His look suddenly changed from puzzlement to understanding. 'Oh, God. How could this happen? What the hell is this thing?'

Richard took the bullet back and stared at it. 'It's a major fuck-up that's what it is. It happened my friend because of that dick of an armoury sergeant, our glorious leader's *mah jai* . By the way, wasn't it nice of him to show up at the hospital?'

'He was on his way back from a meeting at Police Headquarters. No doubt he will be busy covering his arse back at base.'

'Not this time me old son, not this time.'

Superintendent Victor Cummings was sitting behind his desk when Richard, closely followed by Keith, barged into his office. Richard threw the bullet onto his desk.

'Remember these bloody things?'

The OC SDU stared at the black round. 'Looks as though someone has some explaining to do.'

Richard was ready to burst. 'You bastard. You're not going to get out of this one. I told you that little shit of yours had no right being in charge of the armoury. He's a drunk. Just because you wanted your man on the inside to feed you all the gossip, a good man may die. These bloody things were supposed to be returned to headquarters months ago. For the very reason that they could be confused with blanks. Your pet horse obviously didn't do it and issued the fucking things to the training team. He at least should have known what the damn things were. I'll have his balls for this.'

Cummings, crimson faced jumped out of his seat. 'Who the hell do you think you are talking to Chief Inspector. I am your senior officer. How dare you rant at me like this. You are coming very close to disciplinary charges.'

'Go ahead. I'd love a hearing, so I can tell everyone what an incompetent arsehole you are. You have no right being in this job. I warned you about that idiot time and again. God, I wish I had caught him drunk on the job just once.

'You're not going to cover this one up. I have all the evidence I need to go after him.'

Richard was about to turn around and leave when Cummings spoke, in a bitter but calm voice. 'So, you're prepared to see Station

Sergeant Kwan go down as well. Probably other members of the training team and of course that young trainee.'

Keith looked at Richard's face and immediately grabbed him by the shoulders. 'Richard. Don't do it. It's not worth it. Stay calm.' He could feel the older man shaking as he gripped him. Slowly, the rage subsided and Richard turned to face a smug looking Cummings.

Cummings knew he had the upper hand. Richard Stirling would never let others take the blame for the armoury sergeant's mistake. The smugness in his voice nearly sent Richard off again. 'After all, they were in charge of the exercise. They should have checked the ammunition.'

Richard spoke with pure hate. 'You know as well as I do that they did check the ammunition. It would have been an easy mistake for anyone unfamiliar with this ammo. That's the very reason that we decided to get rid of it. The only ones who would have known for certain were the armoury staff who had been briefed on the damn stuff. As I recall, Kwan was on leave when we tested it.'

'Well, I am sure that the armoury staff will say that it was Kwan who picked out the ammunition and that they had been warned not to confuse this stuff with the blanks. Just didn't listen, I suppose. Sheer incompetence.'

This time Keith had to bodily remove his boss from the office. Richard was so mad he couldn't speak. The Assault Group Leader managed to man-handle him out into the open air, where his Team Commander could calm down. Keith thanked the Lord that he had the diversion of looking after his friend. If it had been just him and the OC, he would have probably strangled the man.

Bravo Team's compliment of officers managed to make it back to their office without killing anyone. Kwan was waiting for them. He looked worried. The cover-up plan had obviously reached the unit grapevine. The Chief Inspector who was in charge of the Training Team was on long leave, so ultimately the responsibility for the team rested with the Station Sergeant, his 2i/c.

'*Daai Lo*,' pleaded Kwan. 'What is going on?'

Stirling collapsed into a chair and held his face in his hands. He blew long and hard through his mouth and then looked at Kwan with sad eyes.

'Training ammunition Mr Kwan. Plastic training ammunition. We tested it out last year. You were on leave with your family. It was supposed to be returned to Police Headquarters because it was so easy to confuse with the blanks that we use.'

Kwan was still looking confused.

'The plastic ammo is supposed to recreate the same ballistic effects as the real stuff, but over shorter ranges. So, you zero a weapon over a hundred meters and you can practice on a 50 meter range without altering the sights on the weapon. It really was more trouble than it was worth, so we abandoned the idea.

'Philip probably went for a head shot on Daai Bei. Because of the low mass of the plastic bullet, the drop was much greater, so it hit our man in the side instead. Lucky, huh?'

Keith entered the discussion with a question that was on the mind of all three men. 'Boss, what are we going to do?'

Richard looked at the floor as he spoke. 'I have no idea. I won't let Kwan take the fall for this, but I'm loathe to let that prick get away with it. Cummings has no business being in charge of this unit. He's never even been on selection. Why Ops Wing put him in charge I will never know. I have never been given a decent answer on that one. "Policy" is all I ever get out of them. Well, if that policy ends up costing Daai Bei his life, I don't care what happens to me, that dick-head is going down.'

'Welcome back to the land of the living.'

Richard smiled down at Daai Bei. Tubes were coming out and going in all over the young man, but he smiled as he saw his boss walk in through the door.

'*Daai Lo*, I'm glad to be here. How is the team? Is the kid who shot me alright?'

'Philip's still pretty shaken up. I've told the guys to take him under their wing for a while, try to get him to accept that it wasn't his fault. Do you know what happened?'

'Yes, Ah Pau told me. That damned training ammo. I thought it had been disposed of.'

'We all did. The only good thing that's come of this is that the armoury sergeant has been transferred. He asked Cummings to move him for his own safety. The guys are a little unhappy with the drunken prick. Of course, I have told them that no one has to be caught threatening the guy. So, no one has been caught. I can always be sure that my men follow orders to the letter.

'Doc says you are going to make a full recovery in time. You'll have to postpone your promotion, but Headquarters has assured me that there will be a place for you as soon as you're able to start.'

The constable smiled and slowly nodded his head. 'Beng Jai saved me, didn't he?'

'Yes. I'm making sure he gets recognition for it. Cummings wanted to sweep the whole thing under the carpet, but I went over his head. Unfortunately I've had to swallow my anger and accept a bit of a cover-up, to protect the guys in the Training Team. I can tell you, everyone in the unit is gunning for the OC. If he makes one slip, we'll have him. I can't believe he's staying, knowing that the entire unit hate his guts. He seems to have some powerful protectors. PHQ were perfectly willing to swallow the cock an bull story he gave them. Senior officers, eh? Don't you just love 'em?'

'At least we have men like you *Daai Lo* . Officers who care about their men. I hate to think what the Force would be like if it were full of people like the OC.'

Richard looked embarrassed. 'Daai Bei, I have the same nightmare. It's just a pity that there are any men like Cummings in the

Force. But, somehow we manage to keep going despite them. Don't worry. His day will come. I just hope I am around to see it.'

CHAPTER 16

Jack Garland watched the boy as he walked away from the car, towards the tower blocks of the public housing estate. He made no attempt to hide his distaste. There was no one to see the look that appeared on his rough, deeply cut features. He always made sure that this duty was performed away from inquisitive eyes. It was at times like this that he questioned the remuneration that he received for his loyalty to Li Keung. Distasteful tasks were part of his job description. Some he even found pleasurable, but he hated to be around these people. His master's preferences had always disgusted him, for like many of the perverted, he was the first to denounce the perversions of others. Li liked to fuck little boys. Garland's proclivities lay elsewhere. It was not so much the youth of the boys that disgusted him, his homophobia was totally independent of age. He after all had inclinations toward the young. To Garland this was a different matter. He liked girls, that was alright. That, in his mind, confirmed his manhood.

The thought of any young flesh being corrupted by Li made Garland shiver. To him the twisted body of his boss was a mere reflection of the mind and soul that lay within. Corruption given form. Li paid people like Garland to execute his will, but the evil that resulted came straight form the imagination of the deformed tycoon. It was a wonder that Li had survived to manhood. Chinese families had been known to kill offspring displaying much less deformity than Garland's boss.

It was bad enough that the security chief had to put up with driving these little perverts around, he had to act the pimp, procuring the little sodomites for his master. It had been easier when Li had taken a liking to Thai boys. They could be recruited as house servants and kept away from the public glare. When the time came to change the current model, well then it was easy. Garland smiled at the thought. As the boy entered his block, Jack knew that he would soon have another task to perform, one he would enjoy. Li was tiring of his latest protégé. It would have been easier if he was still attracted to the Thais, but he had gone back to Chinese boys, considering them "cleaner". This one had friends. Jack would have to be smart in the way that this one was "retired". The foreign ones could be returned home and if necessary, disappear when they were out of Hong Kong.

This boy was cocky, not giving Jack the respect that was his due. Li allowed him to test his security chief, taking pleasure in the struggle that Jack had to endure, to stop himself wringing the little bastard's neck. Perhaps that was the intent, to make it all the easier for Jack to do his job when the time came. If that was the intention, it had worked. Jack was already planning something special for the little low life.

Garland started the car and pulled away from the kerb. He felt soiled by the proximity of the boy. He would shower when he got home. Wash away the filth he felt clinging to him, from being so close to the depraved youth. The boys seldom objected to Li's attentions. They were well paid for their services. A few had been taken by surprise, but their silence had been swiftly ensured. Garland was nothing if not efficient when it came to matters of violence. The willing ones had enjoyed the fruits of their perversion for as long as Li enjoyed their bodies. Garland hoped that the current one had made the most of his money. There was little point in saving it. He would have little time left to enjoy it.

Jack started to enjoy thinking about the boy, or rather what he was going to do to him. Yes, something special for this one, he thought. He would make the boy pay for his insolence. This one would indeed be a pleasure.

Li threw the newspaper onto the table. Garland had to shift the paper to read the headline. It was a gesture rather than a necessity, he already knew what the banner said. Li's silence told Garland that his boss was furious. He searched for the right words, something which might ease the situation. Jack knew that the wrong words at this moment might cost him dear. His dilemma was ended sooner than he had expected.

'What is going on?' asked Li. 'Is this man insane? Did you have any idea that he planned something like this, or is it just an outrageous screw-up? If I thought that you sanctioned this…the repercussions of this. I just can't imagine what the Circle will say. I must never be linked with this. No matter what happens now, this must never come back to me. Do you understand?'

'Sir, I knew nothing about this. I can only imagine that the girl was there by accident. I shall let our man know that he has displeased you.'

'Displeased?' Li was black with fury. Garland recoiled from the small man's approach. 'Have you any idea what the Circle will do to us if they discover our involvement in something like this? No amount of power or influence would protect us. The slightest whisper that one of their number should have carried out an act like this will mean the most serious investigation of every member. The chances of discovery then are too great to contemplate.' Li walked to the window of his house and looked out at the gathering storm clouds. 'We may have to terminate the operation.'

Garland was shocked by this statement. He had been angry when news of the girl's death had reached him. He intended leaving their man in no doubt that slip-ups like this were unacceptable, but to end the project because of this, he could not believe that his boss was serious. 'Is that really necessary, we have come so far, the results we want are close.' Li cut him short.

'You just don't get it do you? Most of the members of the Circle would resist any attempt by Vincent Lo to begin a manhunt, so long as the deaths might benefit their own agendas. Many would even applaud our actions, at least inwardly. But this girl's death changes everything. You and I might have the stomach to do what is necessary, but most of them do not. They will fall into line with Lo now. It may be too dangerous to go on. We may have to cover our tracks quickly, if we are to survive.'

If you are to survive, thought Garland. He was under no illusions about his position in the great scheme. He was expendable. Li would find someone to deal with Jack, just as he dealt with others. Perhaps I might have a trick left for you my friend, he thought.

'Let's not rush into anything. I will speak to our friend. Wait and see what the Circle intend. If it comes to it, I will clear away every scrap of evidence. Nothing will lead back to you. I guarantee it.'

Li stared coldly at his security chief. 'I hope you do not cause me to regret the confidence that I am placing in you. You have just made the most important promise of your life.'

'I know,' said Garland. Though he was calm on the surface, his heart was pounding. He always tried to convince himself that he did not fear this powerful man. It was at times like this that he knew the truth of the matter. Jack Garland was just another pawn in the great game. A game that he could not afford to join. He would never be able to afford it. That was the depressing truth which Jack tried to forget. This was Li's game and he held all the pieces. In the end it would be Li who decided who remained in the game. If Jack played his part, he might just survive. If he failed, he would be sacrificed. The King was the only piece that always remained on the board.

Vincent Lo looked at the headline again. He had been looking at it all day and still he couldn't believe what he was reading. Who was behind this? More to the point, why was he having to ask himself this question. As head of the Circle, he should have been on top of this situation from the beginning. The fact that he was powerless to intervene left him feeling impotent and for a man like Lo, that was unacceptable. A real danger was that other members of the Circle might see his impotence. He was exposed. That was an opportunity for those who opposed his policies and held ambitions towards his position. Men like Li Keung.

Vincent despised Li. Not just because the sight of the deformed frame struck some primitive chord in him. Li was a danger to anyone who associated with him. For years, Vincent had tried to find a way to expel this hideous creature from the Circle. Li had allies, though even they would turn on him in an instant, should the advantages of their tenuous allegiances cease to exist, or be important. Vincent had to admit that Li Keung knew how to use influence and harness power. He was a skilled intriguer, but Vincent suspected that his mind was as twisted as his body. The rumours of his sexual perversions disturbed Vincent Lo. Another reason that the tycoon's skin crawled when in the presence of this loathsome little man. Vincent Lo was at heart a snob. He had been born into privilege and wealth. He was a part of the social elite of Hong Kong. Master of his own fate and that of all within his influence, whether they knew it or not. His family were from the economic aristocracy which had flourished before the communist takeover in Shanghai. They had successfully transplanted their wealth to the colony of Hong Kong. Li Keung came from a similar background, but he was from Southern stock, peasants made good. No matter how much wealth and power he accumulated, Li would never be Vincent Lo's equal.

It crossed Vincent's mind that Li might have something to do with these atrocities. Someone as perverse as Li Keung might sanction the killing of a father and daughter. A family, something Li had never had. If the rumours were true about his sexual activities, might he find the murder of a little girl acceptable? But, why? What was the motive behind these bombings. Was it just some madman, exacting revenge from the *Gwailo* , for some slight, real or imagined? Could it really be that simple? In Vincent's mind it could not be that simple. No, someone was manipulating events for a profit motive. In the end, that was what everything in Hong Kong came down to. Profit. It may be as simple as money, but things were seldom that simple. There was a reason for these deaths and Vincent Lo was certain that it was a complex one. He was also certain that he must find out who was behind the deaths and stop them. If it was Li, or another member of the Circle and Vincent failed to detect them before their scheme was completed, he had no doubt that his tenure of office would come to a swift and permanent end. Even the Triad chiefs within the Circle were disquietened by these events. They were too high profile. These men operated from the shadows and feared the glare of publicity. Anything which might shine a light on them or their activities was dangerous and must be dealt with ruthlessly. These men were experts in being ruthless. Vincent saw them as a necessary evil within his elite group, but he also feared them. He had control, so long as he was in control of the Circle as a whole, but should he be seen to have lost his grip on the reins, his fall would be sudden and final.

He must get to the bottom of this and fast.

CHAPTER 17

'Why is this happening?'

The question had been troubling every man in the room. David Lo was the first to bring it into open discussion. The conference room was filled with officers from almost every branch of the Force. David Lo was not the most senior officer there, but as head of the investigation team, this was his baby. In the end, his head was on the block if these bombings continued.

'There has to be a reason,' he continued. 'It may be as simple as an insane grudge against the British. Chances are that it is a lot more complicated than that. Our friends in EOD have shown us that the bomber is highly skilled. They think that his last bomb was staged to show us how clever he is. Clever and I have no doubt insane. But, remember that gentlemen. Mad does not mean stupid. If we underestimate this person, he and I think it is almost certainly a he, will make us pay a terrible price.

'You can imagine the pressure that is being put on the Commissioner over this affair. He has made it plain that all our resources must be put into stopping this character. We have every resource within Government at our disposal on this one. But that also means that the powers above expect results and quickly.'

A moan sounded around the room. Thoughts of sleepless nights and constant harassing from senior officers made their way around the group. This was to be a nightmare for the whole Police Force. In the end, they would either be given a brief pat on the back for a job well done, or pilloried for incompetence. The stage had been reached where, even if they did catch the bomber before he committed another killing, the question would be; why did it take so long? Difficult as it was to be motivated in a situation where you couldn't win, the room was full of motivated men. If they had any doubts about their task before, those had been removed by the latest outrage. Even the toughest and most cynical of men had been struck to the core by the sight of the little girl in that wrecked car. The bomber had made a fatal mistake. He had made the entire Royal Hong Kong Police mad.

'If we can determine the why, we might come closer to the who. It would be wrong to assume that there is a single mind behind all this. The bombings may be carried out by an individual, after all these skills are rare in this part of the world, but there may be another brain behind the bomber. That is the one we need to focus on. Who would benefit from these acts? As I said, it may be a lone bomber with some sort of grudge, but we have to think that there may be a broader agenda at work here.

'The targets have some singular similarities. They are British and they are Taipans. Three deaths among this small group is hardly coincidence. We have to assume that the next target will also be within this group. So, what do we do to prevent it?' David looked towards an officer sitting in the front row. 'Special Branch will coordinate the protection effort. VIP Protection will assign their own officers, but they will have to be supported by other units, as their numbers and other duties will not allow them to cover all the potential targets. We have been fairly generous in our assessment of who falls into the vulnerable category. I think that this is a case where it is better to err on the side of caution. Altogether there are ten men who we consider to be at risk.

'Members of the Special Duties Unit and some Headquarters CID units will be temporarily assigned to the protection detail, but Special Branch will be in overall charge of the assignment. Chief Inspector Stirling from the EOD unit, is to be assigned to us full time. He will help with the technical aspects of the investigation and try to help us anticipate the bomber's next move. He will also be on permanent call to deal with any device that we might locate. He has asked me to emphasise that anything suspicious should be dealt with by him. He will never complain about being called out to deal with a hoax. On the other hand, he will personally throttle anyone who fails to call him out to a real bomb and those of us who know him realise that he is perfectly serious.' A small amount of laughter came from the audience. Those who did know Richard's background knew that he was more than capable of carrying out the threat, or worse.

'Gentlemen, I am afraid that at this juncture, we have precious little to go on. Our man is clever, but he seems to have taken a direction which may work in our favour. EOD have suggested that he may have watched the last explosion and perhaps altered the scene to simulate a well known bombing in Northern Ireland. This man may just become a bit too clever. If he is enjoying himself so much, then he may take greater risks to increase his pleasure. I am hoping that may be enough to help us catch him.

'What I want and I am sure everyone in this room wants is to catch him before he has a chance to take another life. To do that, we have to be proactive in our investigation, we have to be smarter than the bomber and we have to get lucky. Now, if there is nothing more, I will keep you no longer. I'll expect daily reports from the unit commanders. Thank you.'

'So, the *Bing* , have admitted that the explosive was British Military in origin?'

Richard looked at Cassius and gave a wry smile as he replied. 'The Army have said that they concur that the explosive residue is consistent with that you might expect to find from the same type of explosive compounds used in some of their duties. Or words to that effect. I think it was more obscure than that actually.'

Cassius leaned against the wall of his office and sighed like a beaten man. Their lead had just hit a brick wall.

'What about our people? You say that SDU and EOD both use PE 4. How closely are the stores of explosive controlled?'

'Well, as far as we are concerned, I can't imagine that any would escape unnoticed. I had John double check our supplies and records. Not scrap is missing. As for SDU, well, when I was in the unit the controls were very tight. I expect that nothing much has changed.'

'CID officers have been known to walk off range courses with a few extra rounds,' said Cassius. 'Never know when they might come in useful.'

'I know. But plastic explosive is a different matter, particularly in the quantities we are talking about. No, I think that the Force is in the clear, but let's keep the thought in the back of our minds. God, I would hate to think that I'm wrong about this.

'The one good thing is that the detonators used were not British Military standard. The bad news is that they were almost certainly Chinese. Even that doesn't get us far. The same type of cardboard cased dets turn up in fish bombs all the time. If you are in the know, they wouldn't be hard to source, but damn difficult for us to trace. Talking of our friends across the border, are they being of any help?'

Cassius looked glum. 'Not much. Just denying that anyone on their side has anything to do with it. Getting all insulted at the suggestion, which of course no one made and telling us that they are concerned by this failure on our part to maintain the stability of the territory. Just the political bullshit you would expect. God, I can't believe you people are going to hand us over to those jokers in 1997.'

'Don't throw me in with the politicians and the Foreign and Commonwealth Office types. I'm just as likely to be here after the handover as you. Assuming I'm still welcome that is. Mind you, I'm glad I won't be wearing a uniform. Don't know that I would suit one of those little red stars on my cap badge. But, when I come to think of it, you might look good in a baggy green uniform Cass.'

'Fuck off. If it came to that, the only green thing I would want would be a green card. Richard, do you think about 1997 much?'

'Right now my thoughts rarely escape some lunatic who's blowing up kids. But, I know what you mean. It's the uncertainty of it all that gets to me. If we only knew what was to become of us, at least we could make plans. I don't want to leave Hong Kong. I really hope that it won't come to that.'

'Fact is, I don't have much choice. My family is here and I wouldn't think of leaving them behind. I don't have a British passport, so if the communists decide that we can't leave after 1997, I won't have much of a choice.'

Richard looked at his friend. All the rhetoric of the politicians, the promises and the denials, they all meant little when it came to the reality for most people. People like Cassius. They had to stay, for a whole variety of reasons. The fact was, why should they be put in a position where they felt that they ought to leave? Hong Kong was their home. It was also his home, much more now than his native Scotland. When he went there on leave, he felt like an outsider. Richard didn't know where he would go if he was no longer welcome in Hong Kong. At least he had a choice.

'Getting back to the subject in hand,' said Cassius. 'Can you see any pattern developing in the bombs?'

Richard shook his head. 'Nope. The staged bombing came completely out of the blue. I went over the film, but the other two bombs are not similar to any of the other incidents in it. Ok, there is a letter bomb of course, but nothing with the same characteristics. If it was copycatting the film, you would expect them to be as accurately copied as the car-bomb.

'I've looked through every manual and training film I could find, hoping to find some pattern that this guy might be following, but he seems to be making up his own rules. Maybe the car-bomb was a one-off. The next one might be something completely different, no pattern at all.'

'If that's the case,' said Cassius gloomily. 'We're in big trouble. At the moment, short of catching him in the act, the only hope we have is finding a pattern that might lead us to him. Something, anything.'

'At least with the protection teams being in place, life will be a bit harder for the bomber. As long as the protectees let them do their job. I'm sure our guys will face opposition from some of them. People don't like their routines to be interrupted, particularly people who are used to getting their own way. They just don't understand that security can't be at their convenience, it's a full-time effort. Frankly, I don't envy our boys. It will get tough to maintain their enthusiasm for protecting some of these men. The fact that all of them are Brits is bound to wind up the communist press. They will no doubt ignore all the available evidence and demand to know why government resources are being channelled into protecting wealthy Europeans and no effort made to protect the loyal comrades. Just you wait!'

Cassius was silent for a while.

'You OK, Cass?'

'I was just thinking about what you said. Loyal comrades. If you were the Chinese Government, or some part of it and you wanted to cause trouble in Hong Kong, without being seen to do so, mightn't you use someone who owed you a big favour? Someone who would profit from destabilising British led companies, say a Chinese businessman with strong business links to the Mainland.'

'That's a bit of a reach, Cass. Surely any destabilising influence would affect every business in Hong Kong?'

'Maybe not. I've been watching the stock market recently and the shares in British companies have been badly hit every time one of these bombs goes off, but many of the Chinese owned companies have actually seen their share price go up.'

'Oh, come on. This can't be about share prices! Not even in Hong Kong, it would be insane.'

Cassius looked at Richard. 'Tell me one thing about this whole mess that is sane. Remember what David Lo said. There may be more than one person's agenda at work here.'

Richard looked doubtful. 'But, even if a businessman was implicated, not even proved to be involved, surely, especially after that last bomb, they would be finished. No one in Hong Kong is going to put up with that.'

'Perhaps the girl's death came as a surprise to the puppet-master. What if the puppet has started to pull some strings on his own?'

'If there is a third party behind the bombings and they lose control of the bomber, how does that help us? It may make it even more difficult to track down the guilty parties.'

'Maybe I am fishing, or maybe hoping for some divine intervention. It just occurred to me that the more outrageous the bomber becomes, the more likely that his masters might pull the plug and end this for us.'

Richard ran a hand down his face. 'Frankly Cass, I don't know that your scenario appeals to me. To be left, not knowing whether it is over or not. Clueless as to what it was all about. I would almost prefer that the bastard kept on bombing Taipans, so that we had a chance to get him.'

'Richard, I have a funny feeling that you are going to get your wish.'

CHAPTER 18

Garland came today. Loathsome man. Stupid and mundane. He was furious about the girl in my masterpiece. He could never understand the beauty of it. I let him believe that the girl's presence was an accident. It pains me that I need his patronage. If I had time to source more o my materials on my own, I might just make Mr Garland the subject of my art. No, it would be wasted on him. But, if he happened to wander onto my canvas, I would be interested to see the result. My actions seem to serve his purpose, but his demands are so limiting. If he would give me a free hand, I could achieve so much more. The subjects he chooses are of no interest to me and their lifestyles limit my scope. Perhaps that is the way it has always been with artists such as myself. The patronage they have had to endure has coloured the art which they produce. Oh, for the freedom to create without restraint. I must be patient. The time may come when the limits placed upon me become so oppressive that I will need to seek alternative patronage. I am afraid that will not be a happy day for Garland. I dislike leaving untidy threads behind me. I have no doubt that he plans to terminate our arrangement in a similar manner. Oh, do I have a surprise for him. It might lack artistry, but I will derive a different form of pleasure from it.

I refused to discuss the details of the bomb with Garland. How could he understand the beauty of the thing? I had watched the target for some time, gaining an understanding of his routine. Humans are such vulnerable creatures. We love our routines. We take comfort in the familiarity of knowing what the day will bring. How could the man know that the very thing which made him feel safe and secure was the greatest weapon in his enemy's arsenal. Routines make one vulnerable. They give an enemy the luxury of planning. I never allow myself to fall into a routine. If an enemy wants to attack me, they will not have the luxury of planning the assault. They will have to risk all to take me in the moment. A fifty-fifty chance. More than I would ever allow one of the players in my explosive dramas.

The man I had been given as commission was indeed a creature of habit. Within a few days, I had already identified several opportunities for bringing about his demise, but one stood out. I cannot express my delight when the idea came to me. It was sheer inspiration. At first I feared that the opportunity might be fleeting. Perhaps it was unusual for the man to drive his daughter to school. Day after day, as I watched them drive away from the house, I feared that it might be the last time. After one week, I started to feel more secure in the belief that this was indeed a routine occurrence. The daily affection between the two. The look of pleasure on both their faces as the car pulled away. It seemed odd to me that a man in his position would drive his own car to work, but it dawned on me that this was to allow him to spend some time with his daughter, as he usually returned home late at night. A dutiful father indeed. So touching. So perfect.

Happy that things would not change and spoil my plans, I began preparing for the event. Although I had no copy of the film, the image was still vivid in my mind. How could it not be? The first time I saw it, it struck me as one of the most beautiful things I had ever seen. The simplicity of it. The poetry of the figures resting, as if in slumber. The underlying truth that death had laid his icy touch upon them. My heart wept with joy and pain that I had not created this vision.

So, was I merely plagiarising the work of some other artist? No. The beauty that lay in that image was accidental. The man who created it was not an artist, but a technician. I would create a work of art. I would deliberately produce an image that would sear itself into the mind of all who saw it. These idiots who seek to stop my efforts would know that they were dealing with a superior mind. But, am I being too generous to them? Would they understand the significance of the event? Or are they just a bunch of stupid policemen? I hope not, for without an appreciative audience, what is an artist? I do this for myself, but I also do it for others.

The bomb was beautiful in its simplicity. Whether it was exactly the same as the original, I do not know. Nor do I care, for I want to place my own signature on my creations. The materials supplied by Garland are reliable, though I would prefer to use different detonators. The plastic molded nicely into a shaped charge, all the better to contain the blast. The thing which had always struck me about the original bombing was the way that, from a distance, the bodies showed no signs of distress. As I have said, no doubt an accident. I did not want my creation to be spoiled by visible injury, so it was important that shrapnel was minimised and that death was sudden enough to prevent too much movement from the subjects.

I rose in darkness on the day. The excitement I felt was indescribable. Nothing so far has come close to giving me this thrill. Perhaps it was heightened by the fact that I would actually witness my creation coming into being. The package fitted neatly into a small rucksack, the like of which is seen all over Hong Kong. I had no real fear of being stopped by the police, but the earliness of the hour might arouse suspicion, if I was not careful. I decided that I would park my car in a secluded spot that I had found and approach the house from the rear, where I would not be seen.

All was quiet as I approached the house. The car was sitting where I expected it and was pointing in the right direction. A creature of habit indeed this man, almost to the point of obsession. That I could understand. Carefully I crossed the gravel driveway and laid the rucksack on the ground. My heart was pounding as I opened the back-pack and revealed my work. I removed the components and set to my task.

In the dark, it was difficult to maneuver myself under the car. I had to reach in, with my arms outstretched to place the device where I wanted it. The magnets worked well and made the job that much easier. I had to adjust it a few times to ensure that it was in exactly the right spot. Had I been pressed for time, I could have planted the device in a matter of seconds, but I wanted this to be just right and felt that I had the luxury of time on my side.

Reluctant though I was to use the small torch that I had brought with me, I had to switch it on to fit the insulation between the jaws of the clothes-peg switch. Carefully, I unwound the fishing line back to the anchor point. There I adjusted the length of the line, so that it would lie, unseen on the gravel and yet be short enough that the car would not have to travel more than a few feet before the device was detonated. Happy with the length, I secured the line to the post.

I returned to the device and ensured that the insulation had not been displaced by the line adjustment and happy with the set-up, I reached towards the device and flicked the arming switch. This is always the most anxious time. No matter how careful one is in the construction of the device, there is always a chance that a mistake has been made and that when armed, the device will explode. Sometimes I build a delay into the arming mechanism, but in this case I felt that it was an unnecessary complication. Another thing to go wrong. I have great confidence in my abilities, but have seen too many confident men killed by their own bombs to become complacent. Happy that I was still alive, I left my sleeping dragon and retired to the observation point which I had chosen.

They say that the anticipation of a thing can be more exciting than the event itself. It may be true, for the wait was excruciating in a way that I still long for. The physical pain of the anticipation is fresh in my memory, but is a pale shadow of the emotion I felt at the time. Even the fear that the device might not explode, or that I might be discovered in my hide added to the thrill. As the dawn broke, my excitement grew. I was sure that I would remain hidden, but had to be careful, lest my enthusiasm lead me to move my position too much.

Then the moment came. The door opened and he came out of the house. My heart sank. The girl was not with him. My breathing became rapid, my mind raced. What should I do? I could not run forward and stop the passage of events. I could see my dreams fall around me. This was not how it should be. My panic was starting to overcome me and the danger that I would do something stupid became very real. All the planning. The care of preparation. The risk. All for nothing because of this stupid little bitch. She would rue this day, I swore it. Then, my spirits lifted and I sighed with relief. My angel appeared.

Her father was already in the car. I held my breath as he started the engine. There had never been any sign of a mother in this little family group. I could not discover what had become of her. Really, I did not care, so long as she did not make a surprise appearance to spoil my creation. The girl got into the car. Her father reached over to help her fasten her seat belt and gave her a kiss on the forehead. So sweet, so loving.

My palms were sweating as the car inched forward. My eyes were focussed on the two figures inside the car. I must not blink. I forced my eyes wide, to allow the becoming to imprint itself on my retina. A lasting image I would look at again and again in my mind's eye. I had thought about filming the event, but it seemed sordid and mundane. The memory can add so much more to the experience. The sound, the smell, the impact of the blast wave. The experience in many dimensions, not just the two of celluloid and tape.

It was more than I could possibly have imagined. The car seemed to crumple, as if some invisible giant had taken it in it's hand and squeezed. Even my determination to watch every millisecond was not enough to make my eyes take in the whole event. I have lasting impressions though of the figures being thrown back in their seats as the blast tore their legs from their bodies. The music of the blast rang in my ears.

When I was able to look at the scene again, I was initially pleased by what I saw, but as the dust settled, I was horrified to see that the picture had not settled down as I had desired. The front door was flung open and a horrified maid stood there, just staring at the scene, hands to her mouth, seemingly unable to move. I cursed the woman, for I still had work to do. Eventually she gained her senses and rushed back into the house, no doubt to summon help.

I knew that I did not have much time. A less fastidious man might have fled the scene, caring more for his safety than the perfection of his work. Anxiously, I rushed from my position towards the crumpled car, keeping my eye on the doorway to the house, in case another member of the household might appear. I was breathing hard as I reached the glassless passenger door. I reached in and made the final adjustment, moving the girl's head over to rest on her father's shoulder. I had no fear of leaving traces, as I wore rubber gloves. I had anticipated the possibility that a final touch might have to be added to the work. I resisted the temptation to examine the damage to their lower bodies, but had enough of a view to know that my device had achieved the desired result. I stepped back and smiled at the perfection. I have no desire to be caught and reluctantly dragged myself away from my masterpiece and exited the area the way I had entered it. I must confess that I took the occasional glance back at the beauty of what I had created.

As I drove away, the overwhelming joy that I felt started to be tempered by a sadness that the moment could not have lasted longer, but we must not be greedy. I would be able to relive the moment again and again and again. Each time subtle nuances being added as my mind opened up the subtleties which my mental camera had recorded. The anticipation reinvested my pleasure. I was happier, I think, in that moment than I had ever been before. I was anxious for more. My next project would have to be grander still, but that could wait. For now, I could bask in the glory of my latest work.

As I expected, the police have increased security around the targets. So, as with all creatures, I must adapt to the new conditions. Adaptation is the key to survival. In my case I must remain ahead of the changes that occur. Surprise is a tool of my trade, but also my enemy's.

I am glad to have had the intimate experience offered by my last work. It is regrettable that I shall have to be more removed from the experience from now on, but in a way it will force me to be more ingenious in the way I approach the next problem. In order to derive satisfaction from the experience, I shall have to pool all my resources towards the statement that I shall make. Here lies danger. The temptation to be elaborate in the design of the device is already making itself felt. I must resist. Vanity can bring death. I must remember that the purest examples of my superior skill are often the simplest. Within that simplicity lies a sophistication of expression that no elaborate contraption could ever hope to match.

A statement is required. What the experience will lack in intimacy, it can compensate in blood.

CHAPTER 19

'Bloody half-arsed measures,' thought Peter Lee. The Police Inspector didn't like the set-up one little bit. In the VIP Protection Unit he was used to having more men, technical back-up and the opportunity to plan ahead. To add to his troubles, he had men working for him who had no real experience in close protection. The SDU lads could shoot, but they just didn't get the fact that their first priority was the protectee, not capping the bad guys. The CID men were almost a liability. They weren't the most disciplined individuals he had ever worked with. Peter had to assign them donkey work and that only compounded their complacency. The nightmare was completed by the fact that the man they had to protect was totally uncooperative. He wanted them there, but didn't want to be inconvenienced by them. Some people just didn't understand security and David Rankin was one of them. He may be a very successful businessman, but when it came to his personal safety, he was an idiot. An arrogant idiot. Peter was used to being treated like a servant by protectees. Some were better than others and in despite of his training, he did feel more inclined to protect someone who showed him appreciation and respect. Human nature he supposed, but hardly professional.

Today was a classic example of the problems he faced. He had begged the Taipan to vary his schedule and to minimise his exposure, all to no avail. This ceremony was a bad idea. The new factory was a personal project of Rankin's. He had beaten off strong opposition from the rest of the board to move this project ahead. Many had wanted the facility built in China, where the labour and construction costs were much lower, but Rankin had argued that the high-tech nature of the business could best be served by the higher education standards and more stable workforce that were available in Hong Kong. It had been a hard fought battle, but the Taipan had his way. This opening ceremony was personal. It was a public victory display. Nothing that Peter could say would dissuade the man from attending.

Events like this one were commonplace for someone in Peter Lee's line of work. The problem here was that he didn't have the benefit of all the normal support. No sniffer dogs, no technicians to sweep the area. Not even enough manpower to give the area a proper going over and then to secure it. 'Just not good enough,' he thought. How was he supposed to protect this man under these conditions?

Peter was sitting in the front passenger seat of the Jaguar as they made their way through the Lion Rock Tunnel, on their way to the factory in the New Territories. At least Rankin had allowed him to use a G4 driver. Small enough comfort to have one of his own men at the wheel. Not that Peter expected the need for evasive maneuvers on the Tolo Highway. The threat was unlikely to come on the road. It was their time at the factory that he worried about. He had requested enough manpower to check the place out ahead of the ceremony, but the Force was stretched to breaking point. They had to rely on the company security personnel. The thought made Peter cringe. Rent-a-cops. Security guards were amongst the lowest paid members of any organisation. The old English adage came to mind, "You pay peanuts and you get…". He had seen enough private security forces to know the truth of it.

Rankin sat in the back and talked to his companion in animated style. He was obviously excited, if a little unhappy about Peter's presence. He had tried to persuade the Inspector that he should travel in another vehicle, but Peter had insisted, even going to the extent of threatening to remove the security detail altogether if they were not allowed to do their job. The deaths of the other Taipans had frightened Rankin enough that he drew short of risking total exposure. The man just didn't understand the realities of close protection. He wanted the comfort of it without paying the price in terms of his personal freedom. The man might as well paint a target on his forehead.

The sight of his men did little to remove the unease that Peter felt. As the Jaguar pulled up to the entrance, Peter looked at the crowds of workers waiting for them. He didn't really believe that the bomber would deliver his deadly package by tossing it from the crowd, but from the briefing he had attended at Police Headquarters, it seemed likely that the man enjoyed watching his handiwork. It was what lay inside the building that worried Peter Lee. One of his men approached him as he exited the vehicle. Another took over the job of watching the protectee.

'This is hopeless, sir.'

Peter looked at the sergeant and nodded. 'Yes, it's out of control. Keep the men sharp. If they pick up on anything odd, I want to know. And I mean ANYTHING!'

Peter stood to one side of the VIP party as it entered the building. Quite a turnout, he thought. The project had brought three hundred new jobs to the area, with the promise of more if the business did well. A boost for the image of the diverse group of companies that Rankin headed and a message to the mainland authorities that the Group was investing in the future prosperity of Hong Kong.

The schedule of events was due to commence at 1400hrs. They were right on time. First, the Managing Director of the new facility would speak, introducing the press to the business and the job opportunities that it presented. Next, the local District Board member would give the government's thanks for the siting of the factory in an area which it was keen to develop. After him, the head of the Heung Yee Kuk, the long established organisation representing the villagers of the New Territories, would speak on behalf of the residents who had been so handsomely compensated for relocating their homes and given work in the new facility. Finally, after much mutual appreciation and back slapping, Rankin would speak and unveil the plaque commemorating the opening of the factory. That done, everyone would be ushered off to a reception where the prying eyes of the press would be excluded and the real business of the day could commence.

Peter looked at his watch. Another forty-five minutes until his charge would deliver his speech and then only if the others didn't run over time. Probably would be longer, this lot looked like the sort who loved the sound of their own voices. He looked around the faces in the crowd, looking for clues in the expressions he saw, anything that might spell danger to the protectee. All he saw were enthusiastic locals and jaded journalists. Many familiar faces among the latter. He wished he could share their obvious boredom.

Peter's gaze moved from the people around the presentation area, to the area itself. He scanned the podium and the public address system. Suddenly he had the feeling that something was wrong. He couldn't put his finger on it, but something wasn't right. Damn, he thought. The lack of preparation for this event was getting to him. He was becoming paranoid. But was that it? He just couldn't shake the feeling that something was wrong, out of place. He had learned to trust his instincts. When you had trained as long and hard as Peter had, some things became instinctual, awareness lying just below the conscious level. Something was wrong.

Just as he was beginning to become annoyed by his feelings, he saw it. Peter gestured to one of his sergeants, calling the man over to him. 'That ashtray over there. Is it my imagination, or was that in a different position this morning after we did the sweep of the area?'

The sergeant looked at the cylindrical rubbish bin, come ashtray. There were identical ones throughout the building. They had moved all of them away from the podium area that morning, but this one was sitting against the wall, behind and to one side of the place where all the speeches would be delivered. 'Sorry sir, I didn't notice it. About two hours ago some workmen were in doing a final clean-up of the area. They replaced some of the trash-cans. Said the management wanted everything in view to be new.'

'What! This is a new building. Everything in it is new! Come on.'

Peter led the flustered NCO over to the rubbish bin. It looked just like the others. Peter carefully looked around the metal tube. He couldn't see anything out of the ordinary. Reaching into his pocket, he removed a tiny mag-lite torch. He twisted the end to produce a tight beam and pointed it into the oval aperture in the side of the tube, where rubbish would be placed. The internal compartment was only about five inches deep, despite the fact that the tubular receptacle was about thirty inches tall. Peter quickly looked around and spotted another bin close by. He hurried over to it and shone his torch inside. The cavity in this one extended to the bottom of the tube. He hurried over to another, sitting beside the lobby lifts. Again, the full length of the tube was hollow.

'Get everyone out of here. Grab the uniform guys and tell them that we will be moving everyone out of the lobby.'

Peter marched over to David Rankin. 'Excuse me sir. We have a suspicious object in the lobby of this building. We need to move everyone out now. I will make an announcement, but I want you out of here at once.'

The Taipan looked at Peter Lee as though he was crazy. 'What? Are you mad? What suspicious object?' The businessman looked around the lobby with untrained eyes, giving the area the most cursory of glances before speaking again. 'There's nothing out of the ordinary here. You are talking nonsense. I won't let you spoil this presentation with your idiotic paranoia. My God, where do they get you people?'

Peter stayed calm, at least on the surface. 'Sir, see that rubbish bin over there,' he said, pointing at the offending object. 'First of all, it shouldn't be there. Second, I have examined it and it has been tampered with. It is my professional opinion that there is a strong possibility that it is a bomb. Now, I would like you to make your way with the other dignitaries to the front of the building. If you do not, I will remove you myself. It is my job to protect you, whether you like it or not.'

Rankin was about to come out with an outraged outburst, but something in Peter Lee's eyes changed his mind. Instead he took a deep breath and issued a warning. 'I hope for your sake Inspector that you are right.'

So do I, thought Peter. As one of his men escorted Rankin out to his waiting car, Peter stood on the podium and asked everyone to leave the area, as there was a security threat. He apologised for the inconvenience, but assured the gathering that the delay was necessary for their safety. As with most gatherings in Hong Kong, there was the minimum of trouble when confronted with rational directions from the police. In any other part of the world, the press would have kicked up a fuss. Here, the Chinese reporters did as they were asked. Only later would they make a bloody nuisance of themselves. For now, they picked up their gear and walked out of the building.

'Aren't you people going to do anything? What the hell is that man doing, just standing there? Get me a senior officer, I want to speak to whoever is in charge here.' Rankin was becoming apoplectic in his frustration. There seemed to be nothing happening, yet he was being held back from the building. He had refused to leave the area, still believing that Peter Lee had overreacted and that the ceremony would continue in due course. Afterward, he would make the Inspector rue the day he had joined the Police Force. The young man obviously didn't know how much influence that David Rankin had in this town.

'Bit of an arsehole, isn't he,' said Richard.

'Tell me about it,' replied Peter Lee.

The two men were standing next to Richard's vehicle, which he had set up as his command post. They were about fifty yards away from the Taipan, but they could hear every syllable of the tirade which the local superintendent was having to endure. The senior policeman was one of the good guys and was making sure that Richard was not disturbed by even this influential member of the public.

'Just as a matter of interest,' said Peter. 'Are you actually thinking of doing anything?'

'I am doing it,' replied Richard. 'I'm waiting. You said that the ceremony had a fairly strict timetable. In the past our man has shown that he has inside information which he uses to attack his targets, so we wait until after your man was supposed to speak. If nothing has happened by then, I'll try something else. No point in me going up there just at the very time that a bomb would be likely to go off, now is there? I may be crazy to do this job, but I'm not a complete imbecile.'

'I see your point. But I'm not sure that he does,' said Peter with a slight nod in the direction of the, still vocal, Taipan.

'Bollocks to him. If he wants someone to just walk in there, let him do it himself. Contrary to popular belief, I don't get paid to get myself killed. Quite the opposite actually.'

Richard looked at his watch. Rankin would have been about halfway through his speech by now. Odd, he thought. Difficult situation in which to assure that you would get your target. Not as controlled as the other bombs. Something had changed. If the rubbish bin had been converted into a bomb, the bomber had been forced into an imprecise attack. Why? He turned to look at the man standing next to him and realised why. Of course, the close protection. He couldn't get as close to the targets as before. His hand had been forced. Good, thought Richard. Maybe now we might start to get the upper hand with this bastard.

The size of the suspect device suggested that, all that had to happen would be for Rankin to be reasonably close. A lot of other people would die as well, but the bomber had already shown that a bit of collateral damage didn't bother him. Richard took a puff at the cigar he had lit on arrival. The Cuban tobacco helped him think of things other than the prospect of walking up to something that might separate his body parts at high velocity. It was something to do while he waited. He didn't often have the luxury of this sort of wait. Usually he was too busy planning his attack. In this case, waiting to see what happened was the best course of action. Perhaps that was true for him, but as he looked at Peter Lee, he could see that his colleague was impatient for something to happen.

'Worried?' asked the bomb disposal officer.

'If this turns out not to be a bomb, my balls are going to be hanging from Rankin's belt.'

'Not if I have anything to say about it. You did the right thing. It was a gutsy call, considering the pressure that you must have been under. If Rankin can't see that you are acting in his best interests, then he is a fucking idiot and deserves to get blown up. Just think of the other people there. At least one of them will know that you did the only thing you could do under the circumstances. From what you told me, it's at the very least a bit odd that this one bin is so different from the others and replacing brand new bins is a bit suspicious to say the least. Any clues as to who did the replacing?'

'No. The guys were so wound up by this fiasco that they weren't paying too much attention. If this had been a full G4 team, the guy would have been eating the carpet and we would have had our man. This half-baked protection detail is a liability. But I suppose it is better than nothing.' Peter looked as though the weight of the world were on his shoulders. Richard had a lot of sympathy for the guy. He had been in similar positions before. Lee probably didn't think that Richard's three "pips" were sufficient protection from the flack that would erupt if this were to come to nothing. Richard swore that he would look after the lad. In Richard's book he had done a good job.

'Nothing is happening,' said Rankin. 'Why is nothing happening? Tell that man to get in there and sort this out, so that we can get on with the ceremony. This is so embarrassing. Do you realise how this looks? It is an outrage. If you are in charge, do something. Tell your men to sort this out.'

Superintendent Lai was a patient man, but his tolerance of Rankin was wearing thin. 'Sir, I am the Incident Commander, because it is taking place in my division, but as far as handling the suspicious object is concerned, the EOD Unit has final say. They are the experts, not me. It may seem that nothing is happening, but I assure you that the bomb disposal officer is waiting for a good reason. I am sure that he will be happy to explain everything to you when he has dealt with the object, but until then, I am not about to disturb his train of thought. It is his life that will be at risk when he approaches the device, if that is what it is. If I were him, I would be doing exactly the same. It is his decision when to take action. Now, if that is not good enough for you, there is a complaints procedure which you can use. All complaints are taken very seriously and will be investigated, but I have to say, that there are no grounds that I can see for any complaint.'

'Really? Well, let me tell you Superintendent, I know enough people in this town to make your life and that of…'

The explosion silenced the crowd. Most ducked, as fragments of glass flew in their direction, as the plate glass around the entrance was shattered. They were too far away for the glass to reach them, but it was an instinctual reaction.

Richard looked down at the crouching figure of Peter Lee. 'Well, sport. Looks like you were right. I don't expect that Rankin is the sort to apologise, but on his behalf, may I thank you for saving his ungrateful hide.' Richard looked at his watch again. 'Let's give it another seventeen minutes, just in case there is a second nasty surprise in there. Then I'll pop in and see what we have.'

Peter let out a long sigh of relief. 'Thank God. I was starting to have visions of my career being flushed down the toilet.' He was silent for a moment and went very red in the face. 'That was an awful thing to say. I should be happy that lives have been saved, not worrying about my job.'

Richard laughed. 'Peter, don't be too hard on yourself. I can't think of a soul who would have had any other thought under the circumstances. I'm just impressed that you didn't fold under the pressure that Rankin must have been bringing to bear. I'll be mentioning that in my report by the way. You me old son are going to come out of this smelling of roses, despite the moaning that Rankin is bound to do. Once he has recovered his wits, I'll lay odds that he is over here complaining about the damage to the building.'

'You're probably right,' said Peter. 'Probably his way of dealing with the fact that someone tried to blow him up.'

'No,' replied Richard. 'It's just the fact that he is an ignorant, self centered son of a bitch.'

Richard was tempted to send the robot in to have a look around. He hadn't used it in a while and it usually impressed the crowds, but today he would do it manually. No point in dragging the affair out too long and further aggravating the assembled dignitaries, all of whom had insisted on staying to see what happened.

When he entered the building, he saw much less damage than he had expected. Most of it was centered around the podium on which Rankin would have been speaking when the bomb detonated. The broken windows had made the blast seem more destructive than it actually was. They would have this lot cleared up in no time, thought Richard. The objective had not been to damage property, this bomb was designed to kill. There was a surprising amount of the casing left intact, he saw. All the better for the forensic guys to find something which might lead them to the bomber. After having checked the area and giving the remains of the bomb a good going over, Richard walked back out to his command post and told the scene of crime officers to start doing their thing. He had recovered pieces of the device and placed them in evidence bags. He would record everything that he removed from the scene in his notebook and the report he would write up back at base.

Well?' asked Peter.

'An interesting one,' replied Richard. 'Anti-personnel device. Probably a limited amount of explosive, not enough to do serious structural damage, but enough to fling these out at seven thousand meters per second.' He held up a clear plastic evidence bag in which were a couple of ball bearings. 'I dug these out of a wall. Our man made himself a Claymore mine. Clever really, the tubular shape of the bin was ideal, gave the projectiles a good spread pattern. If you hadn't evacuated the area, we would have been clearing up a lot of bodies in there, not just Rankin.'

'This guy just doesn't care, does he?' Peter Lee looked horrified. He wondered how anyone could be so callous about human life.

'No Peter, he cares. He cares about his bloody bombs. He enjoys the mayhem they cause, the pain and suffering. This guy is getting his jollies from the destruction. I wouldn't mind betting that he is really pissed off right now. We foiled his little plan, no one died. I hope the bastard is climbing the walls with frustration. Only trouble is, when he calms down, he is going to be even more determined with the next one.'

CHAPTER 20

'We really must get a new sofa in here,' said Richard.

Ah Pau looked at the green government issue furniture that they were sitting on and grunted in agreement.

'Any more holes in this thing and it's going to fall apart. Not very comfortable either. I think the springs have gone.'

'Wonder what caused that?' enquired Ah Pau. 'Must have a word with the lads, I hope they haven't been bringing their girlfriends up here again.'

'God, I hope not. Remember what happened the last time, I thought the OC was going to can the boys when he heard about that. Just as well that I can lie through my teeth, or we would have lost half the team. Can't say I was too impressed myself. Getting laid is no excuse for a breach of security. Mind you, the boys were young. Did you ever get up to any of that sort of nonsense when you joined the unit?'

Ah Pau feigned surprise at this outrageous suggestion. '*Daai Lo*, don't you know that I was a dedicated young man, didn't even have sex during training, didn't want to sap my energy.'

'Yeah, right. I remember that time in Macau...'

Just then they heard a crash off to the right. In an instant, two figures stood before them, pointing automatic weapons in their direction. Gunfire resonated around the small room, as 9mm bullets ripped into the targets, six inches from the heads of the seated men. Richard could feel splinters of wood strike his cheek as the MP5s spat out their bursts of lead.

Just as suddenly, the firing stopped, but the weapons were now pointed directly at the two men. One of the figures screamed out an order and obediently, Richard and Ah Pau hit the floor, arms outstretched, face down. Richard coughed as the dust from the wooden floor stuck in his throat. A barked order and a swift kick in the side had him crawling on his belly towards the exit. Any time he tried to raise his head, he would receive a sharp thump in the small of the back, just to remind him that a gun was pointed at him.

The glare of the sun which greeted him at the exit made him stop. His continued forward progress was ensured by another carefully applied boot. Loud voices met him outside the building. Following their instructions, he placed his hands on the back of his head. His legs were then crossed, his right foot placed in the hollow of his left knee. A body pressed against his legs and he could feel the probing hands systematically start to search him. Richard decided to put up a bit of resistance to this treatment. His answer was the full weight of the searcher being placed on his leg. The resultant pain was enough to discourage him from this foolish course of action. From the periphery of his vision, he was aware of a weapon being pointed at his head, more cause, if any was needed, for his cooperation.

Richard could hear Ah Pau, somewhere close, putting up more of a struggle. It was short-lived. Sufficient persuasion had been applied to silence the tough Sergeant. Having satisfied themselves that the pair were no threat, their unseen guards backed away.

'Alright, on your feet,' came the familiar tones of Keith Symons.

Richard and Ah Pau stood up, dusted the grime from their uniforms and stretched their backs, easing the cramps that had developed during their search. The pair were greeted by a group of smiling faces. It wasn't every day that the men had a chance to put their Team Commander through "the treatment". The only face that was showing any concern was that of Philip, the young trainee sniper. He looked nervously at Richard.

'OK, not bad. Let's go see the damage to the terrorists.'

Richard and Ah Pau led the two men who had executed the assault back into the Close Quarter Battle House. Assault men and snipers both did CQB training. This was their bread and butter, the most basic skill they had to master.

The tight grouping of holes in the target brought a smile to Richard's face. He turned to Philip and nodded his approval. 'Good shooting. Your control was excellent. Good focus during the entry, but I think you have to be a little more aggressive. There was a slight hesitation as you engaged the target. Perhaps not enough to give the enemy a chance to fire, but it's something you need to work on.'

Turning his attention to Keith, who had been the other member of the assault pair, he continued his debrief, although it was more for Philip's benefit than his experienced Assault Group Leader. 'Exit phase was OK. It's tricky getting the right balance of authority, without angering the hostages. Chances are that they won't know why they are being treated like this. You are looking for terrorists who might be hiding among them and there's the chance that some of the hostages may have been turned during a lengthy siege, so you can't take any risks. Get them to a safe area, search them for weapons or explosives and then bring the tempo down slowly. Don't take any crap, but don't dish out a kicking unnecessarily. It will just anger the subjects and make them more difficult to control. If applied at the right time, it gets a message across. If not, it's pointless and counterproductive.'

'Ah Pau, how did Keith's target look?'

'Not so bad,' said the Sergeant, obviously enjoying his role. 'You know how his shooting is. I was worried that the last bullet was going to get me.'

'Oh, bollocks! Look at that group, I was never near you.'

Richard and Ah Pau laughed in unison. It never failed. The young Englishman was so easy to wind up. He had been the worst shot in his selection group, but had worked hard to remedy the situation. He did not have the seemingly natural ability which Richard possessed, but he was more than above average for the unit. Everyone appreciated the dedication that Keith put into his job, but they couldn't help hitting this raw nerve from time to time. Besides, every member of the unit had their vulnerable spot and every other member of the unit would attack it occasionally. It was all done in good humour and it served a useful purpose; it stopped them taking themselves too seriously. The job on the other hand was taken very seriously.

Richard looked at Philip. 'So, Philip. How do you feel after your first live firing session?'

'Better than I did when I started, *Daai Lo*. I was very nervous.'

'Well, it didn't show,' lied Richard. 'Everyone is the same and that is a good thing. This training can be dangerous and no one should go into it with anything less than a serious attitude. Your colleagues are risking their lives by sitting inside the CQB. It's a test and a display of confidence, as well as skill with a firearm. It's a way of saying, "I trust you with my life". As a part of this Team, that's what every man does. He has to trust every other member of the team with his life. So, fancy being a hostage and letting me get a bit of my own back?'

For the first time that day, Philip smiled as he nodded his assent. Richard clapped the young constable on the shoulder as they exited the room to prepare for the next session. This had been the first step in rebuilding a young man's shattered confidence. Richard was pleased by the way it had gone.

It was a hot day. Richard stripped off his DPM jacket. The SDU men made an odd sight when on the beach. Well tanned, muscular torsos, but strangely pale from the waist down. At the beginning of summer, most of them made a concerted effort to redress the balance. The culprit for this melanotic imbalance was the amount of time they spent on range courses such as today's. The pale earth which covered the range reflected the sun's rays and amplified the effect of the relentless onslaught of the bright ball. There was no refuge, unless inside the CQB. There, the problem was breathing, as the sun produced an atmosphere akin to the inside of an oven.

Placing the three-point sling over his head, Richard adjusted it for fit, moving his shoulders until the MP5 was sitting in the right position. He raised the muzzle, pushing against the sling, checking the stable shooting base that made the weapon become a part of his body. Satisfied, he pulled back the cocking handle and locked it in place. He lifted the curved magazine and checked the seating of the top rounds. Canting the sub-machine gun to the right, he pushed the box magazine into the magazine well and checked that it was held firm. He then straightened the weapon and with his left palm, slapped down on the cocking handle, knocking it out of it's locking point. As the breach block travelled forward, it picked up a round from the magazine and pushed it forward, into the breach. Richard checked again that the safety was on and moved into position.

Richard took the number one position, to the left of the door. Ah Pau positioned himself right behind his boss, close enough that Richard could feel the other man's arm against his back. When he was ready, Ah Pau touched Richard's shoulder with his left hand. A constable, who was acting as range officer, seeing the signal, gave the order to begin. 'Stand by, stand by, go, go, go.'

Before the end of the command, Richard and Ah Pau were through the doorway. A short corridor lay before them. They cleared the distance in a second. As Richard entered the room, the first thing that he saw was the image of a woman off to his right. In her hand was a pistol. As Richard moved, his MP5 was already brought to bear. Where he looked, the muzzle of the weapon followed, like a third eye. He brought the weapon onto the target, not really aiming, but knowing exactly where the fall of shots would be. He fired on semi-automatic and put two "double taps" into the centre of the target.

To his left he heard gunfire and turned, all the time tracking the MP5 with him. His eyes engaged another target, inches from the head of a seated, and worried looking Philip. Richard pulled the trigger, but nothing happened. He yelled out, 'Stoppage!', to let Ah Pau know what was happening. At the same time he moved his position, to make himself as difficult a target as possible in the cramped area, swung the MP5 behind his back and drew his Browning from its holster in one fluid motion. He fired another double tap to the centre of the target, then another two shots to the head of the figure. He checked that there were no other targets in the room and moved back to the door, keeping his pistol on Philip, who was moving into a prone position on the floor, at the insistent instructions of Ah Pau. Richard called out, 'Clear', to let the rest of the team know that the entry and room clearance had been satisfactorily completed. The Assault pair then proceeded to mete out some of the treatment that they had received a short time before, exiting the hostages as quickly as control would allow.

When the exit and prisoner handling had been completed, Richard and Ah Pau went to a safe area to unload their weapons. As Richard unloaded his MP5, he discovered why his weapon had malfunctioned. A dummy round had been loaded in the magazine. He turned around and was greeted by the sight of several grinning faces.

'You bastards!'

Keith Symons spoke for the group. 'Just wanted to see if you still had the skills, boss.'

Richard smiled, not so much at the test he had been given, but at the sight of the smile on Philip's face. The lad was becoming part of the team. Richard had been worried that the incident with Daai Bei might be too much for the lad to bear and that a good man would be forever ruined. That was the reason for his visit to the range on this occasion. Although Richard still trained with his men, the opportunities to have days like this were fewer than he would have liked. It wasn't his job to be first through the door anymore, but he never knew when he might be required to make up numbers on an assault. Anyway, he enjoyed it.

In the rehabilitation of the young sniper, Richard felt that stage one had gone well. He was also aware of the fact that there was a long way to go. There was resentment over the accident within the unit and particularly within Bravo Team, but none of it was levelled at Philip. The anger was all reserved for the OC, who ultimately was held responsible by the men. From the first days of his tenure, he had shown himself to be the wrong man for the job. Most of his blunders had been covered by men like Richard, for the sake of the unit. This last one had almost cost one of their own his life. That had been too much for most of the unit. They now looked even more to Richard and the other Team Commanders to support them and protect them from the imbecile in charge. He had no idea how he was going to do it, but Richard was determined that the OC's days were numbered. Even if it cost Richard his job, the man was going down.

CHAPTER 21

Continuous noise rang around the rafters of the barn-like building. The floor was a scene of perpetual motion, people milling around or purposefully barging through the crowds. A network of drains flowed with water and the detritus of commerce. The tiles on the floor were awash. This was, after all, a "wet" market.

Split into areas, according to the produce on sale, these markets were where ninety percent of the population did their shopping. Fresh fruit and vegetables from the New Territories and the Mainland. Fish from the waters of Hong Kong and far beyond. Meat, freshly slaughtered or air dried. The mix of aromas was astounding, even forbidding to those unaccustomed to shopping in the raw. Richard wandered through the market, casual in his pace, intent in gaze, as he sought inspiration from the produce on display. He had not always been so blasé about the wet markets. It had taken him a long time to come to terms with the smells and sights of this environment. For years he had been like most westerners in the Territory. Supermarkets, with their over-priced and often dubious quality food had been the only places he would have considered shopping. The wet markets were not for the uninitiated. Richard at least had the benefit of speaking Cantonese, an anomaly in the largely linguistically retarded expatriate community, but he still had the prejudice of the western "pre-packaged" society to overcome. The food in the wet markets was as "raw" as it got. Freshness of ingredients was the key to good Chinese cooking. When you went there to buy a chicken, the creature was still breathing when you chose it. The shopkeeper would ring the bird's neck before your eyes, just to assure you that it was what you would get. It was up to you if you wanted it whole, or if it was to be placed in a large rotating drum which would wrench the feathers from the still warm corpse. Sensitive westerners usually baulked at the thought, ignoring the fact that the chicken would be as fresh as you could get. Their grandparents would have been considerably less sensitive to the process, but we had after all progressed in the last fifty years. Why have fresh meat, when you could have some that had been sitting under plastic on a shelf for a few days?

Richard had finally been convinced by Cassius that it was worth giving the wet markets a try, particularly since he would halve his grocery bill in the process. Richard was a keen cook and enjoyed playing host to friends around a dinner table. So, biting the culinary bullet, he ventured out, with Cassius, on a wet shopping trip for dinner party supplies. He never looked back. Now he rather enjoyed the experience. Some of the smells, particularly of dried seafood, he would never call "pleasant", but he loved the hubbub and energy of the place. He delighted in haggling with stall holders. Initially they had been surprised that a *Gwailo* could argue in their own language. 'Obviously a cop!' would be their thought, for they were usually the only foreigners they came across who had a serious grasp of Cantonese. Through time, Richard had become known to the people who worked in the market which served the housing estate at Lok Fu. He was still a curiosity to many and he almost certainly paid more than a Chinese person would, but there was good humour in the faces which greeted him on his frequent visits and he was always happy with the quality of produce that he bought. Some of the shopkeepers even kept him right on his buying decisions, telling him what was the freshest and had the best flavour.

Freshness of ingredients is of paramount importance to Chinese gourmets. If the meat, fish or vegetables are not fresh, you can be sure that a Chinese person will be able to tell, even after the food is cooked. The Cantonese have the reputation of eating just about anything. The truth is that they have one of the most sophisticated palates in the world. If proof is needed, all anyone has to do is take a five minute walk around the streets of Central or Tsim Sha Tsui and see the world in culinary form.

That having been said, they are also incredibly arrogant about their own cuisine, believing it to be the best in the world. Having tasted the highest quality Chinese food, Richard had a hard time arguing with them, though his own tastes tended towards European cuisine and although he sometimes cooked Chinese food at home, he tended to favour European dishes for his dinner parties.

Richard's dinner parties had become legendary. People made very unsubtle hints about how much they would like to be invited to one. This usually meant that a party of six could end up being twelve at dinner (there was usually at least one surprise guest..."Janice just happened to pop round while we were getting ready. Haven't seen her for ages."). Richard didn't mind and always cooked far too much food anyway. It had become a standing joke. He could never make up his mind though, whether his parties were so popular because of the food, or because of the liberal quantities of booze that flowed before, during and after them. Keith usually turned up a good hour before everyone else to aid in the last minute panic to get everything ready. His main job was to mix the potent Pimms that was his specialty, or even more lethal gin and tonics. Just the thing to get the guests loosened up for excellent dinner conversation. Of course chef and assistant would have to test the quality of the drinks before the guests arrived. They were never disappointed.

Although most guests made an effort to dress for the party, Richard's garb was invariably a T-shirt and in winter, jeans, in summer, shorts. It was hard work cooking for a ravenous multitude. He would plan to change before dinner, but always seemed to be too busy cooking or keeping the conversation flowing. His informality now seemed to be accepted as part of the show.

The meal he was shopping for now would be an entirely more intimate affair. For the first time he was cooking dinner for Natalie. He wasn't entirely sure what he would cook and so was looking to the freshest ingredients on offer to give him some ideas.

The seafood section of the market was Richard's favourite. A great fan of the fruits of the sea, his eyes scanned the tanks of lobster and prawn, the piles of shellfish and the languid movements of garoupa and a dozen other varieties of fish. None of these attracted Richard. Walking among the tanks had planted a seed in his mind. He now knew what he was looking for. All he had to do was find it. At last, he found the one stall that carried the thing he sought. The fan-shaped shells were large, holding the promise of great bounty within. Richard knew the stall-holder and started to ask about the quality of the scallops. Assured that they were fresh, he set about choosing the best, with the aid of a now well trained eye and the friendly owner of the stall. Armed with his marine prize, Richard wandered off into the throng, his mind moving on to the next purchase.

'Good morning heartache, what's new?' Lady Day addressed the room in that voice that could break your heart no matter what the words were. Richard, dressed in his traditional chef gear, black jeans and T-shirt, opened the bottle of Barolo. He had chosen a wine with real gusto to accompany the main course. He laid the bottle on the sideboard and looked at the cork. Good red base, no sign that the wine had migrated up the side of the cork, an indication that the seal might not have been airtight. He sniffed the cork, no musty smell that would show that fungus or bacteria had ruined the contents. He would let a bit of air get to it before he tried the wine.

By the time he walked back into the kitchen, Billie Holiday had moved on to 'God Bless the Child' Richard's taste in music was broad, but this music made him feel sad and happy at the same time. There was something about her voice that could manipulate his emotions more than that of any other singer. It set the right mood for the evening. Mellow, but with an underlying passion.

Turning his attention to the white wine that was chilling in the refrigerator, he felt the bottle and was happy with the result. He didn't like leaving white wine in the fridge for too long. He had a good supply of ice, but would wait until Natalie arrived before opening the bottle. He had chosen a New Zealand wine. This one, a Cloudy Bay Sauvignon Blanc, was growing in popularity. He preferred the Chardonnay, but wanted a fresher, less overpowering wine for the scallops that he would serve as a starter. They were being simply cooked, in the Venetian style, *Capesante alla Veneziana* , pan-fried in olive oil with garlic, parsley and lemon juice. He had opened the shells and removed the unwanted yellow 'skirt', leaving the plump meat ready for cooking. The stall-holder had not let him down, the scallops looked magnificent. He was looking forward to seeing how they held up when he seared them on a griddle and then quickly cooked them with the simple ingredients. Shellfish this good deserved to be allowed to demonstrate their flavour with the minimum of help.

Richard checked around the kitchen. Everything was ready, all he needed now was his guest. Keith had offered to come over and help him prepare, but Richard knew what that usually meant. He didn't want to be half-cut before Natalie arrived. Besides, he had a feeling that getting rid of Keith would be a problem. The young man took an inordinate interest in his boss's love life, no doubt in order to fuel the rumour mill at work. Richard had expected the man to turn up anyway. He lived in a block of flats only a couple of minutes walk from this one. Richard's flat was in a private block, one of only four apartments reserved for the Hong Kong Government. The developer had been required to hold these flats as part of their purchase of the land. At the time there had been a shortage of accommodation for senior civil servants and a number of private developments had been likewise "commandeered". Richard liked the arrangement, as he was surrounded by a mix of people. Not that neighbours in Hong Kong tended to have too much to do with one another, but it meant that his every move was not under the close scrutiny of other police officers. They were dreadful gossips!

Just then, the door buzzer rang. Richard looked at his watch. Early. God, he loved this girl. He went to the control panel and saw Natalie on the CCTV screen. He pressed the button on the intercom and opening the door, told her to come up. Richard went to the front door and opened it, watching the light on the lift display bring his guest closer and closer. As the numbers climbed, his heart seemed to quicken a little. Finally, it reached eighteen and the doors opened. Richard's face cracked into a smile as Natalie walked towards him.

'Good evening. You look wonderful,' said Richard.

Natalie was matching him, with a black Max Mara dress. It's neckline showed off the curve of her bosom and the length gave her legs the opportunity to take Richard's breath away. Almost as a reflex, his hand went to his mouth. He was afraid that he might be drooling. Gathering his composure, he invited her in.

'Billie Holiday, I love her!' exclaimed Natalie as she walked into the flat. 'Nice flat. Very, what's the word I'm looking for? Male!'

'You mean Spartan?'

'Let's say minimalist, that makes you very fashionable. Could do with something for the walls. Just so happens that I might be able to help you there.'

'We'll see. Just remember that the days of the corrupt copper are pretty much over in this town, so my art budget isn't exactly huge.'

'Don't worry, I can pick you up something reasonable. I just have to find out what your taste is like. Though, I can't argue with your taste in photography. Where did you get the prints?'

'I picked those up at the Museum of Modern Art when I was on leave in New York a few years ago. Couldn't quite get a Liechtenstein in my suitcase. Drink?'

'Please. A glass of white wine.'

Richard walked into the kitchen. Natalie followed him and stood at the door. 'Mmm. Something smells good,' she observed. 'God, you really do like to cook, don't you? I thought you were exaggerating. Look at this kitchen!'

Richard had spent more time and money on his kitchen than any other room in the flat. Every conceivable appliance had been installed. One of the things which he had liked about the flat was the size of the kitchen. It had been like a cavern when he had moved in. With all his additions, it had taken on a "homey", almost cluttered look. He had separate fridges for drinks and food. He even had a commercial ice maker which he had picked up at an auction of the contents of a bar which had closed down. From this he took a couple of scoops of ice and placed them in a silver ice bucket. He opened the Cloudy Bay and poured Natalie a glass. He watched her as she took the first sip of the wine. She announced the quality of the wine with a raise of her eyebrows and a nod of her head.

'Good, isn't it,' said Richard. 'A friend of mine in the Force put me on to it. He comes from Marlborough, where the wine is produced. I get it from an importer he knows, who's trying to get the local hotels interested in it. Personally, I hope he fails. All the more for us.'

As Natalie browsed around his flat, Richard turned his attention to the kitchen. Occasionally he would call out to her and pop his head around the door. She seemed intent in her scrutiny of his books and music collection. Richard understood. He thought that you could tell a lot about a person from the material on their bookshelves and the music they played. Not that he had ever made any profound discoveries from his rummaging through the personal tastes of others. He had discovered the obvious; whether they shared the same taste in music and books. Obvious, but to Richard very important.

This was particularly important with women. Richard didn't expect a woman to share all of his interests, but in the evening, after a long and tiring day, it was nice to settle down with a glass of wine and listen to music which relaxed you, rather than sounds which drove you mad. At least this evening had started well, Natalie enjoyed Billie Holiday. So far so good.

Natalie scanned the shelves. He was a complicated one, this Richard Stirling, she thought. Her eyes passed over an eclectic collection of books. The latest techno-thriller vied for space with cookery books, covering the globe. Management books had such strange bedfellows as a collection of Ginsberg. A number of Lonely Planet travel guides sat together at the end on one shelf. They had the dog-eared appearance of having seen service in the countries that they covered. Well travelled and obviously happy to rough it at times. She picked up the one for India. It was filled with margin notes and underlined passages. The writing was small and neat, for the most part. She had to turn the book around to read the entries, as they were often written at odd angles. The observations had an almost poetic quality. She had expected annotations about the service in a particular restaurant or the cleanliness of a hotel. Instead she found descriptions of the light falling on a building at a particular time of day, or the characters who had shared a train compartment. There were some entries about the poor health that Richard had suffered for about a week of his stay. Even through the suffering his besieged gastro-intestinal tract was giving him, he managed to see the joy in the world that he passed through on his journey. He had evidently been travelling for a good part of the time on his own. It seemed as though he had been alone while he was sick. Natalie's heart went out to him. Being alone and sick in an unknown land was not an experience she would relish.

Richard poured a little oil over the griddle and watched as the smoke rose from the hot surface. One by one he placed the scallops on the ridged surface of the cast iron pan. They only remained on the griddle for a few seconds on each side. Just enough to seal the surface and give them a slightly "smokey" taste. They were transferred to another pan in which some garlic had been cooking in olive oil. The shellfish were pan-fried quickly in the pungent mixture. Richard squeezed the juice of a lemon into the mix and finished it off with a little chopped parsley. He transferred the scallops back into their shells which were sitting on two plates. A simple dish, but from the smell, Richard knew that it would be delicious. He picked up the plates and took them to the dining table.

The scallops did not disappoint. The wine was an excellent accompaniment, bringing out the flavour, without overpowering it. Richard was pleased with his choice. Natalie was enjoying the meal a great deal more than she had expected. The truth of the matter was that she had been rather skeptical about Richard's culinary skills. The shellfish which had quickly disappeared from her plate had surprised and delighted her. Cookery books on a shelf were no guarantee of skill in the kitchen. The only unhappy thought that crossed her mind was that she might have to return the compliment. Cooking was not high among Natalie's list of skills. In fact, her kitchen's most used item was the microwave, for heating up ready cooked meals.

Having cleared the plates away and checked the progress of the main course, Richard sat down and enjoyed the conversation of his guest and the remaining Sauvignon Blanc.

'Where did you learn to cook like that?'

Richard smiled. 'You saw the cookery books. Those and lots of practice. Believe me, some of my early attempts would have had you running for the door. Being a bachelor, necessity made me learn to cook. You must be the same, living alone.'

Natalie visibly winced. Richard noticed the look which spoke more eloquently than words. 'I take it that I am not receiving an invitation to dinner at your place.'

'Not unless you like pizza. There's a great little place just around the corner from me and they deliver.'

'Actually I love pizza. Next time I'll make you one.' Richard looked over the table at his companion. 'Is all this domesticity making you feel uncomfortable?'

'No, not at all. It's just a little surprising. Most of the men I have met in Hong Kong spend so little time at home that their kitchens are as badly equipped as mine. An invitation to dinner anywhere other than a restaurant is unusual. I think that for a lot of people in this town, home is somewhere that you sleep between drinking sessions.'

'Yes,' laughed Richard, a knowing look in his eyes. 'The truth is that I know that scene all too well. My first tour in Hong Kong was just like that. I was in danger of developing a serious drinking problem. Luckily I recognised the fact. When I started my second tour of duty, I resolved to make a home for myself. One that I would look forward to coming to at the end of the day. That's when some friends and I started to have regular dinner parties. Not that they were exactly teetotal affairs, but they made us spend some time and effort on our flats, turning them into homes rather than doss-houses. So, my cooking skills started to develop. In fact I really enjoy it. I love good food and somehow, when you prepare it yourself, it tastes all the better. Of course, the company is what completes the evening and tonight, the food will have to be great to match it.'

'Oh, that sounds like a well worn line,' laughed Natalie. 'So what is next on the menu?'

'*Piccioni alle olive.* Roast pigeon on a bed of olives. The birds are stuffed with prosciutto, pigeon livers, spring onion, bay leaves and juniper berries, all cooked in olive oil and marsala. It's pretty rich, so I'm going to serve it with a salad of blood oranges and shallots. The salad will cleanse the palate between mouthfulls of the pigeon. There's a good, robust Barolo to go with it. Any objection to red wine?' Natalie shook her head. 'Well, why don't I pour us a glass and get the pigeon. It should be just about ready.'

Richard and Natalie sat on the sofa with the poise of two satiated diners. They sipped the last of the wine and seemed happy to be alive.

Natalie broke the satisfied silence. 'Where did you get that ice-cream? It was incredible!' Richard didn't answer, he merely smiled at her. 'Oh, God. Don't tell me you made it. You did, didn't you.'

'Guilty as charged. Last year I treated myself to a Gaggia ice cream maker. I've been experimenting with flavours, but that praline is still my favourite. It is a bit of a hassle to prepare, but it's worth it.'

'I'll say!'

'Well, if you like it that much, I'll give you some to take home with you.'

Natalie moved along the sofa and looked Richard in the eyes. 'Give it to me tomorrow then…and that's not a well worn line!'.

Both tried to suppress an embarrassed laugh, but seeing the effort in the other's face, they released the tension. Suddenly the awkward corn was gone and they were in one another's arms.

A well manicured fingernail ran over the scar. Broad and ugly, it ran over the top of his shoulder. Natalie looked at it with curiosity and sadness. 'An operation?' A question begging an explanation of the cause rather than the cure.

Richard looked at his left shoulder. 'The joint kept dislocating. In the end they had to open me up and shorten the tendons to hold the thing in place. Not very pretty, but it saves me the discomfort of having my shoulder put back in place. That's one sight you wouldn't want to see, unless you like watching a grown man cry.' He was only half joking. A shiver went up Richard's spine as he remembered the visits to the casualty department at Fanling Hospital. He had eventually managed to find a doctor who had the "knack" of getting his arm back in with the minimum of discomfort, but there had been some younger guys who made a real meal of it. Perhaps the sight of hovering SDU men had made them nervous. His guys could be very protective, sometimes with negative results.

'This could give you a lot of pain when you're older,' observed Natalie.

'That and a dozen other injuries,' said Richard with a cheerless smile.

'How did it happen?'

'Sports injury…' Richard stopped short of finishing the stock answer to the question. He looked at Natalie. A voice inside him spoke words of caution. Perhaps it was his heart, or maybe his conscience. Either way, he knew that he had to be honest. 'Actually, that's not entirely true. It's a training injury. Wear and tear really.

'Look, don't ask me why, but I feel as though we might go somewhere in a relationship. I don't want to come on all strong, but if we do spend some time together, it would be wrong to start off with a lie. My job…well I can't tell you a great deal about it. Not yet anyway. You're a smart woman, so I have no doubt that you will work it out for yourself. You might find this silly, all this secrecy. It's a bit of an open secret anyway, but I have to play the game. We're not supposed to tell.

'My job involves a certain degree of risk. It's very physically demanding, which accounts for the injuries. It's almost a badge of office actually. Quite a few of my colleagues have had similar operations, to one part of their body or another. We push ourselves to the limit and sometimes bits of the body just aren't up to it. They need some help from the miracles of modern medicine.

'What I'm trying to say, not very eloquently, is that I have a dangerous job. Through time, you will learn about it, but there will always be things that I can't tell you and there will always be the risk that I don't come home one night. That's a risk that any policeman takes when he puts on his uniform, but in my line of work, we tend to go looking for trouble. Also, our training is hazardous at times. We do everything we can to minimise the risks, but accidents do happen. I want to get to know you better, but I would understand if you found my job too much to handle. Being with someone like me isn't for everyone. It would be no reflection on you if you didn't want to get involved with me. Frankly the sensible thing to do would be to run like hell.'

Natalie placed her finger over his lips. 'Shhh. I get the picture. I'm new in town, but I think I can guess what you do for a living. Your physique is a bit of a clue as are the guys you hang out with. You all have a "look". I like the fact that you are thinking like this. That you think enough of me to consider the future. It may be tough, but I'm sure it will never be boring.

'Look, as you're being brutally honest, I suppose that I should be just as truthful with you. The fact is, I'm really a man.'

Natalie laughed at the look on Richard's face. Just the slightest flicker of shock, maybe even belief. 'Just joking. What I'm trying to tell you is that you don't have to be so serious. Let's just see what happens. I appreciate you telling me all this and the fact that you don't want to lie to me. We don't know much about one another yet, but we will...I hope. It takes time. I think it will be worth the wait.

'Now, don't you think it's about time you put some of that physical conditioning to good use?'

Richard looked deep into her eyes as he pulled her tight against him, his hands started to explore the contours of her body. Gently he massaged the nape of her neck and was rewarded with a soft groan. He felt the passion within him grow like a fire run out of control. He was lost in her, nothing outside her existed. Nothing else mattered. He had never felt like this about a woman. He was safe here. He never wanted to leave.

CHAPTER 22

Lau peeled away the paper stencil. The arrow pointed off to his left, to nowhere in particular. Soon enough it would indicate the direction to Fanling, in the New Territories. It would guide drivers on their way, drivers who were free to travel anywhere they wanted to go. Unlike Lau. His world was this prison, finite and strictly defined. Even within the walls of Stanley Prison, there were areas that were closed to him. Some because they were for the prison staff only, others because they were the territory of rival Triad gangs. Segregation was purely voluntary in this ghetto. The prison officers turned a blind eye to much that went on in here. Only when the activities of the Triad members caused obvious trouble did they intervene. Partly it was because the activity took place under the surface of prison routine. There was the corrupt element within the community of warders, but for most of the men whose job it was to cage their fellow man, it was a matter of indifference. What went unseen was none of their concern. They were paid to do a job. Why invite trouble by stepping over the boundaries of their job description? In this world, crusaders were hard to find.

Work was supposed to keep the inmates busy, keep their minds off any mischief. Unfortunately, the work tended to be so mind-numbing that the smarter members of the institutional community would find themselves hatching plots at an almost unconscious level. It was while working in the sign shop that Lau had come up with the idea of bringing drugs into the prison using the model aircraft. Strange the directions that idle minds could take. It had turned into a lucrative business. Demand always outstripped supply when it came to easy distraction from tedium.

A bell indicated that it was time for the workers in the sign shop to have lunch. Didn't time fly when you were bored, thought Lau. Today his mind was ticking over in idle. He found no enthusiasm for anything. He had been through this before. There were always times when the oppressive tedium of this place became too much, even for someone of his strength and imagination. It was like a weight pressing on his soul. Dangerous if it persisted for any length of time. That was the recipe for suicide. There were remarkably few in prison, but if the will was there, nothing the prison staff might do could prevent a man from taking his own life. Self destruction brought about the most remarkable leaps of imagination.

Perhaps it was boredom which lowered his guard. Whatever the cause, Lau didn't see them coming. Before he realised what was happening, four men dragged him from the corridor, into a storage area. No official eyes were there to see the act. It took less than a minute. The blades were sharp, the cuts many. The men sliced, rather than stabbed. A "chopping" was seldom intended to kill the victim, it was a message. This message was being delivered with mute savagery. Lau would wonder later why he did not cry out during the assault. The pain was real, but the blows that accompanied the cuts seemed to hurt the most. That would change when the air hit exposed flesh. Time stood still as more of his exposed skin felt the touch of razor sharp steel. His prison uniform gave little protection. A short-sleeved shirt and shorts ensured that there was plenty of exposed skin to attack. The four assailants made use of every inch they could reach. Then, as suddenly as it had begun, it was over. The four men disappeared through the wet fog that covered Lau's vision. He lay on the concrete floor, not moving, only listening to his own breathing, looking for assurance that he was still alive. Then the pain hit and he found his voice.

Hospitals didn't just have a certain smell, the air itself seemed harder to breath, as if it was denser than the air outside. Richard hated hospitals. The operation on his shoulder had taken place in the sister hospital to this one, on Kowloon side. Queen Mary Hospital sat on a hillside, overlooking West Lamma Channel, on the western end of Hong Kong Island. He had first stepped through its doors while at Police Training School. He had suffered an attack of heat exhaustion during a run. A heavy bout of drinking in the mess the previous night had probably been the main contributing factor to his collapse. Some intravenous fluids had seen him right as rain in about an hour, but he had the fear of God put into him, as he lay on the bed in the Casualty Department. The sights he saw around him made him swear that he would avoid any more visits to this place. As he walked past patients lying on camp beds in corridors, he renewed that particular vow.

It wasn't that the doctors and nurses in the hospital didn't care, quite the contrary. Resources were stretched to the limit. Just as there was insufficient housing for the population of Hong Kong, so too was there a shortage of beds in hospitals. The government was trying to put both matters right, but good deeds took time. Disease was no respecter of timetables.

At last he found what he was looking for. The barred windows on the door and the Correctional Services officer sitting at his desk were sure signs that he had found his way to the secure ward. Richard walked up to the desk and produced his warrant card for inspection by the young prison officer. The man took a little too long perusing Richard's badge of office, much to the policeman's annoyance. He knew it was a little dance that they had to do. Inter-disciplinary rivalries existed the world over. In this case, Richard suspected that a slight inferiority complex had much to do with it. Correctional Services were not the most respected of government departments. They did a difficult job, but some of their men had an unfortunate attitude that put other people's backs up. Just like now, thought Richard.

'Who do you want to see, sir?' asked the young man, his tone of voice negating the courtesy of calling Richard "sir".

'Lau Kam-hung, the prisoner who was chopped in Stanley prison yesterday,' replied Richard. He kept his manner cool, trying to overcome his anger at the insolent attitude of the young prison officer. He thought that they seemed to put on a bad attitude along with their uniform. Richard knew that this was unfair. He had met plenty of good blokes in the Correctional Services Department and the Police Force had its own share of obnoxious characters.

'Nature of business?'

'If you look at that clipboard in front of you, I think you will find a memo from your headquarters granting me access to the prisoner.'

The prison officer looked down and flipped through the papers on the clipboard eventually finding the relevant memorandum. He checked the name against Richard's warrant card and then handed the small plastic card back to its owner. Still, the young man was persistent. 'What do you want to see him about?'

Richard had had enough. 'None of your business is what I want to see him about. Now, you have the paperwork granting me access to the prisoner, so kindly open the door and let me in. Unless of course you would rather pick up that 'phone and call the man who signed the memo.'

Richard hated treating other government servants like this. They all had enough aggravation when dealing with the public, without one of their "own" dishing it out, but this guy had crossed the line. The signature at the bottom of the memo was a very senior officer in the CSD, who happened to be a friend of Richard's. With little grace and an obvious loss of face, the young man opened the door with a key attached to his belt by a thin chain. Richard thanked him as he entered the ward and was given a grunt for his trouble.

The ward was quite busy, Richard saw. Many of the patients would be men who had tried to avoid arrest and suffered injuries as a result. Usually the injuries were slight, but they had to be treated, to cover the police officers concerned as much as the criminals. The first thing these men would do would be to make a complaint of assault against the officers who arrested them. It would be likely that the policemen had also been injured in the struggle and would be at present receiving treatment in the casualty department. Richard knew that some policemen crossed the line at times. He had no time for the cowboys who bragged about torturing prisoners. They deserved prison terms more than the targets of their abuse. Violence was no substitute for intelligence. Perhaps an odd attitude, considering his previous line of work, but he had always felt that deploying the SDU was the last possible option. They may employ violence, but it was to save lives, innocent ones. The people who would feel the edge of their sword were violent men, with little regard for human life, not some drug addict from a housing estate, strung out and desperate.

Richard had seen chopping victims before, but as he caught sight of Lau's bed, he realised that it was different when it was someone you knew. He had seen worse, but it was bad enough. The doctor had told him that many of the cuts were superficial and would heal quickly, but Lau would have plenty of scars to show off. Most of his body had received cuts, including his head and face. Richard straightened himself and put the best attempt at a smile on that he could muster.

'Well, you're a fucking mess, you old bastard.'

Lau turned to look at his mocker. This movement exposed a nasty wound down his left cheek. Despite the obvious damage, he raised a smile when he saw Richard standing beside his bed. 'I'm still more handsome than you. Fatter than ever, I see. You'll never find a wife looking like that.'

'You're probably right about that,' said Richard as he pulled up a chair and sat down. Turning serious, looked straight at Lau as he spoke. 'So, they made a pretty good job of it. Silly question, but how do you feel?'

'Probably better than I should. They were vicious, but they were not out to kill me. Before you ask, I don't know who they were, but I'll find out who and why.'

'I'm sure you will,' said Richard without enthusiasm. 'But I think it is fairly obvious why. Should narrow down the possible culprits. I thought your friends were looking out for you in there.'

Lau managed a brief laugh. 'So did I, but you are never completely safe. I let my guard down. I don't think you want to know what will happen now. A message has to be sent out after this.'

Richard knew exactly what that meant. The Correctional Services Department were going to have a few more woundings on their incident reports. Courtesy of the man in front of him, though he doubted that Lau would do the work himself, not unless there was a particular individual he thought deserved his personal attention. Lau was no coward and he could handle himself. They really must have caught you off guard, you old bugger, thought Richard.

'How is Cassius?' asked Lau.

Richard was slightly surprised by the question. 'He's fine. We're working together on something at the moment. It's keeping us busy, but more so him. You know Cass, once he gets his teeth into something there's no stopping him.'

'Yes, I of all people should know that.' The words were spoken with bitterness.

'Lau, what did you expect him to do? He was your friend, you were one of us. Cassius didn't have a clue that you were a Triad member. Not until you were filmed by his unit taking part in an initiation ceremony. No, sorry presiding over an initiation ceremony as an office bearer. You know Cass better than anyone, did you really think he would let you go. You may feel betrayed, but so does he and every other member of the Force. Well most of them. I'm sure a few of your other colleagues are still in the ranks.'

Lau looked at Richard for a moment and smiled. 'I know, but he hasn't once come to see me, even now he won't come. None of the people from training school, only you. We were all so close before.' Lau looked hard at Richard's eyes. 'Why do you come Richard? Have you forgiven me?'

Richard Stirling took a deep breath, looking off to the far wall. He turned to look at the man lying on the bed. 'Forgive you, no. The betrayal was too great Lau. But, I still consider you my friend, for all your failings. I can't begin to understand what you did. I don't even want to think about the damage that you may have caused to cases that you were involved in. But I know that you were a good cop at least some of the time. Maybe only when you were dealing with rival Triads, but at least you put those bastards away. One hell of a lot of them. I also know that there is a decent man beneath the veneer of corruption. I can't begin to imagine the upbringing you had Lau, what brought you into the 14K, but I do believe that you are my friend and that doesn't change just because you are behind bars.'

Lau looked toward the foot of the bed. 'I was a good cop, Richard. You have to believe that. I had other loyalties, but there were times when I thought about leaving those behind. But the money, well when you grow up with none and then have the chance to make so much, most of the time by doing nothing more than turning a blind eye…' The ex-cop turned to look at his friend. There was just the hint of shame in his face. 'Thank you for coming Richard. You may not believe me, but it means a lot that you didn't turn your back on me. I would have understood if you had. You owe me nothing and I owe you so much. I can understand if YOU were to feel betrayed.'

Richard allowed himself to smile. After all, he was here to try and make Lau feel better, not go over old accusations. 'Lau, as far as I'm concerned the only person you betrayed was yourself.'

CHAPTER 23

The rolling drum-beat of the rain on the bodywork of the Land-Rover drowned out the sound of the engine. Inspector Peter Walker heard nothing as he stared out of the steamed-up windows of the police vehicle. His mind focussed on the vision in his head. Water ran in torrents down the concrete steps which led up to the graves. Wind lashed the hillside, sending spray up from the artificial waterfalls and sending the banana trees at the base of the slope into a wild dance. This was his first typhoon. It was one he would never forget.

At first the call had sounded almost like a joke. "Dead body found in Tsuen Wan Permanent Cemetery". He had been tempted to say something inane, like "So?". He was glad now that he had not. In the three months since he had left training school, Peter had come face to face with death many times. He was almost becoming blasé about it. Part of his job was to look at bodies in cases of sudden death. He was no expert, was not expected to give a medical opinion, but his task was to look for obvious signs of foul play. All he was really required to do was look for wounds, anything that would make it clear that the body should not be moved and the experts called in. He had never before had to make such a call. Usually it was just old people whose time had come, or the occasional suicide. The sight of death no longer seemed to bother him. He had started to crack the bad jokes that were part of coping with this unpleasant aspect of his job. If you could laugh at death, then perhaps it wouldn't touch you too much. That had been the reason for his ill-conceived thought when the call had come over the radio. Now he felt ashamed for having such a thing enter his head. Peter didn't think he would ever crack another joke about the poor souls that he had to man-handle in an attempt to see if they had been a victim of violence. Not after today.

He had been annoyed when he arrived. The sight of the rainwater surging down the steps of the cemetery had made his heart sink. The cabin of the Land-Rover was dry and comfortable. Peter felt cheerful watching the wretched weather from the safety of his vehicle. Now he would have to go out there and be soaked with his men. Leadership had a price. Within seconds of leaving the cab, he was drenched. Despite the heat, his skin rose in gooseflesh as the water, driven by the wind, soaked through his uniform. Peering through the stinging rain, Peter could see one of his men waving from the top of the hill. 'Great,' he thought. These things never happened somewhere easy to get to. Keeping his footing was difficult as he slowly made his way up the concrete staircase. The strength of the surging water was enough to knock him off his feet. He crouched and gripped the low coping-stones which edged the stairway to maintain his balance. Behind him, the occasional curse in Cantonese told him that Sgt Wong was still with him. Peter didn't want to have to turn around, as he felt in imminent danger of following the plunging water back down to the base of the slope. The higher he went, the greater his anxiety at the prospect of this unwelcome trip.

When he reached the summit, Peter breathed a long sigh of relief. The climb had been no more than a hundred meters, but if he had lost his footing it would have been a long, painful and perhaps fatal drop to the bottom. He wondered why they made these cemeteries so steep, then realised that if the land was not like this, developers would have built quarters for the living rather than the dead.

As the constable who had signalled him gave Peter a salute, all the Inspector could think about was the uncomfortable squelching in his shoes. His socks were sodden and would soon turn his feet into a couple of pale prunes. Seeing the look of anticipation in his subordinate's face, he returned the salute with as much enthusiasm as he could muster.

'OK, what do we have? Some old mendicant drop off to sleep with his ancestors and then fail to wake up?'

Peter's mood changed as he gave the young constable's face a proper inspection. There was real sadness in the man's eyes. Peter Walker changed the tone of his voice. 'Show me what you found.'

A gravestone had been broken and knocked over. It partially covered a storm drain that would normally carry torrents like today's off to the side of the cemetery. Now, though, the duct was not fulfilling it's role. Something was blocking it. It was difficult to see, as the fallen gravestone was blocking the view. Peter walked to the other side of the stone and took a sharp inward breath when he caught sight of the body. 'Oh, Jesus Christ.'

There would be no doubt about the fact that this body could not be moved. Peter didn't have to touch it to know that this was out of his hands. He quickly rallied his thoughts and started to give instructions to his men. The area would have to be cordoned-off and as much evidence preserved as possible. The appropriate people would have to be called out on what for many of them would be their day off. Peter tried not to think about the amount of "brass" that would be hovering around here in a very short while. With any luck, they would let him get the hell out of here and back to his other duties. Away from here. Away from this sight.

Peter didn't want to look at the body, but he would have to report what he saw, so he turned his attention to the corpse and scanned it with his full attention. He was no more than a boy. Peter couldn't guess at the age, the side of the face that was visible was so badly bruised. All the features were puffed-up, the face resembling a balloon rather than a human countenance. Both hands and feet were bound with thin twine. The cord had cut into the flesh, possibly when the boy had struggled, thought Peter. The cuts were deep and bloody. Another length of the same twine was tied around the throat, tightly enough that much of it was buried in the flesh of the boy's neck. Whether this was the cause of death was unclear, as there was a gaping wound in the back of the head. Without moving the body, Peter could not see if there was an exit wound, but it certainly looked as though the boy had been shot in the back of the head. The pathologists would have to determine which cruelty had actually caused death. The body was naked, except for some underpants. At least the boy had been allowed that small degree of dignity. Every inch of exposed skin was covered in bruises and cuts and had taken on a livid purple-red colouring.This boy had been very badly beaten. It might even turn out that the beating had killed him. This lad's last hour had been a painful one. Peter shook his head at the thought that one human being could inflict such cruelty on another. He thought that the boy was possibly a Triad member. This had the look of a ritual killing, but no one deserved this sort of treatment, no matter how corrupt their lives.

Peter Walker stared out at the rain, but all he saw was the mutilated body of a young boy. He wanted to go back to the station. He wanted to change out of his sodden uniform and be dry and warm. He wanted to go to the Mess for a beer and listen to amusing stories told over the bar. He wanted jolly lies and humorous exaggerations. He wanted to hear words like "You think that's bad, wait 'til you hear what happened to me…". He wanted to be told that the images would fade and that he would feel better soon. He wanted contact with human beings like himself. Men with morals and compassion for their fellow man. Men who would never consider doing to another human being what had been done to a scared boy in a dark, wet cemetery. He wanted to be anywhere other than where he was now and to be thinking thoughts other than those which haunted his mind.

'The boy didn't suffer, did he?'

'No, of course not,' lied Garland. No trace of mendacity was betrayed by his coarse features. 'I had to damage the body somewhat after death to complete the appearance of a Triad execution. You know how extreme these people can be, but the boy was dead already.'

'Oh, the poor boy. That lovely body. Was it really necessary to abuse him?' Li almost convinced Garland that he felt something for the little faggot, but the security chief knew better. The order had come from Li's lips. He had tired of his plaything and wanted it disposed of. The boy was becoming too cocky, even for Li. It was obvious that the youth thought himself untouchable. His demands were becoming excessive, his mouth too loose. He had to go.

'It was the only way,' replied Garland. 'Now he will just be another boy from the estates who got on the wrong side of some Triad thugs. A queer with a big mouth who pissed someone off.'

Li began to grimace at this bold statement from his head of security. Could it be a dig at him? Perhaps. It would not be the first time that the Englishman had tried to bait him. Li knew that Garland thought his liaisons with local boys was too great a risk. The Englishman preferred to find foreign friends for his master. Individuals who would not be missed when it became time for them to "retire". But, Li preferred the purity of his own race. His dalliances with foreigners had left him dissatisfied and with the bitter taste of having allowed someone beneath him to enjoy the warmth of his embrace. The foreign boys were accommodating to his every whim, that was true. But their eagerness to please felt sleazy and contemptible. The local boys were more coy, their favours had to be won. This gave an excitement to the encounters which Li craved. Once their secrets had been plundered, Li's fascination for the boys quickly waned and when they no longer interested him, or as with the last they became a danger to him, he had to reluctantly hand them into Garland's tender care. Li suspected that the treatment that the boys received was less than kind, but he did not like to think too hard about it. He thought himself a compassionate man. After all, did he not make the lives of these poor boys rich in their last days. A short life well lived was surely better than a long miserable existence.

Li sighed. 'Well, probably the fate that would have befallen him anyway. At least he had some delightful days in my company. Now, let me see the photographs of the dear sweet boys you were telling me about.'

CHAPTER 24

It was always a risk. The security around the target forced me into a corner. It was a good plan, though. It should have worked. Was I sloppy? Or were they lucky? Lucky, I think. It would have been perfect. I could have watched it on television. The cameras were there. They may have been destroyed in the explosion, but some tape would have survived. Enough to give some journalist the scoop of his life. I didn't use too much explosive for that very reason. To have actually seen the target torn apart by the projectiles from the Claymore, that would have been a joy! There would have been so many deaths and injuries from this event that the whole tableau would have been magnificent. All of it centered around the European on the podium. Such beauty!

No, they were lucky. I wonder who discovered the device? From my observations, they seemed a rather incompetent lot. Except for one or two who appeared to know what they were doing. Yes, luck.

Then the bomb disposal officer turned up. Interesting character. Very cool. He took his time, did the sensible thing and waited. He knew the schedule as well as I did. Must have been under a lot of pressure to do something. Ordinary people just don't understand. If there is no obvious activity, they think that nothing is happening. They are so wrong. The greatest weapon against my devices is a smart brain. That EOD officer has one. The way he smoked his cigar.

So calm, so relaxed. He must have enjoyed my device in the cigar box. That would have amused him. Perhaps I should send him a little gift.

Who is he? I must find out. It is always wise to identify your adversary. Determine his weaknesses, in case he starts to get too close. Perhaps I should have devoted some time to looking at the police capability with respect to bomb disposal. Funny that the military are not responsible for EOD in this town. Yes, I must find out more, especially about this man.

Garland will complain about my "failure", as I am sure he will put it. That man is becoming more intolerable by the day. I hope he is enjoying his life, for I have a feeling that it is shortly to come to an end. If he is too aggressive with me the next time we meet, his demise may come soon. Not before he furnishes me with information about my friend the EOD officer, though. He is an interesting character this one. He has the look. Someone who has been through a lot. Someone who would appreciate my work. So rare to find a man with the sensibility to appreciate the splendour of the explosion. So few people understand the complexity of the event. It is all over so quickly for them. They lack the knowledge and eye to see the grandeur in the spectacle. Because it lasts such a short time, they assume that there is no real trick to producing the event. How can they appreciate the ingenuity and skill which is required to produce such a wonder? But, he knows. He understands. I shall have to devise something special for my new friend. Something to take his breath away. And I must be there to see the flash of understanding in his eyes, right at the end, when he knows that he has been undone by a superior craftsman. He must take pride in his skill, but he and I both know that the real skill lies with the man producing the device, not the one who so selfishly prevents it from fulfilling its destiny.

I wonder just how smart this man is? He approached the blast area without a bomb suit. Did he not think that there might be a secondary device? No, he waited for some time after the explosion. He had thought of that. Does he not care? Could it be that this champion of law and order has a death wish? Or does he believe in his own invincibility? Such vanity deserves to be tested and if proved, punished. Yes, I must discover more about this man. Garland can use his police contacts, if he still has any. I find it hard to imagine that such a loathsome man could possibly be in favour with the authorities, unless of course he managed to mask his true nature while he was an officer of the law.

A challenge. To see just how clever this EOD officer is. Does he really have the instincts for the job, or is he merely a technician? An exciting exercise. It is strange how fate brings us stimulation, just when it seems to thwart us. A short time ago, I was angry at the blow the Gods had dealt me, now, I see the opportunity to up the stakes in the great game. A European policeman, a bomb disposal expert, now that would be a masterpiece. Public and spectacular, that has to be the goal. Suddenly I feel energised. Preparation, that is the first stage. Let us find out who our friend is and the best way to get at him.

CHAPTER 25

The doors of the lacquered chinese cabinet were wide open. Inside, a bank of television screens silently shed their phosphorescent light upon the room. Images changed, producing a constantly moving collage. Most of the pictures were of mute faces, their lips mouthing unheard words. Li watched allowing his eyes to wander between the screens, not looking at the immaculately preened presenters, but at the figures that scrolled along the bottom of some of the screens. Stock prices. Over the last few weeks he had been carefully tracking the movement of certain key stocks, or rather some of his employees had been doing this tedious task, updating him on the movement of the share prices on an hourly basis. Occasionally, he liked to watch the movement himself, particularly when he expected that there would be a dramatic fall. Today he was disappointed. The one stock he was interested in had fallen, but not nearly as much as he had hoped, as he had expected. The figures mocked him as they slid from view across the screens.

Li cursed silently. What had gone wrong? The plan had been moving along beautifully. The share prices of the targeted companies had plummeted after the untimely deaths of their Chairmen. Li had gobbled up stock, through a number of companies. Companies which, when the time was right, would come together to form a group with enormous power. A group which Li would control. The plan had stumbled. Li knew that the increased security which surrounded the Taipans would make things more difficult. They had foreseen this probability when the plan was being put together, but the man they had been given as their instrument in this affair was supposed to be good enough to overcome such obstacles. Li's associates would soon be asking awkward questions of him. But, what had he to fear? They had been the one who had supplied the bomber. If fault lay at any door, it was theirs. Li tried to console himself with that thought, but deep inside, he knew that the people he was dealing with would see the situation in a very different light. They may have approached him with the proposal, but they were not the sort of people at whose door you could lay blame. This was an operational failure and Li was in charge of the operation. The plan had always been a gamble and Li knew that if his associates' involvement were likely to come to light, his life would be worth less than the lowest figure to cross the screens before him. It could not be allowed to come to that.

A knock at the door announced the arrival of Garland. His face was flushed as he walked into the office. He had been in a hurry to get here, sensing his master's displeasure when he spoke to him on the telephone. Li said nothing, merely continued to look at the television screens. It didn't take Garland long to realise what was expected of him.

'He says that the police were lucky,' the lack of substance in the statement became obvious to him as soon as the words came out of his mouth. 'I don't agree with that evaluation,' said Garland, trying to place himself at a distance from recent events. Li was still behaving strangely towards him after the boy's death. He wondered how the man could hold something against him which had been done at his own instruction. Not a direct order, but Garland had been left in no doubt that the boy had to go, permanently. Now, the security chief was being held responsible for the actions of a man over whom he was supposed to wield control, but who in reality was his own master. Of course he could not say this to Li. If Garland was not in control of the bombings, then he was nothing more than a messenger boy and that he could not tolerate.

Garland tried a different tack. 'There may have been an element of luck in the discovery of the device, there always is. But the men who have been assigned to protect our targets are very good at their job.'

Li at last turned to face his subordinate. 'You assured me that they were not that competent, that they would be stretched too thin to cope with attacks in a professional manner. What has changed, or were you wrong?'

'The men they have assigned are from Special Branch, their VIP Protection Unit. Section G4 they call it. I didn't think that they would have enough manpower to be assigned to duties such as these. I expected CID officers, maybe SDU men who are not trained for this type of work. G4 must have been expanded. Special Branch are very secretive about their strength.'

'Either that, or your contacts within the Police Force are not as good as you claim. Which is it Garland? I would really like to know.'

'The Police Force is highly compatmentalised and the personnel move around a great deal. I cannot be expected to have access to significant information within every branch of the organisation. The specialist units in particular are very closed communities. Other officers know of their existence and of the men who are a part of them, but are less informed about their operations, unless of course they are exchanging bullshit over a bar. I gave you the most accurate information that I had at my disposal. As it turned out, it was inaccurate, but I have provided you with plenty of accurate information in the past and will in the future. I didn't plant the bomb. Maybe you should be asking him what went wrong. He wants me to find out about the bomb disposal officer that they called out to the scene. Says that the man may pose a threat to the operation, but I'm not sure that he is telling me the real reason for his interest.'

Li's interest picked up at this last remark. 'What do you mean by that?'

'I mean that our friend is beginning to act even more irrationally than usual. I suspect that he has his own agenda working here and that the error with the last bomb may be a result of his mind being on other things. He is supposed to be working for us, but sometimes I get the impression that he thinks that it is the other way around.'

This worried Li. Was Garland making excuses, or was the man his associates had provided turning rogue? Li had never met the bomber. Garland did not know of Li's associates. That was the way that he had wanted things. A buffer on both sides. If Garland knew the full extent of the operation, it would be a weapon which he might use against Li. On the other hand, if the bomb maker was unstable, Garland was his only contact and therefore the only possible target for his deranged behaviour.

'Garland, I suggest that you bring this man back under control. After all, that is what I pay you for, is it not? You are the source of his materials, so use that as a lever to make him toe the line. Without your help, he is nothing but an asset without resources. Give him the information that he requires, but again use it to extract his cooperation with our cause. You can get him the information that he requires, can you not?'

Jack Garland was a man used to giving abuse, not receiving it. He sucked in his fury and spoke in a noticeably level voice. 'I can get the details of this EOD officer. It will be common knowledge. I am sure that I can find out about him from my contacts. These people also like to drink. Perhaps it is the strain of the job, but they can be very eloquent when they get into an environment in which they feel safe, like an Officers' Mess. They travel around a lot to incidents and are generally treated to a few beers after the job is done, so there will be plenty of people with plenty to say about this character.'

Li looked at him very coldly. 'In that case, I am surprised that you have not generated details of this man before now. I would have thought it inevitable that we would come up against a bomb disposal specialist in the midst of a bombing campaign. Don't you think?'

Garland said nothing for some seconds. 'If only I had your foresight, sir. I will remedy my shortcomings at once. If you have nothing further for me that is.'

Li dismissed the security officer with a gesture and returned his attention to the television screens. He might have to start looking for another security chief, thought Li.

CHAPTER 26

Sleep was obviously not on the minds of the chickens in their coops. The large shed resonated to the sound of the garrulous birds. It was partly because of the noise,certainly because of the smell, that the poultry farm was situated some way back from the village, encroaching on the surrounding bush. There was plenty of open ground around the small collection of buildings, but for the farmer, it was a constant struggle to keep mother nature at bay.

Poultry prices were falling, as greater numbers of birds were imported from the Mainland. The man who owned and operated this farm was not too worried about the trend. He had, for the last year, found an additional source of income and all he had to do to earn his money was turn a blind eye. Initially, he had little say in the matter. They had turned up one day and told him that he had to clear out the single storey building at the rear of his property. The welfare of his family would depend upon his cooperation. Subtlety was not a Triad attribute. Unhappy to be drawn into their activities, his unease had been meliorated by the cash which they "forced" into his palm every week. Soon, he learned to temper his resentment with acceptance and grudging gratitude for the bonus income. He still feared the presence of these men, gangsters brought police and police meant trouble. Chinese people stayed away from police as much as possible. To have police involved in your life meant that you had trouble in your life, so stay away from the police and trouble stayed away from your door. So went the logic of his thinking.

The farm was an ideal location. A quiet corner of a quiet village in the New Territories. The tell-tale smell of their operation was masked by the awful stink of the farm. The building they had chosen was well hidden from view. They still had to be careful, but it was the best site yet. Ideal for converting the block morphine into number three heroin. The lab had remained undetected for almost a year. There had been some talk of moving and holding this place as a back-up for the future, but the decision had been made to remain for at least another month. If another prime site could be found by then, the move would be made. For now, the operation was working smoothly. The farmer had been more than cooperative, though he had to be reminded from time to time that he could not flash his new found wealth around. At least not until they had moved on. This was just another night, like all the others that had produced so much of the precious commodity that was their livelihood.

The nullah was like hundreds of others to be found throughout Hong Kong. A concrete trench which carried water away from the hillsides during the heavy rains which could turn those slopes into surging walls of death. The conduits were also channels for all manner of liquid run-off from the villages that they protected. This one ran up the side of the poultry farm and captured all the foul residue from the activity that took place there. On this night, there was an unusual object in the nullah, moving silently in the opposite direction to the flow. The figure was almost invisible in the blackness of the deep trench, his black clothing melting into the shadows. His step was careful on the slippery surface of the nullah. Each footfall methodically placed, the outside edge of a boot placed down and then the foot rolled over flat onto the ground. Even without the barnyard chorus, the figure's movements would have been inaudible. The man stayed close to the wall of the nullah, making him invisible from the farm, even without his camouflage.

The figure stopped and slowly felt the wall of the nullah. At last, he found what he was looking for. Heavily rusted rungs formed a ladder up the side of the fifteen foot wall. Carefully, he inched his way up the ladder, until his head was just below the rim of the nullah. The man paused, listening to the disembodied voice softly speaking into his left ear, telling him that the lookout was on the other side of the building. The human eye detects movement, even in peripheral vision. One of the secrets of fieldcraft is to make movements slow and infrequent. A well camouflaged man will remain undetected, even at close range, if he remains perfectly still. The slightest movement will give him away. The man raised his head over the rim just enough to give him a view of the building. He remained stock still when he was in position. The black Nomex balaclava and cam-cream on what little of his face was exposed, made it almost impossible to pick him up in the darkness. He watched for no more than fifteen seconds, more than enough time for his trained eyes to pick up the detail he sought. Painfully slowly he descended below the rim and started his descent down the ladder. Back in the comfort of the dark nullah, he began to methodically retrace his steps, back to where his colleague was waiting, still covering the edge of the nullah with his pistol.

'Enjoy the nullah, did you?' asked Richard Stirling with a huge grin on his face.

Keith Symons gave him a "stop taking the piss" look. 'Jesus, what an stink! That's bad enough, but the footing is very poor, boss. But, I think you're right. It's our best approach route to the target. We're going to have to be damn careful when we are carrying all our kit. If one of the blokes slips, there could be a godawful racket.'

'Then no one had better slip,' was the unsympathetic reply.

Keith shrugged off the minor rebuke. 'Can I send some more of my guys up to do a close recce?'

'No,' said the Team Commander. 'I know everyone wants to get up close and do a bit of night-crawling, but you've been there and that is enough. The more people that go up, the greater chance of discovery. You brief your men on what you saw. Sometimes you might not even get the chance to get up that close before an op. Be grateful that you did this time.'

Keith sniffed at his overalls. 'Yeah, bloody grateful. Next time, why don't you go the whole hog and find a nice cess pit for me to have a swim in.'

'I just might, young man. Now, go get cleaned up a bit and come back with your guys for the briefing.'

Richard turned to a Chinese officer in plain clothes. They were looking at a diagram of the farm which had been drawn on a white-board. 'Ben, how sure are you that they are armed? We haven't seen any sign of firearms so far.'

Ben Hung was a superintendent in Narcotics Bureau. On a tip-off from an informant, NB had been keeping the farm under surveillance for the last two weeks. Their informant had told them that he had seen guns in the building that was being used as a narcotics lab, so he had asked for help from the SDU. It was rare for the counter-terrorist unit to be used in criminal cases, mainly because the senior officers in Police Headquarters resisted their use. The men of SDU welcomed any opportunity to use and hone their skills. 'The informant was pretty clear on that point, Richard. He's been reliable in the past and the sight of the guns seemed to shake him up a bit. Not just handguns, he said. There were what he described as "soldier's guns", long weapons.'

That had been the clincher for the powers that be in PHQ. They didn't want to send NB officers into a situation for which they were not trained. If there were weapons like those described inside, the SDU men were the ideal people to effect an entry. The Narcotics Bureau detectives would take over the scene once it was secure. There were plenty of cowboys in the Force who would have tried to take this job on themselves and probably caused the death of some of their men, but luckily Ben Hung had his ego under control and knew when to ask for help.

'It's very odd,' said Richard. 'If your informer is right, then we have an escalation in the level of threat posed by criminal elements. I hope to God that this is not the beginning of a trend. There's always been the potential for military arms to make their way down here from China, for example. But we've been lucky up 'til now. Mind you, having the weapons is one thing, being able to use them effectively is quite another.

'So, we have snipers covering all sides of the target building. So far they have reported only the one guard. He seems to be concentrating on the front of the shed, watching for any approach from the main road. He only went to the rear of the building once and that was to take a leak. Not exactly smart, these boys. You would think that the blind side would be covered. Two entry points on the front. Windows left and right. We'll use the nullah to approach the building. The bush around here is pretty thick, we're more likely to make noise going through it than using the nullah. We exit on the blind side, just here.' Richard indicated the position on the diagram.

'The doors look pretty solid. When one of the suspects entered the building, it took about thirty seconds from the time he identified himself, until the door was opened. That might indicate that the door is bolted and barred on the inside. It's quite usual for these labs to be well secured, so I'm not going to take the obvious way in. We'll blast a hole in the wall, just here.'

'What, explosives?' Ben Hung looked horrified. 'Richard, these labs use a lot of flammable chemicals. If you start using explosives, you might get a bigger explosion than you bargained for.'

'Relax, Ben. We have a thing called a water-damped frame charge, for just this sort of thing. Anywhere there is a risk of fire. It's a tubular plastic frame, with a shaped charge of plastic explosive inside. You fill it with water and place it against the wall, or door. The explosive forces the water forward at extremely high velocity, turning it into a liquid knife, I suppose you could say. The water cuts through the wall and moderates the blast at the same time. So, no fires. Well, that's the theory anyway.'

'Please tell me you have used this thing before,' pleaded Superintendent Hung.

'Of course. In training. But never with a building full of explosive fumes. Should be an interesting test.' Richard grinned at his colleague. 'Ben, trust me.'

Most people are afraid of the dark. It covers unknown dangers, hidden threats. For the men of SDU, darkness was a friend. They were the unknown danger, the hidden threat. Darkness was a blanket which protected the men from the icy fingers of death. These men were trained to blend into the night, until the time when they would emerge, suddenly and without warning, like a bolt of lightning.

The line of men knelt at the base of the nullah. Two men pointed their MP5s at the rim while one climbed the ladder and exited the water-course. He turned and took hold of the rectangle of plastic that was being handed to him. With the explosive package in his hands, he quickly, but quietly moved off to the rear of the building. On the orders of the snipers, each man in turn climbed the ladder and disappeared into the night. The guard at the front of the building was none the wiser to all the activity that was taking place only forty yards from where he stood.

'Relax Ben,' said Richard.

Ben Hung was nervously picking at his fingernails. The tension was obvious from his posture and his silence. 'How can you be so calm?' he asked.

'Believe me, I'm not. I just have a lot to think about, so it doesn't show so much. The guys are moving into position.' Richard was listening to the sniper commentary through his earpiece. The Assault

Group would change to another channel when they were in position, with the exception of one man, who would monitor the sniper channel, just in case the targets had any nasty surprises up their sleeves. The assault channel would be on speaker in the command centre. A house in the village had been commandeered by the police. It was out on its own and had allowed them to set up unseen.

'Ben, you had better get your guys ready to go. When this goes down it's all going to be over in a hurry. When I give you the word, I want your men in there as fast as possible to protect the chain of evidence. The less my men have to do with it the better. Ideally I want as few of them as possible to have to give evidence in court.'

'Understood Richard.' Ben spoke into a radio in Cantonese. His men were waiting in two unmarked vehicles, ready to move in when the SDU men had done their part. Both sides would be learning here. If the raid was successful, it might well be the beginning of greater cooperation between the units. For SDU, it was an opportunity to put their skills to practical use and break up the tedium of continuous training. For NB, it meant not having to send their men into dangerous situations for which they were neither trained, nor equipped.

The sergeant placed the frame charge flush against the wall and extended a plastic leg from the rear of the all-in-one unit. This he positioned on the ground in such a way as to brace the charge securely in place. The positioning of the demolition charge had been determined earlier, during a close recce, which Richard had led. Using a fibre optic camera, he had looked through one of the windows without being seen. The lab was quite spacious and luckily the end nearest the nullah was fairly clear of equipment. Richard was fairly sure that the blast would do little permanent harm to the occupants, unless of course one of them happened to be leaning up against the wall when the charge went off. That would be just too bad. Just as important, the explosion would not damage any of the evidence that Narcotics Bureau would need to bring a successful prosecution against the men inside. He had been a little concerned that there was no sign of the weapons that were the main reason for he and his men being involved in this operation, but that didn't mean that they weren't there.

When the sergeant was happy with the set-up, he backed away, following the firing cable back to the assembly point. The detonator had been placed in the charge before the dems were put in place, a reversal of normal range procedure, where the last thing to be done was putting detonator and explosive together. Back with the rest of the Assault Group, he took the bare ends of the firing cable and plugged them into the Shrike, the battery unit which would detonate the charge. He pressed a button and was rewarded with a green light, indicating that he had a circuit. He signalled his readiness to Keith Symons and waited for the command to go.

Richard listened to the sniper commentary through his ear-piece. He stiffened as he heard one of the snipers report that the guard was on the move. The man hadn't budged for almost half an hour. One hell of a time to decide to go for a stroll, thought Richard.

'Bravo One, this is Bravo. Guard is moving to rear of the building, over.'

Richard listened to the acknowledgement from Keith and held his breath.

It was going to be a long night. The guard had drunk some beer before taking up his post and now his bladder was telling him that some room was needed. Nature's own toilet was at hand. He headed for the rear of the building and the dense bush that started there.

Keith only took a second to make the decision. The guard was going to be taken out of the picture anyway, so there seemed to be no better time than the present. Four of his men were stationed at the opposite end of the building to the rest of the team, hiding in the bush. The guard was heading straight for them. Keith depressed the radio key in his left hand and softly spoke his order into the microphone at his collar.

The SDU men allowed the guard to pass their position and then silently two of them emerged from the darkness, quickly covering the ground between them and their target. The guard was a 426 in Triad terminology, a fighter. Normally he would have put up a formidable resistance to his attackers, but now he was given no chance. He was on the ground and incapacitated in a few seconds. The takedown made little sound, certainly not enough to alert the occupants of the building.

Keith knew that he had to get on with it now. He asked Richard for approval to go and was given it straight away. Most of the Assault Group had donned their NBC6 repirators for the assault. The explosive would kick up a lot of dust. The respirators would prevent choking or vision problems as the men moved into the building.

Richard handed control over to Keith, as he had sight of the target and could best judge when to go. The group who had disposed of the guard got ready to play their part. They would let off two stun grenades immediately after the demolition charge had gone off, to provide a distraction and draw the attention of the occupants to the opposite side of the building to that which the Assault Group would enter. They had decided not to use stun grenades inside the building for fear of causing the flammable chemicals to go up. When he was happy, Keith spoke into his throat mike in a calm, but positive voice. 'Stand by, stand by, go, go, go!'

On the first "go" the sergeant punched the firing button on the Shrike. The blast shook the ground and immediately the Assault Group were rushing to the hole which the frame charge had opened in the concrete wall. It was low, so the men had to stoop as they went through. Keith was the first man through the ragged gap. As he entered, he heard the twin booms of the stun grenades. There was a lot of dust before him, but he caught sight of a figure off to his right, he made for it and brought his weapon to bear on the target. Behind him, his Number Two covered the opposite angle, engaging a target ahead and slightly to his left. Neither target had an obvious weapon, so the SDU men told them to get down on their bellies. They had to shout to be heard through the respirators, but they would have done that anyway, they weren't inviting these men to join them for a drink. Behind the first assault pair, other men moved quickly into the building and moved forward, dealing with targets as they came into view. There were six men inside the shed. Four were lying on their stomachs, with their hands behind their heads within ten seconds of the entry. The last two made a dash for the far door. The elaborate security arrangements worked against them, as they were grabbed by two SDU men before they managed to get a thick metal bar off its mounts. They too were face down in the dirt before they were sure of what was happening.

The members of the Assault Group called out the all-clear in turn, when they were happy that their targets were going to pose no threat. One of the team opened the door through which the two Triad members had tried to escape. One by one, the targets were moved out of the lab, into the care of the SDU men from the back-up team, who lined them up on the ground while they waited for the NB team to arrive.

Ben and Richard arrived shortly after the Narcotics Bureau men. Under their supervision, the suspects were searched by SDU for weapons. The NB officers would search their belongings for anything which could be used as evidence. Keith was standing at the door of the shed. The two older men approached him. Keith spoke to Ben Hung first. 'Target is secure, sir. I am ready to hand the scene of crime over to you and your men.'

'Thank you Keith. NB now has control of the scene.'

With that formality over, Ben would later make an entry in Keith's notebook to the effect that he had taken over the scene at this time. It was at moments like this that the SDU men were reminded that they were still policemen, even if their job was more akin to that of a soldier.

Richard allowed Ben to enter the building with his men and turned his attention to his own subordinates. Keith looked relaxed, but Richard knew that the blood would still be coursing through the young man's veins. 'So, how do you think it went?'

Keith smiled. 'Strange one. Boss. As I engaged the first man in the building, I had this strong urge to shoot. I had a real moment of indecision when I saw he had no weapon. It only lasted for a fraction of a second, but it gave me a nasty feeling.'

Richard nodded his head. 'Yes, we train largely on the assumption that the bad guys are going to try to kill us when we go through the door. When we come across some poor bastard who is shitting himself, it throws us off a beat. If we have more of these gigs, we had better think about some specific training for them. Of course, we still have to assume that the guy in our sights is a potential threat, but we can't prosecute a corpse.

'The one thing that worries me is that if we do this a lot, the training for our primary mission might suffer. I don't want the guys to get soft when doing an assault. If they start to assume that the bad guys will be unarmed, then this sort of op becomes counter-productive.'

Keith nodded his agreement with his Team Commander's assessment of the situation. 'Everything went smoothly apart from that. The guys did their jobs well and no one got hurt. I think most of the evidence is intact as well, though a couple of glass beakers may have been smashed as our guys went after the last two. The frame charge worked pretty well, but it was a bit of a tight squeeze. If there had been someone with a weapon and the nerve to point it in the right direction, we could have been in trouble.'

'Yes,' said Richard. 'We'll have to look at that. If the manufacturer doesn't produce any bigger units, we might have a go at making our own. The idea is certainly sound. What about the dust? Did the water affect it?'

'Not much,' replied Keith. 'We would still have had visibility problems without the respirators.'

Just then, Ben Hung called out to the two men, asking them to join him in the lab. Richard saw that Keith was right. The lab was pretty much intact. That was probably due to the size of the place. There was plenty of empty space, where his men had been able to move around. If there had been a clutter, the SDU Assault Group would have gone right through anything that got in their way. They were trained to be very single minded when they had an objective or a target to tackle.

Ben was standing over in a corner of the lab. One of his men was bent over a long wooden box. The Superintendent gestured to Richard and Keith. 'Come and have a look at this.'

The Bravo Team Commander peered into the open box. 'Fuck!'

'Looks like our informant was right,' said Ben.

In the box were four weapons. Two were Chinese versions of the AK47 assault rifle, the Type 56, their 30 round box magazines in place. The other two were handguns. Type 54 pistols based on the Russian Tokarev and chambered for the 7.62 x 25 round. 'Do you mind?' asked Richard, gesturing towards the weapons.

'Go ahead,' replied Ben.

Richard reached in with his gloved hands and removed one of the weapons. He removed the magazine and saw that it was loaded. Then he pulled back on the cocking lever and checked the breach. No round was expelled, so the weapon had not been ready to fire, but damn close to it. He pulled the trigger on the empty weapon and placed it and the back in the box. Richard removed the top round from the magazine and looked closely at it. 'We'll have to get the ballistics boys to check this lot out. They should be able to tell us where it all came from, but I suppose a good guess might be from across the border. This is ball ammunition, so nothing special there. Christ, if one of these had been pointing at that hole over there,' he said pointing to the damaged wall, 'our friend here would be mincemeat.'

'That's a nice picture,' said Keith. But he was thinking exactly the same thing.

Richard looked grave. 'Looks as though the game has just stepped up a few significant levels. Ben, the guys who put this place together are going to be pretty pissed off to lose this lot, but I have an awful feeling that if they were willing to leave these weapons just lying around here, there are more out there. Looks like we are going to be busy boys from now on. I don't expect that they will make the same mistake twice. Next time we come up against these weapons, they will be in the hands of someone willing to pull the trigger.'

'Well,' said Keith. 'Looks as though our training is not going to have to change that much after all.'

CHAPTER 27

Richard draped his arm across Natalie's shoulders and stared at the painting.

'So, is this good?'

Natalie turned her head to look at the face of her lover. His face had an amused look as he surveyed the canvas. 'My boyfriend the Philistine. Or so you would like everyone to believe. Do you honestly think I would have a painting in my gallery that wasn't good? Anyway, do you like it?'

It was an old question and Richard had plenty of old answers for it. There was the old "I don't know much about art, but I know what I like" tack. The truth was that he didn't know much about art, which caused him a great deal of pain. He wanted to become more enthusiastic, if for no other reason than the fact that it meant so much to the woman he loved. Richard had tried to get involved in discussions at parties, he had read about art. He just didn't get it. When people in Natalie's circle started to engage him in a deep conversation about an artist's intent with a particular piece, he just thought, well the guy is over there, why don't we go over and ask him, rather than trying to second guess someone who is in the same room. He knew he was being unfair. Art was about more than daubing some paint on a canvas. It was about emotions and ideas. It was not as though he was left cold by art, quite the contrary. Richard couldn't understand why one image would bring out strong feelings and another would leave him cold. His personality didn't like such mysteries. He liked to know why things were the way they were, how things worked. But, most of all he wanted to share Natalie's passion. So long as this eluded him, he felt that there was a barrier between them.

For Natalie, her boyfriend's search for meaning in art was both touching and amusing. She knew how much he wanted to share this part of her life, but after four years of sustained effort, she felt that it was probably a lost cause. The thing was, she loved him all the more for the fact that he would not give up on the quest for enlightenment. Not because it meant so much to him, but that she did.

'How are things going for the show?' asked the artistic dunce.

'We'll get there, but one of the artists has been refused permission to leave China for the exhibition. He has either upset someone or they are just using him to demonstrate their control to the others.'

The gallery would be showing the work of some young stars of the new Chinese movement that night. Four artists would be represented, two from Beijing, one from Shanghai and one from Tibet. The artist from Tibet was Han Chinese, but had been known in the past to speak out against oppression in the annexed country. It was not really surprising that he was the one artist who would not be making an appearance at the show that evening.

'Will you make it tonight?' asked Natalie.

'Well, I'm on call, but unless our friend decides to plant any more bombs, I should be here to let your friends tell me what an ignoramus I am.'

Natalie allowed herself a little laugh at her man's discomfort. 'My poor darling. You do try so hard. I think you just have a very low threshold of tolerance for pomposity. And I have to admit that I have a lot of pompous acquaintances. It's a price I have to pay for the line of work that I am in. The only thing that matters is that I know you are not ignorant.' Suddenly, her face became grave. 'Do you think this bombing is going to continue?'

Richard had made a decision some time before. At the start of their relationship, he had kept a lot of his work away from Natalie. He thought that he was protecting her, but it soon became apparent that Natalie's intelligence and sensitivity to his moods made her suffer even more living in ignorance of his work. Some things he couldn't tell her, he signed the Official Secrets Act every six months, but he had tried to be more open with her. She seemed to relax when she knew what was happening. She would always worry about him, but she had faith in his abilities and with knowledge, she left her imagination powerless.

'I don't see any reason why it should stop, particularly now that we have stymied one of his plans. That last one could have been very bad, darling. The first ones were very target specific. Then there was the little girl. This one, well it was indiscriminate. A lot of people would have been killed along with the primary target.

To some extent we are to blame for that. By putting security measures in place around the target, we made it more difficult to get at him without causing a lot of damage.'

'Are you any closer to finding out why this is happening?'

'No, not really. Cassius is developing some theories. It could be that we are just dealing with a crazy, but there are no notes, no signs of an ideology, no matter how twisted. Cass even thinks that it may all be about money. Knowing this town he could be right.'

'Money?' Natalie looked horrified. These acts were unspeakable in their viciousness. To suggest that the underlying cause was only money made them even more atrocious.

'Yes, Cass has been monitoring the stock price of the companies involved. He has asked Commercial Crimes Bureau to investigate any large purchases of stock after the bombings. Of course a lot of people will take advantage of significant drops in fundamentally sound companies. The market here is so volatile, that even a nasty rumour can affect a share price. It will usually bounce back, but by then the speculators have had their bite at the cherry. The CCB guys are looking for patterns, purchases that are perhaps just a little too quick, the same company popping up in all or most of the cases. Anything that might give us a lead to work on, because we have precious little at the moment. I'm afraid my side of the house isn't giving the investigators much help. We still don't know where the guy is getting his explosives from. The Army have been noticeably uncooperative in that department. Makes my blood boil when I see them close ranks like that. They still think that the British Empire is alive and well.'

Natalie looked at Richard and wondered at his passion. He couldn't get animated about the images that lined the walls of her gallery, but his work was a different matter. It wasn't so much the job itself, as the people that it affected. Whether it be the victims he encountered, or the men he worked with, Richard was as passionate in his approach as he ever was in their private moments. The bottom line was that he cared. She knew that he would never let anything happen to her if he could help it. He had his personal pain to haunt him, but it made his resolve to protect those around him all the stronger. Right now, he was hurting because he felt impotent in the face of this new threat to the community. He might feel no particular warmth towards the individuals concerned, but it was the people around them that he worried about, their families or the unfortunate bystander who dies simply because he was standing on a specific spot at a particular moment. Richard waged a war against fate as much as against the criminals in society.

Natalie leaned over and kissed him on the lips. 'Tonight you can put your cares to the back of your mind and be annoyed at all the arty types you will come across. At least you should enjoy the wine.'

'I don't know how you put up with it,' said Sarah Chan.

It was time for Natalie's weekly reminder that she was in a relationship with the wrong man. That was certainly her friend's opinion and Sarah was not one to allow her opinions to be hidden. Natalie was beginning to wonder how much longer she could put up with this.

Sarah continued. 'It was bad enough when he was doing the other job, which he would hardly talk to you about. At least that was mostly running around playing soldier. But bombs! And now, with this maniac blowing up all these good people, how long will it be before Richard ends up getting blown to bits. It's not as though there's nothing else he could do. He's a policeman for God's sake. He should think of you.'

Natalie sighed. How many times had she gone over this with her friend. 'Sarah, it's who Richard is. I knew that when I met him. It was the fact that he was different that drew me to him in the first place. Sure, I worry about him, but if I ask him to be someone other than who he is, I'm asking him to change from the man that I love. Anyway, you know as well as I do that he either wouldn't do it or would and then resent me for asking him to. He's good at what he does and he loves it.'

'Obviously more than he loves you.'

'That's not true,' said Natalie forcefully. 'In his own way he feels that he is protecting me by doing the job he does. Richard doesn't for a moment think that he is going to get killed doing his job. If he did, I don't think that he would do it any more. He's not an idiot you know.'

Sarah looked at her friend with sadness in her eyes. 'When I think of all the men you could have and you pick him. Look around this gallery. There must be a couple of dozen young, attractive, successful men who would jump at the chance of being with you. You must have had offers.'

Natalie gave a cynical laugh. 'Oh, I've had offers alright. Plenty of men ask me out, even when they know that I am in a relationship.

They try to impress me with their wealth and status in the community. They even try to put Richard down for being a policeman. That's usually when I show them the door.'

'Well, let's face it cops are not exactly very high on the social ladder, unless they are very senior and even then…'

'I wonder what that company chairman thinks of the social standing of police officers after they saved his life and that of a lot of other people?'

Sarah had a touch of venom in her voice. 'I doubt that he gave it a second thought. They were just doing their job.'

'Then that says more about him than them, doesn't it?' Natalie wondered at that moment why she considered this woman to be her friend.

Natalie had been right, the wine was excellent and all courtesy of one of the socialites attending the showing. Crystal Li was one of the beacons of Hong Kong society and it was one of her engaging quirks that she only drank one brand of champagne; Louis Roederer Cristal. Richard mentally raised his glass to her, wherever she was in this mass of people. He was trying to find a nice quiet corner and let things go on around him. Natalie was working, he would keep out of her way for now.

'You look as though you are having a really shite time.'

Richard turned at the sound of the voice. The gravelly tones brought a smile to his face before he had even seen the man who had uttered the obscene observation. Brian Steadman was a columnist with the South China Morning Post and a writer on subjects from art to politics, wine to wildlife. A bon viveur and without a doubt the single best friend that Richard had made outside the Police Force. He had met Brian through Natalie and felt his spirits rise every time his friend appeared at a social function. Life was never dull when Brian Steadman was around, particularly if, as now, he had a drink in his hand. That was pretty much all the time.

'Is it that obvious?'

'My boy, if someone had just farted in your face, you couldn't look more uncomfortable. My advice is to drink heavily.' With that Steadman downed the remaining wine in his glass and started scanning the area around him for a waiter, like some sort of booze seeking radar. It didn't take long for him to home in on his target and summoning the young man over soon had two glasses of the golden liquid in his hands. Uncharacteristically, he handed one of them to Richard.

'So, this is quite a business with the bombs. You received a nice piece of coverage when you saved the miserable hide of that dreadful bore David Rankin.'

'Yes,' said Richard with a slight grimace. 'He didn't seem too grateful. Buggered off without so much as a thank you to anyone. Just seemed to be in a huff about the fact that he had missed a photo opportunity with him at centre stage. And, he even had the gaul to complain about the damage to the building. Not that he made the complaint himself of course, it came from his company. Felt that I should have made more of an effort to prevent property damage. Nice to know your life is worth less than a bit of poured concrete.'

'Should have let the bastard be blown up, I say. You know of course that if it had been me, you and the rest of your mob would never have had to buy another drink in your lives. Of course, with your choice of profession, it might not be such an expensive way of saying thank you.' Brian raised his glass in salute to his friend with the absurd job.

'Thank you very much Brian, but with the way you fling booze down your neck, I still think I have a chance of outliving you, you old sod. How's Peter?'

Peter Wong was Brian's partner. In a town where, under certain circumstances, homosexuality was still a criminal offence, their love affair was one of the least well kept secrets around. Peter was an artist of international standing and had helped Natalie when she was starting out with the gallery. Both she and Richard had a huge soft spot for the two men, who enriched their lives by their presence. Brian was what some would describe as a "man's man". Hard drinking, an accomplished sportsman in his youth and not averse to the odd sexist comment. If there was anyone who could shatter sexual stereotypes, it was him. Peter was from a wealthy Chinese family, who had disowned him when he had announced his sexuality. They were an odd couple. The sophisticated, handsome artist and the bluff, worldly writer. Yet they had found love and acceptance in one another's arms and somehow, the couple together seemed to be more acceptable to Hong Kong society than they had ever been separately.

'Couldn't be here tonight. Had to nip off to New York for one of his own shows. He'll be in touch when he gets back and we'll have the two of you round for dinner.' When Brian spoke about Peter there was no affectation, no gay innuendo. He may put on an act with other people, but where Peter was concerned, his heart shone through the crusty exterior.

'Any clues as to who is behind the bombings?'

'Ah, I see we are wearing the journo hat now,' commented Richard.

'Just curious dear boy. You must be getting a hell of a lot of pressure from upstairs.' Brian pointed upwards with his champagne flute. 'I've heard rumblings that the other Taipans are becoming a bit unhappy with the way the Police Force is handling the matter. Their grumbling usually ends up directly in the ear of the Governor.'

'Actually, I haven't been affected, but I know a lot of the bodies in Headquarters are beginning to worry about their futures. Pensions can be such fragile things. The investigative team is probably getting the brunt of the flak. Thankfully David Lo is a good guy and seems to be protecting his men.

Political pressure is counter-productive. Particularly in a case like this. It's not as though they can haul in any poor bastard off the street and stitch him up. The next bomb would make it fairly plain that they had the wrong man. Anyway, Cassius To doesn't work that way and he's the guy on the sharp end.'

'Pal of your's, isn't he?'

'Yes, Cass and I go back to training school. He's one of the best there is.'

Brian looked thoughtful for a moment. 'Isn't he the officer who had to arrest a friend for membership of a Triad Society?'

Richard looked deep into his glass. 'Yeah. Lau and he were best friends. They even worked together at one point. One hell of a team. It broke Cass's heart to have to haul Lau in. They haven't spoken since the trial.

'Actually, I saw Lau the other day.'

'Oh?' Brian looked genuinely surprised by this revelation.

'He was in Queen Mary Hospital. Some members of a rival Triad Society decided to make their mark, by making their mark all over him with some sharp objects. Nasty, but not life threatening.'

'So, why were you visiting him?'

Richard looked at his friend, straight in the eyes. 'I suppose that I believe that a friend can be as human as the next guy. We all fuck-up at some stage in our lives. God knows I have. I don't forgive Lau for what he did. He probably caused a great deal of damage. But there is a bond between us which I can't really explain. When I heard what happened to him, I couldn't just ignore him. I haven't exactly been a regular visitor to Stanley Prison, but I do drop him a line from time to time.'

'Isn't that a bit awkward? I can't believe that your bosses will be too chuffed by that.'

Richard laughed. 'Too right! They told me they thought that it was inappropriate for a serving officer to associate with a known Triad.'

'What did you say?'

'I asked them if they were going to refuse half of the contributions to the Police Welfare fund and stop attending social functions attended by certain high profile chinese businessmen. Then I told them that if they were so concerned they could always fire me.'

'My boy, you are going to play that card once too often. You have a lot of friends in this town, but I gather you have your fair share of enemies as well. Mainly because you are not afraid to speak that mind of yours.'

'Perhaps you're right Brian, but if they did throw me out, I think I know of at least one person who wouldn't be too upset.' Richard looked over at Natalie, who was charming a group of potential art buyers. 'I sometimes wonder if I am being fair to her. She puts up with so much. My job must scare her stiff.'

Brian put his hand on Richard's shoulder. 'She loves you, what else is there to say. She's a strong girl and I think she knows that you are the sort of man who has to follow his heart. I for one can't see you sitting behind a desk. Not yet anyway, though if they do decide to give you the boot, I'll find you a job. You did learn to read and write, didn't you?'

'Yes, Brian,' said Richard. 'Joined-up writing and everything.'

'Bugger!' said Brian. 'You'll never make a journalist then me old son.'

CHAPTER 28

'You are sure that none of your people are responsible for these attacks?'

Vincent Lo stared at the man seated before him. Sung nodded his head, without uttering a word. As head of the largest Triad group claiming the title Sun Yee On, he was unaccustomed to being interrogated in this way. He didn't fear Vincent Lo, not in a physical sense, but he knew how much he and his fellow Chiu Chow gangsters had to lose by falling from favour within the Circle.

Vincent continued his probing. 'And you have heard nothing about these bombings, or who might be responsible?'

Sung at last decided to speak. 'Nothing. It really is of no concern to us. It makes no difference whether these Gwailos live or die. It would not affect our business interests in any way.' By "business interests" he meant drugs, gambling, prostitution and extortion, among other activities.

'Yet it seems strange to me that you have no knowledge of these acts whatsoever. With the number of eyes and ears that you have in every corner of this city, how is it that you are so completely in the dark?'

Sung looked hard at Vincent. 'What did the heads of the other groups have to say?' He meant the other Triad leaders with whom he held a fragile truce when conducting Circle business. 'Did their eyes see more, or their ears hear whispers of these things?'

Vincent Lo turned and looked out over the busy harbour. 'No, they know nothing at all. I cannot understand it. Someone is profiting from these killings, yet no one seems to know anything about them. It is as though they were being perpetrated by ghosts.'

'Maybe that is the case,' said Sung. 'You assume that a Chinese must be behind the bombings. What if it was a Gwailo conspiracy. The targets have all been Gwailo.' He used to the derogatory term for westerners, Gwailo, literally "ghost man, or devil man". The word had achieved such common usage that it was even used by Hong Kong expatriates to describe themselves. An example of the abused taking the sting out of an insult by adopting it themselves.

Vincent shook his head. 'No, I have contacts in the Gwailo criminal community, what there is of it. They would betray themselves too easily and they do not have the resources to mount such a campaign. Even if terrorist groups outside the Territory were responsible, we would know. The Circle acts as bankers for most of the major groups worldwide. They would be jeopardising a great deal of money and a valuable resource by causing waves in the financial markets here. We have to identify who would profit from these deaths.'

'There is of course another possibility,' said Sung. 'Our comrades across the border. We are not exactly their favourite people. If they were attempting to destabilise Hong Kong, we would not be made aware of their activities.'

Vincent considered this for a moment. It had crossed his mind before, but he could not find a rational reason why the authorities in Beijing would take action such as this. There were plenty of other ways they could cause a lot more damage in the Territory. Shut off the water supply for one. 'I doubt that this is official, but of course there is always the possibility of individual action being at work here. We have contacts at very high levels within the Party in Beijing. I know that they keep us at arms length and only tell us what they want us to know, but to mount a bombing campaign like this makes no sense. If it were uncovered that Beijing were responsible, it would make the negotiations over the 1997 handover even more difficult. There is absolutely nothing to gain by it. In fact, that is the problem that I have with the whole thing. I can't see anything worth the risk. There has been a lot of speculative buying of shares in the companies involved, after the bombings, but you would expect that. There is no single large buyer. There seems no reason for it.'

Sung stood up. He was announcing that this audience was over. 'Then perhaps we are dealing with a madman.'

'A well equipped and skillful madman,' said Vincent. 'No, I can't believe that it is as simple as that. Sung, please get your people to start looking into this thing. It has to stop. It does the Circle no good. Sooner or later the Police are going to start digging into the backgrounds of the business rivals of the targets. I don't want them to start getting close to our group. We profit from our anonymity. Scrutiny by the authorities could mean an eventual end to our association. None of us want that, do we?'

He still suspects me, thought Sung. 'I will try to uncover something. Perhaps now that all the Triads in Hong Kong are looking, we might find something.' Sung just let Vincent know that he realised that every other gangster within the Circle would have had this conversation. At least they had better have had the same treatment.

The combined resources of the Triads made for a formidable intelligence gathering tool. If there was any chance of uncovering this conspiracy, if indeed there was one, the criminal bloodhounds would succeed.

When he was alone, Vincent Lo withdrew a file from his desk. He opened the brown cover and spread out the documents inside. The sheets bore the names of companies and columns of numbers. All these companies had bought significant amounts of shares in the affected businesses, just at the point when their share price plummeted after the bombings. None of the purchases on their own would make a change to the control structure of the companies. His company and others within the Circle had made purchases at the time. They all had people whose job it was to look for opportunities within the volatile market that was the Hong Kong Stock Exchange. Many of the company names were unfamiliar to him, but that was not the thing that had caught his attention. One familiar name was missing and it nagged at Vincent. The one man he knew who hated the British more than anyone. The one man who would love to get control of British companies. A man who would normally jump at any chance of financial gain. A small deformed businessman called Li Keung.

The girl placed another ticket into the plastic cup. Another "Ladies Drink". Another thimbleful of Coke costing almost as much as a bottle of Scotch. Of course, you weren't buying a drink, you were buying the girl's time. Puerile conversation and perhaps the odd flash of tit. And company. Loneliness seeks strange companions. Wanchai was the most famous of the red light districts in Hong Kong. Immortalised in the "World of Suzie Wong", a world that probably never really existed, except in the minds of lonely and romantic expatriates. Describe that romantic picture to a Hong Kong Chinese and he would have been hard pressed to know what you were talking about. This was commerce pure and simple. Romance lay elsewhere.

One of the oddities of Wanchai was that it lay right on the doorstep of Police Headquarters. The "strip" was easy walking distance for thirsty cops. Expensive drinks and nostalgic, if faded reminders of lost youth lay behind the thick velvet curtains over the entrances to the bars. For most, it was a bit of fun, their profession left outside, their eye blind to the reality that lay within. For some, it was family. In times past, they would have been put into a taxi by the mama san, when she had been their favourite bar-girl, with almost the entire contents of their wallet intact. Policemen were generally treated well in the bars, so long as they behaved themselves and didn't cause too much trouble. For the bar owners, it was polite insurance. If there was trouble, having some tame cops on the premises did no harm. More than one situation had been prevented from turning bad by one of the Gwailos propping up the bar.

Some on the other hand were bad news and were only welcome because of the money they spent. Jack Garland fell into this category. When he had been a serving officer in the Force, he had made the lives of the bar-girls misery. He didn't expect to pay for drinks, or anything else that took his fancy. With a reputation for violence, the sight of him walking into the bar was enough to provoke a sudden epidemic among the staff. Bar owners would have to remind the girls of the debt that they still owed the bar and that to refuse a customer was not an option. Nowadays, he no longer had any influence in the bars and would not have been welcome if he had not been in the company of a regular.

The Panda was one of the smaller bars in "the Wanch". It had yet to succumb to the introduction of Filippina and Thai dancers. This was an old style Wanchai bar and attracted men whose main preoccupation was drinking. The bar-girls were somewhat vintage, but some new blood was injected from time to time. For Bill Blair, this was the place to start an evening in the Wanch off. When his funds were low, it would also be the place to end up, as the drinks were a little cheaper than some of the other bars and he would get less hassle from the girls.

Bill was a Chief Inspector of Police. He had been a Chief Inspector of Police for almost twenty years and would remain so until the day he retired. He no longer bothered to even try to present himself before a promotion board. Any thoughts of becoming a Gazetted Officer had been shattered the day one of his bosses had let him read his Record of Service. Too much damage had already been done. Once an ambitious, if none too bright CID man, what was left was a bitter remnant of a bygone age. The cops had become smarter and less keen on the bottle. People like Bill Blair were being left in their wakes. Jack Garland saw himself in Bill, only he had been smart enough to get out while the going was good. Bill had never been able to take the plunge and now marked time until he could retire with his pension. Placed in jobs where his apathy could cause no harm, he was one of the forgotten men of a Force trying to ready itself for an uncertain future. With a lot of time on his hands, Blair was the font of all knowledge, or at least gossip within the Force. He was an old friend of Garland's and his main source of information about the activities of his former colleagues.

'Richard Stirling. Know anything about him?'

Blair replied without taking his eyes off the breasts in front of him. 'The EOD guy. Of course.'

Garland realised that this was going to be a long night. His companion would want to suck as much hospitality out of him as possible. He had promised Blair that the evening was on him, but Bill was obviously afraid that it would come to an abrupt end when Garland had the information that he required. The truth was that Jack was looking forward to a night in the Wanch, something he hadn't done in quite some time. He planned to get out of here as soon as he had the information he needed and move the party to somewhere with fresher and more active meat.

'So, what do you know about him?'

Blair realised that it was time to pay the piper and turned to face his ex-colleague. 'Used to be SDU. Tough fucker by all accounts. Of course, never was a real policeman.' He left out the "not like us Jack" part. 'Too busy running around the hills playing soldier. Made CI on the back of it, but he wasn't too smart our boy Richard. He'll be like me, stuck in the rank.'

'How so?' Garland's curiosity had been aroused now. He felt that he was about to get something on Stirling, something he might be able to use to his advantage.

'He left SDU under a bit of a cloud. Volunteered for the EOD job, even though he knew that he might never be promoted. If you ask me, he was probably trying to find a hole to hide in.'

'Pretty high profile hole!' exclaimed Garland.

'Yeah, with this bombing business he is making the papers a lot, especially after the last one. I've only met the man once, but he seemed personable enough. Bloody University graduate though, but I suppose I can forgive him that as he wasn't a real policeman. He chose the paramilitary side of the Force, so I can't complain about him too much. Doesn't take himself too seriously and has a healthy disrespect for senior officers. Bloody lovely girlfriend. She runs an art gallery up Hollywood Road way. Stirling has a lot of friends outside the Police Force, mainly through her I think. But he's still one of the boys. Popular in the main, although he has his fair share of enemies. Don't think it worries him too much. Has a reputation for not giving a shit about anything. He'll happily tell a *Gingsi* to go fuck himself, if he thinks he is in the right. Very protective of his men. That's part of what got him kicked out of SDU.'

This was it, thought Garland. 'Tell me about that.'

'Well, about three or four years ago…'

CHAPTER 29

Richard Stirling. My enemy has a name as well as a face. Yes, he is my enemy, but also my rival. An equal of sorts. He has trained to build the same types of device that I use in my work. He may even share the vision. He may be able to appreciate the beauty of what I do. Garland has found out much about this maverick cop. An unusual man, not the bureaucrat that I had imagined. A man willing to bend, if not break the rules in order to achieve his goals. Loyal to those who deserve it and ruthless with those who do not. A chequered past. He has fallen from grace, only to climb back up to a position of respect and authority. He is his own man, not afraid of rank or position. He is dangerous to my plans, for he will not allow himself to be drawn into a situation he is not happy with. No pressure seems to reach him. He knows how to say no, even to those who expect only yes. It will be a challenge to kill this man.

How do you reach a man like this? His personal safety will be secondary to those he is sworn to protect and those he loves. A passionate man, who may allow himself to be drawn into a trap to avenge an injustice. How much is he ruled by his passions, I wonder? What would I have to do to make him act hastily, out of passion, rather than reason. Touch someone he loves perhaps? Loyalty makes him vulnerable. His actions have shown him to be reckless with his own security when it comes to the lives of his friends. He is a man who believes in futile gestures. Just how far would he go?

A direct approach is called for in the first instance. I want to see just how good this man is. Are his instincts strong enough to protect him, or is he merely a skilled mechanic? If I test him, then I will see if he is worth pursuing. If not, he will no longer be a problem and I will be able to focus on the original task. A task which I have to say is starting to bore me. This Stirling is a welcome diversion from the tedium that my assigned job has become. I feel as though I am going over well trod ground. The security on the targets has made it impossible for me to be as ingenious in the application of my art as I would like. Some might think that I am making excuses for a lack of imagination. They would not understand. I could have disposed of the rest in much more mundane ways, but I chose to be creative in the way that I brought about their demise. I gave them the gift of my talent at its brightest.

This man is just the challenge that I require to bring my gifts back on stream. Assuming of course that I am not overestimating this Stirling. We shall soon see.

Garland has been tasked with finding out more about this man. I can tell that he is suspicious about my motives. He has expressed his opinion that I should be concentrating on the other targets, particularly after the failure of the last device. I told him that the device did not fail, it was mere chance that the police were alerted to the possibility of a threat. Sometimes the Gods are against us. Time seems to be a problem for Garland and his master. Their schedule has been affected by the missed attack and the increased security around the rest of the targets. They should have accounted for that when they drew up their plans. I cannot be held responsible for their shortcomings. Perhaps it will be sooner than I thought that I shall have to turn my attention to Mr Garland and his mysterious paymaster. The only mystery lies in Garland's mind. For now, he is useful, but not indispensable. I shall not make him aware of this fact, however. Let him think that he is in control. When the time comes, I want it to be a surprise. I shall take pleasure in that brief look of realisation as his fate catches up with him, courtesy of a few pounds of explosive. In the mean time, he can find out what I need to know about Chief Inspector Richard Stirling.

I already have the basis of a plan of attack. It will be simple, but will test his abilities. If he survives, he will have proven himself to be a worthy opponent. Then the information supplied by Garland will become important. It will give me the opportunity to develop a campaign to break and finally defeat my new adversary. Garland will of course be annoyed. This course of action will distract me from the attacks on the Taipans, but I shall persuade him that it is necessary in order to distract the authorities sufficiently to open up the protection around the primary targets. He may still harbour doubts, but what can he do? He, or rather they need me. They have no alternative if they are to execute their plan to its completion. I wield the power, no matter what they think. I shall have my way.

So, Richard, I think I may call you Richard, as it is my firm intention to end your life, my friend. Our game begins.

CHAPTER 30

The shopkeepers in Peking road were arguing with the incident commander when Richard arrived on the scene. It was quite a picture. One of Tsim Sha Tsui's busiest streets deserted, cordoned-off back at the Hyatt Hotel, almost right back to the main thoroughfare of Nathan Road. A crowd had gathered behind the cordon line at all the access points. The cordon was well back from the street where the device was located, Ashley Road.

'I don't like it,' said Richard as soon as he stepped out of the vehicle, more to himself than the police officers gathered around him. The call had come in to the Command and Control Centre more than forty-five minutes earlier. An anonymous tip that there was a bomb planted at the head of Ashley Road, a no-through road. Crawling through the traffic leading to the cross-harbour tunnel, Richard had been putting together a picture of the incident in his mind, using the available information. It just didn't make sense. What was the target? The only things at that end of the street were offices and an Italian restaurant. Was someone pissed off about the tagliatelle al funghi? A little alarm was sounding in Richard's head. It was one he had heard before, usually just before he was about to land in the shit.

Richard pulled out a pair of binoculars from the cab of the Transit. He looked towards the head of the cul-de-sac, about a hundred meters away. There it was. A package sitting on the pavement. It didn't appear to pose a threat to anything in particular. Even if the thing was packed with high explosive, as long as people were kept away from the area, the structural damage was not going to be significant. Plenty of broken windows, but not much else. The same question ran through Richard's head like a skipping record; what is the target?

The caller had said that the device would go off at four o'clock, in about another forty minutes. Plenty of time for Richard to have a go at the thing, assuming the information was correct. If not, it didn't matter too much, he could send the Ro-Veh, the remote control vehicle up there and blow the shit out of it without placing himself at any risk whatsoever. Plenty of access, an easy approach for the robot. All he had to do was sit where he was and man the controls. What is the target?

Richard looked around him. This was the obvious place for a command post, wasn't it? He turned to the Emergency Unit Inspector in the group who had met him. 'When you arrived on the scene, did you search the area around the CP for any other devices?'

The young expatriate officer looked a little flustered. 'Eh, actually, no sir, we were too busy closing off the area and moving the people out.'

'Get everyone the fuck out of here,' ordered Richard. There was no anger in his voice, but very definite urgency. 'Get them behind the cordon line. Ah Pau, take the Transit back up there, towards Canton Road. At least a hundred meters.'

Ah Pau nodded and headed for the drivers door of the EOD vehicle. Suddenly, he stopped and turned to look at his boss. 'What about you?'

'I think I will have a little look around.'

Ah Pau looked anxious. '*Daai Lo*, do you think that is a good idea? Why not let the EU guys do it, there are more of them and they should have done it in the first place.'

Richard smiled at the concern of his friend. 'They can join me once they have cleared the rest of the personnel out of here. I promise I won't hang around, I just want a quick look.'

Reluctantly, Ah Pau climbed aboard the vehicle. He knew there was no point arguing with Richard, all it would achieve would be to lengthen the time that he spent in the danger area.

As people and vehicles were moved away from the vicinity of the command post, Richard headed for the small park just across the road from where he had alighted from his van. It was typical of those found in the urban area. A small patch of grass and concrete, with swings for children and seats for their parents, old people and drug traffickers. The oasis was bounded by a line of low bushes. Richard's eyes scanned the area, looking for anything that might hold an explosive device. He rapidly became frustrated at the lack of results from his search. Time was ticking away and he had already spent too long in an area which might hold a bomb. Just as he was about to join Ah Pau at the new Command Post, his eyes wandered across the street, close to where the Emergency Unit vehicle had been parked.

No, he thought, it couldn't be. Richard ran over to the dirty yellow trash can. It was like thousands to be found in the street of Hong Kong. It became unlike any other when Richard peaked through one of the large semi-circular openings in its side. Instead of discarded fast food containers, Coke cans and other assorted detritus, he saw something which had him running in the direction of his vehicle. Now he knew the answer to the question that had been plaguing him since his arrival…he was the target.

'Cheeky bastard,' said Richard.

Ah Pau looked worried, although his boss showed no signs of anxiety. 'What is it? What did you find?'

'Not sure yet, Ah Pau. Looks as though our friend is starting to repeat himself, either that or someone is copying his style. If I am not mistaken, there is a bloody great bomb in that rubbish bin, the one our friends in EU parked right next to. Only one way to find out.'

Richard checked his watch. 'Well, there's no way of telling when this thing might go off. Get me the Hook and Line set, will you?' Richard always tried to look for patterns in the timing of devices, based on the time warnings were given, or devices were discovered. He avoided approaching suspect objects at times like, on the hour, a quarter past, half past, quarter to. All the chronological "round numbers". People tended to be tidy about things like setting timers, of course the really smart ones knew this and might set a bomb to go off at an odd time, but you played the odds and did anything which might increase your chances of walking away from the device in one piece.

Ah Pau returned with a reel of rope and a wooden box. The Allen Hook and Line set was the most primitive of contraptions and one of the most useful. Richard opened the box and extracted what looked like a large karabiner. This he attached to a shackle at the end of the rope. While Ah Pau attended the reel, Richard ventured back towards the now empty street and the trash can. When Ah Pau had been getting the Hook and Line, Richard had been planning his route and the way he was going to tackle the problem. He reached a lamp-post on the opposite side of the street to the trash can and passed the rope around it. This would allow him to pull the can in the desired direction, hopefully with the desired result. Quickly, he moved towards the suspicious can. The rope was becoming heavy as it played out from the reel, plus the friction caused by the lamp-post meant that Richard had to put a fair amount of effort into his forward progress. On reaching the can, he attached the end of the rope to the handle which allowed the belly of the can to be removed for emptying. Happy that it was secure, he high-tailed it back to the Command Post and the relieved features of his number two.

Between them, Richard and Ah Pau could have moved the trash can by pulling the line, but Richard had something more in mind. He attached the rope to an anchor point on the rear of his vehicle and explained to Ah Pau what he had in mind. Richard watched the can as Ah Pau got into the Transit and started the engine. Richard guided Ah Pau, getting him to take up the slack in the rope. When he was happy, he signalled his number two to get ready. Ah Pau revved the engine hard, with the clutch depressed. Richard made a rapid gesture with his arm and Ah Pau released the clutch, sending the van jolting forward. Almost as soon as he had begun, Ah Pau came to a stop and exited the vehicle. He found Richard with a satisfied grin on his face. Down the deserted road, they could see the trash can on its side and the belly section lying clear of the shell. The sudden "yank" had achieved the desired result.

'Well,' said Richard, 'at least we know there isn't an anti-handling device.'

Slowly, the squat metal caterpillar made its way down the ramps at the rear of the vehicle. A short length of cable connected the robot to the control box in Ah Pau's hands. While the number two was unloading the Ro-Veh, Richard busied himself with preparing the weapons that he would attach to the arm of the robot and would use to disable the suspected bomb. From the look he had managed to get at the device, it seemed to be covered in plastic sheeting, so he had no idea what the case was made of. It could be metal, plastic or wood. He was betting that the material would not be too thick, or strong. From the look of the device, the trash can itself was probably intended to provide any shrapnel. A secondary case would be redundant. Richard finished filling the Pig-sticks with water and placed the end-caps on the barrels. These he handed to Ah Pau, who secured the weapons in their clamps on the robot arm. The Ro-Veh had already been connected to the reel of cable which would link it to the console which Richard was now readying.

The control console was self-contained, allowing Richard to move the Ro-Veh via a joy-stick and watch through one or both of the vehicle's cameras on a black and white television monitor. There was a great deal of skill involved in maneuvering the robot, particularly in the confined space of buildings. Today's little trip would be an altogether easier matter, in the open space of the street. Still, Richard had to judge just where to position the weapons attached to the arm of the remote vehicle. As the target was quite large and he had no idea of the internal structure of the device, he was going to hit it with two Pig-sticks simultaneously. Blow the shit out of it. He could have X-rayed the object, but that was another manual approach to the device and he felt that he had been up close and personal enough with this thing already.

When at all possible, firing two Pig-sticks at once on the Ro-Veh was to be avoided. The vehicle was more maneuverable, but less robust than the model it had replaced, the venerable "Wheelbarrow". The arm might be damaged by the double recoil, but if Richard used only one weapon, he might detonate the device and destroy the remote vehicle altogether. The only other option was to manually position two Pig-sticks and that was again an unwarranted risk.

Ah Pau gave him the thumbs-up that the weapons were secure and armed. He had screwed the breaches onto the Pig-sticks and placed the ends of the firing cables in the terminals. The cables he had then lashed to the robot arm with duct tape and ensured that they would not foul in the tracks of the vehicle. On the end of the barrels of the Pig-sticks were loops of tape, into which were stuck lengths of cardboard. These allowed Richard to judge when the weapons were in the right place. As he approached the device with the arm, judging distance through the monocular camera was difficult. When he saw the card move, as it touched the device, he would know that he had reached the ideal stand-off distance for the weapons. With a slight lurch, the Ro-Veh set off towards its target.

Richard sat in the rear of the Transit. The cover ensured that the small screen was free from glare and that his actions were hidden from the eyes of the public and press. All eyes would be on the small metal creature that was making its way towards the eviscerated bin.

It had been a while since Richard had used the little robot on a job. It took time to get ready and he usually wanted to get ahead with things. Today, he felt strangely happy that his little metal friend was taking the risks for him. It was an odd sensation, being back from the sharp end of the action, but on this hot day, Richard was glad not to be making the lonely walk back to the device. His little voice was telling him that he was in exactly the right place.

The innards of the bin started to become larger and larger on the monitor screen. Richard maneuvered the Ro-Veh to approach the target from what would have been the side of the bin. Richard wanted to angle the shot through the package. The metal container would provide a reflective surface, bouncing the high velocity surge of water, causing even more disruption to the device. The open ends of the bin would allow plenty of room for the components to separate. A back-stop could be useful sometimes, but on this occasion, Richard felt that there was a danger that firing into the top end of the bin might actually hold the circuitry together and that was the last thing he wanted. This package was going to be blown to hell and back.

As he got closer, Richard slowed the progress of the remote vehicle. From his position. He could see the vehicle and the bin. He stopped the Ro-Veh and moved his attention to the controls which would extend the arm. The targeting camera which he was using was on the arm itself. He could have put another camera on the body of the vehicle, but he felt that he could drive the machine with one camera under the present circumstances. If the damn bomb blew up in the face of his mechanical friend, he might as well save one of the cameras. Using the monitor, he moved the arm until it was pointing the Pig-sticks at an angle, down into the body of the device. Happy with the set-up, he returned to the track controls and moved the Ro-Veh forward, very slowly. The machine stopped and rocked slightly on its tracks. Richard eased the arm forward, watching the lengths of card on the end of the weapons for his visual cue that they were in the right place. It happened very suddenly. The card bent as it struck the body of the device and Richard quickly let go of the control. He gave it a quick visual check and then told Ah Pau to inform the Incident Commander that there would be a "controlled explosion" in about two minutes time. At least he hoped it would be controlled.

Ah Pau returned and gave him the thumbs-up that the cordon was ready and he could go ahead with the attack. Richard flicked a switch to arm the Pig-sticks. Ah Pau had wired them through the same firing circuit, so that they would go off at the same time. Richard yelled out a warning. 'FIRING!' and pressed the button.

The bang was fairly muted and this told Richard that at least the device had not gone off, assuming that it was a real bomb. He grabbed his binoculars and surveyed the scene. The Ro-Veh was still in one piece. That much was good news. There was a lot of debris. On the Ro-Veh monitor, he couldn't see much detail, but he returned to the console and pulled the vehicle back slightly. This gave him a better look at the scene, but he still couldn't see much in the belly of the can. He would have to take a little walk.

Richard found what he was looking for and placed the items separately into plastic evidence bags. Detonator, power supply, timer and explosive. The latter had worried him. Homemade by the look of it. That didn't fit. Could he have another bomber to worry about? Somehow, he didn't think so. There was something about the device. It was clean, well constructed and seemed to have the same "signature" as the others. Richard's instincts told him that this was the work of the same man that they were chasing. The analysis of the explosive would be interesting. The quality of the substance would let them know just how skilled this man was. It was one thing to construct explosive devices with commercial components, but the true artists could make a bomb out of just about anything.

Ah Pau looked on as his boss and friend sifted through the debris of the device. Why wouldn't he wear the bomb suit? The older man worried about Richard. They had been through a lot together Ah Pau felt that he was taking the sort of unnecessary risks that he would have bollocked one of his men for when they had been in SDU. You always tried to minimise the risks that were inherent in any job. It was common sense. To take unnecessary risks was stupid and Ah Pau knew that Richard was not a stupid man. So why?

Richard popped as much of the explosive as he could gather up into the evidence bag and started to stand up. He wasn't sure what came first, the searing pain in the side of his head, or the sound of the explosion. Of course it must have been the flash, though he was only vaguely aware of that. These thoughts ran through Richard's head as he lay on the ground, stunned. The blast itself was too far away to have given him anything more than a nasty fright, but the shrapnel had sliced through his temple and given him a nasty knock. Ah Pau was with him in seconds.

'*Daai Lo*, are you OK? Stay still, don't move.'

The sergeant checked Richard for wounds, other than the obvious gash in his head. Ah Pau reached into a pouch on his belt and took out a wound dressing. He tore open the packaging and took hold of the ends of the bandage. Pulling the ends apart, he shook the wound dressing, making it unravel itself. Head wounds always bled badly and generally looked worse than they were, but there was always the danger that the brain had taken a jolt, so it was best to treat head wounds with care. Ah Pau placed the dressing pad against Richard's wound and started to wind the bandage around his head. As he was doing this, he told one of the Emergency Unit officers to call for an ambulance. Richard started to protest, but was told to lie still by his worried friend.

'Guess the other device was getting a little impatient with me,' said the still stunned EOD man. 'Two devices. Our friend doesn't do things by half measures. Thorough bastard.' That was enough talk. Suddenly Richard felt very tired.

CHAPTER 31

So, the man has instincts. Sharp and focussed. Perhaps I have found a worthy opponent after all. He is a risk taker, this one. He was lucky today. The Gods were smiling on him. He will need more than divine patronage to defeat me. I have my own Gods on my side, the Gods of detonation and cunning.

I could hardly believe it when the police vehicle pulled up right next to the second device. In a way, I cursed them, for this gift was not for them. Luckily this Stirling had his wits about him, otherwise the plodding cops could have inadvertently foiled my plans. Stirling might still have been killed, but I would never have known if he would have been worthy of my attention. Now I know.

He looked puzzled as he searched through the remains of my beautiful bomb. I cannot say that I enjoyed watching him vandalise my work, but I could see that the explosive was causing him concern. Yes, my friend, I do not need to rely on a supply of plastic explosive to carry out my work. A lesson which Garland should learn. It is merely an opportune convenience for me not to have to create my own. The task gives me pleasure, but there is a price to pay in time and effort. There is also the possibility that impure ingredients will affect the result. No matter how skilful the chef, he cannot create a masterpiece with second rate ingredients. In the past I have been taken advantage of in this regard, but never twice by the same person. I take revenge very seriously.

The coolness he displayed, in not immediately attacking the second device, was impressive and disappointing. Having determined that he was the primary target, he may have thought that the other package was a hoax. After all, there was no logical target for that device. I was a little kind to him in that respect, if there had been an obvious target for the primary device, he may not have thought to look for a secondary one. But, then again, he has displayed good instincts and to have changed the game-plan so drastically on him would have been less than sporting and the British do so love their sport. Well, my friend, the game has well and truly begun.

CHAPTER 32

'What the fuck is going on?'

Li paced the deck of his yacht, his footfalls echoing the fury in his voice. Garland watched the robed figure with a lump in his throat. He would have to choose his words carefully here. This, he was sure, was one of the moments when his future hung in the balance. He focussed on the diminutive figure now staring at him. Although the sun was shining Li wore a thick toweling robe. He never exposed his twisted body to the members of his staff. That privilege was reserved for his lovers. At least that is what Garland assumed, or did Li make the boys adopt positions where they would not see his deformed body, merely provide him with a receptacle for his lust. The mounting fury on the face of his employer dragged Garland away from his bizarre reverie.

'Well?' shouted the businessman, barely containing his fury.

'He is out of control. The cop at the scene was the one he had me find out about. I think he is going off on his own little adventure here. He assured me that Stirling posed a threat to the operation, but I am now sure that my doubts were justified and that he is playing some kind of game at our expense.'

'Really?' Li made no attempt to hide the sarcasm in his voice. 'You have come to this masterful conclusion all on your own? Well of course he is out of control, that much is fucking obvious. What I want to know is why you are not keeping on top of the situation and what you intend to do about it.'

Garland swallowed, to try and clear the billiard ball that was currently blocking off his windpipe. He needed to breathe. He needed air, so that his brain could catch up with the conundrum of his own salvation. His own body was mocking him. 'I…I will give him one more chance to start focussing on the operation and then, if he has failed to comply, I think that we should terminate our relationship with him.'

Li took a deep breath and turned his back on Garland. As he did so, the Englishman took a deep breath of his own, one of relief. Somehow, he never felt quite as uncomfortable when those dark eyes were not piercing his soul. If he had his way, Garland would have conducted every interview with his boss looking at the back of the latter's head.

'To have come this far, only to be thwarted by a madman,' said Li, half to himself.

Garland thought that the idea had been the work of a madman from the beginning, but he decided to keep the irony to himself. This was not a situation where humour would win him any points.

'Do you really think that he can be brought round?' Li was starting to think rationally again, the fury slowly subsiding.

Garland thought carefully about his reply. Often he would give his employer the answer which he thought the little man wanted, rather than the one which expressed his true feelings. On this occasion, candor was called for. 'Honestly, no. I think he is too deeply immersed in this grand theatre that he has conceived. I do not know what the objective is, but I think he is enjoying himself too much to be of further use to us. He should disappear.'

Li turned to look at Garland. As he did so, he thought he caught a look in the other man's face. Almost a wince. That pleased Li. Fear was an emotion that he liked to instil in as many people as possible, even those close to him. 'Give him one more chance.' As Li spoke, he could see that this was not the order that Garland wanted. His head of security wanted to kill this man. Badly. Li would hold back that particular pleasure for now. A morbid carrot to be dangled before his minion. In fact, he was not sure whether he had the power to order the bomber's termination. Li would have to ensure that when the time came it was an order that would not come back to haunt him. After all, the bomber was a "gift" to aid the project. Still, Li had to give his subordinate the impression that all was under his control. 'If your attempt fails, I will be the one to decide when and how he is to be disposed of. His demise must leave no trail.'

Garland was somewhat put out by this last statement. When had any of his garbage disposals ever come back to the "great man". He was a professional. The fact that he enjoyed his work was a bonus. 'Whatever you say, sir.'

Li looked at his security chief. He could see that there was a battle going on below the surface of the man's obedience. How long could he maintain Garland's loyalty, he wondered. Money was important to the Englishman, he had proved that in the way he enthusiastically went along with the corrupt practices rampant in the Police Force when he had first joined. He had reinforced the fact with the relish with which he expedited actions on Li's behalf. Actions which might strain the moral limits of most men, but not Garland. He would do anything for money. Anything? Was Li really sure of that any more? Sometimes he had the impression that a "palace coup" might be brewing, but to what end? Li had his organisation so tightly drafted that without him, the whole structure would collapse. In any normal business environment that would be a completely unacceptable state of affairs, but in the egocentric, paranoid world in which Li lived, it could be no other way. Without Li, Garland was out of business.

'Have some lunch,' said Li, in a milder tone of voice. Time to play the sympathetic employer. He had brandished the stick, but he knew that the carrot always worked better with Garland. A carrot with lots of zeros. 'I have some calls to make. Relax and enjoy the sun.' The aft deck of the yacht was laid out with a large buffet, far too much food for the two men, but excess had never worried Li, as long as it was for his own benefit. Leaving the slightly less disgruntled Englishman to enjoy his food, Li walked into the main salon of the large vessel and headed down into the bowels of the boat.

Li's Superyacht was a one-off. Built in the Hudong Shipyard in Shanghai, it had cost a fraction of the price Li would have had to pay the Italian boat-builders who had originated the design. There had been some rough edges when Li had taken possession, but they had been easily ironed out by a boat-yard in Hong Kong.

The design had come into the hands of the Chinese shipyard courtesy of the energetic libido of a salesman Italmarine. On business in Shanghai, trying to sell his company's designs to the rapidly expanding government shipyards, the Italian had fallen under the spell of a leggy Shanghaiese goddess. The working girl had easily persuaded the lustful Italian to take her back to his hotel room. Before matters reached a climax, police burst through the door and arrested the salesman and the prostitute. Sex outside marriage was an offense in China, whether money exchanged hands or not.

While the honey-trapped salesman was being given a hard time, the girl counted the money and the plans for Italmarine's latest products were being copied.

After a brief appearance before a magistrate, the confused Italian was fined and sent packing, with a warning and a stamp in his passport, the characters of which translated as "Fornicator". This fact he would hide from his wife, but take great pleasure in relating to his male friends over several drinks.

The original design had been changed somewhat, not by Li, but by the men who had sponsored the construction of the vessel for him. They had included some non-standard equipment in the package.

The communications room of the floating palace was like something out of a nuclear submarine. The windowless room had subdued lighting, allowing the displays on the equipment to be easily read and to ease the strain on the eyes of the crewman who monitored them. When Li had entered, he had dismissed the radio operator and now sat in the semi-darkness on his own.

Li faced a high resolution monitor. Leaning forward in the chair which was always kept at the right height for his small frame, he started to type commands into the keyboard in front of him. These instructions connected the satellite communications system to a Chinese satellite in geostationary orbit over southern China. It took a few seconds for the transaction between his computer and that on board the satellite to be completed and several more for his call to be linked through the ground station outside Beijing, through to the terminal of the man he wanted to contact. Li watched the cursor on the screen blink. A visual metronome, his heart seemed to beat in time with it. Li knew fear when he spoke to this man. Good news was all that he wanted to hear. Problems were for Li to deal with. The Motherland had been good to Li and the man he was calling took every opportunity to remind him of the fact.

Some years before, Li's businesses were in trouble. Poor investment strategy and a decline in key markets had hit Li, just as the Tiger Economies of Asia were really starting to take off. Lack of foresight, conservative business methods and sheer incompetence, had nearly cost him his entire fortune. But help had been at hand. One day a man had entered his office unannounced and thereafter, Li's destiny would be forever entwined with that of the People's Republic of China. Li was baled out, at a price…loyalty.

The man he was calling had first come up with the plan. It had immediately appealed to Li's vanity. A blow against the business interests that Li blamed for his near downfall and the British, whom he loathed. In the businessman's mind, his failures had not been his fault, but that of foreign business interests who had manipulated markets and undercut him again and again with lucrative contracts. Li was a man who could never admit that he was at fault. It was his greatest weakness. One man never feared to tell Li when he was wrong and to let him know the consequences of failure. A bleep from the satellite system announced that that man was logging on to his terminal.

Li sat as straight in his chair as his twisted frame would allow. The monitor blinked into life and a figure sitting at a console came into view. The uniform was that of the People's Liberation Army. A chest full of medals proclaimed the seniority of the man wearing it. His features were grim, expecting the worst from this unexpected communication.

The PLA was a self-funding army. Government funding was kept to a minimum, the army itself had to supply everything from bullets to missiles. As a result, it had extensive business interests, everything from manufacturing to nightclubs. In recent years they had begun to invest heavily in Hong Kong, both openly and as in Li's companies, through the back door. Li's non-executive directors were the Chiefs of Staff of the Chinese military. The man on the screen was his liaison, the only person within the government that Li was allowed to contact directly. He was also, Li knew, a man who could terminate all agreements. That included Li's continued presence in the land of the living.

The face on the screen stared impassively at his monitor, which would be displaying an image of Li. The businessman wished that he could see his own image, see if he was displaying the fear that he felt. It soon became apparent that Li was expected to speak first, after all he had been the one to initiate the communication.

'Your man is behaving erratically.' As soon as he uttered the words, Li regretted the implication that his mentors were somehow at fault. Still the face on the screen looked at him without displaying an ounce of emotion. Li was becoming even more unnerved. 'That is to say, he seems to have started to act on a mission other than that for which he was recruited. His attention has been redirected away from his designated targets. He seems to be obsessed with some police officer. A bomb disposal expert. My man Garland is having difficulty controlling him.' That was better. Shift the possibility of blame towards Garland. Li knew that the men in Beijing would hold him ultimately responsible for the conduct of his employees, but there was always the chance that he could escape recrimination by offering Garland's head on a platter.

At long last the Chinese Officer leaned forward and spoke. 'Tell me everything.'

CHAPTER 33

Cassius To walked slowly down the main corridor running through the heart of the Explosive Ordnance Disposal Unit. The walls were covered with photographs of bombs and incidents involving bombs. Reconstructed devices displayed their ugly ingenuity to anyone with an eye to see and a heart to cry for the evil skills of mankind. What was it, wondered the policeman, that drove men to create bigger and better ways to destroy one another? That was what these images were all about. These creations didn't just kill people, they obliterated them. As though the objective was to wipe away any evidence that the victims ever existed. What did it take to create the sort of hate that made men want to erase their victim's existence?

'Cassius!' It was John Gray. 'Come on in, we're just about to have some coffee. Want some?'

Cassius followed the older man into a pantry at the end of the corridor. There he found Richard watching a kettle boil. His face looked more solemn than he could ever remember seeing it. When he looked up at the new arrival, Richard tried to put a smile on his face, but it was a half-hearted effort. A dressing on his right temple was testament to the close shave that he had recently had.

'Hi Cass. Tea? Or would you like to risk a cup of John's coffee?'

Cassius smiled. 'Tea please.'

There was an awkwardness about the room which was unusual, considering the company he was in. These two men were normally the most life-affirming pair you could imagine. Doing the work they did, they grasped life with both hands and squeezed every ounce of joy out of it that they could. Today, they looked as thought they were in mourning. John Gray was still trying to be cheerful, but Cassius suspected that he was worried about his colleague. Richard was definitely not being his usual self. Cassius thought perhaps he should get down to business in an attempt to clear the air.

'Have the test results on the bomb you dealt with come back?'

'Yes,' said John, 'and very interesting reading they make too. Takes the game on to a whole new level. The explosive was home-made.'

'What? Are we dealing with someone else? Oh, God. I hope this isn't the beginning of a spate of enthusiastic amateurs.'

John Gray shook his head. 'There was nothing amateur about it. Quite the contrary. I would say our man is showing off. Trying to impress us with his skill.'

'So, you think we are dealing with the same man?'

Richard spoke at last, much to Cassius's relief. 'Almost certainly. The first device, the one that nearly got me used the same military spec explosive that we have seen before. It was almost as if he wanted to make sure that we knew it was his handiwork. Only, he seems to have taken a little change in direction. That whole set-up was a "come-on". Intended to get me into a position where the secondary device would end my participation in the human race. The first bomb that the call was about had no real target, at least none that we can fathom. Looks as though I have an admirer.'

'What about this home-made explosive? Can we trace the ingredients?'

'I think it will be pointless,' said John Gray with a slow shake of his head. 'It's called "HMD", Hexamethylene tetramine dinitrate. I'll give you a list of the components required for its manufacture. It's not easy to make and it's pretty unstable. You have to use it within a few days of making it. Powerful though. Velocity of detonation of over 7500 meters per second.'

Cassius hated all this techno-talk. 'How does that compare with the military stuff he was using?'

'In terms of power, not far off. Probably more interesting is the fact that the guy made his own detonator. Now that is just plain showing off. They are tricky as hell to make and the explosives you have to manufacture are likely to blow your hand off if you so much as look at them the wrong way. Even the most experienced bomb technicians will use commercial dets if they are available. Making your own is always a last resort, unless you are a flash bastard like our pal.

'No, there is no doubt. He's sending us a message, trying to impress us with how clever he is. He's telling us that he's smarter than we are and he's throwing down the gauntlet.'

Cassius looked puzzled. 'What do you mean?'

'What he means, my dear friend,' said Richard, 'is that he is challenging me to a little contest and the loser ends up dead.'

'What? You mean he is personally targeting you?'

'Looks that way,' replied Richard. 'He knew exactly where to place the secondary device. The first one was so obviously a "come on" that I would have had to have been half asleep not to spot it. The guy was testing me. From now on, we're going to have to watch our arses every time we get a call-out.' Richard looked pointedly at John. The men took turns to be on call. Richard felt grateful that he had such a good teacher. John's experience and his willingness to share it had probably saved Richard's life. His own instincts had played a part. Instincts born of years of placing himself in harms way.

'Tell you what,' said John, 'I have some paperwork to get out of the way. Why don't you two wait for me up in the mess and we'll swap the tea and coffee for something a little stronger. I think we all could do with a small libation.' John left the two friends alone. He knew that Cassius was as worried by Richard's appearance as he had been all day. Perhaps the detective could get his old squad mate to open up about what he was feeling. John was not one to pressure anyone into talking about their troubles, but he was always a good listener. People just had to be ready to talk. Sometimes he wondered if it would be better if he and his fellow countrymen were as open as the Americans who bared their souls for daytime television. Probably not, thought John. Real emotions were complex and dangerous things. John Gray knew better than to take dangerous things lightly.

'Want to talk about it?' Cassius was never one to beat around the bush.

'About what?' Richard looked genuinely puzzled by the question.

'Come off it Richard, it's me. Even John looks worried sick. You've got something on your mind. Can I take a guess? Something to do with almost getting your head blown off?'

'That's a bit of an exaggeration. Yes, I had a close shave, but I've had them before.' Richard looked frustrated, as though he couldn't find the words to express what he was feeling. 'This is different, though. Before, it has been…I don't know…impersonal. When I went through a door and there was a man with a gun on the other side, he wasn't aiming at ME, it could have been anyone. This, it's definitely personal. The bastard was trying to kill me, or if I hadn't been there, John. There's some arsehole out there with my name on his hit-list. Someone I have never met. Someone I will never meet, if he has his way. I knew this was always a possibility. In a sustained bombing campaign, the bomber usually gets around to having a go at EOD personnel. I didn't think it would bother me this much.

'When I was in SDU, there was always a person to take down. A target in your sights. If they were able to get you, there was a good chance you might get them first. But this. I can't get the man, only interrupt his plans. He always gets another go at me or some other poor bastard. It's like chasing a fucking ghost.'

Cassius looked at his friend. Personal danger had never seemed to worry him before. It had always been something which Cassius had failed to understand about Richard. He seemed to have an almost cavalier attitude towards his own safety. Always deeply concerned about his men and those he was sworn to protect, Richard had taken some terrible risks with his own life. Cassius had heard all sorts of rumours, even ones about Richard having a death wish. The Police Force was a real rumour mill. Most of the gossip had little basis in fact, but there had been an awful lot about Richard since he joined the EOD Unit, since the incident that had forced him out of SDU. But now, the opposite seemed to be true. Perhaps the awful truth had finally dawned on his reckless friend. He was mortal.

'I suppose we had better catch him then.'

Richard looked at Cassius through dark eyes. 'How, Cass? We have bugger all to go on. Not a single lead. At the moment the best we can hope for is that the bastard blows himself up mixing his "bathtub" explosive. So far he hasn't struck me as the sort to make stupid mistakes.'

Cassius looked pensive. The germ of an idea was growing in his mind. 'This attack on you. It really is a major departure.' He looked at Richard, who seemed about to congratulate him for stating the bleeding obvious. 'No, wait. I mean a REAL departure. What if our friend has lost the plot? What if he has gone off on a little sidetrack of his own? His lords and masters, whoever they are, are likely to be a bit unhappy with our boy.'

'Well, I suppose if it takes the pressure off the Taipans, we are gaining some sort of victory. Can't say that I am too thrilled to be playing the decoy though. But if he stops following orders, won't he be replaced?'

Cassius frowned. 'I don't think that it would be that easy. You said yourself that the skills required are not easy to find. How many mad bombers do you know?'

'You mean apart from John and myself? Actually you have a damn good point, assuming there is someone controlling events, other than the bomber himself. Whatever the master plan is, if it is of sufficient importance, this little distraction is not likely to be tolerated for long. Might even shut the plan down altogether. So, what are you suggesting?'

'Richard, I really don't want to suggest anything, but what if we play his little game? Place some stories in the press about how you foiled the plans of this "second rate" bomb maker. Really hit him where it hurts, in the ego.'

'Get him mad, you mean? Hope he will get sloppy and expose himself?'

'Either that, or as you say, blow himself to hell and gone. I'll take either option.'

Richard looked less stressed than before. Somehow the prospect of playing moving target seemed less worrying, not if it lead to the demise of the guy who was targeting him. It was almost as if Richard was taking control back. As long as there was a plan, he was on the offensive and that was where he liked to be. 'You know, suddenly I feel like that drink. Let's have a little chat about your idea with John. He's not going to like it, I can tell you that now.

'One thing though. If we do this, I want John out of the picture. It will work better if the bomber only has one person to fixate on. So, I go on permanent call. John can act as back-up.'

Cassius looked at a man gone through a transformation. The dejected, hunted look that Richard had displayed when he had arrived was gone. In its place was something quite different. Richard was back in the role of the predator. He might be hanging himself out as bait, but he was determining the course of action. He was laying a trap, luring his prey into a course of action that could bring about his capture, or death. There were terrible risks to be faced, but the knowledge that such peril existed was a form of armour in itself. Richard was grasping control of his own destiny. He was declaring that he would decide when his time was up, not some madman with a bomb.

'Don't you want some time to think this through?' asked Cassius.

Richard smiled in a way that almost made his friend shudder. 'I have thought it through. It's the only way I can see of getting this fucker. If you have an alternative, please let me know. Until then, lets go get him.'

CHAPTER 34

The Vinho Verde glugged as it left the bottle and swilled around the glass. There seemed to be an endless supply of the stuff and a fair proportion of it was ending up in Richard's gut. For the umpteenth time that evening, he raised his glass and toasted his hosts, Corpo de Policia de Seguranca Publica de Macau, in short the Macau Police.

The yellow-green liquid was sharp and raw, tart enough to draw Richard's cheeks in, but with enough fruit to make the experience a pleasure. It was an ideal accompaniment for the table full of seafood that stretched out before the Hong Kong policeman. You could fault the Macanese for many things, but hospitality was not one of them, even if Richard had to close his mind to the fact that none of his hosts would be required to dip into their pocket to pay for the meal. That was just a fact of life in Macau. As far as graft was concerned, they were where Hong Kong had been fifteen years before. Yet here there seemed to be an acceptance that belied the evil nature of corruption. As anti-graft as Richard was, there was a larger issue to consider...face. This was Asia and despite the best efforts of the colonial authorities on both sides of the Pearl River Estuary, face played a very important part in the Chinese way of doing things. Richard was on a liaison visit with Macau's version of SDU, the Portas do Cerco Comando da UTP. To refuse their hospitality would be to seriously endanger the relationship. As much of a rationalisation as that seemed to Richard, he knew it to be the truth. Besides, he was having a great time with these guys. Their way of doing things may differ from his, but they had shown themselves to be capable allies in the fight against the Triads who plagued both Hong Kong and the Portuguese enclave.

'Darling, of course I love you. I know it hasn't been long, but I really have strong feelings for you. Oh, damn. Look, I'll have to call you back, my pager has gone off, it's work. Yes, love you too.'

Keith Symons hung up the telephone and immediately picked the receiver up again and dialed the number. The line was engaged. He tried again. It took him four attempts to get through. 'It's Bravo One, what's happening? What? Really? OK, where's the RV? OK, I'll be there as soon as I can. If my guys get there before me, tell them to start getting organised. What about Bravo, has he been informed? Well, tell the OC that he can be here in less than an hour, I'm sure we can lay on a chopper for him.'

Keith grabbed his crash helmet on the way out the door. It was time to see if he could break his record for the journey from Kowloon to SDU Headquarters in Fanling. This time he was sure he would be excused the odd speeding ticket.

Richard had spent the last week training with the Macau Police and exchanging ideas on counter-terrorism. It had been a bit of a one-way street, as the Macanese unit was fairly new and were making the same mistakes that Richard's group had made years before. SDU were rapidly being recognised as the most capable force of its kind in Asia. Units from all over the world were approaching them for liaison visits and exchanges of personnel. From relatively humble beginnings, successive generations of men had developed the capabilities of the unit to the point where they now taught others.

One thing that the Macau Police had in abundance was enthusiasm. They trained hard and were anxious to learn new techniques. They shared something else that was common to all such elite units, extreme pride. They were all volunteers, doing a hard job and loving it. Praise for other units was restrained, but sincere. Tonight's celebration was their way of telling Richard that they appreciated everything that he had passed on to them and the fact that he had never laboured the point that they still had a lot to learn. In fact, Richard's opinion was that in this game, you always had a lot to learn, no matter how experienced you were. Forget that fact at your peril.

He had to admit, these guys knew how to party. Keith had been champing at the bit to come with him, but they couldn't afford to leave the team without a commander. The unit was badly hit by injury and officers being forced to take much overdue leave. It had been touch and go whether or not Richard would make this trip, but the order had come down from Police Headquarters. The Hong Kong and Macau Governments enjoyed a special relationship. These exchanges were a tangible example of that.

Keith would cover for him and Alpha Team Commander, Mike Jessop, would help out if required. What Richard hadn't told his younger colleague was that he had lined up a visit to Hereford for him later in the year. He was saving the news for his return, when the jibes about "skiving off" would start. The news would take the wind out of Keith's sails and earn Richard a few pints for his trouble. Richard could hardly wait to see Keith's face. The lad had worked hard. He deserved the trip as a pat on the back. Not that it would exactly be a holiday. The SAS would work Keith very hard indeed, just to knock any cockiness out of him and remind him of the fact that he was still in the junior league as far as they were concerned. Richard thought about his own visit a few years before. Then SDU had much less of a reputation than they did now, but he still thought he was something special. The boys at Stirling Lines had rearranged his thinking for him in short order. He might have the same surname as their illustrious founder, but he would have to prove that he deserved to breathe the same rarefied air as them. He had done well and been a credit to his unit, but it had been the hardest month of his life. Richard put the satisfying, though tortuous memory to the back of his mind and dug in to another crab claw.

Keith had smashed his record. He doubted he would be able to better the time, even if he bought a faster bike. Richard would probably have bollocked him for taking the risk of such speed, for all the time it would really save, but Richard wasn't here and Keith was pumped up with adrenalin.

Four of the team, who lived locally were already getting each member's kit bags in the back of a Transit van. Keith checked that they had everything under control and headed for the briefing room. The Ops officer was there and looked pleased to see Keith. 'Keith, we're going to be briefing in the field. The OC is at the scene and the HQ lads will set up a command post where we can fill you in with all the details. Just get your guys ready and move out to the RV point as soon as you can. The drivers have the location. I'm just off myself, but I wanted to wait for you.'

Jimmie Tong was basically a nice guy, but too much of a "yes man" for Keith's liking. He had backed up the OC after the training accident and been party to the subsequent cover-up. But, he was good at his job and had smoothed things over between Richard and Victor Cummings in the past.

'Has Richard been informed?' asked Keith, almost in passing. He didn't like the look he saw on Jimmie's face. 'Jimmie, has Richard been called back from Macau?' Although the Ops officer outranked him, it was customary for the members of the unit to use first names, except with the OC who insisted on having his rank acknowledged.

'Look, Keith,' began Jimmie, 'everything has been a bit of a rush. Richard will never make it back from Macau in time anyway. I've paged Alpha, he'll cover as Team Commander for both teams if you have to lead an assault. I know it's not perfect, but it will just have to do.'

'Jimmie, there is no "just have to do" about it. I have every confidence in Mike Jessop and we've worked together before, but Richard should at least be informed. If the Macau Police can get him on a chopper, he could be at the rendezvous before us!'

Jimmie Tong was looking increasingly uncomfortable. 'Keith, it's not as simple as that. Why don't you concentrate on getting yourself and your team to the scene. Leave me to worry about letting Richard know what's happening.'

Keith shrugged and turned for the door. He almost made it through, when he turned and looked at the Ops officer. 'Has the OC told you not to inform Richard?'

Now Jimmie broke out into one of his famous blushes. He would never make a criminal, he couldn't hide his guilt.

'That bastard,' said Keith. 'What the hell is he playing at? This is a breach of Standing Orders. I can't believe that he is being so petty.'

'Look,' said a restored Jimmie Tong, 'just get your ass downtown. I promise I will get word through to Richard. I doubt if he'll arrive before the show is over, but if he does, I'll blame someone else when the OC blows his top. Fair enough?'

Keith gave the Chinese officer a smile. 'Fair enough boss.'

Dinner had passed very pleasantly. Richard wasn't feeling the effects of the wine too badly. He was grateful, as the evening was just getting started. The whole party had piled into a couple of police vans and were now heading for a nightclub which was owned by a senior officer who was among the revellers. Most of the men that Richard had trained with were only mildly corrupt, if at all. This guy was a heavy hitter and quite open about his wealth. Richard only hoped that the alcohol that was going to end up going down his neck didn't loosen his tongue too much. He had to maintain the air of cooperation that existed between his Force and this one, no matter what his personal feelings were.

The conversation was a mixture of Portuguese, English and the language they all shared, Cantonese. Richard was impressed with the language skills of the Portuguese officers in the party. There were far fewer expatriates in the Macau Police than in the Hong Kong Force and many of them were seconded army officers, as well as policemen. There seemed to have been a great deal more inter-marrying in Macau than in Hong Kong, if the names were anything to go by. Antonio Rodrigues Lin was the officer in charge of tonight's entertainment. Tri-lingual and educated in Macau and Portugal, he cut an impressive figure. He was Richard's counterpart and set the standard for the whole unit. Richard knew that this group would be among the best of the bunch. The subject of the conversation, as it was so often at this point in an evening's entertainment, was women. The club they were going to was renowned for the beauty of the hostesses and their willingness to please. Their eagerness came at a price, but tonight, all the entertainment was on the house. Richard thought of Natalie and wondered how the hell he was going to get out of indulging in carnal pleasure. He might have to resort to a simple "no thank you", but it would be better if he could come up with a more creative solution. Again, face was an issue. He could always drink himself into a stupor. He had proved himself perfectly capable of that feat in the past. His only worry was that he might still end up in the embrace of some charming girl, despite his incapacity. Well, nothing to do but cross that bridge when he came to it.

With the equipment loaded, Keith and half of Bravo Team, along with members of Alpha Team, left Fanling to rendezvous with the rest of the teams and the other SDU personnel who had been called out. Other units would be joining them. Although this was not a terrorist incident, the seriousness of the situation had resulted in a number of support units being called to lend assistance. Time was always a factor in these operations. It took time to assemble even the bones of the organisation which was necessary to deal with barricaded suspects. At the moment, all that Keith knew was that some criminals had been located in a flat in Kwun Tong. Who they were, or what they had done he would find out later. All he did know was that these were dangerous people, otherwise he would not be sitting in a south-bound police van, flouting every traffic regulation in the book.

The nightclub was not what Richard had expected. It wasn't even in the centre of town. The vehicles pulled into the courtyard of what looked like a large house, about two miles outside the urban area. The courtyard was dark, except for a lamp which burned over the main door. The group alighted from the vehicles and Richard was led by the arm towards the illuminated portal.

Walking through the door was like entering a different world. In contrast to the darkness outside, the large hall into which they stepped was gaily lighted, a pallet of colours mixing together to provide a festive atmosphere. The place was not full, but there were several tables of people. Men in business suits and women in evening dresses, the latter's attention lifting from their companions only briefly and discretely as they surveyed the new arrivals. Richard was led to a large table against the far wall. It was already full of bottles of wine, whisky and brandy. Preparations had been made ahead of their arrival. The guest of honour was seated in the middle of the table, where he could get a good view of the stage. A Filippino band was playing a creditable version of a "Canto-pop" hit which had been popular the year before. The singer was obviously a Filippina, but her Cantonese was perfect, at least to Richard's ear. He had hardly sat down, when he found himself flanked by two beautiful women. It looked as though the reputation of this place was well founded.

'Gentlemen, Criminal Intelligence Bureau firmly believe that the men holed up in this flat are the ones who ran the heroin factory that we raided last month and that they have a cache of weapons in there, including more of the assault rifles we found at the chicken farm.' Victor Cummings paused to allow the seriousness of the information to have its effect on the audience.

So that's why we're here, thought Keith. Headquarter units had been looking for these people since the raid. The presence of the Chinese AK-47 copies had caused a great deal of concern. The Commissioner had let it be known that he wanted the rest of the weapons found, before they could be used in the streets of Hong Kong. The Territory had a reputation for safety. That would not last long if there were pitched gun battles in the streets. In addition, beat cops would be heavily out-gunned if they had to confront robbers armed with these weapons. It was the job of Keith and his colleagues to ensure that it never came to that. Keith snapped to attention as the OC SDU continued.

'CIB has the flat under surveillance and believe that the entire gang are in residence at the moment. They will continue to monitor the situation, but it is imperative that we are in position to assault the flat as soon as possible. As Bravo Assault Group has formed already and we are still waiting for members of Alpha to arrive, I will assume tactical command of Bravo Team. Keith, I want your men ready to go in ten minutes. I will personally brief you on the situation, but I want you ready to assault as soon as possible.'

Keith nearly fell off his chair. The OC taking charge of his team. What was going on? The young Englishman knew better than to question the OC in front of the other members of the unit. That would have to wait until they were face to face. He really wished that Richard was there.

Richard was desperately trying to stay off the brandy and whisky. The wine was doing a fine job of removing his inhibitions and he was getting into the spirit of the party. The girls spoke little English, but Richard managed to keep them amused in Cantonese and through the pantomime which inevitably developed in such circumstances. Richard played the fool and the girls giggled. It was all part of the deal.

The Scotsman knew that he would be expected to hit the hard liquor at some stage. By sticking to the wine for a while, he was laying the foundation for a spectacular collapse. He had decided that the only way to get out of screwing these girls and saving face, was to be so plastered that he had to be carried back to his hotel. In that state, the worst that could happen would be for him to wake up next to two sleeping beauties, safe in the knowledge that he had been faithful to Natalie in everything but the unconscious comfort of naked flesh. With any luck, the girls would be paid off and sent home and he would be nursing his hangover the following morning on his own. That was the plan, the trick would be to start the brandy at the right time and still keep going long enough to uphold the hard drinking reputation of the Royal Hong Kong Police. That was every bit as important as his own reputation.

The girl on his left challenged him to a drinking competition and Richard saw another possibility of getting out of this situation without having to lie about it to his girlfriend. He picked up the bottle of brandy in front of him and filled the glasses of his female companions. If he could get these two plastered, he might even escape a major hangover the next day. Let the games begin!

Keith was getting more frustrated by the minute. Cummings had given what he thought amounted to a briefing, but which the Assault Group Leader considered a joke. At least it would be funny, if it wasn't so worrying. Cummings had refused Keith's request to do a close recce on the stronghold, or at least see what the CIB surveillance was showing. His OC wanted him to take his men in blind. "Get in there and get it over with".

Keith had suggested that they trap the suspects and try to talk them out. If that failed they could flood the flat with CS gas and flush them out. Cummings was hell bent on an assault. He was right that they had the element of surprise at that moment, but it was all too rushed for Keith's liking. He knew too little about what was going on in the stronghold. What was the door like? Did it have the same sort of security measures that they had encountered at the chicken farm? It seemed likely that the same people would be just as cautious about their base of operation in town. Cummings was sending them through the front door blind. If it took anything more than a few seconds to get through the door, the element of surprise was gone and Keith and his men would find themselves in the middle of a bloody fire-fight. Keith didn't know what to do. Should he refuse? Could he refuse? If he did, Cummings was likely to send the lads in without him and as strong willed as they were, they would probably obey this clown. Keith would never be able to live with his men being injured when he had stood by and watched.

It wasn't really a choice that Keith made. It was an inevitability. He would do as he was told because it was his job to look after his men and if he wasn't first through that door, then one of them would be. With luck, he would be able to watch Richard tear the OC a new arsehole when he returned from Macau. Keith had trained hard for this moment, he couldn't back down now. The key was getting through that door as fast as possible. He would do it, even if he had to blow the fucking thing out of the wall.

'OK, sir. I'll need time to brief my men.'

'Make it quick, Inspector. It's straightforward enough. Just do what you spend all that time training for. Your Team Commander keeps going on about how good you are. Now it's time to prove it. Or is he just full of shit?'

Anger is a dangerous motivation, but when it takes over, rationality disappears. Keith looked at Cummings and even a blind man could have read the expression on his face. He would show this prick.

'I'm sure my team will prove to be worthy of Chief Inspector Stirling's praise. We haven't let him down yet and I'm not about to start now, sir. Anything else before I meet you at the assembly point?'

'Eh, no. I will be taking command from here. You'll get your instructions through the radios. Keep me informed of everything that happens on your approach.' Cummings wasn't even going to get close to the stronghold. He was staying in the remote safety of the Command Post. Blind and yet in control.

Keith couldn't stop the sneer that came over his face as he walked away.

The plan seemed to be working. One of the girls could hardly speak and the other was having trouble making contact with her lips when she tried to drink her forfeit. Richard thanked the Gods for all those evenings when he had learned to play these drinking games. No one expected a gwailo to be very good at them. Richard had paid his dues in the form of agonising hangovers, but the price now seemed worth it. His hosts were too busy getting pissed to worry about the fact that their guest would be sleeping alone that night. Those in his immediate vicinity seemed to have warmed to the fact that the hostesses were failing to keep up with the Scotsman. In fact, Richard had drunk very little brandy, or anything else, since the games began. He actually felt as though he was sobering up a little. That was fine. Once he had dispatched his charming adversaries, he might treat himself to a little alcohol induced oblivion.

His men didn't have to say a word. Their expressions spoke eloquently of their doubts about the situation. Bill Chu, Keith's number two voiced a question which was on all their minds. 'Has the Team Commander been told what is happening?'

Keith had asked Cummings the same thing and been given a dressing down for his trouble. "If Stirling wants to go swanning off to Macau and then misses the action, well that's his fault. We haven't time to piss about contacting him. It would all be over by the time we got hold of him anyway." Keith was certain that if Richard had been contacted as soon as the call-out had been made, he would at the very least be bursting a gut to try and get back to Hong Kong. Cummings hadn't even tried. He didn't want Richard there. Superintendent Cummings planned to rub his nose in it when he got back. Show off what a great leader he was, assuming that Keith did the business in that flat.

'No. The boss hasn't been contacted and Alpha hasn't arrived yet either.'

'Can't we wait, *Daai Lo* ?' It was Ah Pau's turn to voice his concern. He had just come back from deploying the snipers. Keith had taken the precaution of sending the Sniper Group out while the briefing was going on. At least they might be able to feed back some intelligence on the flat and its occupants.

'Sorry Ah Pau. The OC has taken charge and has ordered an immediate assault. The other senior officers on the scene seem to be going along with his decision. He thinks we should make the most of the element of surprise.'

'But, we don't know what's going on in the flat.' It was Ah Fan, one of the constables in Keith's Assault Group. That's the bottom line, thought Keith, a PC can see the problem and a Superintendent either can't or refuses to.

'Look, I know this is bad, but we have our orders and if we don't follow them, someone else will have to. This is our job. Do you want to see Uniform Branch, or CID trying to effect an entry?'

The group shook their heads as one. They knew that they had to go ahead, the loss of face alone was unthinkable, but more than that they had orders to follow and this was a disciplined service.

'OK. Plain clothes officers have secured the building. We'll take along enough dems to blow the door to shit, plus all the other breaking kit we can carry. I want options when we get up there. Slow approach. I don't care how much flak I get from the OC. Let's go.'

That pretty much did it. The girls were basket cases. Richard leaned back and took a long draw on his glass of wine. The boys of the Macau Police were either dancing with some of the hostesses or engaged in animated discussions about the merits of the new Glock pistol or the latest jockey to race at the Happy Valley race track in Hong Kong. Keith would have appreciated his dilemma tonight, thought Richard. Actually keith would have been damn useful tonight. He could have palmed one or both of the now collapsed ladies by his side off on his compadre. The lad tended to be quite willing to perform such arduous duty. Richard realised that he was missing his drinking partner. They had been through a lot together. Richard thought of his subordinate as a brother and best friend. His own brother disapproved of what he regarded as Richard's cavalier lifestyle. They hardly spoke, but as they had never been close, Richard hardly missed the filial contact. Richard sipped his drink and wondered what Keith was doing at that moment.

The lobby was secure. A CID officer had taken the place of the security guard in the entrance hall. A wide cordon was in place around the housing estate. The block which housed the target premises was effectively cut off from the outside world. Keith and his men had slipped into the building as quickly as possible, trying to avoid detection by anyone who might tip off whoever was inside the stronghold.

Keith watched from the number four position as two of his men ahead on the stairs cleared the way for the main party. They acted as *Jin Tau*, "spearheads", one moving while the other covered the stairway ahead with his weapon. Moving in easy stages, their overlapping movement was well rehearsed, smooth and stealthy. It was tiring work, so the pair would act as the back-up men for the assault, waiting outside the flat until required, or to handle prisoners as they came out.

The flat they were after was on the 18th floor. A CID man, or a cynical uniformed officer would have automatically gone for the lift. Under these circumstances, lifts made excellent coffins. Before moving up the stairs, the SDU men had thrown the Fireman's Switches on the lifts, bringing them all down to the ground floor and locking them there. If the bad guys discovered that they were under surveillance and decided to make a break for it, they too would have to use one of the sets of stairs. If they did, they would eventually end up in the arms of a couple of cops armed with shotguns or MP5s. It was at times like this that the SDU men realised why they trained so hard physically. Any of them could have run up the eighteen floors and still been fit to fight. Outsiders laughed at what they considered a waste of effort. They were the ones who would have taken the lifts and probably have ended up dead. SDU men didn't make life difficult for themselves just for the hell of it, they did things because of the lessons learned by themselves and others around the world. Expensive lessons.

They reached the eighteenth floor. At that point they held, while Keith and Bill Chu took over the primary positions in the line of black clad men. They wore balaclavas and had decided not to wear their respirators for this job. If they had to use a demolition charge, they would put them on, but in this confined space, Keith wanted as much peripheral vision as possible. The NBC6 hampered it only slightly, but "slightly" might make all the difference.

In one smooth movement, Keith opened the lobby door and was through, with Bill at his side. There had been hardly any noise. One of the team held the door while the rest filed into the hallway. Ahead the corridor turned left at a right angle. The target flat was around that corner. The Assault Group held just short of the junction.

Richard was rapidly losing interest in the party. His hosts were slowly reaching their limit of imbibing, but seemed in no hurry to break up the gathering. Some had already slinked off with girls in tow, but there remained a hard core who seemed determined to show the man from Hong Kong that they had as much stamina in drinking as in training. Richard looked at his watch. It was only one in the morning. This could go on all night. He had a ferry to catch at midday. The arrangements had anticipated a degree of lethargy the morning after his farewell. Richard could quite easily have gone to bed right away, but he had to let his hosts indicate that it was time to call it a night. If he "did an Oates", it would be bad form and would certainly get back to his colleagues in Hong Kong.

Bill Chu covered the door with his MP5. Keith was close to the metal grill in front of the wooden door. He was listening for any indication of how many people were inside. He had given the entrance a good going over, trying to determine the best way to breach it. He really had a bad feeling about this. How come CIB had been unable to tell him how many people were inside the stronghold? They said "at least three". Big help! He had heard voices, but couldn't determine how many. There were blinds over the windows, so his snipers had nothing to add to the little he already knew.

Cummings voice continued to grate in his left ear, urging him to get a move on. It was a clear indication that the man had taken little interest in the basics of the job for which his own unit was trained. Training which Cummings himself had never gone through. A sore point for the members of the unit at the best of times, a real annoyance to Keith right at this moment. It was hard enough for him to organise his thoughts on the best way to conduct the entry, without some ignoramus hurrying him along.

Keith used hand signals to relay what little he was learning from the door recce to Bill. Finally, he had enough and indicated that they should return to the rest of the men. He covered the door with his weapon while Bill backed away, then followed him, all the time keeping his MP5 trained on the entrance.

The clunk of the door closing behind him sealed the end of the evening and the dance he had performed all night. Richard looked at the bed in his hotel room with longing. He had managed to stay the pace set by his hosts and had engineered his solo slumber. All in all, a good night's work. In the end, he had consumed a good deal less alcohol than he had expected and the mix of drinks had been kept to a minimum. His hangover in the morning might not be too terrible after all.

Richard fell back on the bed and let out a long, deep sigh. Undressing was not high on his list of priorities, but he knew that if he allowed himself to drift off like this, he would not get the full benefit of the little sleep he would get before his departure. Forcing himself back on to his feet, he headed for the bathroom, dragging his clothes off as he went.

The dems were in place. It had taken longer than Keith had expected. The double explosion should remove the metal grill and take the door off its hinges almost simultaneously. Keith was receiving an almost continuous assault in his left ear. Cummings was going ballistic. But now they were ready. The Assault Group were in position. Keith signalled the countdown. Three, two, one, go!

The concrete walls shook with the double blast. Keith was on his feet and moving within a second of the explosions. As he reached the door, he was pleased at what he saw. The grill and door were slightly blocking the entrance, sitting at an angle to the frame, but there was plenty of room for him to get in without crouching.

Keith halted at the door and one of the *Jin Tau* threw a stun grenade through the opening. Keith followed the pyrotechnic into the flat. He felt the blast, but he was expecting it and had experienced the effect countless times in the Close Quarter Battle House. It didn't cause him to lose a beat on his entry. A figure came into his sight over to the right of the room. Keith turned, his MP5 following his eyes towards the target. Then it began.

A 'phone was ringing somewhere. Out there in the dark. Bloody thing. Richard wished that someone would answer it. He was too tired to be bothered with it. Anyway, he had just gotten off to sleep. Maybe it would stop if he just ignored it. But it didn't stop. Slowly, he floated up from the depths of his sleep, the sound getting louder as he reached the surface of consciousness.

The room was dark. Very dark. It was still night. Curious. The thought only half registered in Richard's head. He was too busy trying to focus on finding the telephone. Fumbling around in the blackness, he managed to find it, mostly by luck. As he lifted it, he realised that the ringing had not stopped. It took a few more seconds for his brain to realise that the noise was not coming from the telephone. A few seconds more and his mind had woken enough to register that the sound was the doorbell.

Muttering to himself, he grabbed the robe from the floor, where he had left it and managed to get some lights on in the room using the bedside controls. This had better be good, thought Richard. Opening the door, he was greeted by an officer of the Macau Police. It was not one of his drinking companions. This man looked far too awake to have been a member of the party. He was in civilian clothes. Eventually, Richard recognised him as one of the men who had missed the celebration, because they were on standby. He managed to smile at the young man, but the gesture was not returned. Richard's smile evaporated as his eyes managed to focus on the face before him.

'What's happened?' asked Richard.

CHAPTER 35

Tiny beads of sweat were wiped away as his hands moved down her back. The moist skin was hot, seeming more so against the cold background of the air-conditioned room. He flipped her onto her side and pushed himself against the bed, forcing their bodies even closer together. She groaned with the movement and dug her nails into his shoulders. His back arched with the exquisite pain, just one more sensation to add to the many that were erupting all over his body. As the couple moved around the disarrayed bed, their skin touched in a hundred places, each passing caress causing a tiny surge of pleasure, like a pulse of electricity.

Richard's mouth reached for her breast, his tongue seeking out the erect nipple, finding it, teasing it, feeling her squirm in his arms, half pulling away from him then forcing her breast closer. Natalie pushed him onto his back and sat upright. As he reached up to kiss her, she forced his shoulders back onto the bed and smiling, began to move her hips in rhythmic, but ever changing movement. Richard reached for her, straining to touch her, to gently run his fingers over her body. Her legs were smooth and hard under his hands. He could feel the muscles contract as she began to groan at the results of her labours. He started to feel himself drift into a realm of sensation, being controlled by the woman straddling him. He was the passive recipient of the pleasure being generated by her movement.

Natalie's movements became more urgent. Her eyes closed as she let herself go to the feelings that were radiating through her. Her lover was on the periphery of her consciousness, she felt him under her, responding in time with the pleasure that she was feeling. Richard forced down the urge to take control, releasing himself to her, relishing the feeling of being pampered with such vigour. As she eased the pressure on his shoulders, he raised himself up on the bed and with his mouth reached for her breasts, passionately, but with the gentle touch that he knew she loved so much. His control was rewarded by her response. Their bodies moved towards a single goal, closer and closer. Finally, their muscles tensed as they reached the peak of orgasm, Natalie first and Richard a moment behind. They clung to one another, breathing hard, allowing their bodies to relax in their own time, savouring the taste of sweat on the other.

'We're going to be late, you know.' Natalie was rushing to fix the damage that their lovemaking had done to her hair. They had showered together on the pretence of saving time and as usually happened when their bodies came that close, they had lost time to another bout of carnal indulgence.

'If we were on time, Brian and Peter would think that something was wrong,' replied Richard. He was ready to go, but knew better than to tease Natalie about holding them back. Not if he wanted a repeat performance when they got home. Instead he bent down and kissed her bare shoulder, then left her to get on with it while he called for a cab.

'Good shag?'

Natalie gave him a thoughtful look. 'Not bad, but the old fellow here was in a rush, so, you know. He'll have to do better when we get home, so don't get him too drunk.'

Richard followed her into the flat and handed a bottle of wine to his host. Brian Steadman took the bottle and placed it on a table where two drinks were already sitting. He picked these up and handed them to his guests.

'Martinis. Peter has gone all Manhattan after his trip.'

As if on cue, Peter Wong appeared from the kitchen, a huge grin on his face. 'Well, let me guess. Richard, you were ready to go, but Natalie insisted on jumping you.'

'That's about right,' said Natalie with a smirk, giving Richard a sideways glance as she spoke. 'He has to be encouraged these days. Looks as though the honeymoon is over. Isn't that right darling?'

Richard couldn't help smiling. The grin stretched from one side of his face to the other. God, he loved this woman.

'Well, I'm sure that your bit of exercise has given you both a healthy appetite, so you'll be pleased to know that there is not a healthy thing on the menu.' Brian looked pleased with himself as he said this. Peter was an excellent chef and the couple's hospitality was renowned.

Dinner had been as good as expected, better in fact. Peter had outdone himself. Richard and Brian went out onto the balcony to indulge in the cigars that they both enjoyed, while Peter and Natalie remained inside, happy to be able to enjoy their wine without clouds of smoke billowing around them.

Richard offered the calfskin cigar case to Brian, who withdrew one of the slender cigars. Taking a silver cigar cutter out of his pocket, Richard snipped the end off for Brian and then prepared his own Cohiba. Brian lit a long stem match and held it for Richard. The slender wooden taper was long enough to allow both men to light their cigars. This little ritual complete, the men leaned against the balcony and relished the taste of the cigar smoke. The full flavour would take time to develop, but the Cuban tobacco was of such high quality that even the first few puffs were a joy.

'Brian, how much pull do you have with your editor?' Richard saw no point in beating about the bush, he got straight to subject that he had in mind when he accepted Brian's invitation to dinner the day before.

'Oh, I know where most of his skeletons are hidden, so I suppose I have a fair amount of influence. Why? What are you after my son?'

Peter Wong looked thoughtfully at his guest. Natalie had been great fun at dinner, but was now looking at Richard with a sad expression.

'What's the matter?'

Natalie turned to look at the artist. His handsome features could have made him a fortune in the movie industry in Hong Kong, but his talent was greater than mere appearance. Women adored him, including Natalie, but for more than his looks. His heart was open and giving. If you had a problem, Peter would always be there for you. There was nothing false about his concern and he didn't gush platitudes and sympathy. He just listened and then if he had any constructive advice, he would give it generously and without expectation of reciprocation.

'The nightmares have started again.' Natalie said it in a matter of fact fashion. She might have been telling him that she had been shopping that day. Small talk. Her voice betrayed no emotion, but her eyes revealed the sorrow that the revelation evoked.

'When?'

'Oh, just in the last few days, since the last bomb. The one that could have killed him, though he would never admit that was the case.'

Peter laid his glass on the table. 'So, you think the pressure of this bombing campaign is getting to him? Have you spoken to him about it?'

Natalie sighed. 'I tried. I tried tonight in fact. We ended up making love. Richard tends to use sex as a decoy, not that I am really complaining about that.' She laughed, but it was more to release the tension she felt than appreciation of her own humour. 'I wish though that he would be more open. He just shrugs off any suggestion that he is under pressure and tries to assure me that my worries are unfounded. He thinks he is protecting me, but I know him too well. I know when he is hiding something from me. Richard used to believe that ignorance is bliss as far as my knowledge of his work is concerned. The less I knew, the less ammunition my imagination had with which to torture me. He became more open after he left SDU, but recently I think he has started to believe his old theory again.'

'Is he right?'

'Actually I don't know if it is better to know or not. But at the moment, I am worried about him and I can see that he is concerned for himself, which is the most worrying thing of all.'

'So, let me get this straight. You want to present yourself as a target for this madman, a decoy. If he is concentrating on blowing you to bits, then he will ease off the businessmen that he has been targeting. Perhaps even be forced into a mistake that will help you catch him. That's the plan. That's the best that the best brains of the Royal Hong Kong Police can come up with. And you want me to aid you in this suicide mission.' Brian looked at the lunatic in front of him, for that was surely what he must be to agree to a piece of folly like this.

Richard blew smoke from his cigar through his nostrils and screwed up his face in an expression that said, "well, when you put it like that...". 'I know, it seems like the action of a desperate group of people. Well, that I am afraid is it in a nutshell. We are desperate.

'Look, Brian. We have no leads on this guy. He's a ghost. Worse, he's a clever ghost. That though may be his weakness. He thinks, sorry he knows that he is smarter than us. This isn't really our idea.

It's his. He chose me. He's decided that he wants to cross swords with me, to test me. That just might be the biggest mistake that he has made. Perhaps the only one.'

'So, you want me to bait the trap by antagonising this guy. Make him REALLY mad at you. Not exactly the function of the press, you know.'

'Brian, I won't ask you to print anything but the facts. I'll give you the inside track on the investigation, as far as I can. All I'm asking is that you give as much exposure to this little conflict as possible. Keep it on the front pages. I want his humiliation to be as public as possible. That will attack his weakest point, his ego. As little as I know about this man, the one thing that I do know is that he has an ego the size of a house. That's what all this is about. There may be some hidden agenda at work as far as the attacks on the British businessmen were concerned, but with this attack on me he is working to an agenda all of his own. I am betting that fact will be driving whoever is pulling his strings to distraction. Whatever plot was being hatched has been stalled, perhaps permanently and that's just fine.'

Brian Steadman took a drink of his whisky and turned to look through the glass of the balcony doors. Natalie and Peter were locked in conversation. 'What about her?' he asked. 'Have you thought about the effect that your game will have on Natalie. She loves you, you clot and it is quite obvious that you love her. That is an awfully precious arrangement to be pissing about with.' For all his bluntness and boorish front, Brian was a true romantic. He adored his friends and hated to think that true love, once found, could be squandered. It had taken him a lifetime to find it and the search had shown him just how precious it was.

'I do love her Brian. More than anything. I would give my life for her in an instant, without a second's hesitation. Do you really think that I would be doing this if I thought that I would die as a result of my involvement? But what can I do? Say "Sorry guys, but someone else will have to stick their neck out. I don't fancy this one."? It doesn't work like that. I chose this job and I knew the risks before I started. Natalie has no illusions about the dangers involved, but she also knows that I am good at my job. If I wasn't doing it, maybe someone not so good would be doing it and that just might get people killed. The point here is to save lives, not throw myself to the wolves. If this crazy bastard is focussing his attention on me, then maybe a kid will still have her father tomorrow. Maybe she will still have a life.'

'The bomb that killed the little girl hit him particularly hard.' Natalie's eyes were close to tears. 'It seemed to him that the bomber was playing some cruel joke. There was no reason to kill the man and his daughter, he said that the guy who planted the bomb was showing off. It was a deliberate act of sadism. He's already shown that he has the skill and ingenuity to kill only the person he is after. Richard thinks that the little girl's death was actually supposed to impress the police. Pointless and cruel, that's the only thing that they thought. Half the Force want to put a bullet in the man's brain. The other half have rather less pleasant plans for him.'

'I didn't realise that the girl's death was a deliberate act. I was shocked when I read about it, but I just assumed that she was in the wrong place at the wrong time. This is horrible. How could anyone do such a thing?' Peter's disgust was real. His brain was having trouble dealing with the fact that another human being could commit such an act of barbarism. Most people would. For those lucky enough to escape the influence of the truly evil in society, the concept of such a calculated atrocity was hard to fathom. To even contemplate it was to introduce an unpleasant possibility to their lives; perhaps they were not as safe as they thought.

Peter sighed. 'I can understand Richard's obsession with this case. It has become very personal and I think he is the sort of man who will stand up to a challenge, particularly if he thinks that to refuse would jeopardise others.'

'That's my man, for better or worse.'

A faint smile came across Peter's handsome features, wiping away the frown of worry that their conversation had evoked. 'Why don't you two get married? It's obvious that you are crazy about each other.'

Natalie looked out at the figures on the balcony. 'He hasn't asked.'

Brian looked as though he had just become privy to some information that he would rather not have known. In fact that was just the case. 'Are you sure?'

'As sure as I can be. I could show you the tape, the bomb in the car was an almost exact re-enactment of the one shown in the RUC training film. Even if I believed in coincidences, it's too close. He was showing us how smart and creative he is. If I was anything less than a hundred percent motivated before I saw that crime scene, I got a full tank of determination that day. I want this guy, Brian. The only problem is going to be keeping the prick alive long enough to go to trial.'

'Alright. I'll see what I can do. Our editorial staff has a lot of liberal do-gooders among them, so I think I might have to play the part of the Government Information Service here. I'll channel the stories, but I won't give up my source. One thing I will insist on, though. If I don't like the look of any information that you feed me, I won't do the story. Agreed?'

'Agreed. I'll give you the facts and trust your judgement. But I want this guy fuming and I want all that rage channelled against me. I'll laugh in his face enough that the only thing he will think about is showing me how wrong I am about him. It's a risk, I know, but no one ever told me that bomb disposal was risk-free.'

'Richard, this isn't bomb disposal that you are planning. It's a bullfight and I can tell you, this is going to be one very fucking mad animal that is going to be bearing down on you.'

'What were you and Brian talking about on the balcony?' Natalie and Richard were in a taxi, heading home.

'Oh, nothing much. I was filling him in on the latest events in this bombing campaign, thought that he might be able to make sure that we get a fair hearing in the press. The Police Force has taken a bit of a whipping from the Fourth Estate over this one. I was explaining the problems we are having coming up with any leads. Maybe he can persuade some of his more rabid colleagues to back-off a bit.'

'I thought you didn't care what the press printed.'

'I don't. But the boys upstairs do. A lot of the Taipans in town have been getting awfully nervous and using any lever they can think of to put pressure on the Governor for a quick result in the investigation. It makes no difference that we have absolutely no leads, they think we are all equipped with crystal balls.

'It's people like Cass that I feel sorry for. If this business ends without some form of resolution, ie, we catch the guy, it's going to leave an indelible mark on Cass's record. Through no fault of his own, his career will be over. Not that he gives a monkey's. All he wants to do is catch the bad guy.'

Well, don't worry darling. I don't want you to have crystal balls. I'm happy with them the way they are.' Well, thought Natalie, he's avoiding telling me the truth. At least she could look forward to some sex when they got home.

CHAPTER 36

'Hello stranger.' The smiling features of Frank Duvalier reached out to Richard like the rays of the sun. Frank was probably the most cheerful man Richard had ever met. Nothing seemed capable of bringing this man down. Senior Armourer for the Police Force, he was responsible for the running of every armoury in the Force, maintenance and supply of weapons and ammunition and had a say in firearms policy. Specialist units were fairly autonomous, but when they had a problem, they came to Frank. His knowledge and skill had come to Richard's aid in the past, but the best part about visiting the ebullient Eurasian was that you could never be depressed in his company. It just wasn't possible.

A smile appeared on Richard's face, like an autonomic reflex. 'Hi Frank. Thought I would come down and see how the real workers are getting on.'

'No need to be facetious, young Stirling. We toil away in here just like the rest of you. Fancy a beer?' Frank Duvalier had a reputation as a gun guru, but he also had a formidable thirst. Though he never drank to excess during the day, he did indulge in a couple of beers at lunchtime. After five o'clock, he was a man that few in the Police Force could match in imbibing prowess. For guests to his domain, he kept a ready supply of frosty beer in a fridge, in the corner of his office.

'No thanks, not at the moment, but if you are still interested I'll join you after I have concluded a little business.'

Frank looked quizzically at his guest. 'Sounds intriguing. What kind of business are we talking about?'

Richard reached into his jacket and removed a sheet of paper. 'Your kind. Here's the authorisation for you to issue me with a personal firearm.'

Frank took the paper and looked at it. The signature was that of the Commissioner of Police. Unusual, as normally a formation commander would sign it on the Commissioner's behalf. That fact alone highlighted the odd nature of the order. Bomb Disposal Officers didn't normally carry sidearms, let alone one that they could carry twenty-four hours a day. 'Mind telling me what this is all about?'

'Let's just call it a precaution. I'm about to get involved with an aspect of a case that might make me the target of a vendetta of sorts. So, better safe than sorry.'

'This bombing case you're on. That last one was meant for you, wasn't it?' One thing you could never accuse Frank Duvalier of was stupidity. A nod from Richard was enough to satisfy all the questions that the armourer had. 'Now, let me see. I think we might have just the thing. Come on. I think you know where your old friend is.'

Richard was glad of his jacket in the air-conditioned cool of the Police Headquarters armoury. Normally an item of clothing that he would reject in the oppressive heat and humidity of a Hong Kong summer, he had known that it would come in handy in this walk-in freezer. Frank led the way into the bowels of the facility. Men were busy working on repairs to the little-used, but much handled firearms in their care. Humidity was the main enemy of anything metal in Hong Kong. The warm, moist air produced rust almost instantaneously on any unprotected surface. Although the weapons were oiled every day, constant handling took its toll. Sweat and atmospheric pollution came to the aid of the rust-fest, making a full time occupation of keeping the sidearms of the uniformed officers in serviceable condition. That was the routine work of the Force Armourers. Occasionally, they got to work on something special.

Frank emerged from one of the secure storage rooms with an aluminium camera case. He laid it down on a workbench and gestured to Richard. 'It's all yours. Want to check how we've been looking after your baby for you?'

Richard flicked open the catches on the top of the case and lifted the lid. Inside, a foam rubber insert had been sculpted with recesses of specific shape. In each of these was an item of hardware. There were six magazines. One rectangular shaped recess was empty. This would soon carry a box of ammunition. The largest item in the case was the pistol that Richard had used when a member of SDU. His personal weapon. Operationally it was usually a back-up, the MP5 being his primary weapon, but Richard had spent a lot of time and effort ensuring that if he had to use his handgun, he could use it effectively.

Lifting the Browning Hi-Power P-35 9mm pistol out of the box, Richard felt the familiar grips in his hand. Frank had done a lot of work on this weapon, customising it to Richard's desired specifications. The armourer had made suggestions and given of his time and skill. Much of the gun was non-standard. The original grips had been replaced with rubber Pachmeyer grips. These gave a better hold when the hands were wet, or when the firer was wearing gloves. The barrel had been replaced with one by BarSto, manufactured to lower tolerances, it was more accurate and less prone to "leading" when unjacketed lead ammunition was used. The trigger guard had been squared off and the front chequered. This allowed a better two handed Chapman grip. This was the grip which Richard favoured, where the forefinger of his support hand was wrapped around the trigger guard, exerting a rearward pressure. A Safari Arms ambidextrous safety catch was fitted. Although Richard was naturally right handed, he could shoot equally well with both hands. Tactical considerations made it important that he could do so.

One of the features of the Browning is the magazine safety. If a magazine is not fully home in the magazine well, the hammer will not drop. In Richard's weapon, the magazine safety had been deactivated. This allowed the weapon to be fired in the middle of a magazine change and had the added advantage of reducing the weight of the trigger pull by about twenty-four ounces. This allowed more accurate shooting, but required greater skill and care in weapon handling. Fine for specialist units whose members trained every day, but unsuitable for officers who only attended range courses a couple of times a year.

The standard Browning had fixed sights. On this weapon, they had been replaced with an adjustable rear sight and a ramp fore sight. Even these had received some attention from Frank. The basic sights had been drilled, to produce recesses into which small plastic cylinders had been glued. These cylinders were filled with Tritium. During the 1970s the Israelis had perfected this technology. The radioactive Tritium glowed in the dark, allowing better sight acquisition in low light conditions. In theory, the gun could be fired in total darkness, but in practice, a police officer would find it very hard to justify shooting someone that they could not identify. The cylinders in the rear sight were aligned side-on, producing two luminous lines. The fore sight insert was aligned lengthwise, producing a dot. When the dot was lined up in between the two lines, a pretty fair sight picture could be assured. For additional ease of use, the fore sight implant and those in the rear sight were different colours.

So, anything but a standard weapon, but all the modifications were made specifically to make the handgun more useful in a combat situation. It was Richard's gun, almost a part of him. A part which had been missing for some time. As he racked the slide back and forth and dry-fired the weapon, the old familiar feelings were coming back. But, the real thing he needed to know was, could he still hit something with it?

'Frank, is the indoor range available any time today?'

'Let me see.' Frank went back into his office and looked at a calendar on his desk. Half a minute later, he emerged. 'It's free for the next hour, if you have time.'

'That would be great,' said Richard.

'OK, let me get you some ammunition. Any preference?'

Richard didn't have to think about it. 'How about the semi-jacketed hollow-points we used in SDU?'

'Coming right up. Couple of hundred rounds be enough to be going on with?'

Richard nodded and the armourer went off to get the ammunition, leaving Richard to continue to get the feel of the gun back.

The indoor range at Police Headquarters was situated on a platform roof at the rear of May House, the multi-storey addition to the headquarters complex. Richard had obtained the keys from the duty officer and opened the heavy steel door leading into the blackness of the range. Flicking a light switch illuminated the entrance and control booth. Another key allowed access to this and Richard began operating a bank of controls. One by one, the lights in the range came on, revealing a tunnel-like room at the far end of which was a wall of angled steel plates, the bullet trap.

The range had eight lanes, each with a firing point which was partitioned off from its neighbour. The roof held a set of rails from which hung inverted T-shaped devices which would hold the paper targets. The rails allowed the targets to be positioned at any distance up to thirty meters from the firing point. The targets could be controlled from the booth, or the individual firing points. In addition, the target mechanism rotated, allowing the targets to "edge" and "face", for timed shooting practice.

What Richard had in mind today would be fairly basic. He just wanted to get his feel back and put a couple of hundred rounds down the barrel of his Browning. There would be plenty of time for more advanced training. At least he hoped so. He walked up to the fourth lane and took his weapon and ammunition out of the case. He also removed two magazines and began loading each with five rounds of 9mm ammunition. The magazines could carry thirteen rounds, but for his first practice, Richard only wanted a short load. In SDU Richard had also had twenty-round mags, but for the sort of duty he intended, the longer magazine would be unnecessary and cumbersome.

Richard placed a paper target in the bulldog clip-like jaws of the T-bar. With the control panel next to him, he moved the target out to ten meters. From a hook on the opposite wall, he lifted a pair of ear-defenders and adjusted them on his head. Picking up the Browning, he slid a loaded mag into the magazine well, racked the slide and applied the safety. Standing with his feet and shoulders placed at forty-five degrees to the target, Richard adopted the Weaver stance. The weapon was resting on the shelf in front of him. He raised it several times to eye level, each time adjusting his stance so that the weapon aligned with the centre of the target, without him having to adjust it laterally.

When he was happy with his position, he raised the Browning once more, taking a breath as he did so. As he adjusted the sight picture, he let out half the air in his lungs and held his breath. Gently he squeezed the trigger, feeling the easy pick-up and then the firmer travel as he reached the trigger-break. One millimeter of rearward movement and a bang rang around the walls of the indoor range. Richard let out his breath and lowering the weapon, relaxed his taught frame. It had been a while. Normally he would have been quite relaxed throughout this process, but his muscles, particularly across his shoulders and back, had tightened up. He would have to practise a lot before they behaved themselves again.

Richard repeated the ritual another five times. With the firing of the last round, the slide locked in the rear position, Richard unloaded, released the slide and dry-fired the weapon to ease the springs that operated the hammer. He laid the gun on the counter and threw the switch that would bring the target back to his position.

Frank had really made sure that no one fooled around with Richard's gun. The group was a little larger than he would have liked, but the sights must be at the same adjustment as the last time he fired the weapon. The group was centered on his aiming point, the middle of the centre-mass.

The next group of five shots was better and the next better still. Richard was feeling more relaxed with the weapon by the time he had expended fifty rounds. For the next fifty, he sent the target out to thirty meters and repeated the deliberate fire sequence, taking his time, allowing his body to remember the repeated movements, drilling his muscles into a routine that had once been unconscious and would be again, given enough time and ammunition.

In the control booth, Richard set the timing control to execute a series of edge/face actions on his target. Returning to the firing point, he loaded his weapon and threw the switch on his console that initiated the sequence. With his gun resting at forty-five degrees to the horizontal, he waited for the target to face. When it did, he had given himself five seconds to engage the target and fire. Plenty of time. When he had been in SDU, he could have completed the drill in less than two seconds and engaged multiple targets, facing in random order. But, that was more than three years ago.

The target faced and Richard brought the weapon up, keeping his eyes on the black silhouette. As the sights came level with his eyes, he aligned the foresight in the centre of the rear sight, taking up the slack on the trigger pull as he did so, his breathing following the cycle that he had practiced. The shot was rushed and Richard flinched as he realised that he had snatched the weapon slightly as he fired, trying to rush the shot as the seconds ticked past. The target edged. At least he had managed to get the shot away and it had landed on the target, but without looking, Richard knew that the shot would have fallen outside the Expected Scoring Area. The ESA was an area of the target, the size of his average group and centered on his point of aim. If he did everything right, most, if not all his shots would fall inside the circle that defined this area. Not this one though.

The target faced again. Richard engaged and this time managed to get the shot off without disturbing his basic position. He had been concentrating on the trigger pull this time and as a result wasn't sure that his sight alignment was alright. At close range, he might get away with it, but at thirty meters, a slight error in sight alignment would be greatly magnified and the result could be a miss. So far, he wasn't happy with his performance. The target edged. He had plenty of time, he just had to get back into the way of not thinking about any one thing in particular, but concentrating on all at once. Easy. Richard knew that the key was to relax and let his body remember how this was done.

Face. This time Richard held the gun facing the target after the shot was fired. He listened to all the signals that his body was giving him. He had plenty of time. The target edged, he lowered the gun. Better. He was pretty sure that the shot would have gone where he wanted it to. Concentrate, but relax. Seemingly conflicting instructions. The mind had to maintain its concentration on the job at hand, while the body remained in a relaxed state. The next two shots seemed to take forever to execute. The locked slide on the Browning was like a reprieve from a prison term. Richard let out a long breath as the tension that had been building up was released. He was still not relaxed enough.

As the target came to a sudden stop a foot from his face, Richard winced at the sight before him. Not very pretty at all. All five shots had hit the target, but three of them were outside the ESA. Not good enough by far. Richard used a piece of chalk to mark off the bullet holes in the target. This would allow him to use the same target again. Not a case of frugality, by marking every string of shots off and using the same target over and over, he would be able to get a better picture of his shooting and hopefully how it was improving with each group of shots.

The next group was slightly better, but Richard was still thinking too much about what he was doing. It had all been so easy once, but to reach that level of proficiency had taken years of practice. Half an hour on the range wasn't going to repair the damage done by years of neglect. The annual range qualification had been a formality for Richard. He hadn't even used his own gun. The course of fire was not exactly testing for a man of his skill. Even without the regular practice, he was still a good shot, just not great. Now that he had taken the step to carry a firearm around with him, his pride and his common sense would not allow him to be anything but proficient with the weapon. He just hadn't thought that it would take so much work. Now he knew the truth.

Another fifty rounds and he was starting to be less annoyed with his lack of prowess. Richard looked at his watch. He only had another ten minutes before the range would be in use. Just enough time for something a little more advanced. He bent down and opened a small holdall that he had brought along. He took out a holster, the type of concealed carry holster that fit inside the waistband of his trousers and looped through his belt. He had used this in SDU when there had been a need to wear civilian clothes and still be armed, usually while conducting reconnaissance. Richard undid his belt and threaded it through the loops on the holster. When the rig was in place, he slid his empty Browning into the holster and closed over the securing thumb-break loop.

Richard moved the target down the range to the twenty meter mark. He stepped in front of the firing points and came to a stop ten meters from the target. Drawing the Browning from its holster, he removed a magazine from his trouser pocket and slammed it into the magazine well. He racked the slide, engaged the safety and then removed the mag and re-holstered the weapon. Taking a single round from his pocket, he refilled the magazine, drew the pistol again and pushed the mag home. Again he re-holstered and secured the weapon.

He hadn't had time to program a sequence into the target mechanism, so he would just have to judge for himself how fast he was. Richard placed the palms of his hands together in front of his body. He breathed deep, then allowed his breathing to become more shallow. When he felt relaxed, he began. His right hand reached behind to the holstered pistol. His eyes stayed on the target. His left hand started to move up towards eye level. His right hand gripped the pistol, his thumb breaking the pop-stud that held the securing loop over the hammer and released the gun. Bringing it forward, he released the safety and engaged the front of his right fist into the palm of his left hand, forming a single, solid gripping unit. His left forefinger came over the trigger guard and completed the grip. The sights met his line of sight. Richard placed the foresight over the point of aim and made a "quick and dirty" sight alignment, squeezing the trigger has he did.

A hole appeared right in the centre of the target. Richard re-holstered and repeated the exercise three more times. On the next draw, he engaged the target and fired a "double tap", two rounds in rapid succession. The shots fell within an inch of one another. Again. Again. Again. Again. By the time the magazine was empty, there was a satisfying hole in the centre of the target's chest. Perhaps he had been thinking about it too much before, thought Richard. He knew the truth. He would still need a lot of practice before he would be happy with his performance. Richard packed up his things and cleared the range of spent cartridge cases. By the time he was ready to leave, a group of officers was preparing to go through their annual range qualification. Richard hoped that they would perform better than he just had. Alas, the truth was that he could probably outshoot any man there. The average beat constable had so few opportunities to train, that they were unlikely to become any better than satisfactory and that really depended on your definition of "satisfactory".

Richard's would have failed ninety percent of the Police Force. Practicality won over idealism yet again. Training cost time and money and the latter was never in sufficient supply. Well, it had been said that a society gets the police force that it deserves. Perhaps it would be more accurate to say it got the police force that it paid for.

Well, thought Richard, time to take Frank up on that beer.

CHAPTER 37

'Stop it! Stop the cable car, stop it now!'

'What? I can't just stop it.'

'DO IT!'

The operator threw the emergency stop switch on the control panel and stared at the park manager, as he gasped for breath. The manager's shoulders were heaving as he struggled to drag air into his lungs. The cable car operator was about to ask for an explanation as to why he had been ordered to stop the mechanism, leaving the occupants of the aerial transport literally hanging, when the manager grabbed his employee and dragged him out of the control room. Only when they were out in the open did the manager offer an explanation for his behaviour.

'Had to stop the cars. Received a call. Bombs. One on a car, other in there.' The manager pointed at the control room fifty yards behind them. He was having difficulty talking in his breathless state. 'Caller told me the number of the car. Said he would blow it up if we didn't stop the ride. Police are on their way.' The manager sat down on the cold concrete step. Why had this happened today, he wondered. Tomorrow was his day off. Just then eighteen ounces of plastic explosive destroyed the control room and ensured that the cable cars would not be going anywhere.

'Well there's something there. Probably couldn't have seen it at ground level. It's right on top of the thing that connects the car to the cable, whatever it's called.' Richard handed the binoculars to Ah Pau. This place was so familiar, like returning to a childhood home. Police Training School was adjacent to Ocean Park and the trainees regularly did the "Brick Hill Run", following a steep climb of steps running under the cable car. Tourists used to wave at the young police officers as they dragged their tired bodies up the slope. Now it was Richard's turn to look with pity upon the occupants of the cars. The one with the suspicious package above it was occupied by four very frightened looking kids. Part of a school trip, they had been on their way from the main entrance to the headland, to watch the marine show. Instead of sea-lions and dolphins the children were being treated to the prospect of a plummet to their deaths. If it really was a bomb, it was certainly big enough to slice through the cable and send all the cars on a one-way trip, straight down.

Ah Pau lowered the binoculars. 'This is a sick bastard, *Daai Lo* . Do you think he really is around here with a radio control?'

'With all the stray radio signals that are around, it would usually be a safe bet that he was bluffing. Trouble is, we can't take that chance. We have to assume that he has his finger on a button. At least with the Tactical Unit boys here, they can start searching the area, push him further away perhaps.

'I think though, that this is another little invitation to yours truly. Looks as though I am going for a little trip.'

The car that Richard had been looking at couldn't have been in a worse location. It hung between two towers, out of reach of even the longest ladder that the Fire Services could provide. There was only one way that Richard was going to get anywhere near the thing and as he and Ah Pau made their way back to the car park and their vehicle, they heard the sound of the approaching helicopter.

'Richard, long time no see.'

The smiling face of Pete Bailly came towards the small group of police officers that had congregated in the car park, which now doubled as a heli-pad. Richard had requested the RAF, rather than the Auxiliary Air Force, because of the larger capacity of the Wessex helicopter and the expertise of the man whose hand he was shaking.

'Pete, this is going to be a tricky one. There are six cars that we can't evacuate from the ground, including the one with the suspected bomb on board. What I would like to do is first, get me on to that car, then starting with it, evacuate as many of the people as you can. I don't really want to do anything that might set the damn thing off, until we have everyone back on *Terra firma* . I have to get a close look at it anyway, so I suggest that I abseil down and help you winch out the kids, unless you have a better idea. While I'm doing my bit, you can start to get the rest of the cars emptied.'

'Why don't we get some more choppers in to help,' suggested Pete. I'll call our guys, if you'll do the honours with the Auxie Air Force. We can concentrate on the car with the bomb, while the rest evacuate the other cars. Probably a good idea if we stand off your position anyway, just in case you need us to bring you kit in a hurry. I take it you won't be using a radio. So we'll need to work out some hand-signals with you before we go up.'

'Right, lets get on it. The clock is ticking and I just hope it's not up there with those kids.' Richard went straight to a land-line in order to get the rescue operation under way.

It had been a while since Richard had last exited a helicopter in this fashion. Regular training while he had been in SDU, abseiling from a chopper was not something he had done since leaving the unit. Dropping onto the top of the cable-car was not going to be easy, but Richard had always been good at this. He had put on his old SDU equipment vest, adapted to allow him to carry as much EOD kit as possible, rather than stun grenades and ammunition. Over his shoulder he also carried a coil of abseiling rope. This he would attach to the car, in case a quick getaway was called for. He just hoped if it came to that, that he could get onto the ground before the cable was cut and the car followed him down.

The helicopter held position high above the cable-car. If it got too close, the down-draft from the rotor would set the car in motion. It would make the descent even trickier, but Richard felt he could manage it. Giving Pete Bailly and Billy Parker, the crewman a final thumbs-up, Richard let himself drop backwards, off the step outside the entrance to the belly of the great metal insect. He controlled his descent, stopping occasionally to check on his position relative to the cable-car. The pilot made slight adjustments, keeping him over the target. This was no time for rapid deployment, this descent required finesse.

Richard stopped about three feet above the cable and looked at the unwelcome addition to the top of the car attachment. It looked like a metal box. There was no obvious mechanism on the outside. Richard eased his right arm up, lifting the rope from his side and allowing it to slowly move through the descender on his harness. He stopped when his feet were level with the cable. He was swinging in an arc of about ten feet. Carefully, he caught the cable with his foot and stopped his lateral motion. Lowering himself slowly, he was able to stand on the roof of the car. Once stable, he released the abseil rope and signalled to the helicopter to move off and keep station away from the cable-car.

The children inside the car were screaming, as terrified by Richard's appearance as the fact that they were stranded in this aerial cab. Richard spoke to them in Cantonese, explaining that he was there to help them, not mentioning the word bomb. He had a good look at the device. It was not obvious how the box was being held in place, but Richard thought that it might be with magnets. As there was nothing obvious to be done, he signalled to the helicopter and watched it approach to get the kids off. Richard attached a ballistic nylon loop and karabiner to the cable. Unwinding the rope he was carrying, he tied it off to the anchor and allowed it to drop to the ground. He took another descender from his vest and fed the rope through it. Then attaching the figure of eight to his harness, eased himself down the side of the car and in through the door.

The kids looked terrified as he entered the cable-car. In the back of Richard's mind was the thought that the bomber might be watching what he was doing and that the bomb might really be radio controlled. If that was the case, this was going to be the least successful rescue operation in the history of 28 Squadron. Above, he heard the helicopter. Telling the children not to worry, he stuck his head out of the now open door and saw a harness being lowered towards him. In it was a smiling Billy Parker. Pete Bailly was one of the best. Despite the lateral motion of the human pendulum, he hit the target, right on the money and Richard was pleased to see Billy hanging outside the car, waiting for his first passenger of the day. Although the children were scared, they caught on to the situation very quickly. The first one out was a little girl. Richard helped her into the arms of the crewman. There were tears, but she made little fuss as she clung tight to Billy. In a matter of seconds, they were gone and Richard set about talking to the remaining three children, amazed at the courage that they displayed. He wondered if adults would have shown this much mettle. It seemed to take forever, but as the fourth child was whisked away to safety, Richard let out a sigh of relief. All he had to do now was deal with a bomb, dangling from a wire, a couple of hundred feet in the air.

Climbing back on to the roof of the car, Richard took a plastic strip from his vest and tested the base of the metal box, where it met the top of the cable connection. It was a tight seal. Whatever was holding the box in place was doing so with gusto. Reluctantly, Richard took out a blade and tried to force it into the joint. Slowly, the thin wedge of the blade made its way under the box, raising its edge slightly as it did. Richard wasn't happy about doing this, but he took a screwdriver and opened up the gap even more, stopping short of breaking the contact between box and cable joint.

The air around the park was now filled with activity as another RAF helicopter, one from the Army and two from the Auxiliary Air Force, set about rescuing the trapped cable-car passengers. By the looks of it, they would be finished soon. Then Richard would have to decide what to do about his metal friend.

It occurred to Richard that his being perched on top of the gondola and doing nothing was somewhat redundant. He didn't really want to go through the whole process of getting here again, but every instinct in his body told him to get the hell out of there. The evacuation was almost complete, so he had two options; leave and see what happened, or stay and do something. His mind was made up when Pete Bailly signalled to him that the last of the passengers had been picked up by the other helicopter crews. The cable car was now just a mass of metal, waiting for one man to make a decision.

A couple of weeks before, he might have abseiled to the ground and allowed the box to get on with whatever it might do, but things had changed. He wanted to know what was in the box. If it was explosive, he was pretty sure that the nature of the location precluded any fancy anti-handling devices. The bomber was clever, but he had shown a liking for the simple. Richard prised the box up with the screwdriver and looked at the contents. The inside of the box contained what looked like a shaped charge of plastic explosive. So, his adversary had returned to using commercial materials. The mechanism to one side of the charge looked simple enough. The big worry was the electronic timer that was controlling the firing circuit. Richard had no idea when the thing might go off. There was a single detonator. Richard carefully removed this from the explosive and using a pair of wire cutters, snipped the two leads linking the small aluminium tube to the rest of the circuit. He placed the det in a pocket of his vest and then disconnected the battery which seemed the only power supply.

By this time, the hairs on the back of his head were standing on end and he had the overwhelming desire to get back on the ground. Putting the box under his left arm, he grabbed the abseiling rope and launched himself into open space. His descent to the ground was a good deal faster than his descent to the cable-car. He wanted rid of this thing he was carrying as soon as possible. When his feet touched the ground, he placed the box on the ground, with its open end facing up. He took the detonator out of his pocket and placed that on the ground, away from the main device. Ah Pau was by his side seconds after he had released his harness and started to walk away from the bomb.

'Tell me Ah Pau, was that the single most stupid thing I have ever done?' asked Richard. He felt his skin tingle with the realisation that he had just placed himself in an incredibly dangerous position and had probably stayed there longer than was absolutely necessary. He had gone against every rule of rendering explosive devices safe. By the time he had dealt with the bomb, the only person in any danger was himself. The sensible thing would have been to blow the thing *in situ* . That would probably have caused a great deal of damage to the cable-car, but was a lump of metal worth risking his life for. The answer was no, but his actions had been dictated by something more than a desire to save damage to the property of Ocean Park. He didn't want the bomber to achieve his aim. But Richard had to wonder what the aim of the bomb had been. To kill the passengers? Or to force him into idiotic heroics and get himself killed? Richard realised that Ah Pau was staring at him. 'Actually, I have no idea what I should have done, Ah Pau. What do you think?'

The older man looked at Richard and started to shake his head. 'I think that this man is playing a game with you and you are starting to play by his rules. I think that if this continues, you are going to be killed. You have to start thinking that the one thing this man wants is your death. Don't let him have his way.'

Richard nodded, then turned to look at the metal box. 'OK, let's take this fucking thing apart. I want to get the hell out of here and maybe then I can think straight. Right now, I have no idea what I was thinking of up there. I don't know if there was another way of dealing with that thing, or if I had no option. You start to pack up and I'll deal with our present over there.'

'What should I have done?'

Richard was sitting, his head resting between his two hands, trying to massage away the headache that was cutting through his brain. He wasn't having a great deal of success.

John Gray looked at his protégé and shook his head. 'You were there Richard, I wasn't. Do you think you did the right thing?'

'I don't know…the rules seemed to have changed. It's not enough any more to let these things blow up without hurting anyone. I want to beat this guy and maybe that means not letting the devices blow up at all.'

'Does that sound reasonable to you?'

'Yes…no…I don't really know. A week ago I would have said definitely no. Now, I'm not so sure.'

John let a wry smile appear on his face. 'What has changed in the last week?'

Richard had to think about that. 'Me. I've changed. This has become personal. There's some unpleasant bastard out there who wants to kill me.'

'That's always been a possibility in this job. You've known that from the beginning. The idea is to make sure that the bomber doesn't achieve his aim. Right?'

Richard looked up at his boss, ceasing the cranial kneading. 'I fucked up, didn't I?'

'Actually, in this case, I'm not sure you did. If that cable had blown, it could have caused a hell of a lot of damage, maybe killed someone. The movement of the cable-car made it unlikely, though not impossible that there were any anti-handling devices to give you a nasty shock. You got away with it, there's not much else to say, except maybe to ask yourself if you would do the same again.

'Don't even bother asking what I would have done. For a start, I wouldn't have been dangling a couple of hundred feet off the ground. That's your preserve, I'm glad to say. You do need to think about it. Decide for yourself if you took the correct action. If the answer is yes, then be glad that it worked out OK. If the answer is no, be glad that it worked out OK and don't be so bloody silly the next time.'

Richard Stirling felt very confused. What was it that he had been trying to prove up on that gondola? 'Looks as though I have to get some perspective on this situation.'

John nodded and smiled broadly. 'Well, while you're doing that, why don't you come and see what I was getting up to when you were doing your Tarzan act.'

The debris lying on the table could have been anything to an untrained eye. 'Letter bomb?' asked Richard.

'Yes. Your common or garden variety. Nothing special about it. Sheet PE4, Chinese cardboard det, similar story to our other packages, but this one wasn't particularly well done. It would have done the job if it had reached its target, but with the increased security around our high-risk group, it had little chance of getting close. This one came up on a routine X-ray of the mail for one of the protectees and I was called in to deal with it. I hit it with "Needle" and voila! One nasty little package. It was almost as though it was an afterthought.' "Needle" was a miniature version of the Pig-stick, designed for use against small packages and letters.

'Like he was trying to keep someone happy with this, while the main event was going on over at Ocean Park,' observed Richard. This certainly made it look as though the bomber was working for someone else. Richard made a mental note to discuss this with Cassius.

'I'm going to head over to PHQ. Cass has the security videos from Ocean Park. With any luck, our man may have left us a nice picture.'

John turned to face his colleague, his face serious. 'Don't try to rush things, Richard. We'll get close, without you having to play the human decoy. He's getting sloppy. He'll make a mistake. Just make sure that you are around when we get this bugger.'

CHAPTER 38

Long queues of people stood at Immigration, waiting to re-enter Hong Kong. Most carried the gloomy look of the loser, their hopes and dreams lost at the gambling tables of Macau. A few beamed with the glow of the winner, content with the Gods of Chance, until they were drawn back to the tables, to lose what they had won and more. One face among the crowd bore a grim expression that expressed loss, but of more than money.

'Richard!'

The call came from an unexpected direction. Richard Stirling had to look behind him to catch sight of the face that matched the familiar voice. Picking up his bags, he walked away from the Immigration counters, towards Mike Jessop, Alpha Team Commander.

'Come on, we've arranged to take you straight through Immigration and Customs. Give me your passport.'

Richard did as he was told. Mike led him towards a door. Inside, Immigration formalities were quickly dispensed with and in a matter of minutes, Richard was walking towards the exit of the Macau Ferry Terminal.

'What the fuck happened?' Richard's restraint had surprised even him. Perhaps he had been waiting for Mike Jessop to start talking, but the tall New Zealander showed no sign of opening up.

'Listen mate. I wasn't there. That bastard OC of ours made sure that I didn't get the call-out until an hour after Keith and your boys had arrived at the scene. He was out to make a bloody name for himself, I reckon. The prick has done that alright.

'By the time my boys and I got there, it was all over. Christ, it was a mess. I haven't got all the details yet, but from what I can gather, the bastards were waiting for your guys. Saw them on the building security camera. Cummings didn't think to check the security system, just sent Keith in and kept on his case to get on with it. Your boys tried to stall things, but the pressure must have been too great. When Keith and his Oppo went through the door, the cunts opened up with AK47s. They even had fucking hand-grenades! Tossed a couple of those out into the corridor and took out some of the guys as they were trying to get in to support the first pair. Christ Richard, it was a bloody massacre.'

Richard had stopped walking. He closed his eyes and breathed hard, the rage building in him. He tried to force the blackness in his heart down. He knew that Mike would have stopped Cummings had he been there, he had to avoid taking this out on the Kiwi. 'How many dead?'

Mike bit his lip. This was the part he had dreaded. He knew Richard well enough to know that a volcano was about to explode. 'Five. Three more serious, in hospital. There was a fire-fight all the way out. Two of the gang were killed, one by an Emergency Unit Sergeant, the other by one of your snipers. The rest...well they got away. How, don't fucking ask me. I think everyone was in so much shock, that they weren't thinking straight.'

'Keith?'

'Sorry man, he was practically cut in half by automatic fire. He didn't stand a chance. He could hardly have known what hit him.'

Wasn't it strange, thought Richard, that such statements were supposed to give some sort of comfort to those left behind; "He didn't suffer". "It was over very quickly". "He was cut in half by some prick with an AK47". The fact remained that his friend was dead. Dead for no reason, other than the incompetence and vanity of one man. A man that Richard was determined would pay for his actions.

'Mike, where is our "Glorious Leader"?'

'Richard, I have strict instructions to take you to home. The D Ops will call you when he wants to see you. 'Til then, you're to stay put. He'll probably call this afternoon.' The Director of Operations was the man who oversaw the branch of the Police Force under which SDU came.

Richard looked his colleague straight in the eyes. When he spoke, it was slowly and deliberately. 'Where is Cummings?'

Victor Cummings sat uncomfortably in his chair. Across the desk, Bob MacLean, the Director of Operations, was watching him, waiting for the Superintendent to speak. Cummings had been called in to give his account of what happened in person. This was a black day for the Police Force, to have so many young lives cut short in the line of duty. An explanation was demanded.

'Symons and his men obviously alerted the gang to their presence. They spent too much time at the door, instead of getting in there as quickly as possible. I kept telling him to get a move on, but he ignored my advice. Also, we didn't know that they had grenades. How could we?'

MacLean looked at a file sitting in front of him. 'Did you read the intelligence report from CIB?'

'Of course.'

'And you made your men aware of its contents?'

'What I thought pertinent to the job, yes. Where is this going?'

'This is a copy of the report that I passed to you before this operation began. On page four it states, "there is strong evidence to suggest that the gang have obtained weapons and ammunition from a PLA base in Shenzen. These may include AK47 type assault rifles, automatic pistols, explosives and fragmentation grenades. This information came from a source of the highest reliability and should be considered in any attempt to apprehend the suspects." Remember that section?'

Cummings licked his lips. His boss could see the thought processes at work.

'We were in a hurry. I must have scanned over that section. The words obviously didn't register.'

'They are highlighted in bold print. They form part of the summary of the report, as well as the main body. CIB thought it important enough to mention twice, how come you missed it twice?'

'Sir, this is not my fault. I was ordered to the scene at very short notice. I didn't have time to review the report before calling out the unit. It was made clear to me that there was a degree of urgency about the operation.'

'Made clear by who exactly?' MacLean was a patient man, but his tolerance for Cummings was wearing thin.

'By the chain of command. It was an urgent call-out.'

'Five men are dead. Another may never walk again. Your unit was not made aware of all the facts before they deployed and now you are trying to blame men who cannot speak for themselves. Are you the OC SDU or not?'

'I never wanted the job. It was a political move to bring a runaway group under control. You know that. You wanted someone in there who would make the men toe the line. Instil discipline and respect for the chain of command. That was my job and little thanks I got for it. Those ungrateful bastards never tried to make me feel welcome. Just because I never went through that ridiculous selection of theirs. Why would I have to run ten miles, or abseil off the thirty-fifth floor of a high-rise? I'm an administrator and a good one. Now I'm to be made the scapegoat for the fact that their great unit isn't all it was cracked up to be. No, I'll not take this lying down. I'm a Gazetted Officer. You won't find it easy to get rid of me.

'Symons was incompetent. Stirling was off swanning around in Macau. I did the best I could with the men at my disposal. It's not my fault that they were not up to the job. Stirling trained them, why don't you ask him why they failed?'

Bob MacLean couldn't remember the last time he had hit someone. This remarkable outburst had left him speechless and with the overwhelming desire to rip the head off the man in front of him. He forced his anger back into the depths of his being. He couldn't do what he as a man wanted to do. He had to do what he as a Senior Police Officer had to do. Behave rationally and calmly with a man who was quite obviously a complete arsehole.

'Finished? As a matter of fact, I objected to you being appointed OC SDU. I believe that the man in charge should have gone through selection and training, or at least have the sort of background that would allow him to understand the way that the unit works. You were not there as an administrator. You were there as a leader. The men under your command looked to you for support and protection. One of your jobs was to minimise the jeopardy in already hazardous duty. It is my opinion that you failed your men in this regard.

'Richard Stirling was not "swanning around" as you put it, he was liaising with the Macau Police at the specific orders of the Commissioner. His trip was an important one, though I doubt that this tragedy would have happened if he had been at the scene.

'Why was Alpha not called out at the same time as Bravo?'

'What?'

'Why was half of Alpha Team called out over two hours after Bravo Team, including the Team Commander?'

Cummings looked flustered. 'I don't know what you mean. I knew nothing of this.'

'So, you're saying that you didn't enquire as to why Alpha team took so long to get to the scene?'

'There was so much going on. I had to get on with things. I didn't have time to chase up men who should already have been there. Is it my fault that the armoury staff don't call the men out, or that the Team members don't answer their pages right away. They were probably drinking or in a disco and ignored the call. Probably thought that some girl was calling them. You know what they are like.'

'Not very much seems to be your fault Superintendent, does it? Don't you accept any responsibility for this fiasco at all?'

'No. I did my job to the best of my abilities. That is all.'

'You are a very lucky man. If Stirling were here, I think I would find it very hard to even attempt to stop him doing what I think he would do to you.'

'Is that a threat, sir?'

Bob MacLean was finding it hard to keep his seat, when the door to his office burst open and a figure rushed across the floor and grabbed Cummings right out of his chair. Gripping him by the throat with his left hand, Richard launched a barrage of punches with his right, straight at the man's face. The assault only lasted a matter of seconds, before MacLean and Mike Jessop, who had followed Richard in, managed to prise the furious Stirling off his victim. Richard struggled against the two men, but they were strong and determined to stop the assault.

Cummings stayed on the floor, his hands covering his face, incoherent noises coming from his bruised and bloody mouth. Richard was backed out of the door, into the secretary's office beyond. Bob MacLean closed the door when he had the chance. Then he turned to Richard.

'What the bloody hell were you hoping to achieve in there? Apart that is from ending your career.'

'Stuff my career. That bastard got my men killed. Now it's his turn.' Richard launched himself at the door, but was caught by the other two men before he could reach it. Mike Jessop put an arm-lock on his friend, trying to stop him carrying out what was not an idle threat.

'Listen to me! He'll get what's coming to him, but you lay one more finger on him and he'll win this thing. You will be hung out to dry and that prick will get away with a reprimand. Are you listening to me?' MacLean looked at Richard and was eventually rewarded with a nod. 'There will be an investigation. Everything will be brought out into the open and he'll be shown up for what he is. A spineless weasel. If I'm right about what happened last night, there's a good chance our friend in there is going to face criminal charges. But if you insist on your own personal revenge, you'll be the one in the dock.'

Richard felt about as foolish as he had ever felt. Bob MacLean was right. Who was he doing this for? Keith and his men, or himself? Suddenly he felt very ashamed. He bowed his head and looked at the floor, unable to find the words to explain his stupidity.

Mike was told to take Richard home. MacLean walked back into his office. Cummings bolted slightly as he came through the door, obviously fearing a repeat performance of his recent onslaught. When he saw MacLean enter alone, a look of bravado came over his bruised face.

'See what I have to contend with? How do you expect me to control animals like that? It's no wonder that they get themselves killed.'

That was the last straw as far as Bob MacLean was concerned. He walked over to Cummings and grabbed him by the lapels. Cummings' superior look disappeared and was replaced by one of real fear. When he was younger, MacLean had a reputation for talking with his fists. On this occasion, he resorted to his mouth.

'You are the most contemptible man I have ever met. Those boys gave their lives doing their job and all you can think of is using them to save your own miserable neck. As for Richard Stirling, I wish I had a hundred officers like him and I also wish that I had the opportunity to let him finish what he started a few minutes ago. As far as I am concerned, nothing happened in here. If you try to pursue this, I will say that it was me who gave you those bruises. See how far you get then.

'There will be an inquiry. If you come out of that with your hide intact, there will be no justice in the world. I shall do my utmost to ensure that all the facts come out and that the blame is laid where it belongs. It won't be up to me to decide your fate, but I will do my best to make sure that you are no longer a Superintendent by the end of the inquiry. If you are still in the job it will be an injustice. Now, get out of here. You are under interdiction pending the investigation of last night's events. You will talk to no one about it, other than the officers assigned to the investigation. Is that clear?'

'Yes, sir.' Cummings didn't try to hide the bitterness in his voice.

'Now, get the fuck out of my office.'

There was an inquiry. The finding of the investigating team was that a catalogue of errors on the part of several officers had contributed to the tragedy. The report was several hundred pages long and took six months to produce. The hierarchy of the Police Force felt that to prosecute would be to deal a greater blow to the already tarnished reputation of the Force.

Keith Symons and the others killed and injured during the operation were put up for a variety of awards for bravery. The Governor blocked the submission. None of them were honoured publicly.

Richard was forced to leave the SDU. Confidential entries were made in the headquarters copy of his record of service, entries that he would never be allowed to see. Thanks to Bob MacLean, he was accepted into the Explosive Ordnance Disposal Unit and trained as a specialist, on the understanding that he would never leave the unit and might never be promoted.

Superintendent Victor Cummings was given a verbal reprimand by the Commissioner of Police and then posted out of the Special Duties Unit, into a post which carried the rank of Senior Superintendent of Police.

CHAPTER 39

Garland hated China. He hated the Chinese. In fact he hated most places and most people. Jack Garland carried a lot of hate around with him. His personal baggage was from the house of Loathing and Venom. His vicious nature was fuelled by his hate and jealousy. It took little to ignite the flame of his malevolence. Just being in the streets of a Chinese city was enough to bring out a race hatred which would have made the most dedicated Nazi proud. Watching the shuffling masses from the front passenger seat of the Mercedes made his bile rise. Garland had loathed having to deal with these people when he was a police officer in Hong Kong. No, he reminded himself. The Hong Kong variety were far more advanced than these peasants, with their mediocre designer suits, with the labels still prominent on the cuffs of the jackets. These people were straight out of the paddy fields. As Li's security chief, Garland had to kowtow to these people and oh, how he hated that.

Even though Li had considerable business interests in mainland China, his visits there were infrequent. For that, Jack Garland was grateful. On this trip, they were only just across the border from Hong Kong, in the Special Economic Zone of Shenzen. Garland could remember this place when it was a small town, surrounded by farm land. Now, it was a bustling dynamo of new enterprise, the face of New China. It's high-rise blocks were carbon copies of those in

Hong Kong. The World Trade Centre mimicked the Hopewell Centre on Hong Kong Island, even to the extent of having a circular revolving restaurant on top. The difference was that where the Connaught Centre was a circular building, the World Trade Centre in Shenzen was square, with a circular restaurant perched ungainly on top. To Garland, that summed the place up. It copied Hong Kong superficially, but the people who ran China just didn't get it. They could not understand what it was that made Hong Kong successful, so like their buildings, their economic endeavours were superficially successful, but lacked the sophistication to be players on the world stage. They copied, but they failed to innovate.

As the Mercedes made its way through the traffic, light by Hong Kong standards, along the mud encrusted roads, Garland thought about the story he had heard about the housing estates in Shenzen. A member of parliament from the United Kingdom had been on a visit to Hong Kong and China. In Shenzen, the authorities had been keen to show off their new housing projects, identical to the latest developments in Hong Kong. During the visit, the ample liquid hospitality which the MP had enjoyed over lunch caught up with him. Panic ensued as he indicated that he would like to use the sparkling toilet in the flat he was being shown. It turned out that the block had been built without the proper infrastructure having been put in place first. There was no sewage system for the toilets to flush into, so they couldn't be used. Probably an apocryphal tale, thought Garland, but he had seen enough unbelievable things in China to know that there was probably at least a grain of truth in the story.

The car swung through a gate, into a compound protected by a high wall and a uniformed guard carrying a Type 56 Assault Rifle. The factory produced electronic components for the defence industry. It's main customer, the People's Liberation Army. The security staff were supplied by the military, to protect their own interests. This was one area of Li's business that Garland was not allowed to get involved in. On this trip, he was along as Li's bodyguard and nothing else. The Englishman felt even more enraged by his further demotion in the eyes of the Chinese peasantry. To humiliate him further still, he would not be allowed to sit in on the meeting with the PLA official that Li had come here to meet. Instead, he would wait in silence in an ante-room and suffer the arrogant stares of the Motherland's defenders.

The trip up from Hong Kong Island had not been a pleasant one. Li was furious at the botched attempt to kill the latest target and had reminded Garland in no uncertain terms that he held the former policeman responsible for any failure. The fiasco at Ocean Park had added to the tirade of abuse which Garland had been forced to suffer. There seemed no end to this nightmare. No end but that which Garland had already started to formulate in his mind. Garland was a creature of instinct and right now his instincts were telling him that his life might soon be in danger. As long as Li continued to berate him, he was safe. He knew his boss well enough to know that it would be when Li was at his kindest and most charming that the axe would be poised to fall. Garland's gut was telling him that events were moving rapidly toward that situation. He had to be prepared, ready to make his own strike at the coiled cobra, before he felt Li's venomous kiss.

A factory official in a grey suit rushed up to meet the car as it parked in a space which was always reserved for the Chairman. Garland spotted with disdain the label bearing the name "Pierre Cardin" that was still attached to the cuff of the man's jacket. His contempt became total when he noticed the ubiquitous white socks which lay under the man's black tasseled loafers, their presence made visible by the shortness of the man's trouser legs. Garland shook his head. They never learned, did they, he thought. The manager overflowed with enthusiasm at his superior's visit and totally ignored Garland, failing to even acknowledge his presence as he led Li off to the administration building. Inside, as expected, a sullen lackey pointed

Garland to a waiting room, while Li was given a walking kowtow all the way to the conference room, where his meeting would take place.

The change in Li's demeanor, as he walked into the room, went unnoticed by the lackey who escorted him, but was plain to the man waiting for him in the conference room. Like an emotional chameleon, he changed from superiority to humility, blending in to his new environment, hoping to evade the predator waiting within.

The man's only acknowledgement of the newcomer was the way his eyes followed Li as he entered the room. The door shut quietly behind the businessman, but still his observer made no sound. The uniform was that of a Lieutenant General in the Ground Forces of the PLA. Deprived of structure and differentiation for many years, the 1984 Military Service Law had stipulated that ranks should be reintroduced to the PLA. The process was ongoing, but since 1985 PLA personnel had been issued with new uniforms and insignia to replace the baggy green fatigues which had made it hard to distinguish between officers and other ranks. As a senior officer, this man wore the olive green woolen uniform of the ground forces, with red collar badges and epaulets depicting his rank. A peaked cap sat on the conference table, within reach of its owner. The cap badge was the familiar five-star emblem and the ideographs for "August 1st", the anniversary of the Nanchang uprising, surrounded by wheat ears and machine cogs, the symbols of agriculture and industry. The last two elements were particularly appropriate for this man. Hua Jianying was a senior member of the General Logistics Department.

This was Li's great secret. During the 1970's his business empire had been close to collapse. While others prospered, Li faced bankruptcy and humiliation. Li, as always, blamed others for his own shortcomings. High on his list of those who had "conspired" against him, were the very British businessmen whom he had been trying to eradicate through his scheme of revenge and avarice. The plan had not been his child, but he had adopted it with enthusiasm. Hua had been the architect of the bombing campaign. Li knew that the General had his own agenda in the great scheme, but knew better than to enquire as to what that might be. The less he knew the better as far as the diminutive businessman was concerned.

One thing was certain. Hua owned Li. Hua had been the "white knight" who had bailed Li out of his pecuniary dilemma. With the political influence of his rank and position and the funds within his control, Hua had made "strategic investments" in key parts of Li's business group. The PLA was a self-financing army and had investments in all manner of companies. The backing had been enough to pull Li back from the brink and the access to lucrative government contracts that Hua's patronage had provided meant that Li's star began to be ascendent once more. With the protection of his new masters, it seemed that Li could do no wrong, or if he did, it was soon put right. To the rest of the world, Li was a swaggering success story, but in Hua's presence, the arrogant facade was left at the door.

'Why am I here?'

Li started at the question. Hua's voice seemed almost disembodied. It had come suddenly, without any warning that the man was about to speak. The words were without emotion.

'Why am I here?'

The normally eloquent Li was struggling to say a single word in answer. Eventually he managed to speak. 'I don't understand. You said you wanted to see me.'

'Why am I here, Li Keung?'

Li was beginning to sweat, though the air-conditioning made the room feel like the inside of a meat locker. Panic was not a feeling that Li was used to and he was ill-equipped to deal with it. Soon, it would take over and his iron self-control would melt away in the heat of his own fear. The same question repeated over and over left no room for maneuver. Hua wanted an explanation from Li and though the businessman didn't want to admit it, there was only one issue to be tabled at this meeting.

'I…I explained over the satellite link. Things are out of control. I did as you instructed and made an effort to bring your man back under control. It seemed that he was following instructions again, but recent events have shown that he is merely paying lip service to our instructions. He seems to be pursuing some private vendetta of his own. I don't know what else I can do. Perhaps you have some suggestions?'

The last plea for help was as pathetic as it was tardy. Li knew that he had kept the problem of the bomber's behaviour quiet for too long. Terrified of seeming weak and powerless in front of Hua, he had thought that he and Garland would be able to control the situation on their own. Away from the influence of his Mainland masters, Li had a tendency to become over confident in his abilities. Back in this powerful presence, he was reminded of his previous failures. Humility was a hard pill for Li to swallow, but standing before Hua, the medicine would have to be taken with as much good grace as possible, or forced down. The choice was Li's.

Hua leaned forward, arms lying on the conference table, hands clasped as if in prayer. His eyes bored deep into Li's soul, looking for weakness and finding it in abundance. The General's contempt was open and accusing. When he spoke, the words came out like an artillery barrage. 'We have invested a great deal in you Li Keung. Money, time and effort. It would seem that our investment has failed to bear fruit. A wise investor knows when to cut his losses and look for more profitable ways of using their resources. Can you offer me any reason why we should continue to support you and your activities?'

Li was being challenged to prove more than his financial soundness. His ability to carry out the wishes of his "investors" was in doubt. This was a pivotal moment for Li Keung. His whole future hung on the words that would come out of his mouth in the next few minutes. Tension grew within Li. His mouth dried as quickly as his armpits became wet. Sweat carries the smell of fear. Li wondered if the man at the end of the table could sense the terror that was gripping his gut and tying it in tighter and tighter knots. As the General's eyes continued to burn into Li, the businessman struggled to focus his mind on the problem at hand. Where were the words that would save him from the fire? A mouth full of cotton wool was a poor instrument, if the words would come. Li tried to salivate, bring some lubrication to the dry conduit of his thoughts. None would come. No words. No spit. Li's hands started to tremble. Hua obviously noticed this outward expression of Li's inner turmoil, for a sly smile appeared on his face. The first voice to break the dreadful silence was the General's.

'Let me make it very simple for you Li. If matters are not in hand within ten days, we will terminate our relationship with you. You may now leave.'

So that was it. Ten days to turn things around. Ten days to save his empire. Ten days to save his life. Li was under no illusions about the meaning of "terminate our relationship". It was not merely a matter of the end of a financial relationship. Li knew too much to be allowed to live. As long as he and his PLA backers were of use to one another, there was a bond of dependency. Without that bond, Li was perhaps no real threat, but certainly a potential source of embarrassment. Since 1985, much of the PLA's control over the defence industry had been stripped away and handed over to private enterprise. Li and others like him had afforded them a way of maintaining control behind the scenes. Such knowledge of indirect defiance of Government policy made Li a liability if he was no longer part of the "great scheme".

It took Li some time to realise that he had been dismissed. Hua said nothing further, but continued to bore into Li's inner being with his unrelenting stare. Finally, Li came to something close to his senses and first backed towards the door and finally turned his back to Hua. It was only as he was leaving the room that Li realised that he had been standing throughout the meeting, like some vassal. The truth was that it had not been a meeting. It had been an audience.

Crossing the threshold once more, Li was still stunned by the dreadful importance of the words spoken just a few minutes before. Normally, the chameleon would have taken on the demeanor of the superior once more, ready to dish out some lessons in humility to anyone getting in his way, but today he was too preoccupied to play his petty games. Li walked straight to the ante-room where Garland was sitting, staring straight ahead, with the sourest look on his face that Li had ever seen. Well, thought Li, perhaps the man is in just the right mood for the business that lies before us. 'Garland,' snapped Li, regaining a fraction of his composure. 'Come on, we have a lot to discuss in the car. Let's get back to civilisation.'

Garland looked surprised by this last statement. Li was forever lecturing him on the cultural and moral superiority of the Chinese. The meeting had obviously gone very badly indeed. Far from deriving any satisfaction from this, Garland felt his own gut start to tighten. Whatever was coming his way had bad news written all over it. The moment of truth was certainly at hand.

CHAPTER 40

The smell of rubber was strong from his respirator. The mask seemed to amplify the sound of his breathing as he worked his way up the staircase. Though he was fit, his breathing was hard as he tried to make the climb as quickly as possible. He had to catch up with the rest of the team. Why had they gone on without him, thought Richard? A slight panic started to form in his chest as he pushed himself even harder up the narrow stairs. The walls seemed to close in on him. He couldn't remember the stairwell being this confining when he had started to run up it. Perhaps his imagination was playing tricks with his oxygen deprived brain. As his muscles cried out for replenishment, he began to feel light-headed. He would have to slow down soon, give his body a chance to recover. If he reached the rest in this state, he would be no use to them. He really must get more exercise, less time behind a desk.

Under all his equipment, he was sweating hard. Only the gloves he wore allowed him to maintain a tight grip on his MP5. Richard could hear the communication between his men through the ear-piece of his radio. They were getting close to the stronghold. He tried to contact them, tell them to hold until he caught up with them. He received no acknowledgement of his communication. Perhaps his radio had a problem. Why had they started without him?

His legs were starting to seize up. Lactic acid was building up in his muscles, turning them to fire. Still he pressed on. He had to keep going. Every inch of his body told him that he had to rest. He was pushing on by will alone.

Keith's voice came over the radio. He was going in for a close recce of the door. Richard tried to scream into his throat mic. 'Keep away. Wait for me.' No response. Keith called for radio silence as he approached the door. Richard looked up. When were these stairs going to end? Surely he must be getting close? Still, he pressed on. His passage became more erratic as his brain cried out for oxygen and started to close itself down when the call was ignored. His vision was starting to blur. Richard knew that if he didn't rest, his body would take the matter into its own hands. But he refused to give in to the weakness of his own flesh. His will was all that mattered. He had to go on. His movement up the staircase had slowed, but he refused to stop. He must be close. He just had to be.

Richard stumbled on a step, just managing to maintain his balance. He felt as though he were walking through mud which clung to him, pulling him backwards. Another slip, this time he fell forward and slipped down several steps. Finding his feet, he pressed on. Keith was telling the men to get ready. Stop, wait, thought Richard. He voiced his thoughts, even though he knew that they would never reach the ears of the men. Harder he pushed himself, trying to pick up some speed. He had to be close. He would get to them in time. A mist had descended over his eyes. He could hardly see the stairs in front of him. Still he pushed his body on. In his left ear he heard Keith give the order to go. No! The scream was inside his head. He didn't have the energy to vocalise it. Richard heard the explosion. He had to be close. Maybe it wasn't too late. Harder he pushed. Suddenly his body refused to move. His knees turned to jelly and he saw the stairs rush up to meet his face. The last thing he heard before he passed out was a ghastly symphony of gunfire and screams. One of the voices screaming was his own.

'Richard. Easy. Breathe. Nice and slowly. That's it. That's it. Relax, baby. You're alright. You're in bed. I'm here with you. You're safe.'

Natalie held Richard in her arms. It had been over a year since he had suffered from these nightmares. Natalie had been the one who persuaded him to seek help from one of the psychologists employed by the Police Force, rather than seeking liquid counselling, which was the usual refuge of people in his profession. All had seemed well, until a lump of shrapnel had come close to killing him. Memories that had been controlled, though not forgotten, had resurfaced to wreak havoc with his peace of mind.

Richard's body was covered in sweat, the bedclothes on his side soaked by his unconscious labour. His breathing was starting to slow. He had been hyper-ventilating, his heart pounding against his chest. Natalie could feel it's attempts to escape the confines of his rib-cage. She looked at his face, still showing the strain of his panic inducing somnial experience. His eyes were closed as he tried to bring his body back under control. Natalie wiped the sweat from his brow. Immediately more began to bead between the furrows. As his breathing returned to something approaching normal, Richard opened his eyes.

'Better?' asked Natalie. Richard nodded his head slowly. He had yet to find his voice. Natalie stroked his wet hair, looking down at him as she sat on the bed. They had made love that afternoon and fallen asleep in one another's arms. She had woken suddenly, roused by his flailing movement and muted shouts. This had been the third time this week. 'Same dream?' This time he shook his head. Natalie wanted to say so much, tell him that he should go and see the psychologist again. Perhaps take some of the leave that he had allowed to pile up. But, she knew that he would do neither. Not now. Not while someone was planting bombs on his turf. He wouldn't allow himself to be taken out of the game.

'I could hear Keith scream.'

Natalie looked down at eyes that stared at the ceiling. She thought he looked tired. He always looked tired these days.

'I thought I had made peace with their ghosts. Perhaps I never will. They may lie quietly for a while, but they will always be there. Waiting to remind me that I should have been with them that night. I know it was just dumb luck that I wasn't. Dumb luck and that bastard Cummings. I keep telling myself that it wasn't my fault. But the truth is that it shouldn't have mattered whether I was there or not. I should have worked harder to get rid of that clown Cummings. If someone else had been in charge, the guys would have been safe, even if I wasn't there.

Perhaps if Cummings had gotten what was coming to him, the boys could rest in peace, but as long as that arrogant son of a bitch is still walking around, they never will.'

'I'm not going to nag you. You have gone over this a hundred times. There was nothing more that you could do. The politicians were the ones who had the final say. Everyone thinks that you and your guys got a raw deal. The final insult was promoting Victor Cummings, but it was either that or admit that the hierarchy of the Police Force were wrong, had made a mistake in appointing Cummings to the job. When was the last time the men in the "ivory tower" owned up to a mistake? Certainly not since I have known you and I am sure that you would have mentioned such a monumental occurrence if you'd known about it. Are you sure it's just old memories resurfacing?'

Richard turned his head on the pillow to look up at her. When he looked at her face, he could never feel entirely sorry for himself, not when he had her in his life. He thanked all the Gods that she was with him. Richard knew that if she had not supported him after the death of his men, he might not made it this far. He may have joined the ranks of the chronically morose and spent the rest of his life looking cynically at the world through the bottom of a bottle. She was his guardian angel, his saviour and he loved her for that and more. Ignoring her question, he reached up and drew her head down towards his. Their lips met and Natalie knew that she would not get an answer.

They made love gently, patiently. Richard was still drained from his nightmare, but his ardour remained as strong as ever. He controlled his passion, dissipating it slowly, stretching the moment, on and on. Natalie loved the variety of their sex life. Both she and Richard were aggressive sexual creatures and had the imagination to be creative in the way they pleasured one another. Now, they both took their time. Often they would launch themselves at one another, without warning and when least expected. Then the sex was raw, unsophisticated and hot. Now, the mood was calm, though their bodies were anything but. They controlled themselves, teasing and caressing, pulling back and then submerging themselves in the coupling. They knew each other's bodies so well. Where a light caress would produce the most delightful result, where a more firm stimulation was required. They moved one another's hands, mouths and bodies. Non-verbal communication at its most fluent.

They lay in each other's arms, panting, sweating, happy. Natalie's head rested on Richard's chest. She could hear his heart beat. Faster than normal. When he had been in SDU, his resting heartbeat had been very low, around forty-eight beats per minute. After sex, she used to be amazed at the fact that she could never detect the frantic thumping in his chest that she had been used to with her other lovers. Now, he supplied the soundtrack to their lovemaking. She was half glad, half worried. He was not as fit as he had been, but now there was the added strain of the worry that he would not share with her. She was under no illusions. As welcome as their congress had been, it was another evasion, another attempt to change the subject. Natalie sighed. At least he doesn't just walk away, she thought. Still she knew that they had to discuss this problem some time. She was wise enough to know that it would only happen when her lover was ready.

Richard stroked her head. 'Hungry?' he asked.

'Hmm. Ravenous. We haven't eaten since breakfast.'

'Let's eat out. I feel like being around a lot of people right now.'

Richard had seemed more cheerful over dinner, the memory of his unpleasant dream pushed aside for the time being. They had gone to a "hole in the wall" Thai restaurant in Kowloon City, near the airport. The streets around this location had filled up with these small eateries in the last couple of years, but the original one was still the best and the couple were regular visitors. A few Singha Gold beers had relaxed Richard and tempered the fiery nature of the food. Tom Yam Kung, a seafood soup, Thai beef salad, a green chicken curry and plenty of boiled rice had left the pair replete. A walk was called for. The two lovers left the restaurant and made their way towards the busy streets of Kowloon City. As they walked, they took in the free street theatre that is the hustle and bustle of Hong Kong.

Shops and restaurants cast harsh, but welcoming light into the street, inviting the passing trade to stay a while. Goods spilled from shops onto the pavement, blocking the path of passers-by. Pedestrians shared the road with cars and taxis, showing their indifference to the wares on display. Vehicular noise vied with the shouts and laughter of human traffic for dominance in the hot evening air. Breathless canyons of concrete, filled with people on the move. There was a purpose to the movement, as though the people had to move, or die. Land-locked sharks in a sea of commerce.

Several times, Richard and Natalie looked involuntarily upwards, drawn by the roar of large passenger jets, skirting the rooftops above them. An unnatural proximity. The landward approach to Kai Tak Airport, coming in to Runway 13 was among the most spectacular in the world. A crash would have resulted in a disaster beyond imagination, except perhaps for those whose job it is to imagine such grim possibilities and plan for the unthinkable.

Leaving the bustle of Kowloon City behind, the pair walked towards Argyle Street, planning to walk its length and catch the Mass Transit Railway back to Hong Kong Island. As they neared Kowloon City Police Station, at the airport end of Argyle Street, a familiar figure was coming in the opposite direction. The man's walk was a trifle unsteady, but there was obviously nothing wrong with his eyesight, for as soon as he caught sight of the strolling couple, he let out a roar. 'STIRLING!'

'Oh, dear,' whispered Richard. Then out loud, 'Dave. How the hell are you?'

Dave Price made his groggy way to meet them. His large frame seemed to wobble as he went. On his face was a huge grin which said "Ah, company". 'Richard and the delectable Natalie, how are we on this lovely evening?'

'We're just fine David,' said Natalie. 'And how are you doing?'

'Oh, can't complain. The bastards haven't gotten rid of me yet. They're trying hard mind you. Sending me off on the next "Fatties" Course. Say I have to lose forty pounds, or they'll medically board me out. Silly buggers. A couple of weeks off the sauce and I will lose at least that much. Done it before, I can do it again.

'Talking of having a toot, I was just going to pop in to KC Mess for a quick one. Fancy joining me?'

Richard looked at Natalie and was rewarded with a "why not" shrug. In fact this was not the response that he had been looking for. He knew Dave Price well and knew that "a couple" was shorthand for a raging booze session. If the rotund Senior Inspector had his way, they would still be at it when the sun came up. Not wanting to offend his old friend, Richard accepted the offer, but added that he had to be up early the next day, so could only stay for a couple.

'Oh God, what was his name? What was his name? You know, old, eh...You know, that fellow who was with us on the EOD course, remember? The one with the moustache. Nice guy, even if he didn't drink. What was his name?' Dave had been having this conversation for about the last five minutes. Both Richard and Natalie were looking weary, as they listened to the drunken monologue. Richard had no idea who his friend was talking about. When they had been on a Bomb Disposal course together, there were no mustachioed teatotallers on it with them. Dave must be thinking of something else. Richard didn't have the heart or the energy to argue.

'Bloody hell, the old brain must be going. Anyway, what was I saying?' Dave, spotting that Richard's glass was empty, started towards the cooler for another bottle of beer.

'Steady on Dave,' said Richard, anticipating his friends intentions. 'That's it for me I'm afraid. I don't have your stamina. It's bed for us. Why don't we give you a lift in a taxi?'

The mess was empty apart from the three of them. It had been that way for the last two hours. Richard kept hoping that someone would come in and keep Dave company. He looked as though he had settled in for the night. Natalie had shown a great deal of patience, but Richard was not making excuses when he said that he needed to get to bed. He was dog tired and in no mood for playing straight man to his drunken friend.

It took some persuading, but at last they managed to persuade Dave that heading across the harbour was a good idea. Whether or not he would make it back to his flat was another matter. He seemed in the mood to seek out some alternative company.

The roads were fairly clear and it took less than twenty minutes to deposit Dave outside "The Hermitage", a huge block of service flats. These were usually occupied by Police Inspectors on their first tour in Hong Kong and other single government servants, but there were some long-term residents like Dave. The place had it's own mess, where residents could drink and eat cheaply and it was no doubt to the bar that Dave was heading when Richard and Natalie dropped him off.

As the taxi drove away, Richard placed his hand over his eyes and massaged his temples. 'He wasn't always like that you know,' he said without removing his hand. He sat upright and sighed deeply. 'When I first met dave, he was one of the sharpest men I think I have ever met. Witty, well read, a real font of knowledge. You wanted to know anything about Civil Service Regulations, he was your man. He could turn a long weekend off into a week's holiday, just by playing the system. Good at his job too. He helped me out when I was a "makee-learnee" *Bong Baan* , just out of training school. He took me under his wing and did his best to keep me out of the shit. Did just that on more than one occasion.

'But, when Dave joined the Force, the culture was one of big boozers, men's men. You were either one of the boys, or you ended up getting all the shit jobs. Dave was one of the boys. Even when I first met him, he was starting to get a reputation for unreliability. Get him before lunch and he was fine. Later in the day and it would depend on how many beers he had at lunch, or if his lunch consisted of nothing but beer.

'Then things changed. The guys who had been given the shit jobs started to get promoted and the face of the Force changed. Suddenly it wasn't so cool to be on the toot all afternoon. Turning up late for work because of a hangover was no longer tolerated. Oh, there are still little corners of the Police Force where you can get away with things, but generally, the professionally pious have taken over.'

'Is that a bad thing?' asked Natalie.

'No, it's not bad at all. Probably long overdue, though like any reformed alcoholic, the Force goes to the opposite extreme at times. People like Dave were suddenly an embarrassment. They've been trying to get rid of the poor sod for at least the last four years. Usually it starts with one of these fitness courses that he was talking about. He's always managed to get his weight down in the past, but he isn't getting any younger and the pounds are becoming a bit obstinate. Also, I'm not sure his health is that great any more. He's been downing a lot of booze for a lot of years.'

'Maybe it wouldn't be the worst thing for him to go then.' It was said kindly. Natalie liked Dave Price and her concern was genuine.

Richard grasped her hand and held it tight. 'Trouble is darling, he has nowhere to go. This is his home. His colleagues are his family. His parents are dead, he has no other close family, he wouldn't know what to do with himself if he left Hong Kong. As bad as his lifestyle is, I've seen too many people like Dave leave and turn up dead in less than a year.

'The Force made Dave Price and dozens like him.' Richard turned to face Natalie. 'If you hadn't come into my life, I might well have ended up just like him. Bitter, cynical and drunk most of the time. I have no argument that something has to be done about men like Dave, but it should be in the form of real help, not the cold shoulder. I'll guarantee that he was nothing like that when he arrived from England twenty years ago. It may have been in his character, but it would have been encouraged to surface as soon as he set foot off the 'plane. It was like that for me. Before I joined, I didn't drink a fraction of what I put away on a daily basis at training school. It was only because I joined a unit where fitness was a requirement that I didn't have the same encouragement as Dave. As a young Inspector out in Divisions, he would have been expected to booze it up with the other officers. If he hadn't, he would have been bounced from all the desirable postings.

'The rules changed, but when they did people like Dave were left with the fall-out of the old system and no guidance as to how they could change and adapt. Some managed it on their own, but people like Dave required assistance that just wasn't there. One day his behaviour is encouraged and the next, he is the one who is getting the bum postings and the warnings for dismissal. It makes me mad.'

Natalie looked puzzled. 'But, why has it gone on for so long? I mean Dave has been like that since I knew him.'

'Dave's like me. He has a lot of friends. Friends who shared his taste for the bottle. They would do their best to shield him, but one by one they retired and eventually he would end up in a job where he was working for some self-righteous wanker with a grudge against the "old order". Then the sky would fall in on our boozy friend.

'But, that's not the saddest thing. You saw him tonight. He could hardly remember our names at times. Unfortunately, when I've seen him sober of late, his mind is not much better. The wise, sharp witted man I once knew has gone and been replaced by a jovial shell. It breaks my heart just to think of it. What do the powers that be expect him to do? They want rid of him and they really don't give a damn what happens to him when he's gone. That's the attitude that I have a problem with.'

Natalie leaned over and kissed him on the cheek. 'You're a good man, did I ever tell you that?'

Richard gave her a weary smile. 'My good intentions aren't going to mean much to men like Dave Price. Unfortunately I have my own battles to fight and I may be running out of allies, just like Dave.'

CHAPTER 41

Sweat ran down Richard's face as he concentrated on the task at hand. With the back of his hand he wiped the moisture from his brow, blinking to clear the salt sting from his eyes. The sun was dipping below the horizon, but still the punishing heat of the day lingered in the still air. Richard wished for a breeze, a gentle breath of air to ease his discomfort. The contraption in front of him was aiding the sweltering atmosphere in the assault on his thermostat.

John Gray and Cassius To looked on as the Scotsman struggled to keep up with the job at hand. They were able to relax and cast a critical eye on their friend's endeavours. Both felt pity as they saw his shirt gradually turn a deeper shade of blue, as the sweat soaked in and spread through the cotton. John shook his head. He had offered to help his beleaguered colleague, but Richard had insisted that this was his job.

Relief appeared in the form of Natalie, carrying three ice cold beers. She handed one each to Cassius and John and gave Richard an encouraging kiss as he eagerly reached for his can of liquid salvation. Her mission of mercy complete, Natalie re-entered the flat, closing the balcony doors behind her and leaving her man to the his friends and the barbecue.

'You sure I can't give you a hand?' asked John.

'Just enjoy your beer, I'm fine, though I may need a few more of these by the time the food is cooked,' replied Richard as he raised his beer to toast his companions. His attention was held by the grim look on Cassius' face.

'Come on Cass, this is supposed to be a chance for us to relax and forget our troubles for a few hours.'

Cassius smiled and took a sip of beer. As he spoke, he shook his head and the smile, though remaining, looked less convincing. 'Sorry, I guess I am just one of those types who can't leave his work behind in the office. I can't seem to get this thing out of my head, even for a few pleasant hours with you guys.'

Richard turned over some chicken wings. 'Well, if it's any consolation, you're in good company. Despite the show of indifference, I doubt whether the case is ever far from the front of John's mind, or mine. So, I suppose we can relax the no shop-talk rule.'

It was a basic rule of nature that if you put two policemen together in the same spot, it was impossible for them to avoid talking about work. There were all sorts of rules about not talking "shop", especially in the semi-formal atmosphere of the Officers' Mess, but somehow these rules always seemed to be bent, or broken outright. The job was an important part of their lives and to try and ignore it seemed an unattainable goal.

'Actually,' continued Richard, 'there is something that has been preying on my mind about this whole thing.' a slight smell of burning brought Richard's attention back to the sizzling meat on the barbecue. After some adjustment, removing pieces of cooked meat to a hotplate and replacing them with raw recruits, he gathered his thoughts on the subject that had been causing him concern.

'It's been occurring to me that we might not be asking all the right questions. We seem most concerned with asking why these particular men are being targeted and killed. Why these companies, rather than a dozen others? Good questions, but on their own, will they lead us to the reasons behind this campaign?'

Cassius looked at his friend. The detective was getting one of those feelings, the ones that said that something important was about to come to light. It was always easy to become too focussed on one particular aspect of a case. That was why Cassius liked working with people like Richard and John, in multi-disciplinary teams, it gave you a different perspective and forced you to think about things outside your own frame of reference. 'Go on Richard,' said the detective.

'Why bombs?'

'Sorry?' Cassius was disappointed. This wasn't the revelation he had hoped for, but rather yet another puzzle and a damn ambiguous one at that. He hoped his colleague had more to offer.

Richard saw the disappointment in his friend's face and gave him an encouraging smile. 'Look, John will tell you the same thing. The targets are all individuals. There are simpler ways to kill a man than to use a bomb.

'Bombs take time and skill to build. They require extensive resources in terms of material and expertise. Even the simplest carry a good deal of risk. They might not function at all, or they might function at the wrong time, even killing the bomber himself. For the use of a bomb to be justified for this sort of job, there has to be a bloody good reason for using this method of killing.'

Cassius looked at John Gray, as much for clarification as for confirmation of what Richard was saying.

'He's right,' said John. 'There are any number of ways to kill a single man and most of them are a hell of a lot simpler than targeting him with a bomb. Bombs are good for killing a lot of people, indiscriminately, but for a precise, surgical strike against an individual, it wouldn't be my first choice, unless it served another purpose.'

'Exactly!' said Richard.

Cassius was looking more confused than ever. This sort of speculation could be useful, but it went against the ordered way in which the detective's brain worked. If this continued, Cassius envisioned a huge headache. With a hint of exasperation in his voice, Cassius pleaded with his two friends. 'So, why use bombs? Any theories?'

Richard saw his friend's plight and decided it was time to put him out of his misery. 'OK, we ask the question. So, we look at what bombs ARE good for. Bombs make a statement. You blow someone to kingdom come and you announce your actions to the whole community. It's very difficult to play down a big bang.

'If you make it clear, with an extended campaign, that you are after a particular group of people, then you send shock waves of panic through that group and cause all sorts of secondary effects. Bombs cause fear and spread terror. They shake the strongest foundations in our society. No one feels safe. You can't hide from something that strikes without warning and with such vicious savagery. Dying in a bomb blast probably isn't the worst way to go, in fact it should be pretty quick, but the thought of the damage that a bomb does to a body strikes some deep seated, primitive fears in all of us. No one likes to think of their torn, twisted remains, even if they will never know anything about it. It's for this very reason that the bomb is such a perfect part of the terrorist arsenal.'

'Richard's right Cassius. There has to be a very good reason for the use of bombs here. The killing of the Taipans is of course significant, but so is the manner of their destruction.' John Gray had been having the same thoughts. As an ex-soldier, he knew bombing was never a simple matter of killing. Bombs were a display of strength and a threat of future violence, all aiding a cause, political or otherwise. There was a reason why these men had been killed in such a violent and public way.

'So, a weapon of terror aimed at the heads of specific companies. But, any way you kill them, you are going to create the same effect, surely John.'

Richard left the meat on the griddle to it's fate and faced his friend. 'It's a question of degree Cass. You kill a senior businessman in a prominent company and everyone is shocked and upset, for about five minutes, then it's business as usual. You blow the shit out of the CEO's of the most powerful businesses in Hong Kong and you unleash an emotional Tsunami. Everyone feels the fallout from that event. And who are the most nervous people in this Empire of Commerce?'

Cassius smiled. At last he got it. 'Investors in the stock market.'

Richard took a swig of his beer and returned his attention to the rapidly charring steaks, speaking as he turned over the meat. 'You said it yourself. The Hong Kong Stock Exchange is infamous as one of the jitteriest in the world. Rumours send the price of shares on a rollercoaster ride on a daily basis. Not the sort of environment that would be too friendly towards a company which has just had the Chairman's office dramatically remodelled, along with the Chairman. Look what has happened to the share price of all the companies involved.

'When you first came up with the idea that these killings might be for financial gain, I have to admit that I was skeptical. Perhaps the socialist in me recoiled from such a capitalist plan. But, as I was searching for some reason why a bombing campaign would be used as the means to execute our mysterious plan, it started to make more sense. The sort of ripples that a bombing campaign would send out in the financial community would be ideal for someone with an eye to making gains from the ensuing mayhem. Not just a temporary blip in the share price, but a plummeting drop, no matter how temporary.'

Cassius picked up the thread of Richard's thoughts. 'And if you knew ahead of time that something of this magnitude were about to take place, you would be ideally positioned to take maximum advantage of the situation, ahead of the competition.' The detective leaned back against the balcony railing. His eyes were focussed somewhere in the distance. It started to make sense to him. He had begun to wander off the theory that the bombings were for economic gain, but with the added perspective of the bombing campaign itself, it suddenly began to strengthen as an idea.

'I think I shall have a word with my friends in Commercial Crime Bureau tomorrow,' said Cassius, as his attention returned to his companions. 'So far there has been nothing significant from their investigations, but if we look at the timing of acquisitions of shares in the affected companies, we might find that someone is displaying a little too much foresight for their own good. In fact I think I'll have a look at the data mtself.'

The three men were silent for a moment. It was a theory, perhaps it would result in a lead, at the very least it was an avenue that would have to be explored. Their short moment of pleasure was shattered as the smoke rising from the barbecue signalled that Richard had better pay it more attention, or the dinner was going to be decidedly crispy.

John broke the silence. 'I think I shall get us some more beers, before we all get carried away with enthusiasm.'

CHAPTER 42

I cut the outboard and allow the inflatable to coast under the force of its own momentum towards the shore. The slipway comes closer. I use a paddle to steer the rubber boat in the direction of the concrete wall to the left of the gently sloping concrete finger. The slipway might expose my approach to anyone wandering around the compound. The gate guard will be looking the other way, bored with his vigil of the quiet street. Movement through the gates at this time in the morning is rare, as I have observed over the last few days. This is the "dead time". Those hours of the early morning when nothing much seems to happen and men are at their most vulnerable. The body and the mind want to rest, awaiting the energy of the dawn. For those unlucky enough to have to work through this time, the three or four hours before sunrise are the worst. Night work can be bearable when the mind is occupied, but when even the criminals are sensible enough to be asleep and the world seems to stand still, then the main occupation of these poor souls is merely staying awake. A policeman's lot at four in the morning is most certainly not a happy one.

North Point Police Station. The home of my new friend Richard Stirling. More of a home, I am sure, than his flat or that he, more often than not, shares with his beautiful girlfriend. This is where is life is. For a man like him, like us, work is life. His work defines him, infiltrates every part of his daily routine. When he has had a good day, I am sure that his girlfriend could not wish for a better lover. When the demons are with him, he must be absolute hell to be around. A man like that does not leave his job behind when he closes his office door behind him, it is something which he packs away in his emotional briefcase and carries with him everywhere he goes. Somewhere in that tall concrete block lies the soul of my nemesis. Where better to lay a trap for him, than the place where he must feel most comfortable, his safe haven from the dangers of his profession. Nothing can harm him here. Danger may not pass these walls. Imagine the surprise that will await our confident friend. Imagine the fear. Imagine the confusion.

The boat hits the sea wall with a quiet thump. There is a metal ring nearby to which I attach a rope and secure my means of escape. Everything I need is in the bag at my feet. I sling it over my shoulder and slowly climb up the wall to crouch at the edge of the compound. The police force in Hong Kong take great pains to protect their stations. They build high walls with barbed wire and turrets with gun ports, yet they leave the most glaring holes in their perimeters. Is it laziness, or merely the overconfidence of those who wield too much power in their society? Perhaps the once perceived threat has disappeared and they no longer know who to protect themselves from. After tonight, I think they will know the answer to that question.

The compound looks deserted, but I know that there will be people about, fighting their fatigue, or indulging in some surreptitious sleep. I can see the wooden guard box by the main gate. There doesn't seem to be anyone occupying it, but from this angle I am not certain. I will keep a close eye on the gate, just in case a vehicle does enter the compound, bringing back some unfortunate villain who, like me, decided to take advantage of these lethargy inducing hours. If criminals were sensible, this is the time that they would conduct their nefarious affairs. They would catch the police at their least effective, least attentive. They might have to battle their own fatigue, unless they followed my example and used the wonders of modern chemistry as an ally. My pills are my friends.

I see the vehicle. In the gloom of the night, the van looks black. It does not carry the insignia of the police force, but the conical light on the roof sets it apart from the civilian vehicles when it is on the street. Here, it is one among many, but the registration is the right one. I have seen this vehicle several times now. Its license plate is clear in my mind. This is his vehicle. It is parked under the cover of a low roof forming a lean-to. The entire space is taken up with police vehicles, with an over-spill going into the compound. There are vehicles on three sides of the one I am interested in, which is perfect. Plenty of cover from view, but enough room to work. I cover the ground to the van quickly, crouching in the darkness and keeping my eye on the gate. No one sees me as I reach my target.

I lay the bag on the ground and quietly unzip it. There is not much noise in the compound, but the sound of the city at night intrudes into the quiet. Occasional passing traffic is the loudest noise to be heard, but there is the constant hum of the huge air-conditioning units above me to mask all but the sharpest of sounds. It offers me some comfort, but I must be careful. The same acoustic drape would also cover the approaching step of the local constabulary. Although I am enjoying myself, I know that I must not linger. I reach in and pull out my first little surprise. It is small, about the same size as the one I used for the girl and her father. Not enough to utterly destroy the vehicle, but placed in the right position, enough to end the lives of the occupants of the front seats. I lie on my back and slide under the vehicle. The ample ground clearance of the van makes this maneuver easy and fast. I have already picked my spot and put the device in place. The magnets pull the bomb towards the bodywork. I have to tense my muscles to make the meeting a quiet one. There is a clunk as the magnets hit the metal and then all is quiet once more.

This is where I am most at risk. I pull the Mag-Lite from my pocket and twist the end to energise the beam. I need this light to check the positioning of the bomb and to arm it. I don't want the light to be on for any longer than necessary. In this darkness, the side-scattering of light will give me away. I check the position. It is perfect. There is the switch. Ideally, I would be able to do this remotely, but this is a simple device and I am confident that arming it in situ will be quite safe. I throw the switch. Often I like to include a little LED to show me that a circuit has been completed. It adds to the theater of the piece, but in this case it would draw unwanted attention to my work. I have to trust in my skill and that none of the circuitry has been damaged in transit. I switch off the torch and once again I am lying in darkness. I ease myself out from under the vehicle and crouch in the night, allowing my eyes to become accustomed to the dark, after the retinal assault of the quartz lamp.

The device is a simple one. A mercury tilt switch. The movement of the vehicle will trigger it, or more accurately, when the vehicle comes to a stop, the mercury will keep on moving forward and complete the circuit. I have positioned the device for this effect. I can see now, so I take another look under the vehicle. The device is matt black. Unless you were very familiar with the outline of the belly of this van, you would never know it was there. In daylight, it will be more obvious, but I have kept it slim, so the contour of the underside of the van is not changed too much. A cursory inspection of the vehicle might well fail to spot it. It really depends on the competence of the eyes doing the looking.

Still there is no sign of life in the station compound. I am surprised. During my reconnaissance, there was usually some movement. Perhaps it is just my lucky night. I crouch at the edge of the vehicles. My breathing is deliciously deep, as the anxiety of the moment builds. The adrenalin is starting to move around my system, giving me the high I crave. Danger, or the anticipation of danger, is the greatest stimulant. Stirling knows all about this. Just look at his career choices. Everything he does cries out "adrenalin junkie". His life is the pursuit of the ultimate high. The closer he comes to death, the more alive he is. I doubt that he actually fears death himself. To merely kill him, it would seem, would be no real victory. Garland gleaned some useful information about my dear adversary. His weakness lies not in his love of his own life, but in his fear for those around him. His love of his friends is the weapon most likely to cut the deepest.

Still no movement. It is time. Just one little thing to do.

CHAPTER 43

The weight of the Browning on his hip was starting to feel less awkward. Soon, he wouldn't give it a second thought, in fact he would probably be more aware of its absence than its presence. Richard hated the whole idea of carrying a gun around with him all the time. He had often spoken to CID officers about the handicap of personal issue weapons. One of the main problems was drinking. If you were to discharge your weapon while under the influence, the results could be catastrophic. The best thing was to hand your gun in to the armoury if you knew that a few "toots" were on the cards. Unfortunately many of the drinking sessions that Hong Kong policemen became involved in tended to be on the spur of the moment. Planning was a luxury which few enjoyed when it came to throwing booze down their necks. It just seemed to happen. A few officers took the "leave it at home" route, but this too had its problems. Few officers had secure cabinets at home for their weapons and leaving the service revolver in the fridge wasn't really an option, unless you liked taking risks with your career. So, most just tried to be as sensible as possible and hope that when they did have a drink, the need to get their gun out wouldn't arise.

For Richard, the best solution seemed to be one of abstinence. Since the bombing campaign had started to come close to home, he had cut back on his drinking anyway. A clear head was essential if he was to avoid making stupid mistakes. John Gray too had noticeably cut back on his intake of beer; a certain sign that the head of the EOD Unit was worried.

The sky was clear. It was going to be a beautiful day. Richard's mood tended to vary with the weather. Today he was in good spirits and had a spring in his step as he walked into the office. John was gathering his things, preparing to head out.

'What's up?' asked Richard with a brightness which had been missing from his voice of late.

John turned around and rewarded Richard's brightness with a smile. 'Kowloon. A construction site out near Junk Bay. They've dug up what sounds like an old World War II shell. Back to the old routine, it looks like. Actually it will make a pleasant change from the recent excitement. You seem in a good mood.'

'I am. God knows why, maybe it's the weather. The sun appearing always seems to lift my spirits. If it keeps up I may get my shirt off and lie out on the deck for a while.'

John sighed. 'We really do have a tough job, don't we?'

Ah Pau wished that he and Richard were doing the job on the shell at Junk Bay. At least then they would not be called out should another of these terror bombs be discovered. He was worried. Not for himself, but for his boss. The fact that Richard had taken to wearing his old personal issue Browning confirmed Ah Pau's feeling that for once Richard was worried about his own safety. It should be a relief, but under the circumstances, it was far from it. Ah Pau and Richard had been friends for a long time and been through a great deal together. The sergeant felt that he knew Richard better than he knew his own brother, in fact he liked him a great deal more too. If anything were to happen to his boss, Ah Pau would feel as though he had somehow failed in his duty, which as far as he was concerned was to protect the younger man.

He had washed the Transit the day before. It hadn't moved since then and still gleamed. This had become a daily ritual for Ah Pau. Since the bombing campaign had started to target policemen, he had paid even more attention to this routine. Other drivers joked about his actions, but they hadn't been trained in the same way as Ah Pau. Their thinking was narrow and they feared ridicule more than they feared the possible dangers that the bombing campaign posed. Ah Pau had long ago learned never to worry about what other people thought, especially when it came to the safety of those with whom he worked.

Starting at the front of the vehicle, he looked for anything out of the ordinary, anything that might start to set off alarm bells in his well honed instincts. It didn't take him long to find it. The device might have escaped the notice of some of his colleagues, but to Ah Pau it stuck out like a nipple through a summer dress. It was obvious, maybe a little too obvious. With only a moment's hesitation, he galloped off to get help.

'You're right Ah Pau. Too damned obvious.' Richard got up from his knees and looked around the compound. The hairs on the back of his neck were rising. Always a bad sign. He had to force himself to slow down his visual search. He was scanning the area too quickly to take anything in. Suddenly his head stopped moving. There, on the opposite side of the compound he saw something that made him grab Ah Pau by the arm and drag him in the opposite direction. At the same time he shouted out to anyone who might be within hearing to run for cover. The package was small, but it stuck out from the side of the petrol pump like a carbuncle. He and Ah Pau only managed to take a few steps before the blast hit them, sending both men flying to the ground. Richard wasn't sure which came first, the shock, or the sound of the blast. Whatever the order of events, he lay stunned on the ground, his head ringing, trying to make sense of what was happening. He never heard the sound of the outboard as the rubber boat powered away.

'Dear God. Right in our backyard,' said John.

Richard nodded, then thought better of it as his head throbbed with pain. He was sitting where he had been felled by the blast. He and Ah Pau had escaped with minor cuts and bruises, but others had not been so lucky. The gate guard, hearing Richard's call, had come out from the relative security of his wooden hut and been hit square in the chest by a piece of the petrol pump. The blast had failed to ignite the fumes in the underground tank, but the fuel in the pump itself had been spread all over the compound, not causing a great deal of damage, but giving the area the look of a war zone. There had been a few shrapnel and burn injuries, enough on their own to make this a really bad day, but the death of a young constable meant that the whole Force would be taking stock of this event.

Richard's mood had changed radically. He stared ahead. The anger was building up inside him like steam in a pressure cooker. He breathed hard, trying to ease the boiling hate that he felt for the man who had perpetrated this attack. A Police Station was holy ground as far as the policemen who worked there were concerned. This attack might just have been against the home and family of any man in the station. When working, this was their home and their family. This sort of thing wasn't going to be taken well by any member of the Force. If there was any doubt before that they had to get this bastard, then today would wipe it away forever.

Slowly and with obvious difficulty, Richard stood up. Ah Pau was still having his wounds dealt with by a constable.

'You OK?' John knew that his colleague wasn't alright, but it was the sort of question that just came out at times like this. It was meant more as a show of support than a genuine enquiry.

'Of course I'm not. But, let's have a look at the damage and see if our friend has left us any other nasty surprises. Then maybe you wouldn't mind dealing with the bomb under my vehicle. I don't think I'm quite up to it at the moment.'

'Right. Let's get you and everyone else the hell out of here and I'll get on with clearing that package from under the Transit. Come on lad.'

With as much speed as the confused group could muster, the compound was cleared and John Gray began to organise himself to deal with the bomb under the EOD vehicle. It wasn't going to be such a routine day after all.

'I didn't hear too loud a bang, so I imagine that you dealt with the bomb on the Transit without depriving me of a set of wheels.' Richard was feeling a lot less happy than his words might indicate.

'It's in a lot of little pieces. The bomb that is, not your vehicle. The boys are collecting the bits right now.'

John threw the wire down on the bench.

'What the hell is that?' asked Richard. He was still nursing a splitting headache and feeling a lot less on the ball than he would have liked.

'A command wire,' replied John.

It took a few moments for the significance of this statement to sink in to Richard's throbbing brain, but when it did, the reaction was sudden.

'Son of a bitch! He was there when he set the bloody thing off. Where? Where the hell was he?'

John shook his head as he spoke. 'Well, it looks as though he was in a boat of some kind. The wire trailed off into the harbour. I assume that's the way he approached the station when he planted the bombs. He must have been waiting for the right moment to set off the one on the pump off.'

'What you mean is that he was waiting for me to turn up in the right place before he blew the thing, don't you?'

'It looks that way, doesn't it? He could have detonated it at any time, but he waited for you. Look, Richard, maybe it's time we thought about you taking a break from this. Get away. If you're not around, maybe the guy will lay off.'

'Or, maybe he'll just pick another target, like you for instance. No, running isn't going to help. What we have to do is catch this fucker.'

CHAPTER 44

'Have you come up with a solution?'

Li stared out of the glass wall of his office as he spoke to Garland. He couldn't stand the sight of the man any more. The Englishman had let him down, had become a thorn in his side like all the other British he had ever had the misfortune to encounter. Li knew the answer to his question before he asked it, but he wanted to hear Garland's reaction.

For his part, Jack Garland had just about had enough of his employer. He had never respected anything about this hideous man, other than the size of his bank account. Jack had done his best to help reduce the overly healthy balance, but even the money was not enough to make him continue with this charade of loyalty. He had done everything he could think of, short of removing the dilemma once and for all.

'You know the only thing left to do. Get rid of the problem and cut our losses.' He said "our" to try and show his continued loyalty to his employer, but he had to remind himself to use the word, he really meant "your losses, your problem". Even the thought of killing the deformed figure standing in front of him had left Garland's mind. He just wanted out.

Li turned suddenly to face the security chief. 'No. This matter has been preoccupying my thoughts since we came back from China. There is one more thing that we can do.' Garland suddenly felt a mixture of interest and dread. He was tempted to make a sarcastic remark, but thought better of it and allowed his diminutive master to continue. 'Our man is being distracted from the task that he has been assigned. He has gone to great lengths to show us that he does not require our assistance in the pursuit of his goal and will not be persuaded to return to the path that we have laid out for him. So, we remove the distraction and see if he will return to the fold and continue to do our bidding.'

Garland looked blankly at Li for a moment, then screwed up his face in a look of puzzlement. It was not that Jack Garland was a stupid man, his mind just wasn't attuned to the sort of suggestion that Li had just made. At last, an awful clarity came over his mind and his lack of understanding turned to disbelief.

Before Garland could utter a word, Li spoke for him. 'Yes, that's right. Kill this man Stirling. Remove the temptation and in such a way that we leave our friend in no doubt about our resolve that the project should continue.'

Garland started pacing to and fro in front of Li's desk. He shook his head and breathed loudly, making a show of his frustration and shock. Stopping right in front of Li, he turned to face the businessman. 'You have to be out of your fucking mind.' Garland had never spoken to Li in this manner before and the shock of the outburst was plain on the small man's face. He gathered himself quickly and waited to hear what Garland would say next. Garland placed both hands on the edge of the desk and leaned towards Li. When he spoke, it was obvious that he regretted his aggressive tone and was trying to mend any damage it might have done. 'We are talking about killing a Police Officer. Not just a PC on the beat either, a high profile officer with a lot of friends. And a Gwailo to boot.' The reference to the fact that Stirling was not Chinese was yet another faux pas on the part of Garland. It made a difference to both these men, but in very different ways. Each valued the lives of their own ethnic groups higher than those of foreigners. They were racist peers.

Garland hurried to explain his statement and direct the subject away from racial equality in mortality. 'Look, killing any cop results in one thing; pissing off every other cop on the Force. Killing this one will cause the sort of shitstorm that could end up getting us all hung out to dry. No matter how hard the police may be trying to find our man, the effort would at least double if we kill one of their own.

'Besides, we're not talking about any cop here. This guy is a trained killer. It wont be easy to make his death look like an accident.'

Li looked Garland squarely in the eyes. 'Then don't. Make it plain to all that he was executed. Make a statement.'

He is crazy, thought Garland. The thought had crossed his mind many times before, but right now he knew it to be true. His mind raced as he tried to think how he was going to get himself out of this mess.

'I think that your previous occupation has clouded your judgement in this matter,' said Li in a very level voice. 'The police in this town do not have as high a social standing as they would like to believe. They are the lackeys of the Government, nothing more.'

He just didn't get it, thought Garland. It was just that sort of thinking that made the members of the Police Force rally around one another. They were a very tight group of people and protected every member of the group from outside attack. They might shit on one another from time to time, but no one else was allowed to mess with anyone in the "job".

'Could it be that you do not feel up to the task of disposing of this man?'

Garland looked at his employer and tried hard to hide the contempt he felt. This twisted dwarf could never threaten anyone without his wealth and power. Physically, Garland could have reached over and snapped him like a twig. The only thing stopping him was the threat of retaliation from other members of Li's organisation and more importantly, the Circle. Garland just managed to calm down before he began to speak. 'I can kill him, but it could be messy and in my opinion a mistake.' Garland's pride had been punctured enough to actually make him consider doing Li's bidding. Deep down, some part of Jack Garland resented people like Richard Stirling and wanted to show him that he wasn't as tough as he thought he was. That part was coming to the surface. It would finally make him act in a way that his rational self knew to be a serious mistake.

'I really don't care if you do think it is a mistake. I just want to know if you can get the job done or not. If you can, then it has to be done quickly. You know the schedule that has been forced upon us.'

'Alright. Alright, if that is what has to be done, then I'll make sure that it happens, but I want to get out after it's done.' It was a bold statement for Garland to make, but he had no choice.

'What do you mean?' Li was genuinely puzzled by the Englishman's reticence and the fact that he wanted to "get out" as he put it mystified him even further.

'I mean get away from Hong Kong. There is going to be all hell to pay when Stirling is dead, especially if it looks like an assassination. I would rather be somewhere else when the shit hits the fan. I would suggest the same to you, but I know that you don't believe that you could be caught up in any enquiries. For your sake as well as mine, it would be better if there was no possible way that I was implicated. It would lead straight back to you if I was. That's what I mean. And frankly I don't want to find myself waking up dead one morning, when you realise that what I am saying makes sense.'

Li stared at Garland for a while and then started to slowly nod his head. 'Perhaps what you say does make sense. I am disappointed that you think I would do you harm, but I think that it can be arranged that you "disappear" for a while. A holiday perhaps. If it makes you feel more secure, you can make the arrangements immediately and be on a 'plane as soon as the job is done, before the "shit hits the fan" as you put it.' As Li looked at Garland, the latter seemed to relax a bit at the suggestion. Li smiled inwardly. His reach was much longer than even his security chief realised. No matter where Garland might go, he could stretch out an icy finger to touch him.

Jack Garland sensed the end of his association with this odious little man. He had made a lot of money over the last fifteen years, most of which he still had. Perhaps it was time he called it a day. The thought of one last parting shot at his soon to be former master crossed his mind. Time enough to think about that when he was on his own. Jack had made his mind up. He would do one last job for Li and for the darkest part of himself.

'Give me twenty-four hours to organise the details.'

CHAPTER 45

The death of a Police Officer resonates around the Force like a declaration of war. In effect that is exactly what the murder of a policeman is. Often isolated from the rest of society by ingrained prejudice and lack of understanding, policemen draw strength from the tight community which they build around them. Accused of everything from racism to torture, they accept such attacks on their character in the cause of weeding out the bad elements that exist in any large organisation. To suggest that every one of their number was whiter than white would be naive and naivety has no place among those who have to deal with the harshest realities of our modern world. Even the best of those who dedicate their lives to the preservation of law and order have to make difficult moral choices in the course of their duties. Sometimes they might, with the benefit of hindsight, question the decisions that they have made. Even the best of intentions can result in the worst of results.

In response to the often hostile world in which they work, a close fellowship develops. When one of their number falls in the line of duty, particularly when the death is a result of a deliberate act, then the Force closes ranks. The fallen brother might be a stranger, but his loss will be felt by all who wear the same uniform, or carry the same burden of responsibility. All crime is taken seriously, the crime of murdering one of their own is taken personally.

Richard didn't know Chan Wing-fai. He knew the lad's face only in passing. Chan was less than three weeks out of Training School. Gate Guard duty was one of the boring jobs that all newcomers had to endure. No one would have considered it hazardous duty, just something that everyone had to do at some time. It just happened to be his turn. Pure stupid bad luck. The Chinese believed in luck and the Gods of Chance would be receiving a deluge of offerings over the next few days, as officers in turn thanked them for the fact that they had not been assigned that duty at that time, or asking for protection from any other harm that might be waiting to strike one of their number down.

Funeral parlours were cold places. Cold from the air-conditioners which blasted away to keep the putrefying effects of the Hong Kong summer at bay and cold in their impersonality. This was a business, the business of death and mourning, all carried out with the cool efficiency of any other enterprise in this haven of capitalism. The Funeral business was one of volume. Other families were mourning their dead in this same building, in halls similar to the one in which Chan Wing-fai received his farewells. This great marble barn in which Chan's remains lay was designed to hold funerals for the rich and famous, or those whose death touched many. There were smaller rooms, but the grief they contained would be no less than that which filled the cold air of this hall. There was no intimacy here. This was public grief. Reporters and photographers were milling around the entrance to the hall, waiting to catch their awful record of the suffering that one man could cause. If the young constable had died in different circumstances, there would have been less, if any attention from the press. Chan had become a celebrity by association. He had suffered the same fate as some of Hong Kong's social elite, probably, as far as the press knew, by the same hand that had fashioned the demise of the Taipans. His fame would be transitory and for that the family might be grateful. For now, they had to endure the public intrusion upon their grief, be reminded of their loss by the newspaper headlines and requests for interviews. The Police Force did it's best, through their Public Relations Bureau, to ward off the interruptions in their mourning, but the most zealous of the gentlemen of the press would not be put off by such things as taste and decency. Pain in the name of profit.

Chan's family, clad in white, played their part in the theater of death. Their's was the most human role, the reality within the ritual. Their grief was real, their loss most deeply felt. The others there had their own level of emotion. Some were there to show solidarity from the ranks, others to play politics and be seen to "do the right thing". For Richard, being there was a duty. He felt some responsibility for the young man's death. He had been the target for the bomber, his plan was to invite such attacks. Well, his plan had worked and an innocent had paid the price for his vanity. He had been so sure of himself, of his skill, of his cunning. He had forgotten that he did not work in isolation. In the end, no matter how much he might not like the idea, he was part of a team, a family and one of his family had died in his place.

Richard's body was in the North Point Funeral Home, but his mind was elsewhere, at other funerals, grieving other deaths. They had all been so sure of themselves then too. Arrogant in their self-belief and skills. They had forgotten that in a team you were only as strong as the weakest member and unfortunately that had been the man commanding the unit. Richard had played the crutch for his team, but at the crucial moment, he had not been there to support his men. They had paid the same price as Chan Wing-fai. So many deaths. Young men, with bright futures, cut down doing the thing that they loved. They had thought themselves indestructible. Just like Richard. If you really thought that you could be killed doing your job, you would be insane to carry on doing it. You accepted that there were risks, but in your own mind, you never for one minute believed that death would ever find you with his icy touch. If you did, getting out of bed in the morning would become an impossible task.

Saying goodbye to Keith had been the hardest. Richard was close to all his men, but Keith had been his brother, his friend. A part of Richard had been buried with the young Englishman. For Richard Stirling, one of the most difficult things in his life had been looking Keith's parents in the eye. He wore his guilt like a mask. They had seen the pain in his face and tried to give him the comfort of their understanding. Such strength, such courage. Those who grieve are the real heroes in our society. Their sons and daughters, brothers and sisters may choose to live dangerously, but those left behind are the ones who have to live with their loved ones decisions.

Richard didn't want to feel the pain that seemed to be slowly devouring his gut. He had gone out of his way to avoid this pain. He was supposed to be independent, solitary in his hazardous endeavours, immune from the ache of caring. That had been the bargain when he became a bomb disposal officer. The only one who went in harm's way was Richard. That was the deal. No one else to worry about. No one else to grieve for. But, here he was, reliving the hell of survival. It was easy to allow the feelings of self-pity to overwhelm you. That's what it was after all. The young man in the casket, lying before the assembled mourners, might welcome the pain of grief. A small price to pay for the chance of a few more years of life. Yet, the pain that Richard felt was real. No matter how much he told himself that he should feel lucky to have the life denied so many of his friends, he could not make the pain go away. Perhaps this was the price he had to pay for failing those who had depended on him. Perhaps it would never really go away, just hide in the dark recesses of his soul, ready to grab hold of him and remind him of his shortcomings, his failure.

Richard looked around him. The hall was wall to wall cops. He wondered if there were accusations in the occasional glances in his direction. The word had spread quickly through the grapevine. The attack was obviously meant for the EOD Unit, probably Richard himself. The bomber had missed his target and another mother had to grieve for her son. It was unlikely that anyone held Richard responsible for the constable's death, except Richard. The overwhelming feeling in the Funeral Parlour was anger. The problem was that there was no target for that anger. The identity of the bomber remained a mystery and that meant that the fury that was building in the hearts of the Police Force had nowhere to go. It would build until it spilled out in any direction that came to hand; a speeding ticket delivered with more sarcasm than necessary, an arrest made with excessive zeal, an interview that turned into a complaint of assault. Frustration made human beings act in irrational ways and despite the prejudices of the public, cops were human beings too. Richard knew that finding the bomber had taken on an even greater importance because of Chan's death. Innocent people would suffer unless the case was resolved and it had better happen soon. The tension in the Funeral home was palpable. It could only get worse.

It was time for the body to be taken to the crematorium. The family would accompany the deceased, while the rest of the mourners would find their own way to say goodbye. Many would head to a bar and swap stories of other lost comrades. It was an unfortunate fact that few people in the Royal Hong Kong Police had not seen the passing of a friend or colleague. Most were young men and most of the deaths had made little sense. Tragic accidents, made more tragic by the age of the victims. Richard stood and turned to John Gray and Cassius, who had been sitting beside him. No words were necessary. Under different circumstances they would have done their reminiscing over the bar of North Point Mess. The three men didn't feel that they could afford the luxury of such comfort. There was a job to do, to catch the man who had caused so much pain and anguish. Catch him before another mother had to mourn the loss of a son or daughter. Catch him before his audacity became greater and the human toll leapt beyond the already high price that was being paid in blood. Leads were needed. Questions had to be asked. The one good thing to emerge from the daring attack on the Police Station was that such bravado drew attention to the perpetrator. Hong Kong harbour is one of the busiest waterways in the world. It seemed inconceivable that no one had seen the bomber. They might not realise it, but the right question in the right ear might just yield results. That was the truth of investigation, repetitive and tedious though it may be, results came from thoroughness, covering all the angles.

The bomber had made his escape in a boat of some kind. Boats had to be moored or stored somewhere. They had to be bought, or supplied. They left a trail and at the moment, that was the best chance they had of getting a lead on this murderer. Every other avenue of enquiry had resulted in a dead end. Everyone hoped that the latest road would hold more promise.

The trio parted company at the door of the great hall of grief. Cassius to check on the progress that his team might be making. He had no need to motivate his men. The death of a twenty year old man was more than enough motivation. Especially when he was one of their own.

CHAPTER 46

'No!'

Natalie pushed Richard away from her. He stared back at her as he stood in the middle of the room. His face showed genuine bewilderment and worry as he saw the anguish on her face.

'No, Richard.' Anger had turned to sorrow in her voice. 'You do this every time. Whenever I want to talk to you about what you are feeling, about what I am feeling, you try to distract me with sex. You use it like a weapon. I can't do this any more. I need you to talk to me.' Natalie looked up with tear filled eyes. Her pain was obvious. Richard felt his heart sink at the sight of her. A voice deep inside him spoke, telling him the truth in her words. He took a step towards her, reaching out for her, but she took a step back and halted his advance. Defeated, Richard walked over to a chair and sat down.

'Alright, what do you want to talk about?'

Natalie remained standing, her arms clasped across her chest. There were still tears in her eyes, despite her efforts to wipe them away. She looked like a lost child as she stood there in her flat. This had become their home, even though Richard kept his own place. Now, neither of them felt comfortable in their surroundings. It wouldn't have mattered where they were, a barrier had been raised between them. A barrier of the truth. Perhaps it's appearance was overdue. Perhaps Natalie had been silent for too long. Whether the timing could have been better or not, the time had come to confront the problem which both had ignored in their own way, Richard actively and Natalie passively. They had to talk to one another. They were normally a communicative couple, revelling in each other's ideas and views. One subject had been excluded from their conversation, when it was the one thing that they really did need to talk about. Now it seemed was the time to put that right.

'You know what I want to talk about,' said Natalie. Her voice had regained some of its composure and strength. She would have been happy if Richard had become totally forthcoming, but she knew him better than that. He might want to tell her everything that he was feeling, but he would not make it easy for her, because it was not easy for him. She would have to help him say the things that he was probably desperate to say. 'I am worried sick about you. You can't sleep. When you do manage to get off, you don't rest properly, your nightmares are back. I know that you have started to spend more time at your flat because you are trying to hide all this from me, trying to protect me. Richard, don't get me wrong, I know that you try to deflect my attention away from what's going on in your life because you want to protect me from it, but don't you realise that all you are doing is making me more worried. If things are so bad that you won't let me in to that part of your life, then they must be terrible. I know you too well. You are worried, but you won't talk to me about it. You won't let me help.'

Richard stared at her and then at the floor, the walls, anywhere other than at the woman he loved. He couldn't think when he looked at her, his mind was a whirlpool of confusion, he couldn't pin one thought down. There was so much that he wanted to say, but was afraid to. In the end, anger grasped his speech, anger that was meant for himself, but ended up being unleashed on the wrong person. 'How can you help? Answer me that. What the hell can you do to help me?

'There is a man out there who seems determined to kill me. Oh, not quickly, he's enjoying his little game far too much. He places bombs for me. Not very clever bombs, ones he probably knows that I can deal with, unless I get stupid. But as a result, other people end up getting killed. That's his way of getting at me. It eats away at me little by little, until I am so desperate to prevent anyone else being hurt that I end up doing something that I know I shouldn't and then it's all over. He wins. But, you see I won't let him win. I can't let him win. It would be easy for me to end this dance. All I have to do is let one of his devices get me. It would be over as far as I was concerned. I wouldn't be there to see what petty revenges he might inflict on other people. I wouldn't be there to suffer the consequences, just like I wasn't there for Keith and the rest of my guys. I get it easy and others suffer.'

Natalie stared at him with wide eyes as he got to his feet and walked over to the window. The nightly display of lights was at it's most glorious, as Hong Kong put on it's evening dress. Richard didn't see it. Natalie had wanted to hear what was troubling him and now that he had started to tell her, part of her wished that he had kept it to himself. The best part of her wanted to hear the rest, to know everything that was troubling the man that she loved. His tone frightened her. Richard was normally calm, even in tense situations. The anger that she heard in his voice now was something alien, something from the darkest part of his soul. It was something she had never heard before. For the first time, she saw that her man could hate. What was unclear was who it was that he hated, the bomber, or himself.

'I know that I can't do anything to help you with your job, but I want you to be able to tell me all your troubles. You treat me like a porcelain doll, you seem scared that you'll break me if you tell me what is troubling you. Richard, you should know by now that I am made of stronger stuff than that.'

Richard continued to stare out of the window, afraid of what he might say if he looked at Natalie. He loved her so much that the thought of hurting her produced a pain in the middle of his chest. Why couldn't she understand that he wanted to protect her from the horrors that he had to face in his job. She lived in a world where people were basically decent. He knew that another world existed, a world inhabited by the perverse and the ugly, the truly evil. He didn't want Natalie to see that world. What he did tell her of his work, he kept superficial. How could he explain that other world to her without changing her forever. He wanted to protect her, to keep her safe, yet now she challenged him to reveal the dirtiest secrets of that black world. It was quite clear what she was saying. "Tell me, or lose me". Reluctantly, he turned to face her.

'You want to know it all, do you?' His voice was like ice. A shudder went through Natalie as he spoke. 'You want to know how I sweat before a job, how my mouth goes dry at the thought of going near one of those things? About the fear that I live with every day. When my pager goes off, my heart starts to beat faster, my palms sweat. I don't want to pick up the 'phone, but I do. I go to work and I do my job. You want to know why? Because I am good at it and because I'm responsible for one person, me. I'm the one who gets to go and stand over the bomb, I don't have to send some kid out to do it, I do it.

'My nightmares. You've asked me what it is I dream about. I tell you I can't remember. I wish that were true. I remember every terrible moment. It's different every time, but also it's the same. I can't get there. I can't get to my guys in time to do…I don't even know what. Save them? Even I'm not that arrogant. I used to be. Oh, God how arrogant I used to be. Not just about myself, but about the Unit. We were so fucking good at what we did. Trouble was that what we did was train. When it actually came down to doing the business, we fucked up. It didn't matter how good we were on a range, firing at paper targets. It wouldn't have mattered how good we were in a stand up fight. The man sending my guys into a room was an egotistical imbecile and I wasn't there to stop him. I was so arrogant that I thought my guys could deal with anything. It wouldn't matter that the man running the unit should never have been given the job, I thought we were so bloody marvelous that we could win despite the fact that the biggest link in our command chain was made of glass. That's how arrogant I was. And it got men killed.

'I thought that by dealing with bombs, I could escape the responsibility. Sure, I might save lives by doing the job, but it was remote, less immediate than with SDU. Now, I see that I was wrong. It doesn't matter that I am the one who gets sent in harms way. People still die, no matter how good I might be at my job. People still die.

'So, my dear, how are you going to help me with all that?' Richard stared at her. His cold eyes belied the storm that was raging inside him. He knew that his words would sting, but he couldn't stop them coming out. He had challenged her love and now wanted to take back his gage.

Natalie was silent for longer than Richard thought he could take. She looked at him with eyes that seemed to see him for the first time. The man standing in front of her was not the man she had fallen in love with, and yet at the same time it was. She had been hurt by his words. Hurt because of the pain that he had held back from her. She knew that he had been trying to protect her, but she was hurt because he had not trusted in her, in her strength. Now he was telling her that she was useless to him, that there was nothing that she could do to comfort him in his anguish. He was an island and she was a trespasser. She had been tolerated in certain parts of his life, but others would forever be out of bounds. The rational side of her knew that this was an unfortunate reality of the job that he did, another part of her was deeply wounded and wanted to hurt him back. As she wrestled with her own inner turmoil, Richard took a deep breath and started to come towards her. Involuntarily, Natalie took a step back, away from his advance. It was not a deliberate act, but if she had wanted to hurt him, the deed was done. The pain on Richard's face nearly broke her heart. Natalie began to speak, to explain, but Richard was already heading for the door.

'Richard, please. Don't go like this.'

He opened the door as he spoke, not turning to face her. 'You wanted to know what was going through my mind. Now you know. I hope you're happy.' His words expressed an anger that he no longer felt. His pride was driving him out of the door. The best part of him didn't want to go, didn't want to leave her like this. He closed the door and headed for the lift. He hoped that the door would open before the lift arrived. It didn't.

Natalie looked at the blank face of the door. Should she go after him? Richard was a man who needed to be alone at times, alone with his thoughts, alone with his grief. Natalie had wanted him to open up and her wish had been granted, but in the process she had forced her lover into a corner, bringing to the surface things which he had been struggling with internally. At this moment, she wasn't sure whether this was a good thing, or bad. Her own anger had subsided. Would she be doing the right thing by giving him the time to calm down, or should she run after him and reassure him that she loved him and would support him in any way she could. His words had hurt, but she knew that he was right and had to resolve these problems on his own. The best thing Natalie could do would be to tell him that she had faith in his ability to cope with the fear and confusion that were tearing at his soul.

Her mind made up, she rushed for the door. The lift lobby was empty. Natalie kept pushing the lift button. How many times had that irritated Richard. His comment had always been, "Of course that will make it come faster". Right now, she hoped it would.

The chime rang out as the lift came to a stop and the doors slid open. Richard pressed the hold button and stared at the figures illuminated on the panel in front of him. "LB1", lower basement number one, where he had parked his car. His eyes focussed on the bright white letters, but his mind was weighing up his actions. He wanted to turn around and go back up to Natalie's apartment. He also wanted to get away from here. He needed to think about his outburst. Perhaps it was time he brought his worries out into the open. If there was one person who might be able to help him come to terms with his fears, it was the woman he loved. He trusted her in everything else, why couldn't he trust her enough to be honest about the way he felt? That was the problem, he didn't know how he felt. One thing he did know was that he regretted the way he had stormed out of the flat and that the sooner he made amends, the better. Would she want to see him right now? Maybe it would be better to let her calm down. At last he made up his mind and releasing the hold button, stepped into the lift lobby and walked through to the underground garage.

Richard's mind was still preoccupied as he walked towards his car. A sound coming from behind him snapped his brain into the here and now. Someone was there. Richard hadn't noticed anyone as he exited the lift. His mind had been on other things, but normally he was very aware of his surroundings. A little alarm started to ring in his head. He continued to walk towards his car, but his senses were on alert, reaching out into the half-empty garage, seeking out the source of his disquiet.

The man was good. Richard only sensed his presence when he was within a couple of steps. The policeman swung round with a speed that took his assailant by surprise. If Richard was shocked by the sight of the pistol, he didn't show it. With well practiced movements, he stepped towards his attacker and at the same time knocked the man's outstretched hand away from his body. A shot rang out in the confined space of the low-roofed basement. Richard kicked out with his right foot and smashed the man's right knee. With a cry of pain, he fell to the ground, just as Richard's fist made contact with his windpipe, silencing the cry and sending the man reeling backwards.

Grabbing his throat, the attacker dropped the gun, which Richard saw looked like a Tokarev. Automatically, Richard drew his Browning and went for the cover of a nearby pillar. He scanned the car park looking for anyone else who might be a threat.

A shot rang out, almost at the same time as a lump of concrete was smashed out of the pillar Richard was taking cover behind. He backed away slightly, trying to work out where the shot had come from. The man who had attacked him was crawling towards his gun, his shattered knee making it difficult for him to stand. Richard fired a rapid volley of three shots in the direction of the pistol. More by fortune than design, he hit the automatic, sending it flying across the floor. The man understood the message and crawled away in the opposite direction. Richard ignored him for the moment. He wasn't going anywhere in a hurry and a more pressing matter was the person out in the shadows of the basement. The person who was trying to kill Richard.

A movement caught Richard's eye. It was only a glimpse, but it looked as though a figure was moving behind a car off to Richard's left. Whoever was there was trying to flank Richard and get a clear shot at him. Richard moved from his place of cover and got down on his belly, lying behind a parked car. He searched the darkness beneath the cars parked against the far wall, trying to make out any movement in that location. His eye caught what might have been a leg. He brought his Browning to bear. The tritium sights gave him a good sight picture in the semi-light under the car. Just then, off to his right, a chime rang out as one of the elevators reached the basement level. Richard sprang up to a crouch and looked towards the lift lobby. To his dismay, the figure that exited the lift was Natalie. As he was crying out a warning to her, a shot rang out and a bullet slammed into the wing of the car next to him, barely six inches from his head.

In a flash, Richard had turned in the direction from which the shot had come and fired off half a dozen rapid rounds. The bullets hit the car behind which he thought his attacker was hiding like the staccato step of a tap dancer. His intention was to keep the man's head down and to warn Natalie of the danger she had walked into. To his annoyance, she did not move to get back on board the lift, but crouched just inside the doorway of the lift lobby, watching him with a look of worry and fear. He gestured to her to move, but she stayed there, transfixed by the confusion of the moment. Richard's attention was brought back to his most immediate problem by more shots and the thud of bullets in the bodywork of the car beside him. He was crouched behind the engine block, but with cars you could never be sure what bullets would do by the time they had ricocheted their way through the bodywork. He leapt up from his crouching position and amid the sound of gunfire, sprinted the half dozen yards to another concrete pillar.

This position gave him a better view of the car park and had the benefit of placing him between his attacker and Natalie, who was still crouching in the doorway. His first assailant was curled in a ball in front of a parked car. A pool of blood was clearly visible on the floor in front of him. It looked as though the other man didn't want any witnesses left behind. Richard waited. The second man had made a mistake when he moved to outflank Richard. The lifts were now behind the policeman and he had a clear view of the stairs and the ramp at the opposite end of the basement, which were the only other exits.

There was silence in the underground. Richard kept glancing over to Natalie, willing her to turn around and get on board one of the lifts. He didn't want to call out to her, in case his attacker was unaware of her presence. His attention was split between his girlfriend and the rest of the garage. He strained to hear any movement that might let him pin down the location of the other man. Still he heard nothing, saw no signs of movement.

Suddenly the air erupted with gunfire. His assailant's patience must have run out as his rapid fire hit the walls around Richard. The shooting was erratic, as the man tried to keep Richard's head down while he tried to make good his escape. The shooting was desperate. An ordinary cop would have kept his head down as the attacker intended. Richard went down on one knee and peeked around the pillar. He saw a figure quickly backing away towards the stairs. In a lightning movement, he had taken aim on the figure and fired off two rounds in rapid succession. Not quite a double tap, but not much slower. The shooting stopped and the figure slumped forward, dropping the pistol in his hand and flopping on his face.

Richard stood and walked quickly towards the prostrate figure, all the time keeping his gun on the man. As he approached the body, he kicked the pistol further away from the reach of his attacker and walked around the figure, looking for signs of life. He saw none and slowly edged closer. Richard lashed out with his foot, making contact with the side of the man's knee. There was no reaction. Extending his pistol in one hand, he pressed the muzzle into the side of the man's neck and rolled the body over to get a look at his face.

He was a European. Richard thought that there was something vaguely familiar about the face, but he had no reason to recognise Jack Garland. Richard felt the neck for a pulse, but finding none, he rolled the man onto his back. There were two wounds in the chest, one right over the heart. This one wasn't going to give him any more problems.

Richard walked back to the other man, lying in a pool of blood. This one was Chinese. Richard couldn't feel a pulse. He was gone too. In other circumstances, Richard might have started CPR on the man, in the hope that he might bring him back, but he felt no inclination to waste his time with either of them. Instead, he walked over to the lift lobby, where Natalie was still couching, eyes wide, face pale as milk.

Natalie's eyes seemed fixed on a single point in space. Richard realised that she was staring at the gun that he still held in his right hand. He holstered the weapon, but Natalie's unfocussed stare remained still. Slowly he kneeled down until their faces were level. He reached to touch her arm, but she quickly drew away from him and was suddenly looking him straight in the face. She looked as though she didn't recognise him.

'Easy. Take it easy,' said Richard. His voice was calm and gentle, trying to penetrate the veil of shock that hung over his lover's face. 'You're safe, it's all over. You're going to be alright.'

Natalie shook her head. Again Richard tried to take her arm. This time she did not back away. He gently encouraged her to stand up and move away from the doorway, back into the lift lobby, where the bodies of the two men would no longer be visible. Richard pressed the button for the lifts. He could feel Natalie start to shiver, as the shock of what she had just witnessed started to take its toll on her system. She was still silent and kept a distance between her and Richard. The lift arrived and they boarded it in silence. No words were exchanged on the way to Natalie's flat. Richard was just glad to get her away from the basement, back to familiar and comfortable surroundings. He sat her down on the sofa and made a telephone call.

'Cass. It's Richard. You'd better get some of your guys and the local cops over to Natalie's apartment block. There are a couple of bodies in the lower basement car park number one. They jumped me as I was leaving. I'll wait for you down there. Let the local guys know that I am a police officer, will you? I don't want any misunderstandings if they arrive before you. And get a woman constable to come and look after Natalie, she witnessed the shooting. She's in her flat right now, pretty shaken up. OK, I'll see you soon.'

Richard sat down beside Natalie and took her cold hand in his. She made no move to resist him, but she didn't move any closer either. 'Darling, I have to go down to the car park and wait for Cassius and his men to arrive. Someone will be with you soon, will you be alright on your own?'

Natalie didn't look at him as she spoke. 'How can you live like this? Those men…they were trying to kill you. I don't understand…'.

Suddenly it was all real to her. The danger that Richard was living with was no longer an abstract concept, but had taken form in blood. The horror of it stunned her, she was in a living nightmare, totally unequipped to deal with the new reality which had been thrust upon her. She was lost.

Richard stood. He had to get down to the basement and make sure that no one blundered in to the crime scene and destroyed evidence. He didn't want to leave Natalie like this, but he had no choice. 'I'll be back as soon as I can. Try to drink something warm, I'll put the kettle on before I leave. Don't take any alcohol, it'll just make things worse.' He walked into the kitchen and switched the electric kettle on. As he walked to the door, he looked at his girlfriend. She hadn't moved an inch. As he walked out of the door, she continued to stare off into space.

CHAPTER 47

She looked like a child as she lay on the bed, her knees drawn up to her chest, seeking comfort in that familiar childhood pose. He long dark hair was spread out on the pillow, disarrayed, but beautiful. Richard gently stroked the long black locks. Natalie gave no reaction to his touch, her eyes were closed, but he knew her well enough to be sure that she did not sleep. He rose from the bed and quietly left the room.

Cassius was standing on the balcony, watching the deluge. The panoramic view from Natalie's apartment was reduced to a grey wall of water, as the heavens lashed the city with rain. Richard joined him, feeling the oppressive wet heat as he stepped out from the soothing air-conditioned atmosphere of the flat.

'How is she?' asked Cassius.

'I'm not sure. She's strong, but the reality of what happened down there is still sinking in. It's funny, you talk about things. You think that the other person understands what you do, what you train for. Trouble is, we take this life for granted and when one of us get's caught up in a fire fight for the first time, it can be hard enough for us to cope. What must it be like for someone who is not saturated in our culture? Someone for whom the world is basically a decent place.'

The Chinese detective looked at his friend. Richard looked tired. 'You and Natalie have spoken about your job. I've been there when we have all talked about it. She knew what you did when you were in SDU, well pretty much anyway.'

'It's one thing to talk about it. I think perhaps she always thought that we were just "playing soldier", that the training we did would never have to be used in anger.'

'For the most part she would have been right, not many of us ever have to draw our guns, let alone use them.'

'I know Cass, but when we train, we do so in the expectation of actually having to do the job for real. That's the mind set. If we didn't think like that we would be doing nothing more than "playing". It gets into you and prepares you for the real thing, well as prepared as you can ever be, because it is not the same. When the shit hits the fan you do your best and hope that your training will help you come out of it alive.

'For Natalie, she's having to come to terms with something that for her bordered on fantasy. Suddenly it's real and there was her boyfriend, killing someone and coming close to getting killed himself. That's a hell of a lot to absorb in the space of an afternoon.'

'How are you doing?' inquired Cassius. In all the excitement, it was always possible to forget that the guy who survives a deadly encounter might not be too happy about his experience.

Richard took a deep breath. 'I don't think I've really had a chance to think about it. I've been too worried about Natalie. How's the scene downstairs?'

'Oh, the forensic guys are crawling all over the basement. By the way, my boss spoke to the Commissioner. We think that under the circumstances, you'd better hold on to your gun. We'll need it later for ballistic tests, just to tie up the loose ends in the file, but just in case this isn't an isolated incident, the boss doesn't want you walking around with an unfamiliar weapon.'

'That's good of him. Nice to know that someone in the Ivory Tower knows a bit about firearms. What do you think? An isolated attack?'

Cassius laughed. 'You and I both know that we have just got our first real lead to this bomber. If not him, then his boss. My guess is that whoever is pulling the strings got a bit pissed off with his guy's obsession about you and decided to take you out of the picture. Just my guess at the moment, but when we get an ID on those bodies downstairs, I hope things might start moving pretty fast.'

'I don't think the bombs are going to stop Cass.'

'What do you mean?'

'The bomber has shown us already that he is perfectly capable of working on his own. Remember the homemade explosive in the Tsim Sha Tsui bomb? He may be out of control, but he's decided on his own agenda and he'll carry on with it. This guy's not a quitter.'

'Shit. At least the business community will be able to sleep more soundly, when we get to the bottom of this attack. If we take the head man out of the equation, the only poor sod who is going to have to watch his back is you. Sorry, my friend.'

Richard leaned against the rail of the balcony. The rain hit his back, soaking his shirt. He didn't mind, he liked the feel of the cool wetness, as the fabric clung to his skin. It was a wake-up call for his senses which had been dulled after the fire-fight. He was starting to feel more alive again, but the fear was also returning. Fear not only for himself, but for those around him.

'I wish you were right, pal. I wish I was the only one having to watch his back. That poor kid in North Point Station proved that anyone around me is going to have to watch themselves as well. That's the sad truth.

'No Cass, we have to get the guy planting the bombs. His boss might lead us to him, but the main thing is getting that guy, before more innocent lives are lost.'

Cassius nodded his agreement. He knew that believing that the pressure had come off a bit was just wishful thinking. Richard was right, they had to get to the bomber as soon as possible. The one positive thing was that for the first time they might actually have a real lead in this case. After so many dead ends, they had solid evidence; two corpses. The difficult part would be proving a link between the dead men and an unknown bomber. Cassius was not enough of an optimist to hope that one of the dead was the man they were after.

'Listen, you going to be alright up here?' Richard nodded. 'I have to get back down and see how the boys are doing at the crime scene. Why don't you take your time and write out your statement, I'll come back up and go over it with you in a while. I might have some news about our two friends down there by then. OK?'

As Cassius pulled open the sliding doors and re-entered the apartment, Richard decided to stay outside and be alone with his thoughts for a while. He needed to think, to go over the events in the basement in his own mind, before he committed them to paper. It had been his first opportunity to really think about what had happened. He would relive those frantic minutes many times in his imagination, but for now he had to get the order of events clear for the official report.

The wind had picked up and rain was now lashing the windows. The balcony was awash. Richard had taken off his drenched shirt and was sitting at the dining table, pen in hand, as he prepared to write down his recollection of events in the basement car park. The air-conditioned air was cold against his bare skin. Normally it would have made him alert and very aware of his surroundings, but now his mind was focussed on the recent past, trying to piece together the fragments of sight and sound which had bombarded his senses in those frantic minutes.

Stressful situations come back to haunt us in our dreams, sleeping and awake. We relive events, each time adding nuances, real or imagined. In situations where our actions might be open to criticism, there is a danger that influences after the fact can change our perception of events in such a drastic fashion, that we are no longer sure what exactly took place. It is then that the terrible after effects of stress can take hold and bury us in doubt and anxiety. It is to try and counter such damaging effects, that men like Richard were encouraged to record the events as soon after they had taken place as possible, as much to give themselves a clear picture of what took place, as for the investigation that might result. Debriefing was as important to the person involved in the event, as to those trying to discover what happened.

Richard was luckier than most. He had been trained to observe under stress. His mind was trained to organise the disorganised, to bring order from mental chaos. Some things were difficult to put into words. What was it exactly that had alerted him to the presence of his first assailant? It may have been a number of things, a sound which triggered an ingrained reaction, an instinct born of years of dedicated training and experience. Such things could be accepted as existing, because almost everyone who would read the record that Richard was about to make would understand exactly what he was talking about. They would have felt the unexpected tingle along the spine, the raised hairs that warned that there was an unseen danger. These things Richard did not have to analyse too deeply, what was required on the sheet of paper in front of him were facts, as many as his mind could recollect.

At last, he was happy that he had ordered the train of events in his mind and started to put down on paper the images which scanned across his mental slide show. It was not like a movie, the action continuous on the screen, but it came in animated snatches, events broken up into discrete packets. His recording was in this fashion, bullet points leading the reader through the order of events, building a whole from episodic bricks.

Once started, the narrative flowed with ease. As he wrote, little details started to come back to him, minutiae which might or might not be significant, but which anyway warranted inclusion in the record of the attack. At this stage, no one knew what might be significant and helpful to the investigation.

The storm outside had turned the day to dusk. Richard was in full flow and pushed on with his writing, unconsciously leaning closer to the paper as the light dimmed.

Richard stopped writing and leaned back in his chair. Only now did he realise that the room was quite dark. He picked up the sheets of paper on which he had recorded his testimony and prepared to read over his statement. He became aware of a presence. It was a familiar one. Richard looked to his left and saw Natalie standing at the entrance to the corridor which led off to the bedrooms. She leaned against the wall. It was difficult to see her face in the gloom, but her posture said that she leaned against the wall for support, not as a casual pose. Richard put the sheets of paper back down on the table, pushed his chair back and rose to walk over to his girlfriend.

Richard didn't know what to expect, but as he came close enough to see her face clearly, she hurled herself at him and started to lash out with her fists. Richard tried to grab her wrists, desperately trying to avoid hurting her. He was a strong man, but strength can be a burden when the intent is not to harm. Richard took the blows as he tried to catch a moment when he could bring her under control. Natalie's cries were animal and angry, her words confused and disorganised. She accused him of all manner of things. He was a liar, a bastard, not the man she loved, a stranger, a killer. Richard batted off the verbal attack slightly less easily than the physical one. The words stung much more than the blows. Yet he knew this to be what it was, stress.

At last he managed to get a hold of her wrists and stopped the barrage of blows. He pulled her close to him, trying to put his arms around her, without releasing her arms. Natalie struggled like a newly trapped beast, desperate to escape her captor. Her verbal fusillade continued in Richard's ear. He tried to ignore the words which tried to dig into his being, remembering his love for the woman struggling in his arms.

Quite suddenly, the struggle stopped and Natalie slumped in Richard's confining embrace, a wild thing defeated. He grabbed a tighter hold of her and supported her weight. Her cutting words had been replaced by sobs. Richard could feel the tears on her cheek as he pressed it against his own. Her crying became louder and came from deep inside her. Her body shook with the effort of it. Without warning, she pulled herself closer to Richard and held him in a tight embrace. Her voice shook as she spoke through the tears.

'I thought you were going to die, you awful man. I was sure I was going to lose you.'

'It's all over,' said Richard. He knew that this was a lie. She would relive this day again and again over the days, weeks to come, but they would deal with that when the time came. For now, he just wanted her to get through the shock that had turned her mind temporarily against him. She had been terrified by what she had seen, yet her fears were for him, not herself. In time she would realise that she too had been in peril, but her mind had focussed its attention on her man for the time being.

'Oh, Richard. Suddenly it's all so real. I never really realised before…'

'How could you?' he replied. 'The important thing is that you are alive and that the danger is past.' This was a day for white lies.

CHAPTER 48

Damn them! Damn them all!

Garland paid for his folly, for that at least I am grateful. He underestimated my friend Stirling, a mistake only someone as stupid and arrogant as that Englishman could make. Yes, his arrogance was his undoing and his lack of appreciation of the superiority of a man like Richard Stirling. Superior certainly to a second rate mind like Garland and even his master Li. Li, who would play puppet master with me! His superiority rests solely in his arrogance. In that he is superior. It will make his downfall all the sweeter.

They thought that they could bring me under their control by eliminating Stirling. They were wrong. If they had succeeded in killing my chosen opponent, I would have turned my skills on them sooner than I had planned. Now I have only Li to take care of. Li, who lives comfortably under the erroneous belief that his identity is unknown to me. My friends on the Mainland made sure that I knew all the players in this foolish game.

Garland committed suicide by folly. How could he have hoped to beat a man with Stirling's experience and training? What was going through his mind when he conceived the attack? Was anything going through his mind, or was he acting on a more basic, more primitive level? I have no doubt that the order originated from Li, but the fact that Garland was willing to do his bidding in this ill conceived scheme speaks volumes as to the *gwailo's* stupidity or vanity. Which one is irrelevant now. He paid with his life and a message was sent to his master, one which I hope he will heed. I doubt if Li will have time to bother me from now on. His world is about to come crashing down around him. His Chinese masters will be less than happy about his failure and it will be inevitable that Garland will lead the police back to his master. The dead make excellent witnesses to imprudent action. No, I shall leave him to his fate.

Stirling. My dear Richard. I am glad that your training kept you safe. I have so much more planned for you my friend. At test, I think. A test of your character. And such a test. Yes, I know your weakness lies in your concern for those around you. You worry and you fret about the possible dangers that your actions might bring to your loved ones, but how strong is your love? What is it that you love in another? Shall we find out, my noble friend? Let's test that nobility. Let us see if your feelings go beyond the superficial. Are you better than the herd of humanity, or are you just another beast, drawn by your animal instincts to forge unions with the other cattle? How developed are your sensibilities, my man?

This will take some time and much preparation. There is more risk involved in this test than I would normally allow, but the rewards justify that risk. I will place my head on the chopping block one time to see the result of this test of character. I hope I will not be disappointed. Whatever the outcome, though, one thing is certain. Stirling will weep for this one.

CHAPTER 49

'Mr Li is away on business. I'm afraid that he will not be back in Hong Kong for at least a week.' The Company Secretary didn't seem very concerned that twenty police officers were at that very moment starting to collect every document in sight and open any drawer they could get their hands on.

'I don't suppose you know where he is?' Cassius knew what the answer would be—a lie.

'I'm afraid the Chairman's trip was confidential, even from me. When he contacts the office, I will be sure to inform him of what you have been doing today.'

That last statement sounded awfully like a threat to Cassius. It also seemed highly unlikely that the head of such a large group of companies would be out of touch for a second. No doubt someone was telling Li everything that was happening at that very moment.

Most of the officers pulling the offices on the top floor of Li's headquarters building apart were from the Commercial Crime Bureau. Their specialists would pull Li's financial statements to pieces, looking for anything which might stand as a motive for the bombing campaign against the Taipans. Harbour Holdings was about to be turned inside-out. Cassius would have to leave them to it, though he would be monitoring their progress. He had led the raid in the hope that he could collar Li on the spot, but perhaps he should have known better. If Li had been in the building when they entered the ground floor, he would certainly have not been there by the time the lift reached the executive floors. Still, the businessman would not be getting the use of his plush office for a while.

Not everyone in the offices that filled the top four floors of the Harbour Building were being quite so stoic about what was happening. There were a lot of worried faces watching the men and women of CCB start to identify and record every scrap of paper, file and computer disk that they could lay their hands on. The operation would take days to complete. This was just the beginning. By the time they were finished, every bank account, business and personal, within the control of the top executives of the various companies that made up the Harbour Holdings Group would be scrutinised. At that very moment, fourteen other offices were being raided, all owned by or associated with Li and his business group.

It had been surprisingly easy to get the warrants necessary to let CCB do their job. It was a measure of the power of the men who had been targeted in the bombing campaign that when Garland had been identified, even such a tenuous lead had been enough for the paperwork to be rushed through the Attorney General's office. Cassius and his colleagues had never had it so easy. The evidence that they had presented to obtain the warrants would have been laughed at by a Magistrate, but the nature of this case and the fact that until now there had been no leads, meant that even the possibility of bringing the attacks to an end was enough to get the legal ball rolling. But, thought Cassius, Li would have a lot of friends as well and probably knew about the raid well before the fleet of unmarked cars pulled up in front of the shining glass tower. He would get Li, if his suspicions turned out to be true. It might take him a long time, but Cassius was determined that he would get the man who had caused so much misery. Cassius felt a degree of relief that he and his men now had something concrete to pursue, but Richard's words kept coming back to him. If his friend was right, then the bomber was out of control and they had not heard the last from him.

'Tell your boss that I would appreciate it if he would agree to talk to me regarding certain activities which I think he may have knowledge of. If he's not happy about that, tell him that the document I have in my pocket is a warrant for his arrest on the charge of Conspiracy to Commit Murder. Have a nice day.' Cassius turned around and walked away from the now stunned businessman. They all thought that they were invulnerable, thought Cassius. It was a shock to people like Li to find out that sometimes their money was just not enough to shield them from the laws that ordinary people had to abide by. It was a fact in Hong Kong that there was usually someone with more money. Tangle with enough of them and you ended up being treated like any other mortal in the kingdom of the super-rich.

'So Garland was an ex-Hong Kong cop.'

Richard looked at the photographs of the bodies that were pinned to the wall of Cassius's office. Images taken from every angle, giving a clear view of the two dead men. One dead at the hands of the other. Garland, Richard's handiwork.

Garland was the key, the first step in the chain of evidence that was going to lead them to the bomber. The overall motive for the bombings was no longer the priority. Cassius was confident that the reason behind the deaths would come to light through time. The most important thing now was to get the maverick bomber and put an end to his deadly activities.

'I wouldn't be in a hurry to associate yourself with Garland,' said Cassius. 'A nasty piece of work that one. Even when he was in the job he had a reputation for being handy with his fists and not averse to supplementing his income. Jack didn't just go along with the gravy train, he leapt aboard and gorged himself in the buffet car. He was smart about it though, nothing ever stuck to him. The Independent Commission Against Corruption have a file on him. They pulled him in a couple of times for questioning, but by that time he was working for Li. Every time he was questioned, a squadron of lawyers were right behind him. In his role as Security Chief at Harbour Holdings, he tended to keep a low profile. Whatever he did for Li, he was discrete.'

'Well, we know one thing he did for Li. Remove problems. I wouldn't mind betting that there are a few unsolved murders that could be pinned on our Jack. You think?'

Cassius shrugged. 'He didn't do a very good job with you. I'm glad to say!'

'Yeah. I was lucky. When I walked into that car park, I had a lot on my mind. Pure good fortune that I heard the guy behind me. The old shiver down the spine saved my neck again.'

'Don't knock it. It's a hell of an asset in your job.' Cassius walked over to the incident board and looked at the pieces of the puzzle that they had managed to put together so far. It was a beginning, but they were still depressingly far from any clue as to the identity of the bomber.

'We're going through every record we can find in Li's offices. Garland's was sealed off and every scrap of paper, phone records, anything we can think of is being scrutinised. His home too. If he was still as careful about his activities as he was when he was in the Force, we are screwed. But, if the good life had started to make him sloppy, we may have a chance to find a lead.'

'Lot of "ifs".' Richard frowned at the flow chart in front of him. There were lots of arrows leading from one name, or phrase, or word to another, but they didn't seem to lead anywhere in particular. 'Doesn't look as though we are going to get anywhere in a hurry, does it?'

'The CCB boys know that this is no ordinary commercial case and that we have a bit of an urgent timetable to follow. They'll do their best to try and come up with something. They've already found strong links between Harbour Holdings, actually more specifically Li himself and the PLA.'

'Really?' That piece of news got Richard's attention.

'Yep. And guess what industries that he is involved in.'

'Arms?'

'And explosives. He has plants in Shenzen and Shanghai. Takes advantage of the economic zones. He also has some chemical plants in more remote corners of the Motherland. Well away from large urban areas. You might get the idea that their safety standards are not that high.'

'I thought the PLA had their own businesses,' said Richard.

'They do, but in 1985 the government sent out an edict that at least fifty percent of the defence industry should be farmed out to commercial interests. Li started to get more involved with arms at that time.'

'That must have pissed off a few generals. They would have seen a rather drastic drop in their income.'

'Unless they had a friendly capitalist in their pocket who owed them a few favours.'

Richard smiled. 'Now there's a thought. I'm starting to like this line of thinking. Only problem is that the explosives used by the bomber are not consistent with the composition of Chinese plastic explosive compounds. They're more like British PE 4.'

'Maybe that's where Garland came in. He wouldn't have been above a bit of bribery or blackmail to obtain the materials. I think we had better lean on our Army friends a little. See if they can identify a source.

'Wouldn't Li be able to duplicate the compounds in his factories?'

'It's possible,' said Richard, 'but I think the Garland line is the one that would yield the most fruit. I'll have a word with my friends in the "Bing" and see if I can get at least a sniff of a rumour.'

'I really thought this would bring us closer to resolving the situation.' Cassius shook his head. How do you track down a ghost? If there had been threats or demands, then there was the chance that you could lure the bomber into a trap, fuelled by his greed and vanity. Here, the problem was that the attacks came out of the blue. The only thing that they had on their side at the moment was that Richard seemed to be the target of choice. This fact gave Cassius little comfort. Even this fact might change at any time. The bomber could become bored, or just decide to go off at another tangent. He might even stop altogether. Although this would be a good thing, it would be no victory and Cassius hated to lose.

Richard put his hand on his friend's shoulder. 'As you've said before, we just have to get lucky.'

CHAPTER 50

Vincent Lo looked at the faces of the men seated around the table. He was looking for any sign in their expressions that might mean dissent. He saw none. These men were used to keeping their thoughts to themselves. They showed the world one face and kept another within them, the face that showed what they were really thinking. Vincent knew that many of the men around the table coveted his position, but in the matter at hand, he felt that they were indeed all with him. A rare occurrence, but when the fortunes of their associates were inextricably linked with self interest, it was amazing how this disparate group could pull together. It had taken little effort on Vincent Lo's part to make his case to the members of the Circle. There was no dissent.

'It is agreed then.' Vincent made the statement in a way that made it clear that if anyone did harbour doubts, they had better keep them to themselves. In fact, not one voice had been raised in defence of the man under discussion. That in itself was an unusual fact. Within the Circle there were a number of factions. For one man to stand so obviously alone within this gathering, was a sign of true isolation. But then they were discussing Li Keung.

'So, Li, having placed the existence of this group in jeopardy, no longer enjoys the protection of the Circle. He will no longer be considered a part of our association and is to be held as a threat by all its members. Should he approach any of you for help, I am to be informed at once. He should be left under no illusions about his status. Anyone offering him comfort will be considered to be acting against the best interests of the Circle and will be dealt with accordingly by the rest of the members.' Again, Vincent's eyes scanned the room, looking for any sign that one of the men gathered here might have the intention of coming to Li's aid. Again, his search was fruitless. Lo wanted to smile at this, but managed to keep his joy to himself. He had waited a long time for this moment. Li had been building himself a power base, much against the odds, as there was an ingrained prejudice in Chinese society against the deformed and the handicapped. Nevertheless, Li was beginning to look like a real threat to the leadership of the Circle. Vincent had begun to think about an attack of his own, against his would-be usurper, but the twisted little man had saved him the trouble. All that was left was to close this annoying chapter once and for all. 'If there is nothing further, I will call an end to this extraordinary meeting. Thank you all for breaking into your busy schedules to gather here. We shall reconvene at our regular gathering, then to discuss more pleasant and profitable matters.'

Vincent walked to the door. The sounds of the meeting breaking up followed him out of the conference room. As he walked to the lift, to return to his office, he knew that one group would make their preparations to leave more slowly than the others and that when the room was finally clear, he would be joined in his office, four floors above.

'Even with Garland gone, it won't be easy getting to him.' Vincent Lo paced along the glass wall of his office. The view was of no interest to him, he might as well have been walking beside bricks. It was his inner eye that took the executive's attention. Normally the intellect of this man would be attempting to deal with a number of issues at once. For now, he was totally focussed on one thing. The elimination of Li Keung. 'We have to find something, some weakness that will let us get in through the wall of people that he places around him. I honestly think that if he could get someone else to take a crap for him, he would.

'There has to be a way in. There are a dozen Garland's waiting to fill his slot in the organisation, but they may not have Li's total trust at the onset of their new role. It will take time for him to find another attack dog that he can trust with his most intimate secrets.'

Vincent stopped his pacing. He turned to look at the man sitting on the sofa in the corner of his office. The man had said nothing since entering the room. He knew Vincent well enough to know that there would be a good deal of this audible ruminating before he got to the point. So, he relaxed with the brandy that he had poured himself when he arrived and let the head of the Circle do what he had to do.

'I don't want any of this to come back to haunt me. The others are quite happy to have Li ostracised from the Circle, but they would balk at the thought of killing him. They can be a sensitive bunch, our colleagues. Also, it might set a dangerous precedent. We balance on a knife edge in our relationships within the group, to introduce killing as a means of censure might offend the sensibilities of some of the members.'

A vicious look came over the face of Vincent Lo. 'One person I do want to know is Li himself. When it happens, I want him to be aware of who has sent Death knocking at his door. I want the last words that twisted dwarf hears to be my name.

'As if he could ever take my place! The arrogance. He should have been drowned at birth. Instead he was allowed to grow and fester among us like an open wound, polluting the air around us, fouling the place where we work and live. I wish the opportunity to rid us of this creature had come sooner, but now that it has arrived, I have no intention of allowing it to slip away.'

Vincent walked over to a tall antique chinese cabinet and opened the lacquered doors. A variety of drinks and glasses was arrayed inside. He reached for a bottle of Ardbeg. He was unusual among his fellows in that he preferred Malt Whisky to brandy. The Islay brand that he was pouring was one of the many that he savoured. Vincent's palate was as educated as his brain. He poured a few drops of water into the glass, to release the esters within the golden liquid, allowing the full flavour and aroma to emerge. He allowed the first drink of the whisky to linger in his mouth, savouring the flavour and feeling the fumes reach his nose. As it slipped down his throat, it radiated a mellow warmth through his chest, easing the tension that had been building there. With glass in hand, he turned and walked back to the centre of the office. This was his stage, his performance was as much for his own benefit as for that of the man on the sofa. The role he played was as close to God as you could get. He had decided that a man should lose his life. There was no other reason for the killing, other than the fact that Vincent had decreed it. Li had endangered the Circle, but ejecting him from its ranks would normally have been punishment enough. Li's empire would be irrevocably damaged by the fact that none of the other members would do business with him. There would always be the threat of physical retribution, should he choose to open his mouth about the group, but few in the Circle would feel comfortable with the execution that Vincent had determined would take place. The only thing left to decide was, "how?'.

Vincent Lo turned and faced the seated figure of Sung, the Triad boss.

'Li has one weakness which he thinks is his little secret and I think it may be the opening we need. That and your man.'

CHAPTER 51

'I wasn't having any trouble with the old one.'

Natalie was anxiously looking at her watch. She was expecting Richard soon and wanted to get on with preparing dinner. The two had a lot to talk about this evening. The workman had been waiting for her when she arrived back from the gallery. As he hurried to complete the job, she started to take pity on him. He had obviously had a long day, this was a big apartment block and replacing the security intercoms would be no small task.

'Sorry, miss, I don't know why the property company has decided to replace the system. Everyone seems perfectly happy with the one they have, but I have my orders. Maybe it's something to do with the insurance. You know how they can be. If they decide that a particular system is not good enough, well I suppose it must be cheaper premiums or something.' The workman saw Natalie glance at her watch. 'I'll be as quick as I can. Actually, there's not much to it, the whole thing is just one module. There are just a few wires to link up and then the rest is just making sure that it is fitted to the wall properly. It'll only take ten minutes or so, now that I have the old one off.'

Natalie smiled at him. He was a good looking man, well spoken for a workman. The usual colourful expletives were absent from his speech and his accent was strange. Even though Natalie had been brought up in the UK, she had a good ear and could usually place where people came from. This guy had certainly not been born in Hong Kong. He had spent a lot of time north of the border. She thought about asking him, but thought that this might slow him down. Instead she offered him a cold drink, which he gladly accepted. Natalie walked into the kitchen to fetch it and left the workman to his task.

It was on days like this that Richard wished he had been a bit more hard-headed in his choice of car. The Jaguar XK120 had been restored to concourse condition. It had taken Richard eight years to get it this way. Most of the work had been done in the last four, when he had been earning enough money to do the more expensive work. Or rather, pay someone else to do it. When he had bought the car, he had visions of late nights toiling away to the light of a single mechanic's lamp, up to his elbows in oil and grease, his face streaked as he wiped the sweat of honest toil from his brow. Very romantic. It never happened. A few days of attempting simple repairs left Richard in no doubt that his talents lay elsewhere. With time he might have acquired the necessary skills to make a good job of it, but time was one thing that he never had enough of. One of his friends, who had encouraged him to buy the classic car in the first place, owned an old Lotus. It was a well known Elan Sprint, which had competed in Macau in the sixties. Ten years after being bought, it still lay under a tarpaulin in the car park of the building next to Richard's, still in bits. At the end of one particularly frustrating session on his own car, he caught sight of the green carbuncle next door and decided that if he was to have his new pride and joy running, he had better let the professionals do the restoration.

The sleek car, dressed in British Racing Green, was in almost as good condition as the day it had left the factory. Many of the parts had been sourced by Richard during his vacations back in Britain and also Australia and New Zealand. It was a joy to drive, but at this moment, Richard stared longingly at the Honda Accord next to him. The driver looked so cool in his modern AIR-CONDITIONED car. Driving an open-top car in the sweltering heat of a Hong Kong summer was a good deal less romantic than it sounded. The oppressive heat was bearable when you were on the move, but stuck in traffic, as he was now, Richard was sticking to the leather of his seat, sweat soaking every piece of clothing he was wearing. The fumes from the cars and trucks around him covered him in grime and threatened to clog his lungs. But the most worrying thing of all was the steady climb of the needle on the temperature gauge on the dashboard. It was rapidly approaching the red and so was Richard's temper.

He looked at his watch and cursed when he saw the time. This was an important night for Richard and Natalie. It was their first chance to really talk about the events in the basement car-park. They had given one another a bit of space over the last couple of days. Natalie had been the one to suggest it. Richard would have been happier to get things out in the open sooner, but recognised that Natalie might need more time to process things in her own mind. She had called him that morning and asked that he come around for dinner, so that they could have a good talk about things. Richard had been delighted, though apprehensive. She sounded a good deal more cheerful, but there was a lot to talk about and he was sure that the full gamut of emotions would be covered before the evening was done. At least they would start to talk. With luck, he might just have his girlfriend back by the end of the night.

Natalie handed the workman the glass of Sprite. She thought he was rather handsome. His features were strong and well proportioned. He was tall, with the broad shoulders of the Northern Chinese. He looked fit, but that was to be expected with someone who worked in a manual job. Natalie guessed that he was in his mid-thirties, though he could have passed for much younger.

'Has it been a long day?' she asked.

'Yes, it has and I have to install at least another four of these units before I can finish for the day. It will take me a few days to work my way through the entire building.'

Natalie looked at the box that the man was installing. It was larger than the unit that it replaced, though the general layout was the same. A small TV screen next to which were a number of buttons. Below the screen was a microphone and next to it, directly below the buttons was a loudspeaker. Audio was two-way, but the video was for the benefit of the residents only.

'There seem to be more buttons on this one,' observed Natalie.

'Oh, yes. With the old unit, the person ringing the buzzer would activate the appropriate camera and microphone. That still happens, but with this one, you can also check out any of the entrances yourself. This button activates the camera at the main entrance and these three the cameras at each of the basement car-park levels.'

Mention of the car-parks made Natalie shiver and reminded her of the appointment that she had with Richard. She checked her watch. He was late. Not surprising, as the way he would have to come would be busy at this time of night. She imagined him getting more and more frustrated as he watched his car boil over. Poor Richard, she thought, he so loved that car, but it was really impractical in the summer traffic. She had enjoyed their trips to the beach, with the top down and the wind in her hair. Happier times. Times which she had to make sure were theirs to share again.

The traffic was moving, but painfully slowly. One of the concessions to the climate which Richard had allowed when having his car restored was a powerful electric fan to help cool the radiator. Without it, he would have been unable to drive the Jaguar during the hottest summer months. A nerve jangling whine emanated from the engine compartment as the whirling fan battled against the climbing temperature of the engine. It would ultimately be a lost cause, unless the traffic picked up some speed, or Richard arrived at his destination soon.

To drown out the distressing noise under the bonnet, Richard turned up the volume of the car radio. "Synchronicity II" by the Police started to play. The song took Richard back to the time when the record was first released. A time when he used to listen to the radio as he made his daily trek to Fanling, leaving the urban area behind and entering old Hong Kong, a place where you could still breathe relatively fresh air as you ran between the paddy fields and watched the farmers tend their crops. The world he inhabited then was closed to the outside world. The men of SDU trained and worked in blessed isolation, waiting for the time that they would have to enter the "real" world, do their job, then fade back into their cloistered society.

As the car in front of him started to open a gap, Richard was brought back to the here and now, back to the fact that he had an important appointment to keep. These last couple of days, where the possibility of losing Natalie had been all too real, had made him realise just how important she was to him. If their relationship came out of this evening intact, he had already decided that it was time to take things to a higher level. He planned to ask her to marry him. His stomach was turning over more than it had ever done when crouched over a bomb. He was planning to change his life, give it the meaning that it had lacked for far too long.

'So, press this one and you get a view of the entrance vestibule. You can also use the speaker down there to call someone, say they are leaving and have forgotten something. The volume is high enough that you can get their attention as they exit the doors.

'Just press any of these and you can see the entrances to the car-parking levels. It you like, you can leave them all on as a kind of monitor. Press this and they split the screen into four sections, each entrance covered all the time. I wouldn't have it on constantly, as the tube is likely to wear out eventually. They have put a lot of features into the unit, but I'm afraid they have put in a relatively cheap TV tube which isn't up to the task. Best to switch it off if you are leaving the flat.

'Now, why don't you have a go?'

Natalie walked over to the console and started to play with the buttons. It was very straightforward and she had to admit that the new features were a big improvement on the old system. The workman stood close-by as she flicked through the black and white images. He spoke very well for a workman, she thought and then rebuked herself for being so patronising. The man was probably very well qualified. Just because he worked with his hands, that was no reason to put him down. Natalie felt that the innate snobbery that existed in the social circles she inhabited was starting to rub off on her. She hated the fact that some of the people she dealt with through her work even looked down their nose at Richard because he was a policeman. He was smarter, better educated and certainly more worldly-wise than most of them, but still he was a cop and for that they would never really accept him into their circle. He would always be a tolerated curiosity.

'Seems easy enough,' said Natalie. She turned to face the workman. He had a strange expression on his face, almost sad. He handed her the empty glass and thanked her for the drink. He would clear up quickly and let her get on with her evening. Natalie walked back to the kitchen and left him to gather up his tools. As the kitchen door closed, the workman reached up to the security console and started to pressed one button very deliberately. Four, four, four, four. If Natalie had been able to see his face, she would have thought his expression very peculiar indeed.

Richard was soaked with sweat, but much less aggravated as he pulled into the entrance to Natalie's apartment block. He drove down the winding ramp that led to the subterranean car parks. He always thought it odd that the temperature down here was no less oppressive than that outside. It made the basements claustrophobiac, unwelcoming places for many people. He had no such fears. He was just glad that he was close to his loved one. He found a space on the second level and heaved a sigh of relief as he turned off the ignition. The engine clattered to a stop. Clicking and popping noises came from the engine bay as the metal under the bonnet started to relax after the effort of getting through the Hong Kong traffic. Richard patted the large steering wheel and climbed out of the car.

As he walked to the entrance to the lift lobby, memories of the shoot-out came flooding back to him. He tried hard to dismiss the images from his mind. He had to focus on the conversation that he was about to have. He wanted to be up-beat and not dwell on the negative of the last few days.

Out of the corner of his eye, he saw a van driving towards the up-ramp. He just caught the profile of the man driving the vehicle, but paid him little attention. Richard tried to insert his key into the lock on the glass door. It wouldn't go in.

'Oh, bugger! What now?' The lingering traffic frustration was ensuring that Richard's temperature stayed at boiling point and his level of patience at zero.

On the left of the glass doors was a bank of buttons, one for every flat in the building. Richard's eyes quickly scanned the panel and found the number of Natalie's flat. He pressed the button.

The buzzer caught Natalie in the middle of touching up her make-up. She had decided to have food delivered later, as she thought that she and Richard would need all their time to discuss the events that had placed a barrier between them, a barrier which she was determined would come down that very night. She quickly finished what she was doing and placed the brush on the dressing table.

Her shoes clattered on the parquet floor as she rushed to the security console. As soon as she got there, she was greeted by the monochrome image of Richard, distorted by the wide angle lens of the security camera. She was surprised by the sight of Richard looking decidedly hot and bothered. He must have forgotten his key. She smiled at the black and white image of her lover. Natalie pressed the intercom button and spoke into the microphone. 'Hang on darling, I'll open the door for you.' She was pleased by the smile that her use of the word "darling" had produced on Richard's face. Everything just might be alright after this evening. Natalie pressed the red button marked "OPEN DOOR".

The blast spun her like a top, twisting her body as she fell backwards and slid across the polished floor. As she came to a stop, she lay face down and motionless, a pool of blood forming on her right side.

Richard's smile disappeared faster than it had materialised. The sound of the blast was distant, but to his ears, unmistakable. The sudden silence from the intercom told him exactly where the blast had come from. Richard grabbed the door handle. It was still locked. Without hesitation, he stepped back and drew his pistol. Richard fired six rapid rounds into the glass door, shattering it completely. He ran for the lifts and frantically pressed the buttons.

CHAPTER 52

'Christ, what a mess.'

John Gray cupped his jaw in his hand and shook his head. He had seen a lot in his life, lost many friends and colleagues to the evil fire of terrorist bombs, but his heart still had soft spots and one of those was reserved for Natalie Lam.

There wasn't really a great deal of damage to the flat, but the blood on the walls and floor spoke eloquently of the tragedy that had been acted out here only two hours earlier. Cassius was already at the scene when John arrived. The Chinese officer walked over to his older colleague, his own face showing the strain of the situation.

'Hello sir.'

'Hello Cassius.' John Gray let out a long sigh. At times like these, a look was a more effective means of communication than the words which seemed reluctant to come. The Superintendent fell back on the reliable crutch of the professional, the job. 'Let's have a look at what we have.'

The two men carefully made their way over to the wall on which the remnants of the security console still hung. It was immediately obvious to John that the device had been made to deliver the blast straight at the victim, as the wall was relatively undamaged. Although the professional part of him forced John to focus on the device, the part of him that was Natalie and Richard's friend kept making his eyes wander to the blood on the floor at his feet. When he realised what he was doing, John Gray dug deep into his reserves and forced his mind back on to the job at hand. 'Do you know what happened?'

Cassius looked at the remains of the bomb as he spoke. 'Lots of scraps of information at the moment, we're trying to piece everything together as quickly as we can, but we'll have to wait and see if Natalie can tell us anything before we will be sure of the whole picture. It looks as though she was here when the bomber placed the device. Richard saw a workman in a van draw away as he pulled up. We're assuming that he is our man, but Richard didn't get a very good look at him. From what we can gather, the security console functioned normally, but somehow was rigged to blow after the bomber left.'

'That wouldn't be difficult. The damage to the box is interesting. Two separate charges by the look of it. One much more powerful than the other. What were Natalie's injuries like?'

The younger man hesitated before replying. It was as though the words were reluctant to come, as if not uttering them might somehow make the whole thing less real. 'Her right hand was completely destroyed and much of her arm damaged. That accounted for the blood on the walls. Her face…' Cassius had to take a breath before he could continue. 'Her face was practically ripped off. The glass from the monitor screen flew straight into her . I don't know yet the extent of the damage, but the guys who arrived after Richard were pretty shaken up by what they saw. God knows what it did to him when he found her.

'The bastard actually called for an ambulance before he left the building. He used one of the pay phones in the entrance hall. They were here less than ten minutes after Richard broke through the door. What do you make of that?'

John Gray looked grim as he nodded his head in understanding. 'I'll tell you exactly what I make of that. He designed this bomb very carefully. It wasn't designed to kill Natalie, it was meant to do exactly what it did, maim her. See the differential damage to the security console, the way the right side is badly ballooned, whereas the screen on the left side is the only really damaged part? There were two charges. A high powered, probably shaped charge on the right, intended to do the damage to her hand and arm. On the left, behind the screen, a low powered charge, designed to blast glass fragments straight into her face.

'This son of a bitch knew exactly what he was doing. This bomb may have been aimed at Natalie, but it was also targeted at Richard. It's as much an emotional attack as a physical one. This is real terrorism, hitting our boy where he is most vulnerable, in his love of others. I wouldn't mind betting the bastard even intended Richard to be the one who would arrive when the thing went off.

'A hell of a risk, though. Our bomber seems to be getting bolder. And, this is a much more complex device than he has used before. There would have been simpler ways to kill her, but as I say, killing wasn't the intention here.'

Cassius couldn't believe what he was hearing. 'What you're saying is that he wanted to mutilate her, but be sure that she would have to live with her injuries.' The detective could feel the anger building inside his gut. 'And of course, Richard would have to live with the guilt of his part in all this. Natalie's injuries a constant reminder of the fact that she became a target because of him.'

'Diabolical, isn't it? Destroy two lives, without taking a life. God, I hope those two can survive this. Did you see him when you arrived?'

'No, he went with the ambulance to Queen Mary Hospital. I'm going over there right now, why don't we leave the forensic people to get on with their job? I think Richard might need some support right now.'

The two men reluctantly left the flat. Both knew that the scene that awaited them at the hospital would be even more difficult to bear than the one they were leaving.

He cut a sad, solitary figure among the bustle of the hospital corridor. Sitting, with his bowed head in his hands, Richard was an island of grief. The sound of approaching footsteps made him raise his head. No smile could break through the mask of misery when he saw his two friends. He merely nodded an acknowledgement of their arrival and stared at the blank wall in front of him.

'What's the word?' asked John Gray, as he took a seat on the bench beside Richard.

Richard Stirling shook his head. 'She's still in the operating theater. No one will tell me anything other than she is still critical, but that the doctors are doing their best for her.'

'How are you doing?'

'Christ John, she has hardly any face left.' The weariness in Richard's voice made him sound as though he had been on the go for days. He even looked tired, his face drawn, his eyes dark and heavy. After some time, Richard looked up at Cassius and then at John. 'What have you found out?'

The two men looked at one another trying to decide how much of the little that they knew they should pass on to their friend. His pain might be increased or helped by the information that they could give him. In the end, it was the older man who spoke.

'This was a very deliberate act, Richard. The bomb was designed to mutilate Natalie, not kill her. I have no doubt that the grief and self recrimination that you are feeling right now was as much a part of his plan as the injuries she received.'

The anger that had been building inside Richard came closer to the surface. As it did, he changed physically. Suddenly, much of the fatigue disappeared and was replaced with a murderous look. Cassius felt a slight shock as he saw the change in his friend. For a moment, he was afraid of the man seated in front of him. Shaking away the feeling, he added what he knew.

'It looks as though the bomber posed as a workman and replaced the security console in Natalie's flat. It was almost certainly the man you saw leaving the building as you arrived. He called 999 from the lobby of the building a few minutes before you arrived, that's why the ambulance turned up so quickly. That fact adds to the theory that he didn't want Natalie to die. It may well be that he had no thought for her at all. What he wants is to see you suffer.'

Richard looked at his friend. 'He must have broken the locks on the car park entrance doors as well. My key wouldn't go in, that's why I buzzed her flat.

'Cass, I know you mean well and you may well be right about his intentions, but what I might suffer is not really important, is it. It's what he has done to the woman I love that matters. I know this was done because of me. I know I shouldn't blame myself, but I also know that I will. But, our friend has made a big mistake. If he thinks that he is going to break my resolve, he is wrong. Whatever it takes, no matter how long I have to search, I am going to find this guy and when I do, he is going to pay.'

It was a long night. John and Cassius came and went as they tried to support their friend and also keep on top of the investigation. Richard wouldn't budge, despite the assurances from the doctors that he would have a long wait. As time passed, the news from the operating theater started to become more encouraging. There was still a lot that could go wrong, but Natalie was a fighter and seemed determined to hang on.

At three in the morning, the surgeons decided that they had done all they could for the time being and Richard saw Natalie for the first time since her blood soaked body had been wheeled beyond the doors of the surgical wing. Her face was entirely covered in dressings. Her right arm had been cut back to the elbow. Richard's heart sank when he saw her. His mind had been conjuring up all sorts of images of how she would look when she emerged from surgery, but none had been close to the sight that confronted him. He had kept thinking that the damage to her face might not have been as bad as it looked. Modern surgery could do wonders and Hong Kong had a worldwide reputation in the areas of micro-surgery and reconstructive surgery. The bandages around her face drained all his hopes away.

When she was settled in her room, Richard was allowed in to be with her. In order to get access to her bedside, he had told the staff that he was Natalie's fiancé, something he might well have been had the night before gone differently. As he entered the room, a doctor was tending to her. He turned and approached Richard.

'Mr Stirling?' Richard nodded. 'She is a very strong woman, your fiancée. Her injuries were severe, as you saw for yourself. We have repaired as much of the damage as we can for now, but we shall have to wait before we can assess what might be done cosmetically. Her left eye, I'm afraid was damaged beyond repair, but we managed to remove all the slivers of glass from her right one and are confident that it will heal completely in time. The damage to her skull was not too great, but the tissue of her face was badly lacerated. A lot can be done, but she will always be scarred, quite badly I'm afraid. We saved as much of her arm as we could, but the trauma of the explosion had damaged a lot of tissue in the forearm, which was necrotic and had to be removed.

'The healing process will take a very long time. When the physical wounds have healed, I fear there will be a much greater time required for the emotional wounds to disappear, if in fact they ever do. She will need your support and love, as she has never needed them before.'

Richard continued to stare at the bandaged figure in the bed. Only half his mind had come to terms with the fact that it was Natalie. The other half expected her to walk through the door and ask him what he was doing staring at this poor girl. Suddenly, he seemed to snap back to reality.

'How long before she regains consciousness?'

'Hard to tell. The anaesthetic will wear off in an hour or so, though we are keeping her sedated. She will have a lot of pain when she does wake up, but we are dealing with that too. We can call you when she regains consciousness, if you leave us your pager number.'

Richard shook his head and gave a ghost of a smile to thank the doctor for his suggestion. 'No thanks Doctor. If it's all right, I will stay until she wakes up.'

'Of course. If you need anything, ask the staff. I know things look pretty bleak at the moment, but you should be thankful that she will live. Cosmetic surgery is improving all the time, you never know what might be possible. If she is as much of a fighter as she seems, she will learn to cope with the loss of her arm and her looks. The question you have to ask yourself is can you? Can you offer her the support that she will need? You had better think about that and quickly. I don't mean to be harsh, but you have some difficult realities to come to terms with.'

This last comment took Richard by surprise. Up until the doctor had spoken the words, it had never really crossed his mind. How did he feel about Natalie's injuries? He dismissed the thought from his mind, but the doctor was right, he would have to confront his own feeling sooner or later. But not now.

Natalie seemed to be having problems with her make-up. No matter what she tried, it always seemed to come out badly, her face a mess of mixed colours. Her lipstick made her mouth seem out of place, her eye shadow moved her eyes to her cheeks. She kept removing her cosmetics and redoing the job, but each time her features became more bizarre, like one of the cubist paintings that she loved, but could never get Richard to understand. Richard felt a deep sadness as he watched her struggle. He wanted to tell her that she was beautiful enough without make-up, but he couldn't bring himself to disturb her increasingly frantic efforts. Suddenly there was a knock at the door. Richard turned to see who it was.

Richard was woken by the knock on the door of the hospital room. He straightened himself in the chair by Natalie's bed, just as Sarah Chan entered the room. He wiped his face, trying to clear away the cobwebs of a disturbed sleep and stood to greet the new arrival.

Sarah walked purposefully towards Richard, dropped the bag she was carrying and proceeded to slap him across the face.

'You bastard! This is all your fault. Why did you have to come into her life? Look what you've done to her.' The words came as a burst, like gunfire, as she tried to hit him again. Richard blocked the attack as gently as he could and eventually managed to grab her wrists and bring the physical attack to an end. Sarah struggled and uttered a tirade of abuse at him, but that too subsided. When she had relaxed her body, Richard let go of her arms and took a step back from the young woman. 'I hope you are happy. I told her no good could ever come from being with a man like you.'

'Really.' Richard's voice was cold, though he knew that the words that had come out of Sarah's mouth had been rolling around his own head since he had discovered Natalie's bloody body on the floor of her flat. 'If you want to blame me, that's fine, but don't you think you should be a bit more concerned for Natalie. Your bile can wait. Right now she needs those around her to be supportive, not at one another's throat.'

Sarah looked at him with poison in her eyes. She was on the verge of saying something, when they both heard a soft groan coming from the bed.

Richard told Sarah to stay with Natalie as he rushed off to tell the nursing staff that the patient was coming round. In less than a minute he was back with a nurse, who showed a great deal more calm than Richard could muster. After checking Natalie, the nurse said she would summon a doctor and left the room. Richard stood by the bed and held Natalie's hand. To his surprise, he felt her softly grip his hand. He wondered if she knew it was him, or was just responding to the touch. When he looked up, he saw that Sarah Chan was still giving him the evil eye, rather than paying attention to the injured girl lying in the bed. You have some strange friends my darling, he thought.

Richard and Sarah were asked to leave the room while the doctor examined his patient. The two sat in silence on a bench in the corridor. When he emerged, the doctor told them that Natalie was coming round, but that he was going to keep her heavily sedated for the moment. Her injuries would not allow her to speak and he wanted her to get as much rest as possible, so that her body could start the long recovery process. Sarah decided to leave, saying that she would return that evening. Richard was overjoyed by that news! He wanted to return to his bedside vigil, but the doctor looked at him and told him to go home and get some rest. He was no good to anyone in his current state. Natalie would be alright and if there was any change in her condition, the hospital would page him. Richard didn't want to leave, but the voice of reason inside him knew that the doctor was right. It was time to trust these people with Natalie's welfare and get back to his own world and the job he had to do. There was a man out there that he had to find.

CHAPTER 53

'Ah, now isn't this a surprise!'

Lau Kam hung said this with bitterness in his voice as he looked through the wire mesh dividing him from Cassius To. It was all he said. His eyes looked straight at Cassius, measuring the expression on the policeman's face, trying to gauge what was going on in his mind, what could possibly be important enough to bring a visit from the man who had put him behind bars.

'Your anger should at least tell you that my visit is about something important.' Cassius tried to maintain an even voice as he spoke. This visit was as difficult for him as it was for Lau. The man sitting on the other side of the partition had once been his friend, perhaps his best friend. He had thought that he knew this man. He respected him as a good police officer and a decent human being. To discover that what he knew of this man was a cover and that the person underneath was in fact a senior office bearer in a Triad Society had been the greatest betrayal of his life. Richard had once tried to make Cassius understand that not all that he had believed about Lau had been a lie, that there was an underlying decency about this man, but that his life had taken a course that had created a conflict of interests. Richard might not agree with the decisions that Lau had made, but he didn't believe that the man was irredeemable. Cassius could not bring himself to see beyond the abuse of trust. When he had seen the surveillance video which had been Lau's downfall, Cassius had felt sick to his stomach. A part of him wanted to believe that there had been some awful mistake, but as the evidence against his classmate mounted, he felt the hope fade and the anger grow. His boss at the time had given him the opportunity to withdraw from the case, because of his association with Lau. Cassius had agreed that this was probably a wise move, but had insisted that he be involved in the arrest. Somehow he felt that it was his duty to show that his loyalty lay with the Force, not a man who had betrayed it, his friends and the principals by which they lived.

The last time that Cassius had seen Lau had been the day that his team had arrested him. The detective had decided not to attend court for the sentencing, he wasn't interested or so he told himself. Cassius would rather have believed that Lau no longer existed. This visit required Cassius to open parts of his life that he had hoped would be closed forever. On top of that, he had to be civil to a man who had wounded him to the core. Cassius found it hard to look at Lau, not just because of the hurt he felt, but because of the angry wounds that were testament to the attack which Lau had suffered in prison. The cuts awoke feelings in Cassius which he didn't want to have. Pity, concern. These were emotions which Cassius would rather not feel towards this man, not any more.

'I'm here because of Richard. He's in trouble.'

Lau sat upright in his chair. Some of the anger disappeared from his face and was replaced with genuine concern. The only person from his "other" life who had shown him the least compassion had been Richard Stirling. Richard seemed to understand that there was no "black and white" in the world. Our human nature was too complex to allow such a clear-cut view of the society that we created. In order to make life understandable, we build a view of society that includes these sharp definitions of "right and wrong", but the reality is never so well defined. It really did depend on your point of view.

Richard might disagree with Lau, but he respected the fact that he had the right to a different point of view.

'What has happened?' asked Lau. His mind started to race through all sorts of possibilities. With a mind to Richard's chosen profession, it didn't take Lau long to latch on to the bombing campaign that had taken up so much of the news media over the last few weeks. 'Has he been hurt by this bomber?'

Cassius shook his head. 'No, this man is even more vicious than that. He seems to have read our friend's character pretty well. Richard doesn't give a damn about his own safety, but he cares a whole lot about his friends and loved ones. This bastard attacked Natalie, Richard's girlfriend. She's badly hurt. She'll live, but she lost most of her right arm and her face was practically destroyed.'

Lau slumped in his chair. He felt like a man defeated. He knew who Natalie was, Cassius didn't have to explain that she was Richard's girlfriend. Lau knew that she was much more than that, she was the love of his life. How many times had he quizzed Richard about when he would marry the girl? His enquiries had been only partly in fun. Lau saw how much Richard loved this woman, but something seemed to be holding him back from making that final commitment to her. Lau had hoped that his comments might push Richard into realising that he was holding back and allow him to get past whatever barrier it might be that was blocking his path.

Cassius continued. 'This bomber has been deliberately targeting Richard over the last few weeks. Richard encouraged this, as it distracted the bomber from his original targets, these British businessmen. But, other people started to get hurt as a result and now the bomber has hit Richard's weakest spot. He's very badly shaken up. I'm afraid that he might let this son of a bitch get him, just to stop the attacks on those around him.

'We have only one lead. Less than a week ago, Richard was attacked by a man called Garland. He's an ex-Hong Kong policeman, working for a major Chinese businessman called Li Keung.' Cassius saw Lau's eyes light up at hearing the name. He noted the reaction, but pressed on. 'The attack was unsuccessful, but it gave us a line into Li and his business empire. We had suspected that the bombing campaign was being directed by someone other than the bomber himself. There seemed to be no obvious reason for it, so we started to look at who might have something to gain from the bombings. The only answer that we could come up with was that there might be economic gains to be had from the effect of the killings on the share price of the companies involved. We think that the attack on Richard may have been an indication that whoever was behind the scheme had lost control of the bomber and was trying to get him back on track by removing the thing that was distracting him, namely our friend Richard.

'Well, Li has disappeared and so far we can't link him with any of the large, or even small purchases of stock in the companies headed by the dead men. CCB are still looking and it will take a long time to sift through the web of companies that make up Li's empire. Time is something that Richard doesn't have. We need to catch this bomber before he kills Richard or more people that he cares about.'

Lau stared at the table in front of him. He had been keeping up with events in this case, some through the media, others through his contacts in the outside world. This though, had failed to filter through to him. He hadn't realised that Richard was in so much trouble. He felt anger that his "brothers" might have been keeping details from him, perhaps thinking that there should be no reason for Lau to be concerned about the life of a *Gwailo* cop. Lau raised his eyes and looked Cassius squarely in the face. All his anger at the man who had turned his back on him had subsided, back into the dark well where it had been lying before today. His mind was now focussed on what he could do to help his friend, the man who had stood by Lau, even when it might have counted against him with the people he worked with.

'I take it that you want me to use my contacts to find out if they know anything about this, whether Li is involved and if so, how? Alright. This is for Richard. I will see if I can dig up anything, no matter how small that might lead you to this man. I know that you will act on it quickly, so I had better be able to contact you quickly.'

Cassius reached into his jacket pocket an took out a small leather case. He withdrew one of his name cards and wrote a number on the back. He passed the card through a slot at the base of the grill dividing the two men. Lau picked it up and looked at the printing. One side was in English, giving Cassius' name, rank and unit. At the top was the police crest and at the bottom a disclaimer which stated that this was not a means of identification. Lau turned it over. The reverse was in chinese characters. Cassius had written a number on this side.

'That is my home number. I will keep my pager on all the time, so that is probably the quickest way of getting in touch with me.'

Lau looked at the card. Putting his home number on the card was a sign of trust on Cassius' part. Lau appreciated the gesture. He looked up at his erstwhile friend.

'You will hear from me soon, whether I find anything or not.'

Cassius wasn't quite sure how to take that last statement.

CHAPTER 54

Most people have an overly simplistic view of the human character. They look at behaviour and consider it "good" or "bad", "admirable" or "despicable". They believe that they are basically decent and would "do the right thing", whatever that might be. Whenever doubts creep through their moral armour, they dismiss them. The unthinkable is placed to the back of their consciousness with all the rest of the unwanted baggage of the human psyche. It is never let out, for the answers to these unwanted questions are too unpalatable for the ordinary mind to contemplate. What if we are no as noble as we would like to think? How would we react if presented with a situation which required the best part of us to be stretched to its very limits? The answer for all too many would be that they were not up to the challenge of the grim.

I wonder how Richard Stirling is coping with the little test of character which I have set him. What is it that attracts us to another? Beauty? Certainly. But, where does the beauty lie? Is it in a pretty face, a curvaceous body? Do we look for an image of perfection? Finding it, would we be so attracted to it if it were no longer perfect in our eyes? Some might call this form of attraction shallow and state that external looks are doomed to fade with time, but that the inner beauty of an individual will last a lifetime. It is that inner glory that we all believe is the key to lasting relationships. We tell ourselves that although we are physically attracted to someone because of the way they look, we fall in love with the person because of the their character, their inner self. The trouble is, for most of us, that particular claim is never tested. We are allowed to go along through life believing the best about ourselves and ignoring the ignoble truths that we hide from the world. Well, Stirling must now confront his true self and find out if the image he holds of himself is honest, or another lie for the benefit of those around him and his own feeling of worth.

What will he do, I wonder? In the beginning, he will be the very image of the saintly individual, staying with the woman he loves through the most dire of circumstances. But will it be a true reflection of the feelings that will be grappling with one another in his soul? Will it merely be a facade, erected to maintain the honourable image which he wishes to project to the world? If so, will it last? How long can a man live a lie? Perhaps to some extent we all live with falsehood, right up to the end. When our beliefs remain untested, it is easy to exist with a false image of ourselves. We can choose to ignore the little voices within us which tell us that we are not as courageous, or inventive, or thoughtful as we would like to believe. Really we are far less admirable than we would like to think and certainly than we would like others to think. We get away with this mendacious pose because fate chooses to let us off the hook. I am fate's foil.

Watching her as she moved about the apartment, obviously anticipating the arrival of her lover, I was inspired. I could not believe my luck. Or was it fate that brought me there at that moment?

I felt anxious. The job had to be done quickly, lest I face my adversary unprepared. I had it in mind to test the system from the car park level and trigger the girl's unhappy experience myself, but with the imminent arrival of Stirling, I saw a beautiful possibility. Risky, but worth the gamble.

I had to work quickly. It was easy to incapacitate the locks on the entrances to the car parking levels, forcing the event. A simple sliver of metal, broken off in the lock, preventing entry of the key. He would be in a hurry to be by her side. Who would not? An anxious lover as the trigger of his woman's fate. Such events fuel my passion.

As I drove away and caught that momentary glimpse of Stirling at the door, I had to fight the desire to stop and savour the glory of divine accident. I wonder if he wept?

So, how do we end this play? Shall I kill Richard Stirling and leave the devastated princess without her knight in shining armour, if indeed that is what he turns out to be? That would be too easy on our hero. No, by letting him live, I defeat him, no matter what the outcome of his moral struggle. If he chooses to run from the ruined features of his beautiful Natalie, then he will be forever the coward and have to live with the shame. If he stays and holds her hand through the horrified looks and curious stares of an uncaring world, he will have to live with the knowledge that her scars are there because of him. Her life will never be the same, all because she chose to love the wrong man.

She was beautiful. When I was with her, part of my own heart felt a tug towards her beauty. It was delightful. The thought of that face, bloody and destroyed was the most delicious vision that I have ever conjured up. That mass of flesh and sinew which would cause the ultimate defeat of my adversary. Such anticipation as I installed the device. So sweet she was to me. No arrogance, I think she would treat any man the same, be they high or low. I could see what would draw Stirling to her. Yes, perhaps in the end he does love more than the perfect balance of features that will now be nothing more than a memory. She glowed, but will she still retain that warmth and kind spirit after she understands that her body has been ravaged? It is easy to be kind to others when the world is kind to you. For those who have been cursed with deformity, or less than perfect appearance and have to bear the weight of human intolerance and ignorance, it is easy to develop an armour of anger and hate. I wonder if Natalie will retain that sweet disposition after images of repulsion and fear have taken their toll. Will her inner beauty shrivel and die and in its place flourish a twisted, spiteful weed? Only time will tell. I will not see these events, but my legacy to Richard Stirling is the opportunity to die, day by day, as he watches all that he loved turn to wretched ugliness.

Killing a man is easy if one has the will to do it. The manner of his death is where the skill and artistry of the assassin is tested. For a man like Richard Stirling, his own demise is a matter of indifference. He may not welcome it, but he does not dread it. When he chose the sort of existence that he has, he accepted the possibility of an early death. Life is something which he wishes to have on his own terms. He will not be dictated to by others. His existence is in his own hands, to be used as he sees fit. No longer. I have given him his destiny, with its limited outcomes. He may choose to stay or to go, but either path will lead him to damnation.

So, he has been a worthy opponent, but in the end, I had to win. I always had the advantage and I always will. Some might fear that arrogance could lead to disaster, but my arrogance has been earned over many years. I know that I will never be caught, will never fall foul of stupidity or carelessness. Only the cruelest twist of fate would ever lead me into danger and even then, I am sure that I would be able to avoid the hangman's noose. I must leave Stirling to the fate that I have provided for him and move on to other matters.

CHAPTER 55

There was nothing quite like the feel of smooth, firm, young Chinese flesh, thought Li. As he stroked the back of the boy that lay beside him, his mind wandered back to previous lovers, memories of indulgence and submission. None had ever refused him, despite his appearance. Garland may have had many faults, but he had superb instincts for choosing the weak and the vulnerable. They might change with the passage of time, become more confident in the affections of their lord and master, but by then, Li would have tired of them and be ready to move on to fresher pastures. He had to put some thought to a replacement for Garland. The Englishman's deputy, Fung, had stepped in to fill the void left by Garland's sudden demise. He did his job adequately, but he would always be the Number Two in any function, he was not leader material.

Li's attention returned to the boy in his bed. Yes, Chinese boys were the best. They were brighter than the Thai and Filipino boys that Li had sampled. He had once drawn a French youth to his embrace, but had quickly tired of him. His cleanliness was not up to the standard that Li demanded. Europeans were unclean in Li's mind. They seldom showered before bed, bringing the accumulated filth of the day with them between the sheets. The very thought of it made Li shudder. Chinese boys knew how to prepare themselves for the night. The touch of their skin was a delight and did not offend Li's sensibilities.

Li drew back slightly from the warm body by his side, so that he could get a good look at the boy. He was better educated than Li would have expected for a mainlander open to the sort of offer that Li had made him. Well spoken, in both Mandarin and the local Shanghai dialect. This one might just last longer than most of the others. The boy had potential. Perhaps this one would not force Li to take drastic measures when the time came for the youth to retire from his position as plaything to the tycoon. Li knew this to be a vain hope, but at the early stage of any relationship, it was good to think that the future would hold only pleasant prospects.

Li needed all the pleasantness he could find. Word from Hong Kong was not good. The police had turned his organisation upside down. Pressure from Government House had deflected the best efforts of his expensive legal counsel to have the investigation blocked. Li had too many enemies within the British business community. When he had appealed to his friends in the PLA, they had been strangely uncooperative, saying that they would see what they could do, but that the negotiations on the details of the handover of Hong Kong were at a delicate phase, so they were not hopeful that their influence with the negotiating team would be sufficient to be of help to Li.

It was starting to become clear to Li Keung that a fresh start was in the wind. He had done it before, but he had been younger then and had been less accustomed to the trappings of wealth and power. It would be hard to give that all up, even for a short period of time. His influence and accumulated wealth would still allow him an indulgent existence, but everything was relative. Wealth was not an absolute, there were degrees.

As he lay in the semi-darkness of his Shanghai residence, the night seemed quiet to him. This house had been deliberately sited away from the areas marked out for development in the city gone mad.

Although it took him longer to reach his offices than he might have liked, he relished the space that he had around the main house. If he had built elsewhere, he would not have been granted such a generous land warrant.

This must have been what it was like to live in pre-war Shanghai, thought Li. To be a foreign banker with a home set in tree-lined boulevards, travelling to an office with a view over the Bund. Privilege amidst squalor. Then it was the Europeans who wielded the biggest stick, now it was the Chinese. It mattered not to Li that as far as the native Shanghaiese were concerned, Li was as foreign as any European. For them, a Southerner, even one lacking Li's deformities, was like someone from another world. He might call himself Chinese and speak a common tongue, but he was not one of them. He may have spent his formative years living in Shanghai, but he would always be an outsider. Li didn't care. To him, these Northern Chinese were there to work for him, to build his business empire back to its former glory. That was their part in his future, as it had been in his family's past. Many had wondered at Li's victory over the handicaps which life had placed upon his bent shoulders. The truth was that his had been inherited wealth. He had started at the top and managed to come close to destroying everything that his father had reluctantly left him. Li's childhood memories had none of the love and pride that an only child would expect. If the union between his father and his many mistresses had borne male fruit, Li might not have inherited the family business. There were rumours that Li senior's seed could not have resulted in the blossoming of any offspring, even one as deformed as Li. The old man's pride was Li's saviour. To the end, he refused to believe that his wife had taken a lover and that their only child was the result of that clandestine union. So, Li Keung had received the family wealth, to do with as he pleased. Luck, greed and changes in Mainland government policy had saved Li from the humiliation of destroying all that his father had built. Shanghai had been the springboard of the family fortune. Hong Kong had allowed the empire to grow. Perhaps it was fitting that this new beginning for Li junior would have its roots in the same soil that had nourished his father's ambition. This would be Li Keung's opportunity to show the world that he was no pale reflection of his father and that away from the destructive influence of the Westerners, Li could be his own man.

'Sir, may I have something to drink?'

Li returned his attention to the boy. His voice pleased Li. Soft and pleading. It had been more so earlier in the evening. Li had indulged himself with the youth. The frustrations and failures of the last few weeks were laid upon the body of the young man. Li exorcised his demons in young firm flesh. The tycoon smiled. He felt generous towards his new plaything.

'Of course. Help yourself to the drinks over there.' Li pointed to the bar in the corner of the bedroom. 'Pour me a brandy while you are making something for yourself. The Hennessy on the top shelf.'

Li admired the back of the boy as he rose from the bed and walked across the floor. He was fit, well muscled and walked with the poise of a dancer or gymnast. Under any other circumstances, Li would have been intimidated by the physical perfection of the youth. But, a man like Li would never be cowed by one of his own possessions. Power and fear made Li a match for anyone, even a physical specimen so close to perfection as that before him. Never had Li felt in any danger from the boys he had taken to his bed. The threat of reprisal was always made very clear before they were allowed anywhere near the tycoon. Occasionally Li had felt the resentment swell in the body of his bed partners, but it was never manifested in the form of violence, physical or verbal. They were compliant to even his most bizarre demands. They could not be otherwise. They knew the consequences of refusal. Li felt comfortable with this new one. So far he had seemed more than happy to indulge his new master, but the night was young and Li had many more delights in mind. By morning, he would have the true measure of the possibilities of this young man.

The boy's eyes scanned the bar. He knew before he arrived that he would be searched before getting anywhere near the filthy creature that he had been forced to indulge in bed. Men or women, it didn't really matter to him. He had a taste for both, but this twisted horror was almost too much to bear. No matter, it would be over soon. The best part was yet to come. His eyes fixed on an object that looked promising. He pulled the glass stirring rod from the pitcher in which it sat. The end was shaped like a bulb and fit well into his hand. A bead formed the other end of the rod. He could make this do very nicely. Ensuring that his body hid his actions, the boy wrapped the rod in a bar towel and then continued to pour a vodka for himself and the brandy for Li. He placed the glasses on a tray, along with his special package. Turning, he saw Li staring at him from the bed. The lust in the little man's eyes disgusted the young man. But he returned the twisted smile with one of his own, sweet enough to disarm even the most paranoid individual.

Li licked his lips as he watched the young Chinese Adonis cross the floor, back to the increasingly aroused tycoon. The small man shifted himself in the bed, making himself more comfortable as his erection grew. The boy laid the tray on a table beside the bed and handed Li the balloon with an ample measure of dark golden liquid within. The excitement grew in Li as he watched the careful movements of his lover. Suddenly the boy jumped onto the bed, straddling Li. The glass of brandy was knocked loose from the older man's grip. Under different circumstances Li would have been furious at the waste of so precious a liquid, but now he was more excited than ever, caught up in the spontaneity of the moment. He lay back, awaiting the pleasure that was about to come.

The boy reached over to the tray and picked up a small cloth which seemed to be wrapped around something. Li heard a snap as the youth gripped the rolled-up cloth in both hands. A sudden rush of fear ran through Li. Something was wrong with this situation. His fear turned to terror as he looked at the boy's eyes. Instead of the longing that he had seen only moments before, he saw hate, raw and vicious. The boy grabbed Li by the throat, pinning the little man to the bed. Li caught sight of something in the boy's right hand. It glinted slightly in the pale light coming through the balcony windows. Li wanted to scream, but the boy's grip on his throat stifled the sound. The words that came to Li's ears were those that the boy spit out with all the venom he could muster.

'This is a present from Vincent Lo!'

The boy held the bulb of glass in his fist, so that the broken shaft protruded between his middle fingers. He thrust the improvised weapon with a punching action into the torso of the struggling Li. A scream at last came from the little man. The boy thrust again and again at the body beneath him. Some blows were superficial, others went deep into the flesh of the creature beneath him. Li started to make animal noises, like a pig at slaughter. As the squeals of the little man intensified, the boy began to laugh, the ludicrous figure between his legs becoming more ridiculous with every frantic scream. Still, the youth continued his onslaught on the deformed man in the bed. A smile formed on the boy's face as he warmed to the reaction of the older man. It was the best ride he had had for a long time.

The young assassin loosened his grip on the other man's throat. He was enjoying the feral screams that were coming from Li. No one of importance could hear him, the tycoon had dismissed most of his staff in anticipation of the night's events. Only one security man remained and he would not interfere. The boy struck at the source of the screams. The glass shiv lanced into the man's neck. As Li thrashed about, the stem of the rod broke, leaving a length protruding from the man's neck. Blood immediately started to spurt from the wound, in rapid rhythmic sprays. The boy was covered with blood, but remained in position, pinning the wildly lurching body to the blood sodden bed.

Slowly the body's movements began to wane. The screams were replaced by a pathetic gurgling as the body tried to protest at the treatment it had received from hands that had shown such tenderness only minutes before. A last wet sigh told the boy that his work was nearly done. He felt for a pulse and was gratified to find none. The young man climbed from the bed, a look of grave satisfaction on his face. He looked down at his body and decided he had better shower. As he walked to the bathroom, the door of the bedroom opened and Fung, the security man walked in. He looked at the bed and then at the young man. They exchanged nods and the youth went off to have his shower. Fung walked over to the bed to satisfy himself that his erstwhile boss was in fact dead. His expression didn't change as he gazed down at the bloody mess around the motionless body. Blood pooled in the folds of the sheets. Arterial spray decorated the wall behind the bed, like some macabre piece of abstract art. There was no rush. By morning he and the boy would be back in Hong Kong where he would report in person to his real masters that the job had been done.

CHAPTER 56

'Li Keung is dead.'

The statement brought silence to the room. All heads turned to look at Cassius To, as he walked from the door to his seat at the conference table. David Lo watched his detective take his seat and then asked for an explanation.

'Details are pretty thin,' said Cassius. 'When we pressed for information about Li's whereabouts, the Chinese authorities were initially evasive and then, this morning they sent a simple telex to our Interpol office. "Subject of your enquiries, Chinese Male Li Keung murdered in home by person, or persons unknown. Enquiries progressing further details to follow as and when available." End of message.'

'Do you think he is really dead?' The head of the investigation looked questioningly at Cassius.

The detective shrugged. 'Who knows? It wouldn't surprise me. The information that I have received from my informants and the pieces that CCB have gleaned from their investigation seem to make it likely that some of Li's business associates might want him out of the way.' Cassius had been careful to conceal Lau's identity as his main source of information in the case. His former friend had come through in the end. The information he had passed on was patchy and much of it hearsay, but it had filled in a few of the blanks in the great puzzle. If Li was dead, then the whole investigation would have reached a blank wall. It might be the end of the case, but it was a very unsatisfactory ending.

'So far, we have built this picture,' continued the detective. The attention of all the senior officers around the table was focussed on his words. 'It looks as though Li Keung was the brain behind the bombing campaign against the British business heads. He was known to have a chip on his shoulder about the British, but that was only part of it.

'Neither Li himself, nor any of his companies traded in the stock of the targeted companies. Now that omission in itself is significant. A businessman as shrewd as Li liked to think he was would not have passed up the opportunity to capitalise on the misfortunes of his rivals. Most of the other houses in town did just that. But not Harbour Holdings, or any associated company.' Cassius had already begun to think of Li in the past tense.

'My sources though pointed me towards several small companies, all formed in the last year to eighteen months, but with no obvious ties to Li, or any of his holdings. I passed the information on to CCB and they have come up with a theory.'

David Lo moved forward in his chair, but said nothing, allowing Cassius to continue the flow of his report.

'All these companies made significant purchases of shares in the companies affected, almost always when their share price was at its lowest. One or two of these buys might look like fortuitous timing, but you put them all together and it looks like the clairvoyants in town have been having a pretty good run of late. Individually, they were big purchases, but nothing to worry the controlling interests in the companies being bought up. Put them together and they start to look like a very hostile group indeed.

'So, here's the theory. Li sets these companies up through a complex series of secret deals. His involvement can't be traced, but he's pulling the strings. He tells them what to buy and when, because of course he has his own little crystal ball, in the form of a madman with a passion for explosives.

'The deals are made and then everything goes quiet again until the time when Li thinks he can make his move.' Cassius paused and looked at the faces around the table. It took a few moments for David Lo to realise Cassius was giving them all the opportunity to jump in with a theory. David preferred to ask the relevant question.

'So, when would he make his "move" as you put it and what would that be?'

'Some time after the 30th June 1997.'

David looked at his subordinate with a mixture of curiosity and skepticism.

'I know, it seems a long way off, but look at these events as strategic moves. Li buys control of these British companies, without anyone finding out. If he were to declare his interest now, the whole thing would blow up in his face. No matter how low an opinion he might have of our abilities, he would know that we would make the connection back to him eventually. After the Handover, the powers that be in Hong Kong might be very different. Even if things stayed much the same, Li has powerful connections into the ruling elite in China, particularly the PLA. If he was confident enough in the protection that they would afford him, it doesn't stretch the imagination too much for him to "acquire" the companies who bought the shares now. More than ten years would have passed, he might even begin the acquisitions before the handover. Anyway, he ends up with at the very least a springboard for takeover of the British companies he damaged by killing their CEO's a decade before. He increases his personal wealth and scores a victory over the "hated" British. It might even gain him favour with his masters in Beijing.'

David Lo stared at the table and then raised his eyes to meet those of the detective sitting across from him. No one else at the table uttered a word. 'So, that's the theory? All this for because of one man's greed and prejudice?'

Cassius returned the penetrating look from his boss. 'Men have killed for a good deal less. From what we have been able to piece together, it looks like the most likely scenario, no matter how crazy it might seem to us.

'The very nature of the crimes doesn't point to a rational mind at work. Li was mixed up with some very nasty people. His connections with the PLA could have supplied him with a man with the technical knowledge and skill to execute the campaign. Garland, his head of security was vicious enough to act for him and he did try to kill Richard Stirling, just at the time that it looked as though the bomber had been distracted from his task. I can't think of any other reason for the attempt on Richard's life, other than trying to get the bomber back on the job he was assigned.'

Lo sat back in his chair. He didn't like loose ends and this mess looked like ending with a whole lot of them hanging in the air. 'I know better than to quiz you about your sources Cassius, but how sure are you of the information that they have passed on? Where did it all come from?'

Cassius sighed. 'I can't tell you, but you know me and that I wouldn't be so sure of myself unless I was one hundred percent confident in the source of the intelligence. It's not a perfect picture, but we rarely get that anyway. It fits with what we know of Li and his business activities. I get the feeling that he will not be missed by anyone in this town. Frankly, the general feeling is one of relief that he is out of the picture. If he is dead, I am afraid that the evidence suggests that the case has reached a conclusion. We will no doubt dredge up more skeletons as we dig through Harbour Holdings, but with the man pulling the strings gone, the only thing we have to worry about is the puppet. But, that is not exactly a small matter for concern.'

'What do you mean?' David Lo's anxiety was shared by all at the conference table.

'Richard Stirling and I have had a long series of discussions about the way this would end. With Li dead, assuming he was behind all this, we think one of two things could happen; One, it all ends. Nothing more happens and we never find out who planted the bombs. Two, the bomber has already shown that he is quite clearly out of his mind. He went off on a mission of his own when he started to attack Richard and those around him. He might carry on with that assignment, or go off at another tangent. He has a taste for the mayhem he has caused.

'Our one hope might be that although he is mad as a hatter, he isn't stupid. He might feel that to continue would place him in too great a danger and just slip off quietly to wherever he came from. If he is a PLA resource, they might even have pulled him out already. His attack on Richard's girlfriend might have been his parting shot.'

The head of the investigation team shook his head. 'Part of me wants to catch this monster before he gets away. Another part would be happy never to hear about the son of a bitch again. So, I suppose we just have to carry on with the investigation and wait to see what happens. Maybe we might even get lucky. At least now we have a trail to follow, even if it does look like leading us into a dead end.

'Gentlemen, if there is nothing further for Chief Inspector To, we should let him go and discuss the information he has placed before us.'

David Lo rose with Cassius and walked around the conference table. He walked out into the hallway with his subordinate and faced him.

'Cassius. Thanks for that. We have a lot to digest, but I think by the time we sift through the intelligence that you have supplied, our conclusions will match your own. It just seems so crazy, so unreal, but as you said, a rational mind wouldn't have come up with a plan like this in the first place.

'How is Richard's girlfriend?'

Cassius slumped his shoulders. 'She'll live, but the damage to her face is appalling and she lost her arm to the elbow. Her scars will go deeper than that though. Richard is in a bad way. He blames himself. I know he will do everything he can for her, if she still wants him around that is. Who knows what she will be feeling by the time she starts to heal.'

'Tell them they are both in my prayers and if there is anything and I mean anything I or anyone else in the Force can do, all they have to do is ask. We look after our own and those they love.'

CHAPTER 57

Lieutenant General Hua Jianying had worn a uniform most of his life. As a boy soldier, he had first donned the green fatigues of the People's Liberation Army. The pride he felt then was equalled, but never surpassed during his steady climb through the ranks of the largest standing army in the world.

Hua was a proud man. Proud of his achievements, proud of his family and proud of his country. He had been proud of the party which ran that country, until the day he saw the carpet pulled from under his feet. For years the PLA had offered Hua the opportunity of a better life for himself and his family. Business opportunities abounded, as the army invested in companies as a means to fund its operation. Changes had come however, in an effort to open the doors of opportunity to those outside the ruling elite. Men like Hua saw this as nothing short of betrayal. Those dictating reforms would not be affected by them, but men like Hua, the instruments of authority who had kept the decision makers in power, would have to suffer the consequences. Loss of prestige and more importantly, income.

There really was only one option for men like Hua. To suffer a lowering in their standard of living would be to lose face. That was unacceptable. They resorted to other ways of ensuring a regular flow of cash. Men like Hua retained influence, the influence to award contracts to businesses. Such authority had value. Hua considered himself a moral man, so he was surprised at the ease with which he accepted his first bribe. In time, he would further ease his conscience with the realisation that he had been driven to corrupt acts. It wasn't really his fault, it was the fault of those who had decided to change the rules. Rationalisation is the balm of a guilty conscience.

Hua felt he had made the best of a bad situation. The day he had come across Li Keung had been one of mixed blessings. Unknown to Li, Hua had aided the inevitable decline in his fortunes. The businessman's empire would have collapsed without Hua's intervention, but it would have taken longer than Hua could afford to wait. So, the die was cast and Li was made ready to accept an offer of assistance from the rising star of the General Logistics Department. Money and influence, enough to re-float Li's financial ship and springboard him into the business elite of the Crown Colony of Hong Kong. Li won and the General and his associates won, everyone was happy.

Hua was indeed a proud man, but he was also an ambitious man. Some might say that he had a good thing going and that the prudent thing to do was leave well alone. But, Hua had a vision. He saw the future of Hong Kong and he saw a communist flag flying over Government House. As details of the handover agreement between China and Britain emerged, it became obvious to Hua that a lot of mainlanders could make a lot of money after 1997. Hua was determined that he would be one of them. Li Keung was the instrument he would use to ensure his future prosperity. With the mind of the military strategist, Hua concocted a plan to position Li's financial troops in such a way that after the handover, the tycoon could swoop down and in one move eliminate his enemies and vastly increase his wealth and power. Hua of course would reap the rewards of such a move. His hold over Li was absolute and he never let the businessman forget it.

So it was from the mind of the military man, rather than the board room warrior that the bombings had been born. Li had taken to the idea from the beginning. Like many businessmen, he saw himself as the Twentieth Century adventurer. Where, a century before, fortunes and trade alliances had been won by canon and gunpowder, now it was done with a pen and a cheque book. To be a part of something so vicious and exciting gave the small man a feeling of power greater than anything he had felt before. Knowledge of the origin of the plan would go no further than Li. Even Garland would go to his grave believing that his master was the source of the scheme. Had the Englishman understood just how powerless Li was, he might have had second thoughts sooner and bailed out of the whole mess. Li had power only as long as Hua allowed him to have power.

Now, Hua wore a different uniform. This one did not instill feelings of pride, but rather shame. This one bore no insignia, no medals, no honour. Hua was grateful for just one thing on this grey morning, that his family was not here. As he looked towards the horizon, the first glimmer of dawn was lighting the sky. It would not be a bright day, clouds sat gloomily overhead, defying the sun to beat them back. The weather suited Hua's mood. He didn't want a bright day, the dull, overcast sky suited him just fine.

There were no crowds today. A group of fellow soldiers stood some distance behind Hua. There were many ranks present, some by choice, others under orders. For some, their enforced presence was intended as a warning.

Hua looked out over the desolate mud plain that was the public execution ground. He had only been to one of these places three times before. Each time he had thanked any God he could remember that he would never face the humiliation of kneeling in the mud, waiting for the end. But here he was. Events had caught up with him. Li's death had led to an investigation which had, much to Hua's surprise, led straight back to him. Hua was sure that one of the men standing in the group behind him was responsible for his downfall.

Some of the small circle who had been aware of Hua's scheme had voiced concerns, but as ranking officer Hua had silenced them. No doubt one of them had sold Hua out, to save his own neck. Loyalty, it seemed, did not mean much in the world of commerce.

The General only had himself to blame. He was too generous. Li should have been killed, made to vanish, when the plan had gone so badly wrong. The man Hua had supplied was one of the best the PLA had to offer. He had served Hua loyally for over ten years. Any loss of direction could only be put down to incompetence on the part of Li, or his associates, or the corrupting influence of Hong Kong itself. Hua had been too forgiving when he had granted Li his protection. The twisted little man should have been removed.

So, now Hua was kneeling in the mud, waiting for the inevitable end of what had turned out to be not such an illustrious career after all. He would die in humiliation and shame. His family would suffer long after he was gone, but that would be no concern of his. Hua did not believe in an after-life. He had had his allotment of existence. There had been moments to be proud of, but they would all be forgotten, swept away by the tide of corruption.

Someone was saying something in grave tones behind Hua. He wasn't listening, but he knew that it was his sentence, being read out to all present. It was part of the ritual of death, part of the warning to those who would contemplate following the path that Hua had chosen. This was the inevitable outcome of such choices. Yet, the really powerful and the truly corrupt in their society would continue to drain the economy with impunity, of that Hua was sure. In the great machine of Government, Hua was a fairly small corrupt cog. His death would make little difference.

The voice behind him stopped and a hush fell over the open plain. Hua braced himself as he heard the squelch of boots walking through the mud towards him. Hua was a proud man and if his final act would be to collapse face first in the mud, then at least he would face his final humiliation with as much dignity as he could muster.

The footsteps came closer and then stopped. Hua heard a pop, as the cover of a holster was released. A soft scrape announced the removal of a pistol from it's leather home. There was a pause, before Hua heard the click as the hammer of the pistol was cocked and locked itself in place.

The officer aimed at the back of Hua's head, the muzzle a foot away from it's target. He did not hesitate, or draw out the business unnecessarily, but pulled the trigger and executed his duty. The life suddenly drained out of Hua. His body collapsed like a sack of coal, dropped from the back of a wagon. All the signs of life disappeared in an instant, what remained was empty flesh. The officer re-holstered his weapon and waited for a doctor to confirm death. He hoped that he would not have to administer a coup de grace, he never had to before. His attitude was one of ambivalence. This was his duty, he had no feelings for the General, he had never met him. He felt slight shame at the fact that the object of his task was a senior army officer, but if the charges were correct, then the army was better off without this General in its ranks.

The doctor confirmed that General Hua Jianying had drawn his last breath. The young officer walked away and Hua's body was put on a stretcher, to be carried away and delivered to his family.

CHAPTER 58

The caffeine was starting to work its magic, although it would take at least another mug of the strong brew before Richard would feel anywhere near human again. Long vigils at Natalie's bedside had taken their toll, along with the sleepless nights brought on by a guilty conscience. When it came to coffee, John Gray favoured a Kenyan blend which was currently percolating away in a machine in his office. Richard was enjoying his own Italian brand for which a separate coffee machine was set aside. He had contemplated installing a Gaggia espresso machine in the pantry of the EOD unit, but had opted for a filter machine instead. Volume and convenience were more important issues than concentrated strength. He liked to have a ready supply of the dark liquid on hand. As soon as one jug was finished, it was an automatic ritual to brew a fresh batch. Anyone neglecting this particular duty was apt to find themselves on the receiving end of some very pointed words from a caffeine starved Scot.

'Feeling awake yet?'

Richard swung around in his chair to face John Gray, standing by the door of the office. 'Not quite, but I'm getting there.'

'Well, I have something that might shake off the cobwebs. Come on.'

Richard levered himself from the chair and quickly refilled his mug, before following his boss out towards the workshop area.

'What do you think?' asked John.

Richard stared at the package for a moment before replying. 'You have got to be kidding. No, really, you don't think…?'

The padded envelope was addressed personally to Richard Stirling, care of the EOD Unit. Printed on the front were the words, PRIVATE AND CONFIDENTIAL.

John turned from the package to his friend. 'You expecting anything "private and confidential"?'

'He wouldn't be that obvious, would he? I mean, come on. Send me a letter bomb as some sort of parting shot? He can't imagine that we would become that complacent so soon. Or is he really chancing his arm?'

John Gray shrugged. 'There's one way to find out. Let's have a look at the thing.'

Richard placed the package flush against the photographic plate. He used a retort stand to support the plate as it sat vertically on the workbench. The envelope was thick enough to allow it to sit against the plate without additional support. If it was a bomb, it would have to be up to a bit rough handling, having gone through the Hong Kong mail system, but Richard didn't want to fool around with it any more than was absolutely necessary.

Next, he positioned an oblong device, end-on to the package, standing off from the envelope by about two feet. The device was an "Inspektor". This portable X-ray machine had originally been designed for use by para-medics at the scene of accidents. Bomb disposal units around the world had quickly recognised the potential of the machine and adopted it as a part of their kit. Nowadays, the EOD application was the main use to which the system was put. The photographic plate, or cassette contained what was in effect a jumbo version of the photographic system developed by Edwin Herbert Land for the Polaroid company. In fact the sole supplier of film for the Inspektor system was Polaroid.

When Richard was happy with the alignment, he adjusted a dial on the top of the Inspektor. This determined the number of "pulses" of X-rays that the machine would deliver to the target. Richard chose three for the package. He pressed a button on the machine and retired from the room. There was an in-built delay which allowed the operator to get a safe distance away from the X-ray emission. In the corridor outside the workshop, Richard and John waited for the telltale clicks that announced the delivery of X-rays to the target. When they heard them, the pair re-entered the workshop.

Richard removed the cassette from the clamp of the retort stand and walked over to a machine lying on an adjacent bench. This was the developing unit. A tab, which was attached to the film inside, protruded from one end of the cassette. This end he fed into a slot on the developing unit. On one end of the unit was a handle, like that on an outboard motor. Richard grabbed it and bracing the machine, gave the handle a long, fluid pull. Like starting an outboard, the string attached to the handle emerged from the guts of the machine along with the sound of rotating parts. The tab on the film was gripped by the mechanism and the film forced through rollers which would burst the in-built packets of developing chemicals and spread the contents over the surface of the film in an even layer. This done, Richard set the timer on the machine and went to top up on some Italian coffee.

Richard and John had finished most of the contents of their mugs by the time the ringing of a bell announced that the film should be developed. John opened the compartment that held the film and took it out. This was the moment of truth. Although the system was clever and generally reliable, its greatest flaw was the film itself. In the heat and humidity of Hong Kong, it had to be stored in refrigerators, but even with careful handling it could prove a fickle ally in the fight against bombers. Sometimes the chemicals were not spread evenly across the film, resulting in an incomplete image. At other times, nothing appeared at all. John peeled the two halves of the film apart. One side held a negative, the other a positive. He laid both on the bench.

'Well, what do you know.'

Richard tore open the envelope and allowed some of the contents to fall out onto the workbench. He looked inside and drew out the white envelope that remained inside the package. His name was the sole inscription on the inner envelope. He placed this to one side for a moment and concentrated on the objects that had come from the padded envelope. The X-ray had given them a good idea of what lay within the package, but there were still a couple of surprises. They had clearly seen the shape of the Chinese coin, that both men had no doubt would exactly match those that had been used in the bomb that had killed Douglas Fairbrother and inadvertently the unfortunate hawker. The ball bearing would match those that had so nearly been the end of the arrogant and still ungrateful David Rankin. A cigar band made the connection with Ernest Blyth. The final piece of evidence was a small square of what would almost certainly turn out to be sheet explosive. The chemical analysis would no doubt match it with the type of explosive used in some of the bombs Richard had encountered in this case. It was a calling card, an announcement that whatever lay in the white envelope came from the man that Richard, John and the rest of the Police Force desperately wanted to get their hands on. More than thirty thousand men and women had their own ideas of the treatment that they would dish out if that happy event ever came to be.

'I think it is safe to say that the bomber sent these things,' said John. The clincher was the coin, details of which had been withheld from the press. Neither man needed to wait for forensic analysis of the objects lying on the bench. 'Right then. The letter is addressed to you, so I suppose you had better open it.' When Richard made no move to do so, John offered to open it for him.

'No, thanks John. I'll do it. It's just...'

'You're worried that it is going to be something about Natalie, aren't you?'

Richard nodded. His emotions were still racing over the attack on his girlfriend. It would be a long time before he came to terms with his own feelings, never mind the anger that he felt towards the man who had so viciously and callously maimed Natalie. Everyone thought that the act was intended to be an indirect attack on Richard. He feared that the letter would be confirmation of this. If it did, all the recrimination and guilt that he felt would be refueled and burn anew.

Richard took a deep breath and picked up the envelope. It had to be done and now was the time. He tore open the envelope and drew out the sheet of paper within. He was glad of the rubber gloves that he wore. The bastard had handled this letter and Richard didn't want to soil his flesh with the same paper. He unfolded the sheet and looked at the typewritten words. His breath grew heavy as he read, the words stirring up emotions from the very pit of his soul. A ruddy glow on his face became deeper as the rage grew within him. All the effort he had expended in the last few days to control his anger was undone by the words on the page. Richard could only think of one thing, revenge. He was no longer the policeman looking dispassionately at a piece of evidence, he was a man who had seen the most precious person in his life scarred and for no other reason than the fact that she loved him. His reading of the text was personal, his mind making no attempt to link the words with the events that had gone before the attack on Natalie. This was a personal message. There was no case any more, just Richard and the author of the note and unfinished business. As he came to the end of the note, he slowly became aware of his surroundings and the presence of his colleague.

'Well?' asked John. 'What has the bastard got to say for himself?'

Richard didn't make an attempt to explain the contents to John Gray, it would be better if he read them for himself. He simply handed the paper to his friend with a simple summation. 'It's an invitation.'

CHAPTER 59

Richard held Natalie's hand in his own. With his thumb, he stroked the soft skin on the back of the delicate hand. She was sleeping. This was her usual condition now. Even when awake, the drugs that were helping to alleviate the pain of her injuries kept her behind a veil of confusion and blissful unawareness. Yet, something inside Richard made him feel that she could hear him. He felt that the woman he loved lay in some deep part of her being, reaching out to him with unspoken words and heartfelt emotion. It gave him comfort to sit with her and try to explain what was happening in his life. His life had become her life, he was living for them both, until the time when Natalie would once more return to the land of the living.

But would she ever really have a life like before? Hers had been a full existence. Successful, popular, so full of energy and enthusiasm. That was the way she had been, but what would remain of the old Natalie once the bandages had been removed? She faced years of painful surgery just to stabilise the damage that had been done and give her the sort of appearance that society could tolerate. That was the galling thing for Richard. His beloved would have to endure all that suffering because of the prejudice of others. It was easy to love external beauty, much harder to reach below the surface and appreciate the loveliness beneath. Most people wouldn't even try.

Richard understood. To his eternal shame, he had felt the emotions that make us turn from the awful, the horrendous. His inner demons had surfaced and made him take a cold, hard look at himself. In the end, his memory of the woman that lay in the hospital bed came down to much more than a beautiful thing. To his own relief, Richard realised that the things he loved about Natalie were deeper than the flesh on her bones.

He was under no illusions about the difficult times ahead. How he would feel when the extent of the devastation to her face was revealed, he really did not know. That was something he would just have to deal with. All he knew was that she would need him. His concern that she would turn him away had been alleviated by the few moments of lucidity that the drugs had allowed her. Even through the pain, he saw the need in her, felt the love through the touch of her hand. There may come a time when she might try to drive him away, for his own good rather than her own, but he had resolved to resist any such attempt and remain by her side, no matter what. That was the reason why the decision he now had to make was so difficult and why he felt the need to be by her side when he made it.

When John Gray had read the note, his first reaction was "Don't do it!". John had a persuasive argument, it was suicide for the fly to go looking for the spider, especially when the spider knew he was coming. Common sense dictated that the bomber's offer should be turned down flat. Richard, though had seldom allowed a thing like common sense to dictate his actions. He saw it as an opportunity to close the case once and for all. Get the bad guy and ensure that a living time bomb was not allowed to re-enter their lives at a later date. Closure was important to Richard. He hated loose ends.

John's next suggestion was to hand the letter over to Cassius and the investigation team, allow them to use it to trap the son of a bitch. A good suggestion, but one which Richard felt needed some analysis. They were not dealing with a fool. His invitation had been to Richard alone. It was safe to assume that the bomber had an escape in mind, should Richard decide to do the very thing that John Gray was suggesting. His track record indicated that such an escape might involve further deaths, probably of the very police officers sent in to arrest him. For Richard, that was unacceptable. If anyone was going to risk their neck, it would be the man to whom the letter had been addressed. The bomber had issued a personal challenge and Richard was not about to let others take the risks involved in meeting it.

John had insisted that they call Cassius. The detective arrived an hour later and found the two bomb disposal men in the middle of an energetic argument. His appearance and the puzzled expression on his face had brought the debate to an end, at least for the time being. It had taken only as long as it took to read the letter for Cassius to realise what the conversation was about. He had looked Richard straight in the eye and told him that he would be mad to meet the bomber alone. It was out of the question and if Richard tried to go off like some vigilante, he would have no hesitation in giving his friend a night in the cells to think about his decision. It would be unlawful, as well as downright stupid. It was the reaction that Richard had expected and John Gray hoped for.

The three men had sat together and talked the possibilities through. In time, the other two agreed with Richard that to send in a large group of cops would probably result in a large group of dead or injured cops. The bomber had to expect that Richard might pass on the information in the letter with a view to setting a trap. So, what were the options? If Richard attempted to confront the bomber on his own, he would either end up dead, or at the very least being kicked out of the Force. Prison was not an unlikely result either. If Richard had only himself to consider, that might not have stopped him going off to his rendezvous. But there was Natalie. He might get some personal satisfaction from playing the devil may care hero, but he would be no use to her behind bars, or dead. Yet, he couldn't let an opportunity slip away to get this evil bastard once and for all. After nearly an hour's heated debate, his two friends were reluctantly coming to the conclusion that Richard was right. It was too good a chance to miss, perhaps their last and only chance to finish this thing.

The details would have to be worked out in a hurry, as the invitation which Richard had received was for that very night, but it would be done, no matter what it took. Richard insisted that he go alone. Any back-up that was to be arranged would have to stay out of sight. Nothing could give the bomber the slightest indication that he was being set-up. In the end, it might just come down to man against man, but at least Richard would have an official seal of approval for his actions.

The rest of the morning was spent in frantic telephone calls and a trip to Police Headquarters. By mid afternoon, agreement had been reached as to the course of action. Richard had one last piece of approval that he needed before he walked into the firing line and that was what had brought him to Natalie's bedside.

Part of him was glad that she was not awake, even though he thought she just might be able to hear his words through the veil of sleep. As he looked at her bandaged face on the pillow, he wondered what he would have done if John had not been present when the note arrived. Would he have gone off on his own to confront the bomber and damn the consequences. A few years before, he probably would have. Then, he had felt no need to justify his actions to anyone, other than himself. He would never have done anything that he knew would cause harm to those close to him, but he had no one in his life who would suffer too much from the loss of his company. Yes, there would have been sadness and a lot of drinking in the process of mourning a fallen comrade, but nothing like this. Natalie needed him. She would miss his presence.

The plan that had been hurriedly put together was extremely risky. It relied on the belief that Richard's skill would be enough to at least keep him alive long enough to corner the bomber. If he could do that, then the Cavalry could be called in. The reality might be that

Richard would have to take the guy down himself, but that would be just as acceptable an outcome. The question was, would Richard's skill and luck be up to the task?

If Richard were to die in the operation, Natalie would receive his pension and a tidy sum in insurance payments. Money would not be an issue. There would be more than enough to pay for her care. She had some family back in Britain, but they were not close and Richard doubted that they would be willing to take on the responsibility for her. She might end up relying on institutionalised care until such time as she could look after herself. That was unacceptable in his mind. So, what was he to do? Turn away from the job he had sworn to do and ensure that he would be around to look after her, or take the risk that he might die and ensure that no more deaths resulted from the twisted expertise of the bomber.

Richard knew the answer. He had lived with risk all his working life. It came with the job. He could no more abandon his colleagues than he could abandon the woman lying on the hospital bed. His death might seem to some as a form of abandonment, but he felt sure that Natalie would understand that for him to walk away from his responsibilities would be for him to deny who he was. He would never be able to live with himself if others died as a result of his taking the safe path. That was not his way, it never had been and never would be.

What he needed now was some sign that he was doing the right thing. He had not come to say goodbye, he had come for approval. As Richard explained the events of that crazy day to the woman he loved, his eyes moved over her body, looking for any movement that might indicate that she heard him and that she agreed with the course of action on which he had decided. Anything would do. A soft squeeze from her hand, a movement of her body that could give him the confidence to face the dangers that lay in store for him.

Richard needed her strength. His own was stretched to the limit. He was not by nature a fearful man and any fear he had, he conquered. But at this moment, he was afraid. Afraid of making the wrong decision. Afraid of letting Natalie down. He would have to be completely focussed this night, as he walked into the dragon's lair. His greatest armour would be the knowledge that he was doing the right thing and that Natalie would have approved of his actions. It seemed a lot to ask of the frail figure in the bed, but he had to ask. The words were hard. His voice shaky as he pleaded with her to give him some sign that he was doing the right thing.

He gave a start as he felt the pressure on his palm. After the first shock, he thought that perhaps he had imagined it, merely fooling himself with wishful thinking. As if reading his mind, the hand that rested in his own gave another squeeze. Richard knew Natalie so well, that language was not their only means of communication. They could tell one another so much, just with a look or a gesture. At his core, he knew that she was telling him to go ahead with the thing that he had to do. Some might say that this was merely what he wanted to think and they might be right, but Richard felt that the message that his loved one was trying to get across was simply, be yourself, do what you have to do.

Richard felt revitalised as he stood and kissed Natalie on the hand. He didn't want to let go, he wanted to stay by her side. As he continued to hold her hand, tears welled up in his eyes. Richard was an emotional man, but he was not one for whom tears came easily. He laid her remaining hand on the bed at her side and made her a solemn oath. He would survive. If for no other reason than she expected him to. Richard was a man of his word.

CHAPTER 60

I am alone.

My world has become silent. Contact with Beijing ceased suddenly. I have no idea what has happened. I served my masters there for long enough, this assignment has proven that. They have become as corrupt as the man they sent me here to serve. None of them deserve my loyalty. Li, I would hope, has met an end that was fitting and which was long overdue. The men who installed me in this place have vanished, their ambitions gone in a flash. Those ambitions which led them to their demise, self-destructive, greedy and vain. When this drama began, I knew that the only certainty would be that no matter what occurred, I would be the remaining player in the piece. And so it is, or just about.

When I began this play, I had no idea that another man would enter the arena and play such an important part. In the beginning there was merely the mission and even that was only a means to an end as far as I was concerned. An opportunity for me to practice my art, to show the world what I was capable of. Somewhere along the way, Stirling suddenly gave new meaning to my endeavours. His intervention was key to the changes that took place, to the ultimate destruction of the conspiracy that was to be fueled by my creations. I never knew exactly why I was asked to perform my violent art. I didn't care. But my dear friend Richard showed me that the true test lay not in simple creation, but in making my creations blossom despite the best efforts of men such as himself. There lay the challenge. I think I proved myself more than a match for his skills.

And yet, I find that the initial satisfaction of the attack on his girlfriend has not been lasting. I found his weakness and was successful in my assault, but he remains. He is injured, of that I have no doubt, but my victory is incomplete. My prize was to be the knowledge that he would torture himself over the fate of his lovely woman. I suspect that in this I have been successful, but it is only an impression and it would seem that he is determined to stay the course and stand by the love of his life. I can only admire him and damn him for his fortitude. To have seen him run, hide from the awful consequences of his affection, that would have been victory enough. Instead, he flaunts his loyalty and strength of character, tainting the taste of my success. The hours he spends by her bedside chip away at my success, until soon nothing will remain.

It would be easy for me to quietly slip away into the night. That in itself would be a victory of sorts. To leave the final chapter unfinished, with the unspoken threat of a return lingering in the air. It would drive the authorities wild. Civil Servants hate loose ends. They would never be happy until the final full stop had been placed on the last page of the case file. A neat ending to a troublesome affair. If I disappear, I deny them their closure.

After a while they would decide that it was safe to assume that my activities had ceased to be a threat. Some might harbour the fear that I would resume my displays of skill, but it would remain a hidden, unspoken fear. They would pat one another on the back for a job well done, even though the decisive character would be my own, not theirs. They might try to convince themselves that they had been hot on my trail and had forced me to run, but the best of them, men like Stirling, would know the truth, that I had been the one to control the game. If it was over, it was because I had decreed it.

But how can I go? How can I leave it like this? There is one thing that I have to do before I move on to another place and find a suitable venue to display my talents. My victory is incomplete. Before I leave, I have to destroy Richard Stirling.

I can't bear the thought of him being left to get on with his life. I thought I had broken him. I was wrong. His strength has surprised me. If I destroy him, then I can move on with a clear mind. I can't bear the nagging thought that he might be laughing at my ineptitude. His damned morality finally victorious, despite my best efforts to test him. It would stick in my side like a poisonous thorn, slowly infecting my soul and forever tormenting me.

So, I really had no choice. He will have received my invitation by now and should have made up his mind whether or not to accept it. If he decides to decline the offer and instead send in a clumsy battalion of policemen, theirs will be a bloody fate. Such an end would mean that I had overestimated Stirling's moral courage. Something tells me though that he would not allow others to endanger themselves on his behalf. Yet could I have forced his hand? By maiming his girlfriend, might I have realigned his priorities? Would he sacrifice the opportunity to confront his tormentor for the assurance that he would live to support the woman he loves in her darkest hours? No. How could he give up the opportunity to face me? He could no more give up breathing. A man's character does not change so quickly or so easily.

The rage must have built as he read my words. Taunting him with my triumph, challenging him to avenge his sweet love. As I explained the way in which I had delivered the deadly blow to his future, as I detailed the design of my most elaborate device. A device designed to hurt, to maim, to disfigure, but not to kill. He must have felt the bile rise as he read my words. After that, how could he not want revenge? Every fibre of his being must have risen up in anger and demanded that he be given the opportunity to face me.

My hope is that he was able to keep this new knowledge to himself. If his friends and colleagues were to learn of my offer, they would undoubtedly try to dissuade him, even forcibly deny him his chance for revenge. They would have visions of entrapment, using my own arrogance as a weapon against me. Stirling would know that I am not so foolish. He would be aware that I would anticipate such treachery and have an unpleasant surprise waiting for his friends.

Well, I am here. I shall wait the allotted time and hope that my prey is willing and eager to meet his fate. All is prepared. The stage is set. Everything awaits Stirling to make his entrance.

CHAPTER 61

The Tower

Her name was Vera and she was a complete and utter bitch.

She had already killed eighty people in the Philippines and left thousands homeless. The typhoon had cut a swathe of destruction across South-East Asia. Now it was the turn of Hong Kong.

Although much of the energy of the storm had been depleted, there was still sufficient velocity in the winds to cause concern and to ensure that ferry services would be canceled and any seaman with an ounce of sense would be making for the nearest typhoon shelter. The word typhoon is an English version of the Chinese phrase, *Daai Fung*, literally "Big Wind". Vera had more than lived up to the name. The edge of the storm had hit Hong Kong just after midday and the winds had intensified steadily since then. Although rain was being whipped around by the storm, the full weight of the deluge had yet to arrive. In time it would.

The foliage on the hillside gave Richard some shelter from the gathering storm. He had chosen a hide where the movement of the trees would not block his view, but still ensure that he would be hidden from the keenest of observers. His eyes scanned the area, trying to catch any sign of movement. The wind made this sort of passive observation difficult, as it caused the inanimate to suddenly spring to life. Richard, though was experienced enough to be able to filter out the "noise" created by the typhoon. He knew what he was looking for, but was yet to find it.

Below him, the site was open and at the same time cluttered. A sign proclaimed that this was another new development of Harbour Holdings. An illustration gave an artist's impression of how the development would look when finished, right down to landscaped gardens and smiling residents. More flats to be sold at inflated prices to speculators who would sell them on at even more inflated prices, or charge rents that would make a Manhattan landlord blush. In a place where land was at a premium and in limited supply, such costs were said to be justified, unless of course you were a family who lived with the knowledge that you would never be able to afford your own home. Richard wondered if the development would ever be finished. Cassius had indicated that with the Li Keung's demise, his business empire had been thrown into chaos. Work on this site had ceased within a day of LI's disappearance. Someone might buy out the development and complete the work, but in Hong Kong it was more likely that the whole site would be levelled and someone else's vision take shape.

Two tower blocks sat on the site. One was almost complete, the outer cladding reaching almost to the top floor of the thirty storey building. The other was like a giant puzzle which some monstrous child had left unfinished. The lower floors were at an advanced stage of construction, but although the tower reached to its full height, the upper floors lay open to the elements. The entire structure was enclosed in a mesh of bamboo scaffolding. The winds had already started to unravel parts of this. It would be easily replaced when the storm had passed, but right now it gave the structure an even more vulnerable look than normal.

In his letter to Richard, the bomber had stated that he would be in this unfinished building at this time. All the police officer had to do was come get him. It was an invitation to a trap. It was an invitation Richard couldn't refuse.

Richard raised a pair of binoculars and scanned the tower. He didn't expect to suddenly come across another man with a pair of binoculars peering out from the building, he hoped he might catch a glimpse of movement, even artificial light, no matter how faint. All he wanted was some indication of where his quarry might be within the large structure. He saw nothing. Richard concentrated on the roof level, the location of the deadly rendezvous. Still nothing.

There was a lot of clear ground between the base of the tower and the hillside on which Richard sat. His approach to the building would be open and difficult to execute unseen. Security lighting on the site meant that he would not have the cover of darkness to aid his movement. The lights were not particularly bright, but there was enough illumination to ensure that anyone watching from above could not fail to spot him. Even if he arranged for the lights to be cut, that would announce his arrival and indicate that he might not be alone. Richard wanted the bomber to be under the impression that he was acting without the support of his colleagues. For all practical purposes, that was the case. At least for now. Richard shook his head. He would just have to cover the ground as quickly as possible and hope that he might be able to slip in unseen. He might not be able to keep his presence a secret for long, but any time might give him an advantage.

It was time to move. Richard moved slowly from his position to where he had left his equipment. Everything he needed was either in the assault vest that he wore, or the black Bergen rucksack that he now hoisted onto his shoulders. And, of course there was the Browning which he wore at his side. The holster he wore was his old assault rig from his SDU days. It was strapped to his thigh by a broad black nylon band. The rig was designed to allow freedom of movement and still hold the weapon stable enough to ensure a fast deployment. A dark part of Richard's character hoped that he would get the chance to try it out.

Taking one last good look at the tower, Richard made his way down the slope, towards the building site.

Is he out there? Has my guest arrived? He knows how to hide, this one. He understands the dark and shadow, they are his allies, his comfort. No matter. I want him to come. I shall know soon enough if he has accepted my invitation.

Stirling must expect that I will have a few surprises waiting for him. It has taken me two days to prepare, but I think he will agree that the effort has been worthwhile. My interest will be in seeing how far he gets in my maze of peril. And what a backdrop to our encounter! The storm is growing in strength. All the better to aid my escape from what is almost certainly intended to be my capture and final defeat. Oh, I am not so foolish as to believe that my friend Richard has come alone. They are out there, somewhere in the dark, waiting for some sign. They will want Stirling to confirm that I am here and the only way he is going to be able to do that is to face me. The tests I have arranged in this building will be no proof of my actual presence. No, the valiant Stirling is going to have to confirm that with his own eyes.

Then what? Will he triumphantly call in the Cavalry and retreat to some safe corner? I doubt it. If I am any judge of his character, there is one thing on his mind; blood, my blood. If I am wrong, no matter. I shall leave behind several corpses instead of one. I shall get away, that is the only certainty.

Scaling the boundary fence and crossing the open ground of the construction site took less than half a minute. An eternity. By the time Richard stood at the entrance to the tower, he had already made up his mind; stealth was no longer an issue. He would have to assume the worst, that his presence was known and that it didn't really matter. What was important now was dodging any nasty little surprises that were almost certainly waiting for him.

During a long day of preparation, Richard had had time to think through the offer that the bomber had made. A final confrontation. A way to end this whole affair once and for all. The offer was just too good to pass up. It was obviously meant as an invitation to his own death, but Richard had other plans. The bomber knew that the most irresistible thing that he could offer Richard was a chance to tie up the annoying loose ends that would remain if he just vanished without trace. One of the more junior officers on the investigation team had suggested that the bomber might be backed into a corner, cut off from his support system and desperate for a final showdown with his nemesis. Very poetic. Highly unlikely. No, Richard was sure that the bomber had some plan to get himself away from this building site, after he had had the pleasure of bringing Richard's life to a sudden and probably spectacular end. What the guy had in mind, Richard did not know. The only thing that he was certain of was that getting to the top of this building was not going to be a piece of cake.

Richard looked into the lift lobby at the base of the building. It was dark, the low light from the security lamps only intruding a few feet through the gaping entrance. Richard's mind wandered back to his days in SDU. During training they had run similar exercises on the same building, one during the day, the other at night. The point was to show how a relatively simple task could become monumental when you tried to do it in the dark. We tend to take vision for granted. It is so vital in much of what we do. Reduce it's effectiveness and the routine becomes something much more challenging. After a while though, the men of SDU began to grow accustomed to working in low light. It became a home for them, safer than the glare of the day. It wrapped them in security and put their enemies at a disadvantage. Richard needed to regain that mindset. He wasn't feeling at a particular advantage at the moment, quite the opposite.

Richard removed a flashlight from the Bergen. He pointed the long black tube into the hallway and pressed the "on" switch. An intense beam of white light cut across the open space, the side-scatter of light illuminating the whole area. Richard lowered the million candle-power Streamlite, until the beam was about a foot off the ground. He lay down, so that he could look along the beam. He scanned the area, all the time intensely watching the narrow beam. He found nothing to worry about. As his eyes scanned the lobby, he saw the door which led to the stairwell. That was his next target. Richard threw the backpack over his shoulders, but kept the torch in his hand. He would have need of it soon enough. Although it was unlikely that the bomber would decide to tackle Richard physically, so early in this drama that he had concocted, the Streamlite made a formidable night-stick. A comforting object to have at hand. Almost as comforting as a Browning full of nine-millimeter semi-jacketed hollow points. But that was close to hand.

Although the lifts were functioning in the incomplete building, Richard was not even tempted to use them. They were nothing more than metal coffins. Under different circumstances, Richard would have saved himself a walk by using a heli-drop onto the roof, but the storm and the desire to assure the bomber that he was alone, meant that a heli-insertion was not an option. So, the stairs it had to be. Thirty floors, any one of which could hold the bomber or a booby trap. The note had said that the bomber would be waiting for him at the top, but Richard preferred to keep an open mind about the veracity of the man's words.

There was a door on the entrance to the stair-well. Not good news for Richard. Using a Mini-Maglite, which was less intense and easier to maneuver than the Streamlite, Richard inspected the wooden door. It opened towards him. Carefully, Richard eased the door open, all the time checking the crack that steadily opened for any sign of a wire, or line. Nothing. At last the door was open wide enough for him to get through. He checked the concrete floor for any signs of a disturbance, or anything out of the ordinary.

He was sweating freely by now and he had not climbed a single step. Taking a deep breath, Richard stepped into the stair-well and gently closed the door behind him.

The air was cooler in here. The tall tube ran the entire height of the building, a natural funnel. Hot air would build up during the day and climb the stair-well. The circulation had a natural cooling effect. Now, at night, the temperature of the air was noticeably lower than that outside. It was a welcome change, but the effect wouldn't last long. Richard knew that he would be hot again soon enough.

The first flight of stairs lay straight ahead. Richard crouched down and shone the powerful beam of the Streamlite at an angle, parallel to the angle of the stairs. Looking along the beam, he immediately saw it.

The bomb disposal officer smiled grimly as he looked at the translucent thread that stretched across the width of the stairs, about half way up the flight. This was the beauty of the Streamlite. The power of the beam showed up the fishing line that was so often used for trip-wires. It might as well have glowed in the dark. The line disappeared over the edge of the stairs. Curbing his enthusiasm, Richard checked for any other surprises, before walking to the side of the stairs and shining his torch into the shadowy alcove behind the steps. There it was, about sixteen ounces of PE4. More than enough to have demolished the staircase and Richard with it. That's one hell of a welcome mat, thought Richard. The device was out of easy reach, so he went back around to the front of the stairs and carefully climbed up to the tripwire. He cut it with a pair of clippers and tied the line off at the railing which edged the stairs. The bomb would have to wait until later. Richard made an entry in a notebook to remind him of the location and nature of the device. It wasn't that he had a bad memory, but there might be quite a few of these to worry about. There was another reason for keeping a written record; if Richard was killed, someone else would have to clear the building. Hopefully the record would survive the recorder. He tried not to linger on that possibility.

So, it had begun. Richard knew that his worst fears had been confirmed, this was not going to be an easy ascent. He would have to watch every step and try not to become tunnel-visioned. He had to remain aware of his surroundings and be on the lookout for anything out of the ordinary, or any opportunity that he himself might have used to place a booby-trap, if he were in the bomber's shoes. It was going to be a long night.

He's here. A risk taker, our Richard Stirling. Either that or exceptionally confident. He wants me to know that he is here, so he boldly shines a torch, knowing that I cannot fail to see it, unless I am unlucky enough to have my attention diverted elsewhere.

He has no fear of light sensitive devices. Why should he? The circumstances are not suitable for their use. I would have to plant a device and then arm it when the light level had dropped sufficiently to ensure that I would not suddenly join my ancestors. I have heard of their use as booby traps in buildings, but I suspect that the men who planted them were either very fortunate, or incompetent in the extreme. I have no need of such frills. The path will be hazardous enough for my friend below.

His mind must be racing as he takes each tentative step on the staircase. What have I in store for him? That thought must be constantly at the front of his mind. He must concentrate, focus on the many possibilities that have been drilled in to him. The problem with education is that the more we know, the more we fear. Ignorance may be bliss, but in this case it could be fatal. So, Richard Stirling battles with two foes, my ingenuity and his own imagination. Both might kill him, one might save him.

Six trip-wires and he had only reached the fifteenth floor. Richard sat down and took a much needed rest. Time to gather his thoughts. The nature of the devices had changed. Obviously, the bombs would no longer be planted under the staircase like the first one. Richard would spot them as he climbed the stairs, well before he got to the tripwire. Under normal circumstances, this would have made it difficult for the bomber to leave his deadly packages for his guest. The problem was that Richard was walking through a building site. There were piles of sand, bags of cement, wall surfacing tiles, bricks, everything that you would expect to be lying around as indications of men at work. Any one of these could hide a bomb. The general clutter of the site was an ideal arena for the bomber's game.

So far, only half of the trip-wires that Richard had discovered ended up with real bombs. That was the beauty of terror. Once the reality of a bomb had been established, the mere indication of the presence of one was enough to cause the same amount of trouble as a real bomb. Richard had to assume that the slender lines led to a pile of explosive. If he allowed himself the thought that it might not, it was just at that time that it almost certainly would. Goodnight!

As he discovered the lines, he marked them and noted their position. Until he could visually check the device, he couldn't afford to cut the lines. Trip-wires are most commonly attached to "pull" switches, often as simple as the "clothes-peg" switch. Unfortunately, there is another possibility. It can be a bluff. The line is attached to a "release" switch. The tension in the line holds the switch open against some sort of spring. Cut the wire and the spring is released and the switch closes. A nasty surprise for the unwary. Richard dearly wanted to clear the stairwell, just in case it became a much needed route for a hasty exit. In the rush to get the hell out of the building, he didn't really want to have to rely on his memory to dodge the booby traps that he had already avoided.

As he sat, he tried to listen for sounds in the building. If the bomber was at the top of the structure, he would be too far away to give a hint of his presence. Each level that Richard had climbed had had double doors leading out to the floor itself. Richard didn't want his quarry coming out of one of these and creeping up behind him, so he had brought along a good supply of "plasticuffs". These disposable handcuffs he had used to bind the handles of the doors on each floor. At the very least, anyone using the doors would make a loud enough noise to alert Richard to his presence. One less thing to worry about.

Time to move. Richard rose to his feet and started up the next flight of stairs. He had already checked the route, but there was a lot of mess on this one, so he took his time and slowly threaded his way between the piles of construction waste and supplies.

The floor of the next landing was thick with sand. Richard stopped short of the flat rectangular area and shined his Streamlite over the area. His old buddies, his instincts, were telling him to be careful. Richard switched off the powerful torch and took out the Mini-Maglite. The small torch had a band of rubber around the barrel, just in the right location to allow Richard to hold it between his teeth. The band made for greater stability and comfort. Besides, dentists were expensive in this town.

Slowly, Richard started to brush the sand to one side, cutting a channel through the coarse aggregate. Sweat was beading on his brow as he worked. The volume of salty water indicated an effort that seemed out of proportion to the task. Strain comes in many forms. Collectively, those that Richard experienced were more than enough to soak his entire body. The policeman made it onto the landing. He inched forward on his hands and knees. Within a footfall of the first step of the next flight, his hand found something solid lying under the layer of sand. Exercising even more care than before, he cleared enough of the granular covering away to expose the very thing he had expected.

It was home made, by the look of it. An improvised pressure mat. The sort of thing that opened ornate glass doors in restaurants in

Hong Kong, and would just have easily opened the Pearly Gates for Richard. Two layers of foil, or other conductive material, separated by a soft insulator, such as foam rubber. The insulator would have holes in it. Step on the mat, and your weight presses the conductive layers together through the perforated insulation and boom!

Richard determined the boundaries of the mat and clearing the sand away, found the wire which connected the mat to the device, if there was in fact a bomb. The wire seemed to be heading up the flight of stairs ahead of him. It was well concealed against the wall. Time and trouble had been spent on all the little surprises that Richard had found so far. Even the most obvious of the booby traps would have caught out the unwary. Richard deployed his trusty Streamlite, but found no sign of fishing line ahead. Without seeing the device, he had no intention of cutting the wires leading away from the mat. For all he knew, the mat might be a decoy. It was possible that this part of the circuit was in fact closed, not open and that a control relay was at the other end. Cut the wire and he might end up setting a bomb off, not neutralising it. Carefully, he followed the wire to the top of the stairs. There, he found yet another mini-beach waiting for him. Richard took a deep breath and began the laborious process which he had been through on the landing below. Almost immediately he found another pressure mat. He located the wire and saw that it and the one he had followed up the stairs led to a bank of sand against the far wall. Taking his time, he edged towards the pile. It took him a few minutes to clear the sand away from the device. It was enclosed in a cardboard tube. Both sets of wires led into the package. No time for him to do anything other than clear the obstructing mat away. He left the device in situ, not wanting to take the risk that there was a further complication in the form of an anti-handling device. He hated to leave the device intact, but he had no choice in the matter. Retracing his steps, he cleared the first mat out of the way, giving him a better chance of avoiding it, should he have to come this way again in a hurry.

His backpack was starting to make its presence felt, but Richard felt the need to press on more than the weight on his shoulders. With the upper landing clear and another "plasticuff" securing the access to the seventeenth floor, Richard pressed on at his now familiar snail's pace.

He's a stealthy one. Of course, I keep forgetting that was part of his training in his former life. A fact that I really should keep in mind. This one is a hunter, a killer. He wasn't always the one who was on the defensive, playing catch-up to the ingenuity of the bomb maker's mind. He is used to taking the initiative, creeping unseen and unheard towards his prey and then, when the quarry has no chance to defend itself, or make good its escape, he strikes, quickly and violently.

That is his true nature, violence. He must relish it. Garland learned that to his cost in a dark, airless underground. Well, the underground he now occupies is even more airless. Such is the price of folly and arrogance. Another lesson I must bear in mind. I cannot afford to underestimate this man who is navigating his way through my vertical minefield. I wonder where he is right now? He will make slow progress, if he is to survive. There is no sound from below, but then he will be careful not to give me any clue as to his location and progress.

I must be careful to do him the same courtesy. He will no doubt be wondering if I am really here, waiting for him. What does he expect will happen if he makes it this far, I wonder? What fantasies has he conjured up in his mind about our confrontation? He will no doubt play the hero's part in his mind play. Perhaps he sees himself trying to arrest me, or does he simply plan to put a bullet in my brain and claim self-defence? Let him have his dreams of glory and revenge. At least until he reaches his goal, if he makes it that far. In some ways, I hope he does.

He was almost there, but the ladder was blocking his path. Richard had encountered four more booby traps since the pressure mats, all of them involving trip-wires. Either the bomber had run out of ideas, or he was trying to put Richard's mind to sleep. It was all too easy to begin to expect a particular type of device and to overlook the unexpected. This thought crossing his mind may have been the thing that made Richard pay close attention to the aluminium stepladder lying across the stairs. The position might also have alerted him. Builders could be notoriously lax about where they left their equipment, but there was something about the way that the ladder lay that seemed deliberately awkward. It was as though the thing had been placed to give maximum inconvenience to anyone climbing the stairs. It screamed out "Move me!". That was of course the last thing that Richard had in mind.

The beam of the Maglite scanned the edge of the ladder. Richard found the fishing line within a minute. It was attached to the railing and entered the body of the ladder near the top. He couldn't reach it without climbing over the ladder. It was just too obvious. All his experience told him that the fishing line was either a distraction, or not the whole story. The man who had placed this object wanted Richard to move it. He continued his examination of the obstacle.

Richard thought he knew what he was looking at. He couldn't be absolutely sure, but already he had a picture in his mind of exactly what he was faced with. It was the slightest gap. An absolute hair's breadth between the ladder and the floor. In daylight, he might have missed it. In the dark, the light from the torch gave it away, but only just. In his mind's eye, the device took form. Aluminium ladders are hollow. Richard would put money on this one having a quantity of explosive in its long cavities. The fishing line might well be attached to a switch, but his money for the primary trigger was on the microswitch that he guessed was causing the tiny separation between metal and concrete. The circuit would be wired up to the microswitch's "normally closed" contact. Lift the ladder and release the switch and the contact arm would move to the normally closed position, the circuit was complete and Richard's day would be ruined. But not today. This was just what Richard had hoped for.

There was one thing left to check before he moved on. With the torch, he scanned the route that he planned to take to get around the obstacle. Richard was looking for secondary devices. The bomber might have made the ladder bomb obvious in an attempt to force Richard to do just what he was planning to do, climb on the outside of the railing and get past the ladder. He couldn't see anything, no fishing line, no wires, nothing that might give him pause. Still he continued his visual check, going over the same area again and again, until he was confident of his route and how he would negotiate it.

Placing the torch between his teeth, Richard climbed over the railing. Checking the space ahead, he made his ascent in slow, deliberate movements. Each footfall was made with care and precision, each handhold changed only after he was happy that his body was balanced and stable. The weight of the backpack made his maneuvering slightly awkward, but his slow progress ensured that he never over compensated for the extra bulk.

Once past the ladder, Richard re-scaled the railing and was once more on the staircase. He gave the stairs above him another look and then made his way to the next landing. There was some clutter on this flat area of concrete, but after a couple of minutes, Richard felt sure that there was nothing nasty lurking in the shadows.

The twenty-eighth floor. Richard stopped and removed his backpack. As he stood in the dim light, he focussed his hearing on the floors above. Two levels above him he hoped a man was waiting. This was the turning point for Richard, this was where the rules of the game changed. No longer would he play the bomber's game, it was time for Richard to play his own game, by his own rules. This was where the reactive became the proactive, the hunter showed his claws. Richard opened the Bergen and got to work.

Patience is a virtue best not taxed to its limit. Time is on my side, for the moment. There is plenty of night left. Yet my heart is beating a little faster now. The anticipation of this evening's finale is starting to have an effect. There can be only one outcome, but how it will play out is still an unanswered question.

He should be close by now. There have been the occasional signs that he is reaching his goal. Even the most stealthy must give themselves away when confronted by my devices. He will have to take his time, scrutinise them, learn their deadly secrets before he can move on to the next challenge. A few minutes ago I thought I detected a light in the stairwell. Very faint, but to have reached me here, it must have come from a source nearby. The storm outside is acting as his ally. The troubled night masking the sound of his footfalls, the lashing rain a distraction to even my disciplined ears.

No matter. Soon the raging storm will be my accomplice, as I slip through the net that those oh so clever policemen have waiting for me.

Richard wiped the sweat from his palm and continued to tie the line onto the top rung of the ladder. He couldn't afford to move the device at all. It would take only the slightest release of pressure to trigger the microswitch. Carefully he avoided the thin rope as he retreated up the steps to the landing above. One of the doors leading to the twenty-eighth floor was held open by a wedge at its base. Through the door, Richard reached into his backpack and removed a pair of black gloves which he put on. The gloves had soft leather palms for grip, but the backs were made of a flame retardant material. The inner lining would soak up the sweat from his hands. The gloves were long enough to reach a third of the way up his forearm, but like most of his former colleagues, Richard had folded the gloves so that they only reached as far as his wrist. There was no particular reason for this. They were a little more comfortable and easier to get on and off, but Richard suspected that the real reason that the men of SDU did this was because it looked cool. So much for professionalism.

Picking up the small drum of rope, he moved back into the dim grey interior of the building, playing out the line as he went. He allowed plenty of slack.

This floor, like many of the upper levels, was among the least complete parts of the building. There were no doors on the entrances to the flats, or glass in the windows. The elements intruded unhindered here and for the first time, Richard got a view of the intensity of the storm. In the stairwell, the sound had told him that the winds were strengthening, but now he could see that the rain was moving horizontally, defying gravity as it lashed the exterior of the tower block. Of greatest concern was the effect that the wind had had on the bamboo scaffolding around the building.

Richard reached the far end of the corridor and entered the area that might in time be the corner flat. Rain hit him in the face as he approached the open side of the building. The cool rain was welcome relief, but the sight that confronted him was less welcome. The scaffolding, with its exterior covering of green netting, had been badly blown about by the wind. The bamboo poles had bowed out, just at the level on which Richard stood. They were now well out of reach. That meant he would have to jump. He stuck his head out of the gaping hole and looked above him. The full brunt of the rainstorm hit him, stinging his eyes as he strained to see any sign of life that might be coming from the roof level. There was nothing. The sound of the storm blocked anything else out. Good news for Richard as it would help mask his approach.

Richard reached into a pocket and took out a black balaclava. He donned the mask. Not an affectation, but a means to blend in to the darkness.

Carefully, Richard climbed onto the ledge of the opening and perched there like some ominous black bird. In his right hand he held the line which he had played out from the ladder bomb. He began to take up the slack. The line passed round two corners and was proving heavier than Richard had anticipated. He knew he wouldn't be able to accomplish this task in his current position, so climbed back down to the floor of the flat. He grabbed the line with both hands and pulling, felt the line start to become taught. When he felt he had taken up most of the slack, he pulled for all he was worth, stepping quickly backwards as he did.

Damn that's close!

He must be only a couple of floors below. The ladder? I thought he would have spotted that one easily. Maybe he was tired, or…Let's see.

Richard leapt into space. The wind picked him up as he entered the vortex rushing past the face of the building. He felt as though his sideways progress was greater than that forward. A moment of panic hit him right in the chest, then he felt the bamboo in his hands. He slipped as his foot hit the scaffolding and lost his grip. Richard thrust his right arm out. A shudder went through his shoulder as it made contact with a pole. He hooked his arm around the bamboo and grabbed a hold with his left hand. It took him a moment to regain his footing, but once done, he did not pause for breath, but immediately made his way up the scaffolding.

Time was a factor now. The bomber would be checking his handiwork, but would not take long to find out that the bomb had been set off deliberately. The scaffolding swung wildly as the wind and Richard's climbing swung the latticework this way and that. With a determined effort, Richard made it up to the roof level in less than twenty seconds. But would it be fast enough?

At the top, the scaffolding was closer to the wall of the building and Richard was able to step relatively easily onto the ledge and drop silently to the floor. Immediately, his Browning was out of its holster and in his hands. The tritium inserts glowed comfortingly in the dark. Where Richard moved his eyes, so went the muzzle of the gun. He scanned the area with his eyes and his ears, trying to pick up any signs of life. With easy, skillful movements, he started to cover the ground towards the stairwell at the other end of the roof.

The roof of this building was mostly an open area. When completed, it would serve as a recreation and clothes drying area for the residents. A concrete table-tennis table had been constructed. Netless, the concrete block looked like a slab in a mortuary. The roof was partly covered, but gaps allowed the rain to flood the floor. Piles of cement had hardened into mountains in miniature and sand piled up against walls like dunes plucked from a tiny desert. Richard knew that the clutter might conceal yet another booby trap, but he was relying on his luck and concentrating on a stealthy approach to where he hoped his quarry lay. He kept close to the wall on his right as he moved, avoiding the obvious detritus in his path.

The glowering night sky offered little illumination, but his eyes were accustomed to the dark. He kept the sights of his weapon in the lower periphery of his vision, so as to preserve his night sight. His movement was steady. He edged around a corner and saw the figure.

The dark man-shape stood completely still. Richard was too far away to make out features, but he knew that the man was watching him.

'Don't move!' It seemed a redundant statement,but it was part of the routine. 'Get down on your belly! Now!'

A soft laugh came from the unmoving figure.

'I don't think so my dear Richard. It is far too wet and dirty. I wouldn't want to attract undue attention with my appearance when I leave here.'

He has balls, I'll give him that, thought Richard. 'I said get down on your belly, unless you want me to shoot you where you stand!' Richard felt a flutter of uncertainty in his gut as he spoke the words.

'Ah,' said the bomber. 'There lies your dilemma. A part of you must want to gun me down right now. It must want that so very badly. But, the civilised policeman will not let him do that, will he? To your eyes, that would make you as bad as any criminal, worse maybe, for you would have betrayed all that you believe in. Yes, quite a dilemma.'

Richard edged closer. His curiosity was getting the better of him. He needed to see this man's face. He needed to look into the eyes of the creature that had caused so much pain and suffering. Suffering that would continue long after this evening was done.

'Irresistible, isn't it? To look into the face of the Beast. That's how you view me isn't it? Certainly how your colleagues see me. I had hoped that you would see the poetry in my actions. You of all people must understand the beauty of what I do.'

This guy was really starting to annoy Richard. 'Beauty? There's no beauty in what you do. You are a murderer. A criminal, simple as that. All I see is another madman with a little talent.' That ought to get a response, thought Richard.

'Oh, please, don't try to anger me Richard. You are skilled in what you do and you know the skill that went into my creations.'

Richard was disappointed at the level voice. This wasn't going to be easy. Now that he was closer to the man, he could see that he was tall, only a little shorter than Richard. He was well built and had the bearing of a soldier. His English was perfect, with only a trace of an accent. This guy had Officer written all over him. Right down to the attitude.

'You know my name. Doesn't it seem simple courtesy for me to know yours?'

The figure laughed. 'I have many names, my friend. In my profession, I have had to adopt different identities. It has long ago become irrelevant to me. I know who I am, the rest is just a label for the convenience of others. But, if you need to call me anything, call me Chua, Colonel Chua.'

Arrogant son of a bitch, thought Richard. He would have to have a rank higher than Richard's. Superiority to the last.

'How is your beautiful girlfriend?'

Richard tensed. He knew this was coming, but no matter how much he had prepared for it, the anger started to build. Even in the dark, he could see the cruelty lying behind the dark eyes.

'Well, she was beautiful,' continued Chua. 'At night, as you lie sleepless in bed, do you wonder what will be revealed when the bandages are removed? Do you pray to the Gods of Medicine that they might be able to restore some of her radiance?

'Stop praying my friend. If my device did its work as I intended, there will be little left to save. Beauty will become a beast and you will have to live with it for the rest of your life.'

Richard levelled the Browning with the centre of Chua's body. His grip on the butt of the gun was so tight that the sights were trembling before his eyes. He wanted so badly to kill this man. Richard's breathing was heavy and fast. He told himself to calm down. This was not the way. Slowly, he lowered the muzzle.

'I'm impressed,' said Chua. 'Such self control. Yet, I had a feeling that your weakness, your morality would surface and keep me safe from the demon within.'

Richard was getting tired of this. 'Just how did you think you would get away, even if I managed to blow myself up with one of your booby traps? You must have known that I would have back-up waiting out there. Or, are you really that crazy?'

'Of course I know that your friends are out there in the dark. Pretty wet by now, I should imagine. But I also know the way they work. Like you, they wouldn't dream of being so stupid as to use the elevators. They will secure them at the ground floor and take the stairs in search of their comrade. While they are making a less successful ascent than you did, I shall be abseiling down the rope I have rigged in the elevator shaft. There is enough room for me to slip past the elevator car and into the basement level, where there is a maintenance access. It won't be too much trouble to make my exit and fade away into the night, having accomplished my goal.'

'And what is your goal?'

'Why, Richard, your death of course.'

'After all this, that's what you want? I thought you wanted to torment me.'

'I did. But, you've proved to be made of tougher stuff than I imagined. So, the only way that I can win is to kill you. And that is my curse. I always have to win.'

The movement was subtle and quick, but Richard picked up on it right away. His instincts made him throw himself off to his left. Richard had not seen the switch in Chua's hand, nor the wire that trailed from the bomber's feet to the wall off to Richard's right. The blast came for him as he was in mid-air. Richard felt the nails from the bomb strike his right side. Two imbedded in his thigh, another three in the right side of his trunk, his body armour preventing one from puncturing his lung. One hit his bicep, causing his arm to spasm and the gun to fall from his grip.

The pain shot through him. His vision was blurred, but he knew that he had to get to the handgun. Chua would be on him in seconds. With all the willpower he could muster, Richard forced himself to consciousness and spotted the Browning on the concrete floor. He flung himself towards the handgun and grabbed it with his left hand, then swung his body, against the agony, until he was seated facing the direction from which he expected the attack.

It didn't come. Instead, Richard saw the retreating figure of Chua, making for the door to the stairwell. Richard raised the Browning and fired off a rapid volley of shots. The bullets slammed into the wall to the left of the door, just as Chua disappeared through it. The thud of the doors closing behind him was intended as a slap in Richard's face.

Richard fell to his left, the full intensity of the pain hitting him as he struggled for breath. The blast had winded him badly. He still managed a grim smile. Although not ambidextrous, anything Richard Stirling could hit shooting with his right hand, he could hit shooting with his left.

Damn him for his speed! His injuries may yet prove fatal, but if not, I shall have to pay Richard Stirling another visit.

Foresight is a marvelous thing. The abseiling equipment that I left on the floor below will serve me as well as that above. I don't think that my friend back there will be in any state to pursue me, but I will not dawdle. Time to regroup. Next time I will give him no chance to escape my fury.

Mind the steps! None of my little presents to worry about, but I can't afford clumsiness through haste. To be undone by a broken ankle would be tragic.

Until the next time my…

The explosion rocked the floor under Richard.

'Got you, you bastard.'

A little package returned to sender. Richard had taken one of Chua's own trip-wire devices and set it up at the bottom of the flight of stairs leading down to the twenty-ninth floor. He knew that the bomber would not have a single means of egress and just in case Richard managed to spook him in the direction of the stairwell, the policeman wanted to leave a little surprise.

Poetic justice, or just plain luck, Richard did not know. He wouldn't be happy until they had swept up every bit of Chua's carcass. Chua, thought Richard. Was that his name? Did it really matter? What were a few loose ends between enemies?

Richard needed help. He reached into a pocket on his assault vest and pulled out a radio. He spoke into the microphone and called in the Cavalry.

He lay back and waited. Soon, speeding vehicles would bring his colleagues to the base of the tower. He would have to talk them through the minefield that he had already navigated. It would take some time to reach him, but soon enough he would see black-clad figures walking through the stairwell door. He wished that Keith could be one of them.

All he could do was wait. Wait and think. Think about the future and the price of justice.

0-595-21436-3

Printed in the United Kingdom
by Lightning Source UK Ltd.
112071UKS00001B/101

9 780595 214365